ROMANCE

A

Jark

E

Silver Angel

Also available in Large Print
by Johanna Lindsey:

Hearts Aflame
A Heart So Wild
Tender Rebel
When Love Awaits

JOHANNA LINDSEY

Silver Angel

G.K.HALL &CO.
Boston, Massachusetts
1989

Published in Large Print by arrangement with
Avon Books, a division of The Hearst Corporation.

G.K. Hall Large Print Book Series.

Set in 16 pt. Plantin.

Library of Congress Cataloging in Publication Data

Lindsey, Johanna.
    Silver angel / Johanna Lindsey.
        p.   cm.——(G.K. Hall large print book series)
    ISBN 0-8161-4798-1 (lg. print)
    1. Large type books. I. Title.
  [PS3562.I5123S5 1989]
  813'.54——dc20
                                                89-15606

In Memory of My Father,
Edwin Dennis Howard

Chapter One

Barikah, the Barbary Coast, 1796
ON THE Street of the Jewelers, the pearl merchant, Abdul ibn-Mesih, closed his shop in anticipation of the singsong chant of the muezzin calling the faithful to prayer. Abdul had at least ten minutes to spare, but he was getting old, his bones prone to aches that slowed him down, so he needed to leave early each day. As long as he was able, he would walk to the nearest mosque rather than use the prayer rug he kept in the back of his tiny shop, unlike some of his less pious neighbors. So he was the only one on the street at this time, which was why he was the only one to witness the murder.

The young Turk and the large, black-robed man who was chasing him ran right past Abdul, not giving the pearl merchant the slightest notice. If only they had turned the corner and passed out of his sight, he wouldn't have had nightmares that night. Instead, the larger man caught his prey at the end of the street and nearly cleaved him in two with the scimitar he wielded. A quick search of the body produced a paper of some sort, and then the assailant was gone, slipping away without a backward glance, the body of the Turk left lying

1

where it fell, blood running in rivulets down the steep cobbled street in an invitation to the flies to come and feast.

Abdul ibn-Mesih decided he wouldn't walk to the mosque for afternoon prayers today after all. As the muezzins called from the heights of the many minarets in the city, the pearl merchant was kneeling on his prayer rug in the back of his shop and thinking it had been too long since he had seen his daughter in the country. She was due a visit—perhaps a lengthy one.

Later that afternoon, two more of Jamil Reshid's secret couriers were killed before they could leave Barikah. One was poisoned in a coffee house. The other was found in an alley with his throat cut, the bowstring wire used to strangle him left embedded in his neck.

That night, four camels raced west toward Algiers. The man in the lead was yet another luckless palace courier. The three assassins following him slowly closed the distance and finally overtook him. He died quickly, as had all the others.

The one who had felled him was a Greek Muslim, used to this type of work. The two accomplices riding with him were Arabs, brothers from an old family known for their loyalty to the Deys of Barikah, so it was natural the brothers should feel some guilt for their involvement in this night's work. They hadn't killed this courier, but the older brother had killed another one earlier that week.

2

They were as guilty as the Greek, as guilty as all the other assassins, and would be sent to the executioner's block if they were found out. To lose their heads for a purse of gold, to risk their family's disgrace, was perhaps the height of foolishness. But the price of corruption had been too tempting—it was a heavy purse of gold. So they accepted the risk. Still, there was the guilt, but not enough guilt to make them give up their new-found wealth.

Lysander, the Greek, removed the message from the body and opened it. He had to strain to read it in the dim light of the moon, but finally he made a sound of disgust, the urge strong to throw the letter down and grind it into the dust. Of course, he didn't.

"It is the same," Lysander said, passing the letter to the older of the two brothers.

"Did you think it would not be?" the younger brother asked.

"I had hoped," was Lysander's terse reply. "There is another purse for the one who finds the true message. I mean to be that one."

"So do we all," the older brother commented. "But he will still want to see this." And he carefully put the letter inside his robe. "He wants every message, regardless if it is the same as the others."

There was no need to say who "he" was. They each knew. Not that they could have named him, for none of them knew his name. Nor had they ever gotten a good look at him. They didn't even

3

know if he was the one who wanted Jamil Reshid's death, or if he was just a go-between for someone else. But he was the one who paid them so handsomely and collected each letter the palace couriers had carried.

It was discouraging, however. The Dey had an endless supply of loyal men to send out as decoys, all with the same letter, a note actually, written in Turkish, just three short sentences: *I offer greetings. Need I say more? You are remembered.*

The notes were not addressed. They were never signed. They could be from anyone in the palace to anyone in the world. They were more likely meant as a subtle threat for the assassins who read them, a reminder of the Dey's long arm of revenge. There might not even be a true message trying to leave Barikah in the midst of all these decoys. The couriers could simply be a ruse to confuse the assassins and delay them from making any more attempts on the Dey's life.

The first courier who had been captured had sworn before he died that he was to deliver his letter to an Englishman named Derek Sinclair. Even if that were true, if the Dey actually knew an Englishman by that name, which was unlikely, what could be the point of such a letter to him? Why waste the lives of so many men to have such a message delivered? But the assassins couldn't take the chance that there might be another message, the one they had yet to discover, perhaps to the Dey of Algiers or the Bey of Tunis, or even

4

to the Sultan himself across the sea in Istanbul: a letter asking for help. Though what could any of those allies do when no one knew who was behind the assassination attempts?

Lysander remounted his camel but spared a glance for the man he had just killed. "I suppose this one is to be food for the carrion? I am not used to leaving evidence behind, much less the bodies. There are too many ways to dispose—"

"It doesn't matter what you are used to. He wants the Dey to know his couriers are failing in their mission. How else will he know unless the bodies are easily found?"

"It's a waste of time, if you ask me," Lysander shot back, no longer trying to contain his disgust. "I think I will try and work my way into the palace. Who knows? I may get lucky and find a way to earn the largest purse of all, the one for Jamil Reshid's head."

He laughed as he rode away, and the two brothers exchanged a look. Of one mind, they doubted they would ever see the Greek alive again if he did manage to find a way into the palace. After four assassination attempts already, Jamil Reshid, Dey of Barikah, was more protected now than ever. Whoever next tried to take his life would be signing away his own. And if that unfortunate one was tortured before he was executed, he would give names. Not the name of him who was unknown, but the names of the men he had ridden with tonight.

Lysander didn't return to Barikah that night

after all. The Greek had been right. There were many ways to dispose of dead bodies, including his own.

"Do you realize the risk?"

Ali ben-Khalil nodded in answer. He was in awe of the man sitting across from him. When Ali had slipped his note to the palace eunuch in the bazaar, he had expected the same man to meet him, or perhaps another servant from the palace. But not the Grand Vizier, Jamil Reshid's chief minister. Allah preserve him, what had he gotten himself into? What was so important about this message that so many men were dying over, that he himself had volunteered to carry, that would bring Omar Hassan, the Grand Vizier, here to question Ali himself?

Omar Hassan had come in disguise, in a burnoose of the type the Berbers wore in the desert, but then he would have to; few men in the city wouldn't recognize the second most important man in Barikah. And he had questioned Ali thoroughly about why he had volunteered, which had been extremely embarrassing, for what man wanted to admit he was willing to risk his life for a woman? But there it was, his foolish reason. He was a poor man in love with a slave whose owner was willing to sell her, but only for a high price. What other way could he earn that price without stealing it, except in service to the Dey?

But he didn't intend to die in that service, or he would never have volunteered for this particular job. He truly felt he could succeed where so many others had failed, the simple reason being that he was not a servant of the Dey's, nor was he associated with the palace in any way. He was just a poor sherbet seller. Who would suspect him of being one of the palace couriers?

And that was why Ali had not gone to the palace to volunteer his services, why he had insisted on meeting in a house of dancing girls, why he had hidden himself there for two days before the meeting and would not leave for another two days. It was more than likely that Omar Hassan had been followed here, regardless of his disguise, and any men who left this house tonight would likewise be followed.

The Grand Vizier was undecided. He liked Ali ben-Khalil's plan, but the man was so obviously frightened, yet trying so hard to conceal it. Ali was young, perhaps twenty-two. Brown hair and eyes attested to the Berber-Arab ancestry he claimed, with perhaps a few fair-skinned slaves somewhere in his background to allow for the olive complexion and more delicate features. The fact that he had no experience for such a job was all to the good. But still . . .

A week ago Omar wouldn't have hesitated in handing over the letter he carried. But just yesterday Jamil had cornered him to demand, "How many have we sent out now?" What could Omar say? The truth? That there were so many the number was an embarrassment to mention? Jamil would have exploded. He had had to be argued into sending the letter in the first place. It had been Omar's idea, and a good one, he thought. But now he wondered. So many deaths, and for what? By the time the letter bore results, the entire affair could be over, the one behind the assassination attempts discovered and dealt with.

Allah preserve them it had better be over soon. Jamil was not a man to suffer restraints gracefully. The constant vigil, the frustration of not knowing who his enemy was, were already telling on him. If he were older, perhaps he would have more patience. But the Dey was only twenty-nine. He had ruled Barikah only these past seven years, having come to the throne on the death of his older half brother, who had been disrespect-fully known as "the tyrant."

But Jamil's rule had been good for Barikah. His outstanding political wisdom, his spirit of honor and justice, his concern for the welfare of his people, had endeared him to every Barikahian and brought prosperity to the city. Omar would do everything in his power to see Jamil's life pro-tected, even if it meant the sacrifice of hundreds of loyal men, or the sacrifice of this naive young man sitting before him. Why had he hesitated at all?

Omar Hassan tossed a purse onto the table and allowed a slight smile to curve his lips when the heavy sound of it caused Ali's eyes to grow wide. "That is for your expenses," he explained. "There is enough there to buy a ship and crew outright,

8

but you shouldn't have to go to that extreme. A small xebec for speed, rented for your exclusive use, should do you well." Another purse, just as heavy, landed next to the first. "This is for your service. There will be another one like it if you succeed." Omar's smile widened for a moment as Ali's eyes rounded even more, but then his expression turned serious again. "Just remember, if you do succeed, you are not to return to Barikah for at least six months."

This was the only thing Ali didn't understand about his mission, but he was loath to question the Grand Vizier for the reason. "Yes, my lord."

"Good. And don't worry about your woman in your absence. I will personally see that she isn't sold to another and that she is well taken care of. If you don't return, I will continue to see to her welfare."

"Thank you, my lord!"

There was nothing else to say. Omar Hassan handed over the letter.

Chapter Two

My DEAREST Ellen,

I don't mean to complain, but you haven't answered my last letter. Is something wrong? Are you ill? You know how I worry when I don't hear from you. And now that your niece's mourning period is over, I know you

9

must be entertaining. I was expecting a very newsy letter telling me all about it.

Chantelle *is* still with you, isn't she? Of course she must be, since she's not with *them*. I suppose you're too busy getting her ready for the season to write. That I can understand. She's such a lovely girl. She must have every eligible blood in the area trotting after her. *Are* there any eligibles there? No matter, dear. There are certainly enough here in London for her to choose from when she comes. And I am *so* looking forward to seeing you again, and dear Chantelle, too.

You know my daughter's husband—

Ellen Burke lowered the letter to her lap and rubbed her eyes. It was so tedious, reading one of Marge Creagh's letters. Ellen didn't know how the woman managed to write ten to twelve pages of pure nonsense, but she did it every time. And to think that one year of school, shared twenty-five years ago, could account for one of these gossipy letters every few months. But she had to read them. You never knew when Marge might impart some useful bit of information.

She skimmed through several pages until the underlined *they* caught her eye. Ellen supposed she should never have said her American cousins were upstarts, at least not to Marge Creagh. Now Marge felt perfectly free to ridicule the American Burkes at every opportunity. Not that Ellen didn't agree with every word, but it was not for Marge Creagh to say them.

I wasn't surprised when *they* came to town early. Your cousin Charles has made quite a nuisance of himself at the clubs, so I've heard, and so has his son, Aaron. It was bad enough when they brought the older girl out last season, when they all should have been in mourning as you and Chantelle were, but this year they've managed to buy her a sponsor to Almack's. And I wonder whose money paid for that, since it's well known Charles inherited only the baronetcy from your brother, not his wealth. Does Chantelle know how they're squandering her money? How could your brother have made such a perfidious man her guardian?

Ellen crumpled the letter in a rare burst of anger and threw it in the wastebasket beside her chair. So it was true, what she had long suspected. Charles Burke was not only a neglectful guardian, he was also a thief. No wonder he hadn't answered her letters. He didn't dare.

Good Lord, what were they to do? What could they do? Until Chantelle married or reached her majority, cousin Charles had control of her inheritance, and control of her. And since she wouldn't be twenty-one for another two years, nor could she marry without Charles' permission, there was every likelihood that there would be little or nothing left of the modest fortune that Chantelle's father had left her. Even her home had been taken over. Instead of residing in Sackville and the small estate of the baronetcy there, Charles had moved his large family into the more impressive Burke mansion in Dover, which was unentailed and so belonged to Chantelle now.

Fortunately, Chantelle had not yet suggested that she go home, for Ellen had to wonder if she would find a welcome in Dover now. She had come to stay with Ellen when her father died, before his only living male relative had descended on England with his American family. They had come to visit once, when Chantelle was still too overcome with grief to take much notice of them, but they had not suggested she return home either.

Apparently Charles thought the present arrangement ideal. And of course he would, since he was not supplying any money toward Chantelle's support, any of *her own* money. He had obviously thought Ellen was well enough situated to support them both, or he simply didn't care. She had had to disabuse him of that notion finally. Pride was pride, but it didn't put food on the table. Her own inheritance from her father had long ago been reduced to a very modest income, adequate only for one. But several months had passed and Charles still had not answered her letters. And now he was in London again, squandering Chantelle's money on his own family while Ellen pinched pennies and sold heirlooms to keep Chantelle from discovering the truth about the appalling predicament her father had bequeathed her.

No, to be fair, Ellen thought, it wasn't her brother's fault. When his heir, their older cousin, had died, Oliver had made every effort to discover the whereabouts of the younger cousin, who was by default his new heir to the baronetcy. That Oliver had died, too, before Charles was found could not have been foreseen. Nor could Oliver have known what a wastrel Charles was, or he would have made suitable arrangements for Chantelle instead of leaving no stipulation at all —which left Charles, as her only male relative, her lawful guardian.

At least Chantelle had Ellen. With the twenty years' difference in their age, Chantelle was more like a daughter, though Ellen had not helped to raise her. She had always been traveling during Chantelle's younger years, and when she did finally settle down, it was not to come home to live with her brother and his family. She was too independent for that. She had bought this cottage in Norfolk, where she had lived these past ten years, alone. It was how she liked it, though she hadn't minded at all Chantelle's coming to stay with her when Oliver died. She loved the girl dearly.

Ellen had no children of her own, which was perhaps why she felt so close to her brother's only child. By her own choice, she had never married. She was a plain-looking woman of thirty-nine, with light brown hair and blue eyes that were her best feature. She had been asked to marry. She had even had several love affairs that she remembered fondly, so it wasn't that she didn't like men. She just didn't want to live with one. She liked her independence too much.

Perhaps it hadn't been wise to keep Chantelle with her for the past year and a half. Chantelle had learned to be independent as well. That was fine for a woman who didn't plan to marry, but Chantelle would marry.

Unlike Ellen, who had the unremarkable Burke looks, Chantelle was the lone flower in the weed patch who took after her mother's French side of the family. Oliver had always claimed she was the image of her maternal grandmother, who was reputed to have been the mistress of kings, a rare beauty in the French court. Chantelle was even named after her. And it was true she looked nothing like a Burke with her platinum-blond hair and striking eyes the color of spring violets. She might not be small and delicate, but she wasn't too tall at five and a half feet either. She was too lovely by half, actually, certainly too lovely for men to ignore. She would be able to have her pick of beaux. She would be able to marry well—if she ever got the chance with Charles Burke as her guardian.

Ellen sighed. If that man didn't answer her letter soon, she would have to think seriously about taking Chantelle to London herself. She deserved to have her season, to be brought out in a style befitting her means and station. If Charles tried to deny her that, as it seemed he was doing with his lack of communication, he would have a fight on his hands. Ellen still had enough friends and influence in London to make things very unpleasant for her American cousin if he didn't own up to his responsibilities.

"Aunt Ellen, I'm back!" Chantelle called suddenly from the kitchen, and a moment later stepped into the parlor. "I found a nice chunk of beef for dinner and some kidneys for breakfast. Oh, and Mrs. Smith told me to tell you *again*"—she rolled her eyes—"that if you keep sending me to market, she'll soon be ruined."

"Is that why you're smiling?"

Chantelle grinned cheekily. "Last week I was giving her headaches. This week I'm ruining her. I wonder what I'll be responsible for next week."

"Insomnia? She's used that one on me before."

Chantelle laughed. "She's wonderful. I've never met anyone who gets so much pleasure out of haggling."

"Yourself, perhaps?"

"Well, it *is* fun," Chantelle said defensively, ignoring the fact that her throat was slightly sore from spending an hour whittling down the price of one piece of meat. But it had become a sort of challenge, getting the very best prices at the market, better prices than the regulars who had haggling down to a fine art. "And besides, look how much I saved today."

Ellen closed her eyes briefly. So Chantelle did

know that Ellen had been reduced to pinching pennies. Damn Charles Burke.

"I'm sorry, dear—"

"Don't be silly, Aunt Ellen. As soon as Charles sends the money I've requested, I'll make it up to you."

"You wrote him?"

"Of course. I would have done so sooner if I'd realized—well, at any rate, I'll soon set things right. Was there a letter today, by chance?"

"No, not today," Ellen replied, feeling a certain uneasiness at Chantelle's show of initiative. How would Charles react to demands from them both?

"Well, there will be one soon," Chantelle said with cheery confidence. "He can't very well ignore me, now, can he?"

He couldn't? He had certainly done an excellent job of it so far. And both women were to regret that he didn't continue to ignore them.

Chapter Three

THEY HAD locked her in her room, but Chantelle wasn't worried, not yet. It wouldn't be the first time she had gone out through the window, though many years had passed since she had last left the house that way. But it could be done. She did have that option. She just wasn't ready to go yet. She had to wait for the house to quiet, gather a few things, form a plan—but mainly she had to calm down, for at the moment she was so angry she felt she could actually kill Charles Burke.

She had arrived home only that afternoon, but it seemed she had been angry for the past week, ever since Charles' letter had come. Instead of the money she was expecting, she had received an order to return immediately to Dover, and that high-handed idiot hadn't even included the where-withal for the journey. Ellen had to sell another piece of jewelry, which had really been the last straw.

Chantelle was so furious she hadn't even waited for her aunt to close up the cottage to accompany her. Against Ellen's protests, she had left the very next day. She was going to show cousin Charles that she wasn't some silly twit who could be treated this way. He had a lot to answer for, especially his leaving her dependent on her aunt when Ellen couldn't afford it. She had planned to have it out with him. But that wasn't how it had turned out.

She had been shown into the parlor as if she were a guest in her own house. The butler was new. The carpeting, the furniture, were new. She felt like a guest. And the entire clan had been there.

Chantelle remembered them all from their one visit to her in Norfolk, soon after their arrival in England. And the difference between then and now was not immediately noticeable. Before, they had been the poor relations from America come to offer their condolences, mindful that Chantelle was a lady born and bred, whereas not even Charles among them could claim nobility, until now, that is.

Charles was her father's uncle's second son, Charles' own father having been no more than a carpenter's apprentice. It had been Chantelle's grandfather who had won the baronetcy from a grateful monarch, but he had been a rich man beforehand, and it was his wealth that had been left to Chantelle. Charles had in fact left England nearly thirty years ago, escaping debtors' prison in the process.

You wouldn't know it to look at him now. Big, pale, looking older than his forty-nine years, with the stamp of the Burkes on him in his brown hair and blue eyes. He was done up in the finest of fashions, as was his family. And they all exuded the confidence and condescension of the newly prosperous.

There was Charles' red-haired wife, Alice, who, according to the tardy solicitor's report, was the daughter of a tavern owner in Virginia, a tavern where Charles had been no more than an employee. Two of their daughters were present: Marsha, fourteen, and Jane, who was the same age as Chantelle, homely-looking girls with their mother's red hair and hazel eyes not helping to improve their plain looks. There was an older, married daughter, too, but she had elected to remain in America with a new husband, her second, according to the solicitor's report. Charles' son, Aaron, had brought his wife, Rebecca, and their

18

two young children to England, and they were all present, too.

And to think if her aunt hadn't lived near the ocean, Chantelle would have returned sooner to this bunch of interlopers who had taken over her home. She might even have come to like them, especially the younger children, who were rather awed by everything around them. She would have introduced them to the beach below Dover cliffs, which had been her playground as a child. Gathering shells, swimming, sailing with her father, exploring the caves, or just sitting on the cliffs, sometimes for hours at a time, waiting to sight a passing ship, had been the essence of her childhood years.

Yes, if the beach hadn't been within walking distance of her aunt's cottage, she would have missed it too much and come home, maybe before Charles got it into his head that he could marry her off to just anybody, and that *anybody* was Cyrus Wolrige, a man old enough to be her grandfather.

He was present, too, an old lecher who leered at her throughout the entire interview. She knew him. He lived not a quarter mile away from her. She had seen him often in church, snoring through the sermons, ogling the young women afterward in the churchyard. Emmy, her maid, had always called him a dirty old man.

And here Charles' very first words to her had been: "Ah, Chantelle, my dear. Meet your fiancé Mr. Wolrige. You'll be married in the morning."

Chantelle's reaction was to laugh at the absurdity of it. Cyrus Wolrige wasn't offended, though. He just sat there smiling, supremely confident that by tomorrow she would be his bride. His look gave her the chills and sobered her instantly.

Chantelle rounded on her cousin, violet eyes impaling him. "You are joking, sir, and in bad taste."

"I assure you the holy state of matrimony is nothing to joke about," he told her.

She had gathered her breeding around her like a cloak to keep from shouting at him. "Then I assure you, sir, that I refuse Mr. Wolrige's suit."

"You can't, my dear," Charles replied with a tight smile and an apologetic nod to Mr. Wolrige. "I have already accepted for you."

He went on to impress on her that she had no say in it, that they didn't need her permission in order to see her married, that because she was underage, her guardian's permission was all that was required.

It was too much. They all sat there staring at her in different degrees of gloating pleasure, except Aaron, who actually seemed resentful of the situation. And Chantelle found out why later from Emmy.

Emmy had originally accompanied her to Norfolk but had stayed no more than a month, returning to Dover when her mother took sick. And since Ellen's cottage was really too small for three people, she had returned to work here later, tending to the new ladies of the house.

She brought Chantelle a dinner tray that night

and stayed long enough to warn her that these Burkes were serious about seeing her married off. There had been a terrible row in the family because Aaron was already married. They seemed to think it would have been ideal if he could have been the one to wed Chantelle, There had even been talk of his divorcing his wife, who made a big stink about that, and things hadn't been right between Aaron and Rebecca since.

But that news was nothing to Chantelle. It didn't change the plans they had for her now. She was furious, and made no bones about it, but to no avail. In the end, she was still locked in her room, she would still be married to Wolrige in the morning—or so they thought. She wouldn't be here, however. Where she would be she wasn't exactly sure yet, but it wouldn't be here.

It was midnight before Chantelle had calmed down enough to make some immediate plans, and several hours more before she was ready to leave. The main thing was to get out of the house and hide somewhere while she decided what to do next. And she knew the perfect place. The caves. Some of the things she had stashed there as a child might even still be there—blankets, kindling, dishes, her shell collection. Blankets were the important thing, for she intended to spend the rest of the night there, and all day tomorrow, while the Burkes futilely combed the countryside for her. Then tomorrow night she would leave Dover, destination still undecided. London, most likely, and a job, maybe with one of her aunt's friends, where she could also get in touch with Ellen, who might have some other ideas. But the first place Charles would look for her would be in Norfolk, so she would have to be careful when contacting Ellen. In the meantime, she would definitely need some type of employment.

Chantelle grinned for the first time that day. Her stay with her aunt had been a training of sorts for which she could now be grateful. A year ago she might very well have accepted the fate Charles had planned for her, but not now.

Yet it was daunting. Pampered and adored all her life by her father, who had showered her with attention to make up for the loss of her mother at an early age, Chantelle had never known hardship, had never had to make decisions on her own. Certainly she had done without the luxuries she was accustomed to while living with her aunt, but she didn't consider that a hardship. Having no servants to wait on her, learning to cook, to clean, to go to market to buy her own food, had been an adventure, but only because she had shared the experience with her aunt. With anyone else she probably would have felt deprived. But Ellen was special and Chantelle loved her dearly. Her aunt had seen the world; she was independent; she wasn't one to accept only the straight and narrow path, but considered all options, the good with the bad.

Oh, if only she'd listened and waited for Ellen to come to Dover with her, the older woman might have been able to do *something*. No, that wasn't true. Chantelle wasn't that ignorant of the law. No one could do anything if her guardian was adamant about her marrying old Wolrige. There was nothing for it. She had to disappear for two years until she reached her majority, and hope that Wolrige wouldn't agree to a marriage with a missing bride.

If there was nothing left of her inheritance at that time, and her maid had told her how the Burkes had been spending her money as if spending were a new invention, that was the chance she had to take. Marrying Cyrus Wolrige was a worse choice, one to be avoided at all cost. But, by God, if there was nothing left when it was finally safe to show herself again, the Burkes would pay. They would pay anyway. For the first time in her life, Chantelle disliked someone enough to call the emotion hate. It wasn't pleasant. It went against her natural tendencies. But for what they had tried to do to her, what they were forcing her to do, she would get even somehow.

With several changes of clothes, a few personal items, and the last of the money her aunt had given her to get home all tied up in a bundle, Chantelle tossed it out the window, then climbed out on the ledge herself. She was fortunate that spring was already changing to summer so she could wear a thin muslin dress that was tied about her hips, making it possible for her to manage the climb down with ease. She was also fortunate that there was only a half-moon that offered a feeble light to help conceal her progress until she was off the grounds. It was nice to feel fortunate about *something* in this situation.

But she ran into her first obstacle almost immediately. She hadn't counted on the passing of time and the growth of trees. Her tree, which had always been so easy to reach, was still there, but hardly recognizable. The branch that had touched the house and been so easy to climb over now hung far above her head. Even on tiptoes she couldn't reach it. A lower branch would probably be in the right position in several more years, but now it was three feet below the ledge. If she was going to use that tree to get down, she would have to jump for it.

Ten years ago she wouldn't have hesitated, but then children rarely think of the possible results of their adventures. Right now she was looking at a possible broken neck, broken bones at the least, if she missed the branch when she jumped. It was worth hesitating over, but only for a few moments. She still jumped. Yet she had no time to feel elated when she caught the branch, for she heard the crack as it broke with her weight, and she found herself hurtling straight for a collision with the wide tree trunk.

Before she could scream, she let go of the branch and dropped the last eight feet to the ground, rolling as she landed. She stayed there, unmoving, taking note of the aches and pains on different parts of her body, giving a little prayer that none would be serious. When she finally moved, it was with a sigh of relief. Nothing was broken, though she would have a few bad bruises on one knee and hip, and it took her a moment to steady herself when she stood up and untied her skirt.

She had done it, she was free, and she wasted not another moment in collecting her bundle and moving silently away from the house in the direction of the cliffs. This was familiar terrain. It could have been as black as pitch and she still would have found her way to the steep path that descended to the beach and the caves.

Hurrying, she reached the cliffs in five minutes, and then Chantelle was running down the path, safely out of sight of the house, smelling the warm salt in the air, hearing the waves breaking on the beach below. Her playground, and the last place anyone would look for her. Finally she felt she had come home, for that mansion from which she had just escaped was anything but home to her now.

Only this "home" was filled with interlopers, too, as she found to her chagrin when she reached the narrow strip of beach. Twenty yards ahead, a small boat was pulled ashore, and outlined around it, three men. Smugglers? Perhaps. With no lights in evidence, Chantelle doubted they were fishermen. But regardless of who they were, she preferred not to be seen and slowly backed up toward the cliff path, where there was enough bramble and knotty trees to provide a temporary hiding place until the three men departed.

That plan would have worked out just fine, except there weren't just three men, there were five. The other two had been sent down the beach in opposite directions to make sure their own nocturnal landing on the beach would go unnoticed, and Chantelle backed right into one of them.

She was simply startled at first, until a hand smelling of fish closed over her mouth, and then it was too late to scream, even if she were willing to risk it. Better to talk her way out of this so her plans could proceed, and with that thought in mind, she didn't struggle unduly as she was dragged forward to the beached boat.

It seemed an ominous portent that the moon should disappear just as she was brought face-to-face with the other three men. In near total darkness, it was impossible for her to see if she might recognize any of them from the nearby village. And when the hand covering her mouth wasn't lowered so she could speak, she began to feel her first inkling of uneasiness, which quickly increased when they all began to speak at once in some gibberish she couldn't make heads or tails of. The laughter at the end she understood, though, and her uneasiness turned to fear.

Chantelle began to struggle then, but it was too late. With five of them there, for the last man had joined them now, it was appallingly easy for them to get her into the boat. A sweaty cloth was stuck into her mouth, a rope was wound around her a half-dozen times so her arms became useless, and one man's bare foot pressed down painfully into her belly to keep her from rising from the bottom of the boat while the others settled in their places.

A fifth man pushed them off, staying behind on the beach. What difference? There were still four surrounding her, four still talking that gibberish she didn't understand. The foot was removed from her stomach, but she didn't try to rise, afraid to draw their attention back to her. She needed time to think, to calm her fear. There had to be a perfectly logical explanation for their taking her with them, for not allowing her the opportunity to explain what she was doing on the beach in the middle of the night. She need only explain—but to whom? What if none of them spoke English, or French either, which was her second language? Good Lord, if she couldn't understand them, or they her, how was she to find out what was happening?

At least she didn't have long to find out where she was being taken. She was rowed out to a ship riding high in the water, which allowed for its anchorage so close to shore. In short order she was carried aboard, still trussed up, and dumped in a dark cabin, the door slamming shut behind the two who had brought her in, leaving the room in pitch-blackness.

Fortunately, the rope wrapped around her had not been tied tightly, and with some squirming, shaking, and contortions, she was able to unwind herself. Unfortunately, the door opened again just as she had finished, candlelight blinding her for a moment, and then fear took hold of her again, for the man standing there was like no man she had ever seen.

27

Swarthy-skinned, foreign-looking, with a sharp, hawklike nose and black eyes that normally were slightly slanted, but at the moment were quite rounded in surprise as they looked her over. He was short, shorter than she, and thin. She might even be able to overpower him, which idea should have calmed her nerves a little but didn't. He wore loose trousers and a white cloth that wound around his head, but nothing else, not even shoes.

The bare chest offended her; his staring offended her; that she was here was the biggest offense of all. As she stood there facing him, she began to feel resentment in the worst way, which did wonders in making her forget to be afraid. Motionless until now, she recalled the gag in her mouth and yanked it out, noting only briefly that it was just like the cloth wrapped about this fellow's head.

"Do you speak English?" Chantelle asked imperiously. "Because if you don't, you had better get someone in here who does right away. I demand—"

"I speak English."

The fight went out of her as relief flooded in. "Thank God! I was beginning to fear no one would . . . but listen, sir, a mistake has been made. I must see the fellow who captains this ship immediately."

"All in good time, *lalla*." And then he grinned, revealing startling white teeth. "He will want to see you, too, you may be sure. By the breath of

Allah, he will be delighted such a gift has fallen into his lap."

Chantelle tensed noticeably. "Gift? What gift? If you mean me—"

"Certainly you." His grin widened. "You will bring us a fortune in—"

"Don't be absurd," Chantelle cut him off sharply. "You don't know who I am. You can't know if I have the wherewithal to be ransomed or not."

"Ransomed?" He chuckled, a sound of genuine amusement. "No, *lalla,* women are rarely ransomed, at least not one as beautiful as you."

Chantelle stepped back a pace, as if his words had literally pushed her. She didn't understand. She was afraid she did understand.

"This ship—what is it doing here? Why have you brought me aboard?"

"There is no need to fear," he tried to assure her. "You will not be harmed."

She wasn't reassured. She was reaching full-blown panic. *"Who are you?"*

She jumped back when he took a step toward her, so he came no closer. Her fear disturbed him. Hakeem Bektash had never been called on to deal with a captive before, and this was no common captive. His first look at those aristocratic features told him that; her imperious manner confirmed it. She was a lady. But who she was didn't matter, not even her name, for she would be given a new one by her eventual master. Still, he was not used to having any dealings at all with ladies, which was why he had been intimidated into calling her *lalla,* the title for a wellborn woman, even though she was to be a slave.

He simply didn't know how to handle her. Rais Mehmed, his captain, insisted the truth should never be delayed, that captives needed as much time as possible to adjust to their new circumstances. Allah help him, why did he have to be the only one aboard who spoke English?

Before he could say anything, the ship shifted as the anchor was released. "What was that?" Chantelle squeaked, reaching for the wall behind her to brace herself.

"We are sailing."

"No!" she cried out, and then, "To where? Damn you, tell me what's happening!"

"We are corsairs, *lalla.*"

The word was so well known and feared, there was no need for further explanation. But she seemed not to understand.

In fact, Chantelle had heard the word "corsair" before; she was just so upset the meaning eluded her for several long moments. When it finally clicked in her mind what he meant, the remaining color in her face drained away.

"Pirates? Turkish pirates?"

He shrugged. "Pirates, merchants. It is the same on the Barbary Coast."

"The devil it is! Corsairs are white slavers!"

"Occasionally."

"Then you are . . . No, by God, not on top of everything else!"

He was so fascinated by the bright color rushing

30

back into her cheeks, he gave no thought to what she meant. Nor was he prepared for her sudden leap forward. He was pushed aside so forcefully he lost his balance and landed on the floor, the candle flying out of his hand to become extinguished. In blackness, he just barely saw her disappear through the door. Panicked, he leaped up to follow. If she jumped ship, Rais Mehmed would probably throw him over as well.

He was too late. Running onto the deck, he saw her just ahead; saw a man dash forward to stop her, only to crash empty-handed to the deck behind her; saw her not even bother to climb the rail but simply dive over it. He rushed to the rail himself in time to see her silver head break the surface of the water, and miracle of miracles, she could swim. Few men aboard could claim the same, himself included, or he would have immediately jumped in after her.

Beside him, his shipmates were shouting, as amazed as he was that the English girl wasn't drowning but was heading for shore. And then Rais Mehmed bore down on him.

"You stupid piece of shit! I give you the simplest of tasks to do and you bungle it!" The captain's fist accompanied this setdown, and Hakeem skidded across the deck. Rais Mehmed came to stand over him, murder in his dark eyes. "I ought to—"

"Go after her."

"So you're crazy, too?" Mehmed shouted in-

31

credulously. "Go after one worthless female? The sharks can have her," he concluded in disgust.

Hakeem rolled aside to avoid Mehmed's kick and quickly held out a hand to stop any further attack. "She had silver hair and eyes like amethysts. A goddess would envy her beauty."

Mehmed stopped, but now his anger took a new direction. "Idiot! Why didn't you say so?"

Hakeem sighed as the privateer was ordered about and the boat readied to be lowered once again. He had saved himself from further abuse, but what of the girl? He half wished they wouldn't find her, though he didn't understand why.

Chapter Four

"THERE'S A chap here to see you, my lord, waiting up at the house. Just missed you, he did. Wandered in on foot about five minutes after you rode out, but he's still waiting, far as I know."

The Earl of Mulbury dismounted, handing the reins of his prize Thoroughbred over to the head groom. Black brows came together above emerald eyes as he glanced up the narrow path toward the house. He wasn't expecting anyone, and his friends were all known to Harry, so for the moment his interest was piqued.

"Are you sure it's me he wants to speak with, not the Marquis?"

"Asked for you by name, he did. Didn't mention your grandfather. Didn't say nothing else, actually. In fact, I'd say he doesn't speak English. Had that look about him, if you know what I mean."

The Earl nodded, tamping down the urge to grin. Harry didn't trust foreigners, ever since his daughter had run off with a Frenchman many years ago. Anyone with the slightest accent was suspect as far as Harry was concerned. His friend Marshall Fielding had always complained about Harry, because the groom often gave his couriers a bad time when they delivered dispatches here. But the chap awaiting him couldn't be one of Marshall's agents, since at the Marquis's request the Earl was no longer involved with British intelligence, though he had never been seriously involved to begin with. There was no point wondering about it when the fellow awaited him. The Earl headed up the stable path, coming out on the right side of the Palladian-style mansion, residence of the Marquis of Huntstable, his grandfather. The Earl had his own estate in York, but aside from a short yearly visit there to be sure the old manor house was still standing and the tenants were happy with his steward, he lived here in Kent with his grandfather. It was by mutual choice. Notwithstanding the fact that he was the Marquis's only heir, and so the old gentleman was frantic to keep him close and protected, they were also extremely fond of each other.

"Your lordship, there is—

"Yes, I know, Mr. Walmsley," the Earl cut the

butler short as he handed over his hat, gloves, and riding quirt. "Where have you put him?"

"I would have kept him here in the hall, milord, but the way he kept staring at the maids made them nervous, so I moved him to the little parlor."

"Rude, was he?"

"You would think he had never seen a woman before," was Mr. Walmsley's opinion.

Mobile lips turned up slightly at one corner. "Did he offer a card?"

"He didn't even give his name, milord," the butler replied with marked distaste. "If you ask me—"

"Never mind. I'll see him now. And send in my usual tray, Mr. Walmsley, with enough for two."

The little parlor was located to the right of the mammoth hall, down a short corridor there, and at the back of the house. It caught the morning sun, making it a cheerful room, at least at this time of year. The sun was sadly lacking this morning, however, but the rain had held off until after the Earl had enjoyed his morning ride. The room was still light enough with two ceiling-high windows so that lamps were not necessary, and the single occupant was quite visible, standing facing the left wall, clearly fascinated with a shelf of antique clocks.

The little fellow didn't hear him enter, which was fortunate, for the Earl didn't like being taken by surprise, but he certainly was. Even from this side view, he recognized his visitor's nationality, and a dozen questions popped into his mind, along

34

with dread, for he could think of only one reason for an Arab's presence here, and it wasn't good.

With difficulty, the Earl brought his features into a bland mask, and in precise Arabic, he asked, "You requested an interview? "

Ali ben-Khalil jerked around abruptly at the sound of a familiar tongue in this foreign land. It was unexpected, unhoped for, but then Ali was beginning to think Allah had personally seen him through this whole journey, so what was one more blessing? Hadn't he made it safely out of Barikah? Hadn't the weather cooperated and rushed the little three-masted xebec across the seas in less than a month? Even the crew had been blessed in finding an unexpected captive on shore who would add to their profit from this voyage. Then there had been the sailor who spoke English and helped to teach Ali the words he needed to know to reach this place quickly. And there had been the clothes he had easily found hanging in the backyard and stolen, so that he wouldn't look so conspicuous when he had to approach strangers to ask directions. Everything had gone so well, too well, in fact, that he had begun to fear something had to go wrong just to balance the scales. But no, he was here. The tall man who spoke his tongue was obviously the one he sought. He had succeeded, to the very end. Pride and elation swelled in equal proportions within his chest.

"Derek Sinclair?"

At the nod, Ali quickly handed the letter forward, then stood back and waited, for what he had no idea. Perhaps there would be questions. Perhaps the Englishman could recommend where Ali could stay for the next six months. He still didn't understand why he should be banned from Barikah for such a time, but he couldn't complain. He was a rich man now. Besides his own purse, there was still a large balance left from the money he had used to hire the corsair.

He watched the Englishman move to a small desk in a corner and pick up a letter opener before sitting down. The letter itself took only a few seconds to read, it was so brief, and then he looked up to stare at Ali. It was those penetrating green eyes that finally broke through Ali's euphoria to send a cold chill down his back. The eyes, the height, the aquiline features. There was no beard, but . . .

Ali groaned, then immediately prostrated himself on the floor. "Don't kill me, gracious lord! Please, you must lock me away. I am willing, I swear!"

"Why?"

The question was so bland, Ali dared to raise his head slightly. "I—I have seen you."

"So you have. Very well, how long shall I detain you?"

"Six months," Ali replied instantly, finally understanding. "I was told not to return for six months."

The Earl swore softly. Six months? He was supposed to be married next month. Caroline wasn't going to like such a long delay. His grand-

36

father wasn't going to like it either. But if the courier was to be detained for six months, then Derek could expect to be gone just as long.

"Get up off the floor and tell me what you can about this letter."

"I didn't read it," Ali protested as he slowly rose, warily watching his host.

"It wouldn't matter if you had. What else do you know about it?"

Ali briefly told him about the many couriers who had been sent out with the same letter, only to die by assassins. How he had volunteered and succeeded. Then he was asked about the Dey.

"I know only that there have been attempts made on his life, that he rarely leaves the palace now."

"Do they know who is trying to kill him?"

Ali shrugged. "I am not from the palace. That is why I was sure I could succeed in coming here, after so many others had failed. I don't know what goes on inside."

Derek smiled. "You did well, my friend. Now, what am I to do with you for six months?"

"Lock me—"

"I doubt that will be necessary, but you can stay here on the estate. I'm sure we can find something to keep you occupied. What do you do?"

"I'm a sherbet seller."

Derek chuckled. "A sherbet seller succeeding where trained soldiers failed. Well done. If only you could speak a little English."

"A little." Ali was finally able to smile, his relief overwhelming. Allah was still watching over him.

"Splendid," the Earl replied, and stood up just as a maid knocked, then entered with his morning tray.

The girl was pretty, and Ali supposed he would have to get used to seeing women unveiled in this foreign land, as they all seemed to be. The men here must not mind if other men gazed on their women. This girl obviously belonged to Derek Sinclair, for the sensual look she gave him as she set the tray down was extremely intimate.

"Coffee?" the Earl asked.

Ali nodded; then, after the girl left, he asked hesitantly, "She is part of your harem?"

Derek smiled, sipping the beverage he had acquired a taste for in his youth. "We don't keep harems here, more's the pity," he answered. "But if we did, I suppose you could say she would be a part of mine. However, she's not for my exclusive use, if you know what I mean."

"You have strange ways here."

"Strange to you, yes, but you'll get used to them. All things become natural after a while."

The Earl remained behind in the little parlor after Ali was led away by Mr. Walmsley. He sat behind the desk, staring thoughtfully at the letter lying open before him. Three short sentences in a bold Turkish scrawl, easy to read, since Turkish was as familiar to him as Arabic and French. In fact, English had been the last language he had learned, though he spoke it now as if he had been born to it.

His first reaction on reading the letter had been relief. No one had died. But after what Ali had told him, he had to admit: Not yet.

Three short sentences:

I offer greetings. Need I say more? You are remembered.

A child's code, designed by boys who liked to confound their teachers and servants. He remembered fondly the time he had read an essay aloud and no one had understood why Jamil found it so funny. But Jamil had heard the code, and the message only for him: I would rather be eating pomegranates and spying on the Dey. What about you?

This message was much shorter. Three sentences, three words, the three first words of each sentence. *I need you.* Of course Derek couldn't ignore such a message. There had been letters through the years, but sent through normal channels. This one had cost lives. This was no simple letter. *I need you.* Derek would go.

He should have gone two months ago, when Marshall had asked him to, but that had been for a different reason, one that hadn't been important enough to make him postpone his wedding, or break his word to his grandfather. Locating and ransoming some English girl known to be in Barikah, was nothing to him. She had already

39

been in captivity for three months, so it was highly unlikely that she was still a virgin, and thus he could see no need to intervene.

It was the English consul's job to handle the ransoming of slaves. It would just take a little longer for the consul to free the girl, if she could be freed. Few women were, at least pretty women, and Marshall had assured him the girl was pretty. She was aso related to some powerful nobleman, which was why Marshall had become involved. But it still meant nothing to Derek. Only now that he was going to Barikah, he might as well agree to rescue the girl. That way, he could question Marshall about what was going on in Barikah without revealing why he wanted to know.

Kismet. This was meant to happen, at this time, in this way. It was the Muslim philosophy on which he was raised. After nearly nineteen years in England, he was meant to go home. Why, he wouldn't know until it was over.

Chapter Five

BENEATH THE woolen blanket, Chantelle lay shivering. It was a condition she had no control over, and it wouldn't stop. Her hair had dried hours ago. The cabin was warm. It was her fear that was causing the trembling, and twice had made her sick to her stomach.

Dear God, she had come so close to escaping the corsairs. Her feet had actually touched bottom when the small boat bumped into her, pushing her under the water. When she came up for air, hands immediately hauled her inside the boat, and she knew she wouldn't get another chance to escape.

She was brought back to the ship, carried back into this cabin. Only this time two men had stayed to see her stripped down to nothing. Too exhausted from her bid for freedom, she had been unable to stop them. But they hadn't touched her otherwise. They had left her alone in the dark cabin, taking her wet clothes with them. She had eventually found the pillows and fur rug she remembered seeing from before, and the blanket to cover herself with. She had crawled into a tight ball, and the shivering had begun as she wondered what would happen next, afraid she knew.

She didn't sleep, terrified of being caught by surprise. Morning came, and with it light from one small window, and still she was left alone. She would rather have gotten it over with, whatever they would do to her next, than to lie here thinking about it. She was certain she would be raped by the crew, certain that if she survived that, she would then be sold into slavery. Both prospects were so inconceivable that she couldn't bear thinking of them, and so there was just the fear of being hurt and abused.

Several times she wondered what had happened to the little man who had spoken to her before. Why didn't he come again? Any communication at all would have been a relief. But perhaps it was

41

standard procedure to let captives suffer the agonies of the unknown to wear them down. Fear was debilitating. Yet he had spoken to her before. He had said she wouldn't be harmed. But what exactly to a corsair constituted harm?

God, if only she didn't know what they were. If only her tutors hadn't thought to include world history and affairs in her studies. But the Ottoman Turks, who for hundreds of years had been intruding on Christian Europe, were known to her, as were the Barbary States, members of the Turkish empire, and the Barbary corsairs, pirates of the Mediterranean. They raided foreign coasts, they attacked foreign ships, they killed or sold all Christian captives into slavery without exception. So what would such men consider harm to a woman? Certainly not what she would reckon as harm.

When the door finally opened later that morning, it wasn't to admit the sailor Chantelle had spoken with. Four men entered, two bare-chested, one tall, thin man in a long white robe, and one more impressive fellow in a bright silk jacket over loose Turkish pants. All wore turbans. All were sharp-featured, though light-skinned. Only the one in the white robe didn't have a long, curved sword attached to his belt.

Chantelle sat up immediately, but she didn't try to rise with only the blanket to cover her. She held it up to her chin, cowering back against the wall. Trapped in the small room, eyes huge with fear, skin translucent without color, she didn't realize that she stunned them, especially the captain, who was having his first look at her in good light. Eyes like hers were unknown to them. And the hair, silver blond, with a lock falling over the blanket to reveal its glorious hip length, was prized in the East. Circassians were known to have blond hair, but sailors weren't likely to ever see it, and these hadn't. Her face was exquisite. If she had a body to match, she would be worth a fortune. If she was also a virgin, her price could increase tenfold.

It was precisely the latter that Rais Mehmed had come to judge, for her comfort on the voyage depended on her worth. Then, too, if she wasn't a virgin, there was no point in denying himself or his crew the use of her body for the long trip home. Most of his crew were sodomites, but only by necessity. A woman aboard was a blessing— if she wasn't a virgin. Mehmed began to hope she wasn't.

"She is terrified, Rais," the white eunuch said quietly by his side. "Shouldn't you get Hakeem in here to tell her this is just a simple procedure?"

Mehmed shook his head without taking his eyes off the girl. "He must become her friend if he is to help her to adjust. The more he can teach her of her new life, the more malleable she will be, and so the more valuable. If he were here now, even to explain, she would never trust him later, never be willing to learn from him."

"Then get it over with, before she faints."

Chantelle didn't faint. She screamed, piercingly,

until a cloth was stuffed in her mouth to muffle the sound. And she fought, wildly but uselessly. Her blanket was used against her, trapping her arms beneath it as she was pushed down onto her back, the man in the silk jacket lying across her upper body, pinning her to the floor. She kicked, regardless that this dislodged the blanket from her legs, but in seconds, each foot was caught by a different man, and her legs were spread wide and held down with a hand pressed against each knee and ankle to keep them straight and still.

Her eyes were wild with horror, expecting the worst. She couldn't see past the broad chest of Silk Jacket, who lay on her sideways, his hands on her shoulders, his heavy side gouging her stomach. She didn't know that the sailors holding her feet had been ordered not to look at her, that White Robe was a eunuch who couldn't have raped her if he wanted to, that he did this to all female captives. She could only feel what was happening, the shock of something pressing between her legs, being inserted into her body, probing painfully, then withdrawing. She thought she had been raped. She didn't know she had just passed the test that would save her from it, at least while she was on the ship.

The blanket was pulled down over her legs, alerting her that apparently only one man was to violate her for now. Words were exchanged, and her legs were released. She didn't try to move them. Depression was already setting in. She had

44

feared the worst and the worst had happened. Nothing else mattered at the moment.

The two bare-chested sailors left the room before Silk Jacket removed his bulk from her. She didn't care that he pulled her up with him. But she did snap out of her shock when he snatched her blanket away. She reached for it, only to drop her hands instinctively to cover herself instead.

It was the final humiliation, to be deprived of her dignity in this manner. They were animals, and she told them so, though they ignored her words, not understanding them. Her contempt and outrage were more easily understood, however.

"By the prophet's beard, she's magnificent," Rais Mehmed got out, though he suddenly seemed breathless. Never in his life had he seen a woman like this.

"She does have spirit," the eunuch allowed.

"Such curves—"

"She could be plumper."

"I wouldn't change a thing."

"Your tastes are not the usual," the eunuch reminded him. "Nor is she for you. But Hamid Sharif will be pleased."

Mehmed grunted, for the merchant Hamid Sharif, owner of their ship, aready had four wives who nagged him to distraction. "He would rather have the profit, which will put more coins in our pockets. He might even be able to tempt the Dey with this one, though it has been a long while since he has bought any new women for his harem."

"It is not for us to be concerned with whoever eventually buys her, Rais. It is for you to see she is delivered to Hamid Sharif in good condition."

With that he handed the blanket back to the girl, offering her an apologetic smile. Mehmed laughed to see her take the blanket, cover herself with it, then spit at the eunuch's feet.

Chapter Six

CAROLINE DOUGLAS reined in the high-stepping mare and waited for Derek to catch up with her. She hadn't expected him to call this afternoon, or to suggest they ride out when he learned her father had guests. But she hadn't been caught unprepared. This was her chance to wear her new riding habit of dark navy wool, with a light blue satin waistcoat cut like a man's. The masculine style of the outfit, made by a man's tailor, was quite fashionable, and she knew she looked particularly fetching in these colors with her red hair. At least Derek thought so, since he said as much.

Under the brim of her tall hat, she watched him approach, admiring his handling of the half-trained stallion he rode. Raising Thoroughbreds was just a hobby to him, yet his stable produced some of the finest horseflesh in England, many of which were champion racers. Her own mare had been a gift from him when he asked her to marry him. She loved the animal. She loved Derek. She sighed, wondering for the hundredth time if it wasn't a mistake to marry one's best friend.

No, she had to stop it. She had already jilted two men, to her father's vast displeasure. She couldn't do it again, and certainly not to Derek Sinclair, Earl of Mulbury. She wanted to marry him, she really did.

She couldn't think of a more perfect union. They had grown up together on neighboring estates. They knew each other so well. Her father looked on him as a second son. And then there were the incidental things, such as his charm, his handsomeness, his gentle nature. Of course he was a sensualist, but she couldn't really fault that, not when his kisses made her feel like she was the most cherished, beloved woman in the world. The trouble was, she was afraid he made every woman feel that way, and he had had so many women, so many women at the same time.

He used to tell her about each and every conquest, just as she had told him about her first infatuation and each subsequent one. As far as that went, they had no secrets. He had sworn to make her happy. She believed he could. She knew he had given up his mistresses when he proposed to her, and that included half the maids in his grandfather's house. It wasn't that she didn't think he could be faithful to her. So what was it that made her keep having these doubts?

Bride's jitters, no more. She had suffered them twice before as the wedding date approached, and it was no wonder. Decisions came hard for her because she rarely had to make any for herself. She didn't have the confidence to be certain of her choice when she did make one. It had always been so. One of the things that drew her to Derek was that he gave of himself, his own confidence, his strength. When he made a friend, it was for life, as if that person belonged to him. Maybe that was what was wrong. She felt she had always belonged to him. She couldn't imagine her life without him in it. Was that why she had said yes, so there would be no chance of her ever losing his friendship?

No, she loved him, always had. Well, not always. He had taken getting used to when he first came to England. She had been only six years old. He had been almost eleven. He spoke French, acted in strange ways. She hadn't been taught French yet, so their communication was limited, but only for a short while, for he learned to speak English with amazing speed. He had been raised in some Near Eastern country where his father was an ambassador. The Marquis's daughter, Melanie, had married the fellow while abroad and in all those years had not returned to England. But both Derek's parents had died when he was ten, and so he had been sent to live with his grandfather, who had immediately had Derek's name changed to Sinclair since, as the last man of the line, he was the Marquis's only heir.

She remembered Derek's condescension that first year of his arrival, his air of superiority. He had acted like he was a bloody king and everyone else was there just to do his bidding. God, how she had hated him at first. But it hadn't taken him long to readjust his attitude, or to win her over. He had a way with females that was impossible to resist. Soon she adored him, never questioning that her best friend should be a male instead of a female. And even after nearly nineteen years, he was still her closest friend though she knew he had other friends, male friends, with whom he was just as close.

Lord Fielding was one, that scoundrel who had led Derek into a pastime of spying. Pastime indeed, but that was all it was to Derek, who thought it a lark, a bit of excitement, never considering the danger, while the Marquis, and she, too, was terrified each time he crossed over to France, wondering if this time he would be caught and executed. Finally the Marquis had convinced Derek to stop taking risks with his life. The poor man was rightfully afraid that Derek wouldn't live long enough to carry on the line. So he was to get married, at the Marquis's insistence, and his natural choice, the way he had told it when he proposed, had been her. And she had been so terribly flattered. He knew so many women, yet he had chosen her to settle down with.

"Wool-gathering, Caro?"

She glanced down to see that he had dismounted and was holding out his arms to her. She smiled, putting her hands to his shoulders, feeling his sure grip on her waist, the warmth of his fingers. And he didn't let go immediately when her feet touched

49

the ground. Unlike most men, he had the ability to communicate his affection through the senses. It was an endearing quality, because he did it unconsciously, touching a shoulder, a waist, an arm, fingers smoothing over skin. He didn't know what these innocent contacts could do to a woman. Or maybe he did. It was part of his potent sensuality.

She laughed away his question now, unwilling to admit he was so much in her thoughts. "I was thinking of my garden, and moving the rose bushes—"

He pulled her closer. "Little liar."

Caroline grinned up at him, and it was a very long way up, for she was a small woman, and he towered more than a foot above her. "Very well, I was thinking you have very feminine eyelashes."

"Good God, woman, if that was to be a compliment, you failed."

"But they make you very handsome, Derek," she insisted, mischief lighting her gray eyes.

"And if all you have to spout is nonsense, I can think of a better way to spend our time."

"Oh, no." She moved quickly away from him, for once he started kissing her, every other consideration disappeared. "You brought me out here for a reason, so let's hear what couldn't be said in front of my father."

"I have ravishment in mind, little one."

Caroline snorted. "Not bloody likely. If I were going to be ravished by you before the wedding, it would have been done months ago. Now, out with it."

He caught her hand and began walking her through the meadow of wildflowers. "How much of a fuss will be caused if we postpone the wedding?"

She stopped, making him face her. "What's happened?"

"I have to leave England for a while."

"That cad! That scoundrel!" she exploded. "He's done it again, hasn't he?"

"Who?" Derek asked in all innocence.

"You know very well who! Lord Fielding! And after you promised your grandfather you wouldn't get involved in any more of his nasty adventures."

"Marsh didn't . . . well, actually—" He stopped, grinning. "Scoundrel, Caro? Cad? I thought you liked Marshall."

"I did," she grumbled. "Before he recruited you to be a spy."

Gently, Derek pulled her forward to slip an arm around her waist and continue walking. "Marshall never twisted my arm, you know. Whatever I did I enjoyed doing. And this has nothing to do with that. It's something only I can do this time. But there's no danger involved. It's more a diplomatic mission."

"Which I suppose you've been sworn to keep secret?"

"Naturally."

She was torn between relief at the postponement, which would give her more time to get over her doubts, and worry that he was lying to her about there being no danger involved. "How long will you be gone?"

"There's no way to determine . . . possibly six months."

"*That* long?"

He shrugged. "Diplomacy takes longer than spying."

"Father isn't going to like this."

"The Duke and my grandfather will have that in common."

"What did your grandfather say about it?"

"I haven't told him yet. Thought I'd put it off until I'm ready to leave."

"When?"

"Tomorrow, most likely," he admitted. "I'll take ship from Dover."

"Oh, Derek!" She stopped suddenly to throw her arms around his neck.

"What's this, Caro? Will you miss me?"

"Not at all," she mumbled into his jacket.

"Think of me?"

"Not for a moment."

He chuckled, squeezing her affectionately. "That's my girl."

Chapter Seven

DEREK DIDN'T wait until the next day to speak to his grandfather. Finding him in the library on his return home, he laid everything before the old man and left him to draw his own conclusions.

Robert Sinclair's answer was the only one it could be. "You have to go."

"So I concluded," Derek replied. "I've sent for Marshall. He should be here by tomorrow afternoon."

"Are you going to tell him your relationship—"

"Do you see any point in making that known after all these years?"

"No," the Marquis admitted.

"Then you have your answer. There's nothing I can tell him anyway. I won't know why I am needed until I get there. He'll think I'm going after the English girl. That's enough."

"Are you?"

Derek shrugged. "As long as I'm there, I'll look into it. But it's doubtful she can be recovered, even if I can locate her. Once a woman enters a harem, she's lost to the outside world."

Robert frowned. "You say that without the slightest regret."

Derek smiled fondly at his grandfather. Robert's bitterness was understandable.

"What do you want me to say? She's just one girl among thousands. Slavery is only frowned on here. In the East, it is an acceptable institution."

"You don't have to approve of it."

"I didn't say I approve of it. But I was raised in the East. I accept it for what it is, a way of life."

"I know, I know." The Marquis sighed, for this was no more than a rehashing of an old argument. "It's just . . . . do you think you'll see her?"

Derek knew he was no longer speaking of the English girl. "I don't know."

"If you do, tell her she has my heartfelt thanks."

Derek nodded and embraced his grandfather. Affection tightened his throat. The message was clear and as much for himself. It spoke of his grandfather's approval, love, and pride, sentiments not easily expressed by the old man. They might disagree on many subjects, and Robert might disapprove of Derek's hedonistic ways, but a strong bond had grown between them over the years that was unshakable.

An hour later, Derek was still in the library, though alone, when Lord Marshall Fielding was announced. Having handed over his hat and coat to Mr. Walmsley, he was smoothing down unruly brown curls as he entered the room.

Derek rose to greet him, managing to conceal his surprise. That Marshall had arrived today instead of tomorrow meant he couldn't have received Derek's summons but was here for his own reasons.

"And what brings you down from London, Marsh?"

Thick brows over light green eyes gave Marshall a perpetually serious countenance that was hardly relieved even when he smiled. "It's been about a month since I was here last. Thought I'd see how your conscience is holding up."

Derek burst into laughter. Trust Marshall never to give up, especially when he wanted Derek to do something that in his opinion couldn't be handled by anyone else. He had probably come here to give their last argument another go-round, but with little hope of changing Derek's mind. He was in for a surprise.

Marshall was an organizer, not a doer. He and Derek had always made an unlikely pair. With nothing in common save their age and a mutual love of horses, it was surprising that they had become fast friends during school, but they had. It was a matter of opposites: serious, restrained, and conservative on the one hand; bold, adventuresome, and somewhat arrogant on the other. The one pushed while the other held back, perfect complements to each other.

"Sit down, Marshall." Derek led him to a group of comfortable reading chairs. "You're just in time for tea."

Marshall ignored the offer. "I take it your conscience isn't suffering."

"Don't have one."

"Derek—"

"Oh, relax, Marsh. You know you'd never make it as an ambassador in the East. You have to ease into these things, exchange a few pleasantries first. So how's the spy business?"

"You know we don't like that word. Foreign intelligence—"

"A spy's a spy, no matter what you call him."

"I concede," Marshall said good-naturedly. "Now, is that enough pleasantries for you, or shall we discuss the weather, too?"

55

"The climate is rather mild for—"

"Derek, I swear you could try a saint with little effort! You sit here uttering nonsense while Miss Charity Woods suffers atrocities—"

"Come off it, Marsh," Derek cut in brusquely. "You don't know the girl's suffering anything. I happen to know there are women who sell themselves into slavery to end up as your Miss Woods has probably ended up. Harem women are pampered and showered with luxuries. They are rarely ill-used."

Marshall leaned his head back and closed his eyes with a sigh. He should have known it would be a waste of time trying to get Derek to change his mind. If Derek didn't have the legitimate excuses he had used last time for refusing, there was this, the fact that they just couldn't see eye to eye on the plight of women sold into slavery in the Muslim states. Where had Derek lived that the women were so well treated? It wasn't that way everywhere. Didn't he know that?

But it was useless to question Derek Sinclair about his life before he came to England. He never gave details, only opinions, and those were far too Eastern by far.

Derek hadn't offered any opinions last time; he had just flatly refused to leave England for any reason, though his excuse was reasonable. "I'm getting married in a few months."

"Don't remind me. You steal the only girl I can ever love, and you rub it in by inviting me to the wedding," Marshall had answered with a teasing grin that was, sadly, not teasing at all. "You could postpone the wedding."

"Can't do it. And besides, the old man's asked me to stay close. He's ailing, you know."

"Devil he is," Marshall argued.

"He's been bedridden the past week."

"I happen to know he just has a bad cold."

But Derek went one better. "You know his age, Marsh. He wants to see my children before he kicks off."

Of course Marshall couldn't argue against that. The Marquis was nearing seventy, and his health hadn't been that good in recent years. The thought of children, Caroline and Derek's children, depressed Marshall enough to let it go. But there had been so much pressure put on him since then to get results that he was forced to ask Derek again. And then, too, his heart was still hoping that this upcoming wedding might be postponed, though what good it would do him . . .

"You didn't mention what progress the English consul has made."

Marshall grunted. "None. And lately, he can't even get an audience with the Dey. Which reminds me. Miss Woods is no longer the *only* reason we'd like you to visit Barikah, though she's still the official reason, what with her relative demanding the navy be sent in if he doesn't get her back soon."

"Would they send in the navy?"

"Not for something like this, not when Barikah has the only fleet in the world whose size

57

can't be estimated. We'd have no idea what we were getting into, and believe me, we're not eager to find out."

"It's just a small port, Marsh. I'll admit the old Dey had quite a few ships at his disposal, but you have people there who can monitor every ship that comes into the harbor. How can you not know?"

"How indeed, when your friend Jamil uses twins for his captains."

"Twins? Good Lord, that's brilliant!"

"You mean you didn't know?"

"Come on, Marsh. Just because Jamil and I exchange a few letters every once in a while doesn't mean I'm privy to his defenses."

Marshall doubted his hearing. It was the first time Derek had ever called the Dey by name. "It might help, it really might, if I knew what your involvement was with the Dey when you lived in Barikah."

Derek smiled and asked irrelevantly, "Are you staying for dinner, Marsh?"

"For God's sake, Derek! What's the bloody secret? Did you save his life? Is he indebted to you?" At Derek's inscrutable expression, Marshall said in disgust, "Oh, never mind. I should have known better than to ask. But you could at least tell me if I'm beating a dead horse. Is he a friend or not?"

"He was."

"Well, that's something." Marshall sighed, for it was certainly more than Derek had ever admitted before. "And yes, the Dey's strategy with his navy is in fact brilliant. No one knows how many ships he really has, not his enemies, not his allies. It's impossible to tell when one captain could actually be two, their ships' names being the same. And at no one time are all his ships in port, so we can monitor the harbor forever and still not come up with a correct number. But the point is—"

"The point is, England doesn't want to declare war on Barikah."

"Exactly," Marshall admitted. "Our treaty is a good one, an excellent one, in fact, and Jamil Reshid a miracle—an Ottoman who keeps his word."

"So England is happy with the present Dey," Derek concluded. "But what was this about another reason for my going to Barikah?"

"As I said, the English consul, Sir John Blake, hasn't been able to get in to see the Dey. Well, we've only just found out why. Apparently there have been several attempts made on Jamil Reshid's life recently. Naturally enough, security at the palace has more than tripled, and all business except the most important has been suspended."

"And I would guess the ransoming of one slave wouldn't be considered important by the palace officials?"

"Correct, but you don't mention the assassination attempts on your 'friend,' I notice. Could it be you aready knew about it?"

"You deliver the Dey's letters to me yourself, Marsh, and you know it's been a good year—"

"All right, all right, so you haven't received any word. But why aren't you surprised, or even concerned?"

"Good Lord, you're suspicious today." Derek chuckled. "If I'm not surprised, it's because assassination attempts in the Ottoman Empire are a common occurrence. You know that. Why do you think it's legal for a new sultan to kill off all his brothers when he comes to power?"

"Jamil Reshid has younger brothers."

"I know, but Jamil Reshid is not a sultan, and the Deys of Barikah don't practice fratricide. They do, however, surround themselves with bodyguards, who make it nearly impossible to get to them."

"Nearly impossible, but not impossible."

"True, so naturally there is reason for concern. Any ideas yet on who's behind it?"

"Sir John says everything points to Selim, the next in line, because he hasn't been seen in over six months and can't be found. Of course, Sir John isn't privy to everything that goes on in Barikah. He has his spies, but none inside the palace. The fact remains that Jamil's sons aren't old enough to rule. If Jamil dies now, Selim would be the new Dey, and that we would like to avoid at all costs."

"Why?"

"Unlike Jamil, he can't be trusted. We've had our reports on the fellow, believe me. He's everything Jamil isn't. No, we need Jamil to remain in power, not just because he's friendly to England, tolerant of Christians, and has opened trade with us, but because the alternative is unacceptable. If Selim should come to power, the situation just might lead to war."

"I take it there's a rhyme and a reason for why you're telling me all this."

Marshall finally grinned. "If you were to reconsider going in after Miss Woods, we wouldn't take it amiss if you should happen to find out who's behind these assassination attempts and eliminate the problem while you're there."

Derek nearly choked on his laughter. "Hell, you don't ask for much, do you?"

"England would be grateful—unofficially, of course."

"Of course." Derek settled into a grin, adding, "All right, Marsh, you've found the means to sway me."

Marshall sat up, his expression incredulous. "You're joking! You'll really go, put off the wedding, break your word to your grandfather?"

"Well, if you're going to remind me of all that . . ."

"No, no, wouldn't dream of it."

"Then I'll leave tomorrow."

The Earl retired that night well satisfied with the day. He had managed to glean what information Marshall had without revealing his own, he and his grandfather were both in accord about his going to Barikah, and he had parted from Caroline without tears or recriminations. He now had no regrets about leaving. Certainly he would miss

England and all it held dear, but he wouldn't be gone that long. When he returned, the wedding would take place as planned, he would start a family, and his grandfather would be satisfied.

But right now he was looking at his last night on land before weeks at sea and nothing but male companionship. At the top of the stairs, Derek turned to crook his finger at a passing maid below. It didn't matter which maid she happened to be. He knew them all intimately.

He smiled to hear her giggle, and waited while she rushed up the stairs to join him. She turned out to be Clair, a lovely little brunette with an insatiable appetite. A good choice.

"We heard you was leaving, milord," she said as he slipped an arm about her. "Margie and I was planning to come and bid you good-bye later tonight."

"Were you?" he replied lazily, his fingers casually brushing against her breast. "Then we can say our good-byes now, and I'll see Margie later—if you don't wear me out."

She giggled again as he led her toward his room. It was a sound he didn't mind, a sound he had grown up with, having been raised in a harem. That he loved women in general was natural after such an upbringing. He had been afraid that his one regret in coming to England would be that he would never have his own harem. It hadn't exactly become a regret, not with a bevy of housemaids at his disposal, servants accustomed to pleasing a master. Yet he did miss the sensuality of the East, where a man rarely devoted his affections to only one woman. The ladies of quality here demanded eternal devotion for themselves exclusively. It was unthinkable, and yet he accepted this Western idiosyncrasy.

He expected it in Caroline. In fact, he knew she now thought him faithful to her. That he wasn't was not cause for guilt, however. Not that he didn't adore her. He did. If they had been in the East, she would be known as his *ikbal*, his favorite. But she was more than that. She was also his dearest friend, an occurrence that could never have come about in the East, where women were not thought of as companions. So he fully intended to make himself a good husband to her by English standards, to give her no cause for grief. He would just have to practice discretion.

But that was for later. He hadn't taken his one and only wife yet. Right now he was facing the long journey to Barikah, and a long time coming before he found anyone as accommodating as Clair.

Chapter Eight

"COME, *LALLA*, must eat something."

"Why?"

Hakeem stared worriedly at the girl curled up on the low bed. Her eyes were bruised from lack of sleep. Her hair was a tangled skein of silver knots that she wouldn't brush herself and wouldn't let him touch. She wore the same dress she had put on four days ago, when her own bundle of clothes had been given to her—a tight-waisted lilac gown that added to her paleness. She wouldn't change it. She slept in it. The only thing about her that wasn't lackluster was her tone of voice, occasionally peevish, more often coldly hostile.

She didn't appreciate the changes he had wrought in the small cabin. Swaths of brightly colored silk had been hung from the walls. Rugs of soft fur covered the entire floor now. A thick mattress had been found and draped in silk, then adorned with wide pillows. A copper hip bath sat in a corner behind a latticed screen. A small chest of sweet-smelling soaps and oils rested beside it. She hadn't touched it. The water he heated for her each day went unused.

And she wasn't eating, not a morsel since her capture. The captain had even opened his own store of delicacies to tempt her, but nothing did. Hakeem was at his wit's end. He had told her she had nothing to fear. He had told her she had a life of riches and wondrous pleasures awaiting her, that she would probably be bought by some high official wanting a wife, that wives had much more freedom than concubines. He insisted she would be happy beyond her wildest dreams. She seemed not to care, or she simply didn't believe him. He didn't know what to say to her anymore.

"You are wasting away to nothing, *lalla*. If you die, what purpose is served?"

64

"A good one," Chantelle retorted. "I keep a Burke from becoming a slave."

Hakeem sighed. "For men, it isn't desirable. But for women, it is different. I have told you—"

"Nothing that matters!" she cut in heatedly. "I'd still be a slave!"

Hakeem stared at the uneaten food on the silver tray and stiffened his resolve. There was no help for it now. She had to be made to eat.

"Your strength is dwindling to nothing, *lalla*. Soon it will be too late to save you."

"So?"

"So when it becomes apparent to Rais Mehmed that you will not live to reach Barikah, you will no longer be of value to him. He will give you to his crew for what use they can make of you until you die."

She smothered a gasp at such barbarity and glared furiously at the little Turk. "I've already been raped once aboard this ship! A few more times isn't going to matter."

"Raped? Are you mad, woman? Your virginity doubles your value. Rais Mehmed would skin alive—"

"Your bloody captain helped to hold me down!"

Hakeem was speechless for a moment, and then he had to strain to keep from laughing. Could she really be that innocent? But of course she was, or she wouldn't think she had been raped.

"*Lalla*, you are still a virgin," Hakeem assured her gently.

"I'm not stupid!" she snapped.

65

"No, no, of course not. But you are young and—and it is easy to mistake what was done to you. The one who, ah, touched you—he couldn't . . . what I mean is, he was incapable . . . he was a eunuch. Do you know what that means?"

Chantelle's cheeks flooded with color. "Yes."

"What he did was discover if you still possess the prized hymen, and you do. It was necessary, *lalla*, to determine your value. It is done to all female captives."

She was no longer listening to his explanation. She felt like a fool for having drawn the wrong conclusion, but she was surprised, too, at the overwhelming relief in knowing she was still a maiden. But the humiliation of the experience would never be forgotten, and nothing had really changed. She was still going to be sold into slavery.

"It doesn't matter, Hakeem."

He became angry at such stubbornness. "Then you don't mind being raped by a dozen men?"

She flinched, but shook her head. What difference a dozen men now or one man later repeatedly? She was going to be raped either way. At least this way it would be over with, and how long could she last anyway, as weak as she was?

"Then you won't mind a little pain first, will you?" Hakeem demanded.

Chantelle narrowed her eyes on him. "What do you mean?"

"Do you really think Rais Mehmed will sit by and do nothing to change your mind? You have until the end of this day, *lalla*, before he has you bastinadoed. And if you do not understand that this is a form of torture that does not mar the skin, and so does not decrease your value, then I will explain. The soles of your feet will be beaten with a stick. If your feet are sensitive, it is extremely painful. If not, it is still a most unpleasant experience. Are you willing to suffer for your death?"

Her answer was to push herself to a sitting position in front of the tray of food, but her eyes cut into him with furious venom. "You're a bastard, Hakeem Bektash," she said with cold intensity. "Why in hell didn't you tell me about your bloody bastinado sooner?"

"I had hoped you would not prove so stubborn, *lalla*. It is not a good trait for a woman. If you had given in on your own, it would have been easier for me to help you."

"The only way you can help me is to get me off this ship before it's too late."

He shook his head slowly, his expression rueful. "That I cannot do. But there is much I can teach you—the customs of the East, the language. I can prepare you for your new life, if you'll let me. And is it not better to be prepared, to arm yourself with understanding, than to walk in blindly to this new life?"

For a long moment Chantelle stared at him. And then she reached for the bread on her tray, her nod just barely perceptible. But it was a nod. She might be stubborn, but she wasn't a fool.

Chapter Nine

THE DAYS passed with alarming speed for Chantelle. Hakeem became her constant companion, and almost every waking moment was spent learning something: Muslim customs, Barikahian history, the role of Near Eastern women; but mostly Arabic, the language most common in Barikah and which Hakeem had been raised to speak, though he also imparted what little Turkish he was familiar with as well, since this was the language still preferred by the high officials. Chantelle absorbed all she could. Once she had concluded that Hakeem was right—to be prepared was to be forearmed—she not only wanted to learn but insisted on it.

Yet it wasn't easy, taking it all in. Trying to grasp a new language was especially difficult when half her mind was clogged with fear. And she couldn't escape the fear.

She tried. She looked for and found a bright side to this misfortune. She had needed to disappear without a trace for a while, and leaving England had certainly accomplished that. She even managed to dredge up some hope that all was not lost. If she could enter a fairly large harem, it was likely she might never be called on to spend the night with the master. Hakeem had told her that when a man had more than twenty females in his household, not all gained his notice. Of course, Hakeem insisted she would have no trouble being noticed. But she had no intention of drawing attention to herself. And then somehow she would escape, find her way to the English consul, and he would smuggle her out of Barikah and home.

The thought of eventually finding her way home was something to cling to. It was all she had. Yet the fear was still there, for she had her sale to get through, and Hakeem refused to tell her much about that. Until that was over, everything was in doubt, since there was always the possibility that she might be bought by a man who had no wives, no household of women in which she could lose herself, a man who would rape her, though he might marry her and have children by her, God forbid. Then where would she be? Lost. Forever. Oh, horrid, horrid.

And Hakeem, that sometime idiot, thought to cheer her by telling her how likely it was that the man who bought her *would* want to marry her. "He will be extremely rich, for he could not afford you otherwise. And you will be his favorite, his *ikbal*. You will bear him fine sons, and he will honor you by making you his first wife."

First wife. She cringed every time she heard that. It was bad enough that where she was going a man was allowed four wives if he so wanted, but he could also keep as many concubines as he could afford. Potentially hundreds of women for one man. It was inconceivable to her European mind. She didn't see how the women could tolerate it. But then she had to remind herself that they had no choice, for concubines were slaves, captured in war, raids, and by piracy. Theirs was a culture steeped in slavery.

"Was your life so much better?" Hakeem demanded one day when she was particularly resentful of what he was telling her. "Braz says he found you running away with your little bundle of clothes."

That didn't sit well with her. "At least I had choices, Hakeem. I didn't have to stay and be forced to marry a man who was unacceptable to me. But what choices do I have now?"

"You can accept your new life or not. You can go far, *lalla*, if you so choose. Riches can be yours, and freedom of a sort. You need only strive to be the favorite—"

"I won't prostitute myself! I'd rather be a scullery slave!"

He threw up his hands in disgust and left her alone. And she cried—because it was true. She would rather do the meanest chores than warm some stranger's bed, but she would rather not do either. Oh, God, did Charles Burke have more to atone for now! It was *his* fault she was here, *his* fault she was so frightened and helpless, facing a life abhorrent to her.

They would assume she had run away. Aunt Ellen would have come to Dover, and after being told what they had planned for Chantelle, she would assume she had run away, too. But she would also assume that Chantelle would contact her at the soonest opportunity, and she would wait in vain, wondering, and then worrying when time passed and she had no word. And no one would ever know what had really happened to Chantelle. She had simply disappeared from England without a trace.

There had been only one bad storm that delayed the ship's progress for several days. Chantelle hoped for more, but the weather held fine, too fine, the heat increasing in the small cabin soon after they had slipped through the narrow Strait of Gibraltar to enter the Mediterranean Sea. The very next day, she was witness to the corsairs in action.

It came as a shock when the ship began readying for attack, and Hakeem rushed in to explain what was happening. They had passed other ships in the Atlantic without incident, so Chantelle had assumed they weren't after any more prizes on this voyage. Wrong. They simply did their attacking in familiar waters.

"You need not worry, *lalla*. it is doubtful we will need to use the ship's guns. It is nearly evening, so we can take the merchantman by surprise, approaching down-sun of her so it will be difficult for her to identify us. The *rais* has aready raised identical colors, and we have a man who speaks her tongue to hail her and lull her. We will board her before she is aware she is in danger."

Chantelle wasn't worried. But she was excited. This was a possibility she hadn't counted on—

hope from an unexpected quarter. If the corsairs' ship failed in its attack, if it should be captured instead, she would be saved.

She began to pray the minute Hakeem left her, and continued for the next half hour. That was all it took. The noise was horrible, the shouts and screams, the clanging of scimitars on shields, but she was to learn it was only the corsairs who made the racket, which was part of their strategy to terrify their victims. And it worked. The Neapolitan merchantman was easy prey, the crew so taken by surprise that there was little bloodshed. All were made prisoners and the other vessel torched, since the corsairs didn't have enough men to spare as a crew for the prize.

For three days after, Chantelle fell into a depression that nothing could shake, thinking of the men now chained in the hold who, like her, would be sold. And like her fate, what would happen to them was unknown. Hakeem had been willing to enlighten her, but not after she was so appalled to hear the prisoners would be led from the ship near naked and in chains. He refused to continue, assuring her only that her arrival in Barikah would be very different.

It might be different, but it was no less terrifying, as she found out a short twelve days after the merchantman was captured. Seen through the one small porthole her cabin boasted, Barikah glistened on the North African coast, the Barbary Coast, as the long strip extending from Morocco to Egypt was called. It was a white jewel shimmering in the hot midday sun. Flat-roofed, white-washed houses crowded together, rising one above the next on steep hills, flanked on both sides by the verdant green of pastures and fields, with the brilliant blue waters of the harbor below, the cloudless azure sky above. Seen from afar, the Eastern flavor stood out starkly in the green-tiled cupolas of huge domed mosques towering above the houses, each with four minarets rising toward the sky like pointed needles. Cone-topped watchtowers stood out, too. So did a large building sitting atop the tallest hill and surrounded by thick walls that could only be the palace of the Dey.

Closer to the harbor were other large buildings seen just above the high walls that surrounded Barikah: warehouses for the cargoes from the commercial ships of many different nations that crowded the harbor, barracks for the soldiers who manned the walls where twenty batteries protected the bay with more than a thousand cannon, bagnios which housed the huge work force of slaves.

There was also the spire of a Christian church, but Chantelle unfortunately didn't notice this. If she had, she might have lost some of the trepidation now filling her violet eyes, for Hakeem had not bothered to tell her the Dey of Barikah was tolerant of Christians, that many lived here who weren't slaves, that there was a whole European community in the city. A Christian church was a sign of sanctuary, a haven that would be easy to find when she escaped, whereas the English consulate would not be as easy to locate. But

73

she didn't see it, and she didn't see the city for very long either, at least not all of it, once the ship came about to maneuver toward its berth.

Not long after, there was the sound of the male prisoners being led onto the deck after twelve horrid days spent in the hold. The moans, the clanking of chains, sent Chantelle rushing for her bed to cover her ears and stifle her sobs of fear in her pillows. How long before she, too, would be led from this temporary haven? Yes, the ship was now a haven compared with what awaited her ashore.

But time passed and no one came for her. Her tears dried. Her fears gave way to emotional exhaustion. She was almost ready to accept anything just to get it over with so she could stop being constantly afraid.

When Hakeem did finally come to the cabin, it was nearing evening. He had a tray of food for her, and clothes draped over one arm.

Chantelle took one look at the food and thought she would throw up, her stomach was so in knots. "Take it away."

"You will not be leaving the ship until late tonight, when the city is quiet. In the meantime you must eat, *lalla*."

"I'd hate to tell you what you can do with that food, Hakeem."

He smiled at her surly tone, but it was a sad smile. Her puffy eyes gave evidence of her misery. Captives weren't to be pitied. They were merchandise, nothing more, though this one was

74

much more valuable than most. And yet he did pity her. She was such a contradiction with her eyes spitting defiance at him while her mouth quivered with a touching vulnerability.

Hakeem had unfortunately fallen a little bit in love with her, though he didn't know it. But there was nothing he could do about the strange feelings she stirred in him. There was nothing he could do for her either. He wouldn't even be the one to take her ashore, and once she left the ship, he would never see her again.

What she needed was courage so that she wouldn't get into trouble from her sharp tongue, which seemed to be her natural response to fear, and it was a dangerous response. A Muslim admired courage, but no insults; spirit, but not insolence. And Hamid Sharif, to whom she would be taken tonight, was not a man known for his understanding or patience.

"Did you not tell me you were gently bred?" Hakeem asked her, setting the tray of food down on a little stool, which thusly turned the tray into an adequate low table. "An heiress? The daughter of an English nobleman?"

"Bravo," Chantelle retorted. "Your memory does you proud."

"I cannot say the same about your shrewishness, *lalla*." He heard her affronted gasp but went on relentlessly. "If you had not told me these things about yourself, I would think you were a peasant. Peasants have no more sense than to bite at the hand that holds their life. A noble is wiser, having the sense to know when to give up the fight without losing one's pride."

"Don't you dare tell me how to act when you can't possibly know how I feel!"

"No, I cannot know," he agreed. "I can only tell you that you have value, and so will be treated well and with care. But when a slave loses value, it is nothing to have him beaten, sold, or killed. That is never likely to happen to you, because your value is not in a strong back or a special skill, but in your comeliness. Yet undesirable traits will not be tolerated, and there are many punishments that can be inflicted without marring your value."

"Why do you tell me this?" she asked resentfully.

"So that you do not make the mistake of appearing less than you are, and therefore lower your value. You are a lady, one with pride and intelligence. It is your right to expect to be treated is such, and so you will be, if this is how you act. A certain amount of fear is only natural. But how you deal with that fear is the question. Do you show it, holding yourself up to ridicule and abuse, or do you conceal it behind a bearing suitable to your previous class and station?"

"I still don't see—"

"*Think*, woman!" he snapped impatiently. "How you are perceived is how you will be treated. A village wench, no matter how comely, is known to be accustomed to hardship, and so need not be treated with the greatest care. Why subject yourself to that needlessly?"

"Why would I? I am who I say I am."

"Anyone can say they are a lady and yet belie the point with their behavior. I know that when you insult me, you do not do it to hurt me, but to hide your own fear. But I have known you long enough to have discovered this truth. Hamid Sharif will not know you long enough to draw this same conclusion. *Now* do you understand, *lalla?*"

Subdued, Chantelle nodded, and even managed a small smile for Hakeem for caring enough to give her this warning, however unnecessary it was. She had grown used to the little Turk. She felt free to take her anxieties out on him, knowing that he wouldn't hurt her. She would not be as voluble with a stranger. Or would she? She didn't exactly think clearly in the grips of a panic, or react as she would want. She had learned that the hard way. A good dose of courage was indeed needed, only it still wasn't immediately forthcoming.

"*How* do I not be afraid, Hakeem?" she asked in a near whisper.

He would have told her the obvious, that the one who bought her would endeavor to please her so that she would in turn please him, but he knew her well enough to know that that was the last thing to tell her, that one of her main fears was eventually having to please a master. He could only hope that when the time came, she would think differently about it. But what *could* he tell her that he hadn't already?

"No one expects you not to be afraid, *lalla*. But if you remember that you will not be hurt, that

77

you have value, is it not reasonable to find courage in that? And you are prepared, you know what to expect. You also have some understanding of the language now, which will improve with time. Few prisoners can say the same, for most captains do not bother to ensure that the adjustment will be easy, much less that the captives will arrive in the same condition as they were when they were captured. Rais Mehmed saw the wisdom in turning you over to our employer without tears or resistance, and with a knowledge of our ways that could only be beneficial to everyone involved. Hamid Sharif will be pleased, and so the *rais* will benefit, as will you. You truly have no reason to fear your arrival here, *lalla*. Everything will go well."

"Until I'm sold," she couldn't resist adding.

Hakeem frowned at her, but there was nothing more he could say. "I have here the clothes supplied by the *rais* for you to wear to leave the ship. Please be ready three hours after the sun sets."

He held up each piece for her inspection. They were all in dull, nondescript colors and serviceable cotton, except for the yashmak, the veil worn by all women who ventured out in the street, and this was made of a dark gauze. There were pantaloons that looked like long drawers, a long-sleeved tunic that she couldn't know Hakeem himself had supplied for her modesty's sake, a short bolero-type vest with a single button to fasten over her breasts, a wide sashed belt, and a voluminous caftan, the long coatlike garment worn in the Near

East by both men and women, this one full enough to conceal her completely from shoulders to feet. Shoes were not supplied, since her own were still wearable even after their drenching in her one bid for freedom.

Chantelle was not at all pleased by the pantaloons, which in her opinion were no better than unadorned underwear. "Couldn't I wear the robe and veil over my own clothes?"

Hakeem shook his head, but there was a slight smile for her expression of distaste. Clothes had accomplished what all his words had not—to take her mind off her fear.

"Your dress is too foreign in design. The full skirt would bell out even with the weight of the caftan over it. It is our intention that if you should be seen leaving the ship, you will appear a Muslim woman who perhaps had passage with us, and so not draw attention to yourself. Hamid Sharif will want your presence kept secret until he is ready to announce your auction, which will be private, only for those who can afford the high price he will set for you. And besides," he added hesitantly, "your own clothes will be denied you henceforth. In Barikah you will be dressed according to your—"

"New status?" Chantelle cut in bitterly.

Hakeem flushed, but said, "Did you think it would be otherwise, after all I have told you?"

She lowered her gaze to the floor. "No, but can't I keep my pictures, my own hairbrush, my—"

"Nothing, *lalla*. A slave goes to her new master

with nothing, so that what he chooses to give her she will be grateful for."

Her head snapped up. She had been told this, but because she was faced with the immediate loss of her only reminders of home, her earlier anger returned in full force.

"A tradition that serves to undermine confidence and self-esteem, not to mention self-worth," she bit out with contempt. "Will I be begging for my food, too, for even a change of clothes? Because I won't, you know. I won't beg!"

"All will be given to you without your asking for it," he replied patiently. "Why do you persist in forgetting everything I have told you?"

"Because I hate it! Your traditions are designed to break me!"

"What you will do is forget your previous life all the sooner if you have nothing to remind you of it. You will accept—"

"Never!"

"You will, *lalla*," Hakeem said with a sigh. "It is inevitable."

Chapter Ten

RAHMET ZADEH heard the Englishwoman. He had been sent down to the harbor to inquire of the passengers on the English merchantman that had arrived that morning. It was not the first time he had shown up after dark to make the same inquiry. For three weeks now it had been his task

80

to question each foreign ship entering the port, and always at night, by which time the passengers, if any, would have had ample opportunity to come ashore if they meant to. Omar Hassan gave them that chance. It was when the one he sought did not appear at the palace that day that Rahmet had been sent down to the harbor.

It was a task beneath Rahmet's dignity, or so he thought. He was captain of the palace guard. Any of Omar's minions could have been sent to ask these pointless questions, but Omar had chosen him to do it. He did not feel honored. He might if he had been told why the task was necessary, but he had not. The Grand Vizier rarely if ever explained himself.

Disgruntled, feeling as if Omar Hassan were just using this task as a means to punish him, when he could think of no reason he should be punished, Rahmet was not in the best of moods when the sound of that raised, angry voice stopped him on his way back to the palace.

That he knew the woman spoke English was a mere coincidence, since he had only just come from hearing it spoken. He didn't speak it himself. And the dragoman he had brought along to interpret for him on the merchantman had rushed ahead to go about his business, afeard of Rahmet's foul mood, and had already disappeared through the Marine Gate.

What stopped him was the incongruity of it. She was on the wrong ship. The craft that the voice came from was one of Hamid Sharif's ships, also arrived today among much excitement, since it had carried a full cargo of new slaves. There could be no conceivable reason for an Englishwoman to be aboard it, no reason really for anyone to be aboard it at this time of night, when this was the home port and the cargo had already been unloaded. And yet the deck was lit and light spilled out into the water from several cabins.

Rahmet's curiosity was piqued. It wasn't often that Englishwomen were brought here as captives, yet what else could this one be on this particular ship? Then why hadn't they brought her out with the rest of the slaves today?

It was part of Rahmet's job to report anything unusual to Omar Hassan, no matter how trivial, especially now with the threats against the Dey still unsolved. And this was unusual.

Rahmet suddenly struck his forehead with the flat of his palm. What a blind fool he was! *This* could be why the Grand Vizier had sent him down here so often. He could be waiting for word of this Englishwoman but not want Rahmet to know it. It hadn't been necessary to tell him the real reason. Omar Hassan *knew* Rahmet would report something like this.

With those conclusions drawn, which suited Rahmet much better than thinking he was down here as some sort of punishment, Rahmet continued on to the Marine Gate. There he stayed to visit with the guards, keeping his eye on Hamid Sharif's ship and gleaning what information the guards could tell him about any activity that had gone on there. They didn't know much. They had the night watch, and had arrived only shortly after the call to evening prayer.

Rahmet didn't have long to wait to witness some activity for himself. The woman appeared on deck. Not only that, but she left the ship flanked by two men. But there was no clink of chains. She was not restrained in any way. Appearance-wise, she could be any Muslim woman wrapped up in her street robes. Even standing a mere few feet away from her while one of her escorts explained their business to the guards, he could discern nothing about her to mark her a foreigner, not even the color of her eyes, for she kept them demurely lowered, as was only proper.

Rahmet was disappointed, but should have expected no less. It was the bane of all men that on the streets, every woman looked alike. A princess could visit the bazaar unnoticed. A wife could walk down the street with her lover, and if her husband passed, he would never know it. And a female slave could be escorted through the streets in complete secrecy simply by not appearing to be a slave.

A name was given for her that was common, a tale told that could not be immediately disproved. She was said to be resident of Algiers and a friend of their captain, which was why he had agreed to give her passage on his ship to visit a cousin here in Barikah.

The guards accepted this without question. Rahmet didn't believe a word of it, though he chose not to dispute it, for he wanted to know her destination and could do that only by following the three unnoticed. He was more intrigued than ever that they were going to this trouble for the Englishwoman. The only reason that he could think of for it was that she was too valuable to chance passing through the crowds that had turned out to watch the unloading of the Neapolitan slaves that afternoon. If he was right, she would be delivered to Hamid Sharif. If not, he would have to investigate further.

If Hamid Sharif weren't so loyal to the Dey, and a slave dealer besides, Rahmet would have to consider other possibilities with such secrecy and deception involved, like an involvement in the plot against the Dey. Women were not above suspicion. No one was. It was the English tongue that made him doubt this possibility, however, for it was well known the English favored Jamil Reshid's reign and would do nothing to jeopardize it. And, too, it would not be the first time a pretty slave was smuggled into the city for a private auction that the slave dealer wanted kept from the public. Such women were generally offered to the Dey first, and so this woman's particulars would soon be known at the palace, to confirm one way or the other what Rahmet would report tonight.

He set off to follow the three, and as he had suspected, the woman was delivered to Hamid Sharif. Rahmet returned to the palace to let Omar Hassan make what he would of this information.

Hopefully, this was the news the Grand Vizier had been waiting for, and Rahmet would no longer be sent to the harbor after tonight. But he could tell nothing from Omar Hassan's reaction, and for five days, no foreign ships arrived in port. Then an English warship sailed into port for supplies, with two smaller escorts, and Rahmet's suspicions were confirmed. He was not called on again to visit the harbor.

Chapter Eleven

THE NEXT morning, Omar Hassan met the Dey in the hall outside the audience chamber where a crowd had already gathered for the day's business. This hall, leading from Jamil's apartments, was empty except for the two Nubian bodyguards who were never far from Jamil's side.

"A moment, Jamil."

Omar had the privilege of using the Dey's name at all times, though he did so only in private. He had known Jamil Reshid since he was born, had taken an active interest in his upbringing even before he was removed from the harem, and was totally in agreement with the Divan, Jamil's council of advisors, that Barikah had never known such prosperity as under Jamil's rule. His father, Mustafa, had been a good ruler, beloved of his people, but he had lacked Jamil's diplomacy and shrewdness in dealing with Barikah's foreign element, as well as with the consuls of the many foreign governments represented here. Barikah enjoyed peace under Jamil, not so under his father's and older brother's rule.

Of all Mustafa's many children, Jamil and his brother Kasim had been Omar's favorites, each showing at an early age a keen intelligence, but more important in the Grand Vizier's opinion, a sense of honor and justice. They had been their father's favorites, too, which was perhaps why his firstborn, Mahmud, whom he had all but ignored, had grown up with a grasping, vindictive nature that had earned him the title of "tyrant" during his short rule. But by Allah's will, Mahmud had died without issue, and to Barikah's benefit, Jamil had been next in line.

He made a fine ruler, in character as well as in appearance, which not a single one of his concubines could find fault with. From his father he had his exceptional height and coal-black hair tucked away right now under a white turban, but visible in a full beard, the pride of most Muslims. He had his mother's high cheekbones and brow, his father's strong chin and aquiline nose. But the eyes were strictly Lalla Rahine's, not the eyes of a Turk or an Arab, eyes that gave Jamil the look of a European and put foreign diplomats at ease.

It was only recently that Jamil had stopped receiving diplomats, and all urgent business was conducted only once a week now, anything else to be handled by Omar. It showed the depth of Jamil's wisdom that he willingly delegated his power at this time, for his frustration over the continued restrictions placed on him for his own protection had him on a short fuse, which grew shorter with each passing day. He was the first to realize that his easygoing temperament had taken a turn for the worse, which affected his judgment and made it too easy for him to make the wrong decisions or offend someone he shouldn't.

"Skulking about in hallways now, Omar?" Jamil asked as he reached him.

The older man chuckled. "It does seem so."

"What is it, then?"

"Nothing important," Omar admitted. "I just thought you might want to consider purchasing another slave for the harem."

Jamil frowned. "My ears deceive me, correct? You are not suggesting—"

"Hear me out, my lord." Omar stepped back so he wouldn't have to crane his neck to look up at Jamil. That was the only reason that he kept his distance, for he loved Jamil as he did his own sons and liked to think the feeling was mutual. It certainly wasn't that he was intimidated by one of Jamil's frowns. "I know you feel you have too many women already, but I was not actually thinking of this one for you."

A dark brow shot up, and a grin appeared to lighten Jamil's stern expression. "You wish me to purchase you a woman and hide her in my harem? Are your wives giving you trouble again, old friend?"

Omar laughed outright. "No, my lord, not for me. I was thinking of someone else who might make use of her. I am given to believe she is English, which is why I thought of it. She was secreted into the city last night and delivered to Hamid Sharif. The fact that he tried his best to conceal her can only mean she is either so ugly he is ashamed to have her seen, or so beautiful he is afraid to have her seen. You will recall that the last beauty he proudly had paraded through the streets nearly caused a riot. The reason I mention it now is he may not offer her to you this time, having become discouraged after you have turned him down so many times in recent months. If you want to buy her, I may have to contact him, and it should be done before he has a chance to sell her."

Jamil considered this news for only a moment before he slowly shook his head. "No, I don't think so, Omar. It was good of you to think of it, but I prefer not to prepare ahead in this instance, as there may be nothing to prepare for. Our 'someone else' has not arrived yet, nor might he ever. And the last thing I want to do is disturb my women with a new acquisition when they are already displeased with me."

Omar refrained from commenting on that. He simply nodded his acceptance and salaamed, indicating he would detain the Dey no longer. What could he have said that wouldn't have reminded Jamil of his own shortcomings? At least the Dey was not pretending an ignorance of the havoc his foul disposition caused in the palace. He was fully aware that his slaves walked in fear of him, his guards drew lots now to see who would *not* have to show up for duty each day, and his concubines complained constantly of his neglect, or, as the case might be, his favor.

Omar knew that Jamil strived for control, and when he failed to achieve it, his anger only grew worse. The situation had just gone on too long. Jamil's patience was at an end. His temper exploded now at the least provocation, and although he regretted the punishments he ordered and most times cut them short as his reason returned, they still occurred frequently.

Omar sighed and followed the Dey into the audience chamber. Waiting there to speak with Jamil was a servant of Hamid Sharif's whom Omar recognized. Here was a prime excuse for Jamil to lose his temper this morning: having to deal with the same issue twice, since Omar had little doubt that the servant was here because of Hamid's newest acquisition. He should not even have been allowed in, for his was certainly not urgent business. But this was Omar's fault for not being present to screen today's visitors, leaving the duty in the hands of Jamil's harried clerk instead.

Quickly, he signaled to Hamid's man and took him out into an antechamber, giving him no chance to state his business. "The Dey does not require any new slaves for his household or his harem."

"But, my lord—"

"Yes?"

The tone was such that the man lowered his eyes humbly to the floor. One did not argue with the Dey's chief minister.

"Forgive me, my lord. You understand, my master did not wish to offend yours by not offering to him the fairest jewel that has ever come into his possession."

"Ever?" Omar was amused.

"It is so, my lord. I have seen her myself."

"Then my regret is no greater than yours. English, isn't she?"

The man's eyes widened as he nodded, but he should have known the palace spies would have ferreted out this information, probably the moment the girl arrived. If it was not palace spies, then it was spies of the foreign consuls, who tried to keep abreast of things. Very few secrets were kept in Barikah, which was why no one could understand why the head of the man behind the attempts on the Dey's life had not long since rotted away hanging on the palace gate.

"You may tell your master that we appreciate his offering this jewel to the Dey first," Omar continued. "His thoughtfulness will be remembered. And although the Dey has not bought any new slaves for some time, that does not mean he will not in future. But come to me next time. The Dey cannot be bothered with such trifles."

It was a shame, Omar thought later, that Jamil scorned the collection of women for the sake of prestige. Most Turks who could afford it filled their harems to overflowing. Three or four hundred concubines were not unheard of for someone as wealthy as Jamil, yet he possessed less than fifty women, and half of these had been given as gifts or were purchased by Lalla Rahine in her efforts to please her son by providing him with variety when he stopped doing so himself. He had not been pleased, and had finally forbidden her to make any more purchases.

It was not that Jamil did not like variety or love women. What he didn't like was to see women go to waste, and that was certainly what happened to the majority of women in a large harem. There could only be so many favorites, and the rest, though they might catch the master's eye occasionally, spent their days in bored idleness with nothing to look forward to, and their nights alone.

That this should concern Jamil was amazing, but it did. He had felt this way even before the rumors started circulating that he was in love with his first wife, the *kadine* Sheelah. He was a man unique to his culture for the belief that every woman in his harem should feel herself cherished by her master. And he wore himself out ensuring that none of his women were ignored for any great length of time, which was why the thought of even one more woman added to the ranks appalled him.

But it was still a shame, for someone new at this time could serve to take Jamil's mind off his troubles and, in turn, ease what was becoming a formidable temper. But you couldn't tell Jamil that.

What was needed was a day spent away from the palace, for being confined to the palace was

Jamil's main frustration. But the Divan would never agree. It was simply too dangerous, the one thing the assassins were undoubtedly waiting for. What was truly needed was for the many messages they had sent out to bear fruit.

Chapter Twelve

EARLY IN the afternoon four days later, the Grand Vizier was still receiving the more important supplicants requesting an audience with the Dey when his clerk informed him a desert sheikh had arrived with tribute in the form of two Thoroughbred horses. Omar was not impressed and would have put the sheikh off until another day, but his clerk insisted he must see these particular animals himself—they were even now being admired in the outer court.

Omar could not help being annoyed. Jamil's own clerk had obviously thought this fellow important enough to send to him, when all he had to do was accept the tribute and send the sheikh on his way. But then he could see the clerk's dilemma. Most of the desert tribes that paid tribute to the Dey according to their respective treaties did not send their headmen to do so. That this sheikh had come in person with his gifts could only mean that he wanted something from the Dey.

So be it. Jamil's policy was to appease these desert tribes whenever possible, which kept the peace. The desert sheikh might not even be aware of what was happening in Barikah, or why this was not a good time for the Dey to receive his gifts personally.

Impatiently, Omar stepped into the room adjoining his office that had a fretted window facing the outer court. There he could see the horses clearly, for even though a crowd of palace officials and servants had gathered around them, they kept their distance, the two young Arabs in attendance having difficulty keeping the high-spirited animals under control.

Omar was finally impressed. They were magnificent, pure white Thoroughbreds of the like never before seen in Barikah. And then he realized the reason they couldn't be controlled. One was a stallion, the other a mare. By the Prophet's beard! This was a breeding pair.

He shook his head as he returned to his office and bade his now smiling clerk to show the sheikh in. Was it possible the man didn't know the value of such a gift, a tribute worthy of the Sultan himself? These weren't desert Arabians, by any means. Where could they possibly have come from?

And then Omar groaned heavily as it dawned on him how this gift was going to affect Jamil, who was a superb horseman but had had to give up his daily rides since the trouble began. He was going to be delighted with this pair, ecstatic in fact, until he realized, as Omar just had, that he couldn't ride them now and wouldn't be able to for some time to come. This was going to make his present disposition even worse.

Understandably, Omar was glowering by the time the tall desert headman was brought before him. His name had been given as Ahmad Khalifeh; it was a name Omar could not immediately recall, nor find among his papers at first glance. He might have been able to recognize him if it weren't for the bulky burnoose, the hooded robe of the desert that covered him from head to toe, and the fact that he kept his head lowered so that the hood fell forward to further enshroud him.

In his irritation, Omar dispensed with the customary preliminaries of welcome and came right to the point. "Your name is not familiar to me. From which tribe do you come?"

He was answered with a question. "Is that you, Omar?"

The Grand Vizier stiffened. That voice he recognized all too well. "Jamil? What games do you play?"

Laughter greeted this, full and deep. How long had it been since anyone had heard Jamil laugh? Omar frowned darkly, for the man's head had been thrown back, and it was a smooth-shaven chin he could see under the shadowed hood.

"Who are you?" Omar demanded in an ominous undertone.

"Come now, old man, you can't have forgotten me. It's only been nineteen years."

Omar's mouth dropped open in utter amazement. No one spoke to him in such a disrespectful tone. No one! He stood up to call the guards to have the arrogant dog removed, but was arrested by the sight of the hood being thrown back and a pair of laughing green eyes that met his without fear or contrition. He sat back down, or rather, dropped back down on his cushioned pillows, his mouth again hanging open.

"Kasim? Is it really you?"

"None other," came the cheeky answer.

Omar leaped up again and went around the long, low table littered with official documents and letters of petition. "You came! Allah be praised, you actually came!"

"Did you think I wouldn't?" Derek got out before he was enthusiastically embraced. For a little old man twice his age, Omar had sufficient strength left to make him grunt, he was squeezed so hard.

"We didn't know," Omar said, standing back to fill his eyes with the many changes nineteen years had wrought. "We couldn't know. So many messengers were sent out, so many found dead."

"So Ali ben-Khalil told me."

"Then he was the one to finally reach you? The sherbet seller?"

Derek nodded, grinning. "He insisted I lock him up, after he had seen me."

"A smart man. And you were wise enough to come in disguise. I was afraid you would not, but there was no way to warn you in the message without making the simple code obvious."

Derek shrugged. "It seemed the thing to do to avoid confusion."

"Jamil was sure you would realize."

"How is he?"

"Still unharmed, though there was still another attempt on his life last month."

"Do you know who's behind it?"

Omar threw up his hands in disgust. "We have learned nothing. Nothing! Whoever is hiring these assassins does not reveal himself to them."

"Is it Selim?"

"We can think of no other, but then no one is above suspicion."

"Where is he?"

Omar sighed. "He was last seen in Istanbul at the Sultan's court. We have a veritable army out looking for him now, but he hides himself well."

"Have you considered the possibility that he has already been eliminated?" Derek ventured. "How old is Mustafa's last-born son now?"

"Murad is only eleven, and yes, we have considered that, and all of Jamil's enemies, too."

"And his wives?"

Omar chuckled. "You still think like a Muslim, Kasim."

"I can remember my mother telling me of the fierce rivalry among Mustafa's wives and how twice Mahmud nearly died from poison."

"And did Jamil later write you that it was Mustafa's fourth wife who was responsible, and that she also was foolish enough to make an attempt against him which earned her a grave at the bottom of the sea?" Derek grunted. No, he hadn't been told, but he wasn't surprised. To be trussed up alive in a weighted sack and dropped into the sea was the Sultan's favorite mode of doing away with the women of his harem who had displeased him, women kept veiled from other men in life—and so in death as well. Why should Mustafa be any different? Rarely was a woman executed any other way.

Omar continued. "But Jamil's wives? Of course it has been thought of, and security in the harem has been increased also, but Jamil will hear nothing said against them, and I am inclined to look there only as a last resort, too. First, they each of them adore Jamil. But more to the point, none of their sons would benefit unless Selim and Murad both died as well as Jamil, and although Selim is missing, Murad is here in Barikah, and no attempts have been made on *his* life."

"But if every one of Mustafa's sons died?"

"It would be up to the Divan to decide whether to accept Jamil's firstborn."

"It is not unheard of for a *kadine* to rule through her son," Derek reminded him.

"But he is only six years old, Kasim. If he were older . . . It is more likely the Divan will choose a new Dey, and Mustafa's line will rule no more."

"But your vote could sway them either way?"

Omar laughed. "By Allah, you are bringing new thoughts to this problem that even I have not considered. Yes, it is true I could sway the Divan. After thirty-five years of serving as Grand Vizier of Barikah, I assure you my opinion is second only to the Dey's. But it is also true that no one can know how I could vote, least of all Jamil's wives, when I haven't even thought of this possibility myself. But come, Kasim, sit down, sit down. We will have ample time to discuss who is causing all this trouble. Tell me, how did you get here? No new ships have arrived these past few days, and all those before I have had checked."

"A friend of mine got me passage on one of the Royal Navy's warships. I would have been here yesterday . . . only we ran into a little trouble with some Algerian corsairs and became separated from our escort. I imagine they'll arrive either later today or tomorrow, once they regroup. I was dropped off up the coast late last night and rode in this morning. I needed a good enough excuse to get in to see you, and what better way than as Ahmad Khalifeh, come in from the desert with tribute for the Dey?"

"Ah, the horses!" Omar chuckled. "Wherever did you find such magnificent beasts?"

"Find them?" Derek's lips curled with a touch of pride. "I raise them. And Jamil had better be around long enough to start a new line in Barikah."

"*Inshallah*," Omar replied in all seriousness.

"Yes," Derek agreed, just as seriously now. "If God wills."

Chapter Thirteen

DEREK SINCLAIR, Earl of Mulbury and future Marquis of Hunstable, was riding an incredible high in spirits, and had been ever since he had entered the city this morning. The sights, sounds, and smells that greeted him made him realize how much he had missed this part of the world and how easily it was to slip back into the shoes of a Muslim Turk.

There was nothing English about the bazaars he had passed through, where sandalwood and gum scented the air from the spice stalls, camels plodded along with noisy complaint, bells tinkled in the breeze that turned the silk merchant's stall into a waving riot of bright color. It was a sea of turbans and kohl-eyed women enshrouded in mystery. It was the din of merchants haggling over prices, the sweet song of nightingales in bamboo cages, the bubbling of fountains on each corner. It was Barikah, which Derek had never thought to know again.

And the Dey's palace, spread out over more than twenty acres on the highest hill of the city, brought back a wealth of memories long forgotten. Derek moved through the labyrinth now, following in Omar's wake. When he first arrived, he had only gotten as far as the outer court, enclosed in high walls that protected the arsenal, mint, bakery, guards' barracks, and other service buildings. But Omar had taken him through several rooms off his office that led directly into the inner palace, thereby avoiding the second court, where only officials and ambassadors ever penetrated.

Unlike the outer court, which was usually easily accessed by the public, the second court was a cloistered garden with avenues running over its lawns to gates and low buildings. Gazelles and peacocks wandered at will under tall cypress trees, lavish pavilions stood in readiness for any state occasion, and slaves bent over flower beds, toiling beneath the hot sun.

The second court housed the offices of the palace officials and the council chambers where the Divan met several days each week. There foreign diplomats were entertained, the Dey's sons were circumcised or his daughters married, and all ceremonies were performed. And from this courtyard was the iron-studded gate that led to the harem.

Beyond the second court was another gate leading into a third courtyard, the one Derek was most familiar with. It was a more intimate garden with chestnut and medlar trees, and cypresses hung with ivy. The treasury was located there, as well as the throne room and the palace school. And through yet another gate were the richly tiled corridors leading to the Dey's apartments, which abutted the harem.

Omar took Derek instead through the heart

of the palace, through a maze of corridors and chambers that skirted the domed kitchens, the baths, the harem, the courts, and finally led to the very corridor that the concubines used to reach the Dey's apartments.

At last they stopped before a large cedarwood door, flanked on each side by two stiff-backed Nubians. It was only because Derek was accompanied by the Grand Vizier himself that he hadn't been detained at least twenty times by now by the army of guards they had passed at different points along the way, especially when he had remained hooded and with lowered head, a thoroughly suspicious-looking character.

"I hope you have some password or the like to alert these fellows if all isn't right," Derek remarked thoughtfully before Omar could announce them.

"You were searched for weapons before you entered the palace, weren't you?"

"Yes, but what if someone had found a way to get to one of your wives or children, and so coerced you into bringing them in here?"

Omar chuckled. "There is indeed a signal that would have had you or anyone else beheaded in an instant, but I am glad that you are taking such an interest in our security measures. You must feel free to mention anything that concerns you."

A questioning brow rose. "Your family is protected? Killing the one who tells you your family is taken will not save your family."

Omar nodded. "My sons, my grandsons, my

great-grandsons, all are as safe as it is possible to make them. My wives?" He shrugged fatalistically, though there was now a twinkle in his gray eyes. "It would be no great loss were anything to happen to *them*."

Derek suppressed a grin and nodded toward the door. "I suppose you have to announce me?"

"It would be wise, unless you want his personal guards pouncing on you the moment you walk through the door."

"I think I can do without that," Derek replied dryly.

"Yes, it doesn't pay to surprise the Dey, but nonetheless he will be surprised. With so many messengers killed, he had given up hope that one might reach you, Kasim." At the sound of his name, Derek looked pointedly at the guards, but Omar shook his head. "Those who guard Jamil's door are mutes, as are his personal guards."

Omar finally knocked on the door, then waited a full ten seconds before opening it and stepping inside, with Derek following close on his heels. It was a typical Eastern room, large and uncluttered. Finely sculpted onyx columns supported a ceiling that was painted with floral motifs. Stucco panels of floral and geometric designs alternated with bands of calligraphy on the walls. Carved grilles covered the windows but still allowed in ample light to flood the marble floor, in the center of which was set a magnificent mosaic of a hunting scene. What little furniture there was, a few low tables and a single tall cabinet against one wall, was inlaid with mother-of-pearl. There were no chairs or sofas to sit on, nor even a divan in this room, just a low dais strewn with pillows where the Dey was sprawled in relaxation.

But the room was not empty by any means. The coffeemaker was there, Jamil's pipe bearer, and a half-dozen other attendants, all personal slaves. Also present was one of Jamil's concubines, who had had time in the ten seconds Omar had waited before entering to veil herself, and was sitting at Jamal's side with her head demurely bowed.

"Did we have an appointment, Omar, that I have forgotten about?" Jamil broke the silence that had fallen over the room with their entrance.

"Not at all, my lord. But we do request a private word, if it would not be inconvenient. Even your guards should leave, I think."

Jamil raised a brow at this request but did not ask why. He simply nodded his head and the many servants began backing out of the room, the customary way to leave the Dey's presence, salaaming as they went. Even the woman left in this way and managed not to reveal her chagrin at having her hour with Jamil terminated by the Grand Vizier. Jamil wouldn't have noticed in any case. His eyes were on Omar's mysterious companion, whose eyes were likewise on him, though he couldn't tell that with the hood of the burnoose drawn down so low.

The moment the room was empty, Jamil demanded, "Well? Has someone *finally* come forward with information on this cursed plot to see me in an early grave? What did he have to tell you, Omar?"

"Just that he had a pleasant voyage, if more than a month at sea can be considered pleasant without any women aboard to aid a man's comfort."

Jamil scowled at his Grand Vizier. "Is this your idea of a joke, old friend?"

Omar couldn't help himself; he laughed delightedly, then sputtered to a mere grin when Jamil's scowl darkened. He turned watering eyes on Derek. "Reveal yourself before he thinks I've gone mad."

Derek raised a hand and tugged back his hood even as he began walking forward. Jamil sat up, then stood up. One step brought him down from the dais, but he moved no farther than that. Derek had reached him, and they stood eye to eye, one pair of green eyes incredulous, the other identical pair moist with emotion.

"Jamil," Derek said simply, but there was a wealth of meaning in that one utterance.

Jamil slowly smiled, and then he let out a great shout and crushed Derek in a bear hug powerful enough to crack the bones of a smaller man, and grunted when the same hug was returned.

"Allah's mercy, Kasim! I never thought to look on you again."

"Nor I you."

And they both burst out laughing, for one had only to look in a mirror to see the other. Of

104

course, that was not the same thing as being together.

"Nineteen years," Derek continued, his eyes
still roving over Jamil. "God, I've missed you."

"No more than I have you. I don't think I ever
forgave our mother for separating us."

"It made an old man very happy, Jamil," Derek
said in a subdued voice.

"What is that to me when I nearly destroyed
myself in my grief?" Jamil demanded in a burst
of resentment that he had never been able to
overcome. "Did you know that they tried to convince me, too, that you had died, as they did
everyone else? Me? As if I couldn't sense the
truth. I thought I was going mad, with even Rahine
insisting you were dead, when I knew, I knew
here"—he struck his chest hard—"that it couldn't
be so. She finally had to admit what she had
done." That was the day he had stopped calling
her mother.

"You should have told me."

Jamil waved that aside. "I was fifteen before
she would even tell me how I could contact you.
I didn't want to bring up feelings that had been
buried for five years, feelings that I knew would
be read by others before my letters could reach
you."

"And I was afraid to ask why you never answered my letters, which I began writing immediately."

"I never received them. Our father saw to that,
again at Rahine's request."

"Why?" Derek demanded, some of his own resentment resurfacing.

"She wanted no reminders. There were two of us, so one was easily sacrificed. But she wanted no reminders."

Derek looked away before saying, "I remember her words when she took me down to that ship. 'I can't go back, Kasim,' she told me. 'And even if I could, I can bear no more children. You are the only one who can carry on my family line, and that means as much to the English as it does here. Jamil was the firstborn. Your father would never let him go. But you, you are all I can give my father, and I love him, Kasim. I can't bear to think of him dying alone, with no hope for the future. You are all that he will have of me. You will be his heir, his joy, his reason to live. Please, don't hate me for sending you to him.' "

"She had no right!"

"No," Derek agreed softly. "But I also remember her tears as I sailed away."

They looked at each other for a long, silent moment before Jamil finally admitted, "I know. I often heard her crying when she thought she was alone, but I was young and unforgiving then. I hardened my heart to the fact that she missed you as much as I did. I refused to believe that she could still love you after what she did. And I hated Mustafa for a long time for letting her convince him to go along with it."

"He had many sons at that time, even if we were his favorites."

106

"Don't make excuses for him, Kasim. Serves him right that he began to worry later when half of those sons died before they left the harem."

That spiteful statement made them both suddenly grin. "You don't mean that." Derek said.

"No," Jamil replied. "But he did finally bemoan the fact that he only had five sons left, one of which he had willingly given away, and as everyone believed this son dead, he might as well be. Of course he could rail at Omar, the only other one to know about it, for not stopping him from being so generous with his favorite *kadine*."

When they both turned for Omar's comments on this, they found that he had quietly left them alone for their reunion. They smiled at the old man's thoughtfulness and moved onto the cushions scattered about the low dais. Jamil offered a long Turkish pipe with an amber mouthpiece, but Derek declined. He sprawled back in a very English pose, leaning on one elbow, his other hand resting on a bent knee. Beneath his now-open burnoose was revealed a white linen shirt with open collar tucked into clinging buff-colored trousers, likewise tucked into knee-high boots.

Jamil's Turkish trousers were large and loose, ending at the knee, easily accommodating the Eastern fashion of sitting cross-legged, as he did now. His feet were bare, his collarless tunic green silk and lined with yellow gems about the neck and in several layers about the cuffless sleeves. An emerald the size of a walnut was in the center of the turban that he removed now that they were alone, giving his head a shake to loosen coal-black hair that was worn at least three inches longer than Derek's.

When their eyes met again, Jamil asked pointedly, "Did *you* forgive her?"

"I think I understood her motives better once I came to know Robert Sinclair. I came to love him, Jamil, just as she does."

"And how I hated him for being the reason you were taken from me." This was said quietly, without the earlier heat Jamil had displayed.

"I did, too, at first. I hated everything English. But then a little girl of no more than six put me in my place, demanding of me, 'What have you to be so high and mighty and god-awful arrogant about? You're just a boy, and an orphan at that.' "

"An orphan?"

"It's the story our grandfather put out, to explain why I showed up alone on his doorstep. My father was supposedly a foreign diplomat my mother had met and married while abroad, and both parents died, leaving the Marquis to raise me. It kept things simple and generated sympathy. Ah, the sympathy." Derek chuckled. "When I was only twelve, there was the prettiest little kitchen wench who insisted on showing me how very sympathetic she could be."

"Twelve?" Jamil snorted. "And our father made me wait until I was thirteen before any female slaves were allowed to serve me."

They both grinned, remembering their first attempts at making love and how very hesitant and scared they had been at that early age. Then Jamil added, "And the unwise female child who insulted you?"

Derek laughed. "She became my closest friend." He laughed harder at Jamil's incredulous look. "It's true. She made me realize what an utter ass I was for taking out my loneliness and resentment on everyone around me. I was there, and there to stay, so I began to make the best of it."

"But a female friend, Kasim? I know Europeans feel differently about women, but you're only half English."

"I had only just left the harem, Jamil. It felt more natural for me at the time to associate with this girl rather than with the men of the Marquis's household. And as you say, Europeans feel differently about it There, it was all right for me to remain friends with Caroline, even as we grew older. And now," he added with a grin, "I'm going to marry the lady when I return."

Jamil shook his head. "You have waited a long time to marry."

"It takes a bit more time to think about it when you're stuck with your first choice."

"Yes, only one wife." Again the Dey shook his head. "Can you be satisfied with only one?"

"Come on, Jamil. You know very well that Europeans enjoy as much variety as you do. We just have to be discreet about it. Actually," Derek added truthfully, "I still wouldn't be getting married just yet if the Marquis hadn't insisted on it. He wants to see some children before he passes on."

"You have none yet?"

"None that I know of. And you? How many are there now?"

"Sixteen, but only four are sons."

"Then you've had three more daughters since I last heard from you? Congratulations."

Jamil started to shrug that aside, for daughters were not considered at all important except when it came time to marry them off, but the fact was that he adored all his little girls, and they were all still young, under the age of six.

He was grinning proudly when he replied, "My first wife has given me two daughters now, as well as my oldest son. They are angels, Kasim, the youngest only three months old."

"I hope I'll get to see them while I'm here. I am their uncle, after all."

"Of course," Jamil said with some surprise, for if Kasim agreed to Omar's idea, he would see not only Jamil's children while he was here but all of his women as well. "Didn't Omar tell you—" He fell silent at his brother's bland look, only to explode, "That son of a camel's turd! He didn't tell you why you're here, did he? He left it to me!"

Derek grinned. "Actually, it didn't come up. We ended up discussing horse breeding instead."

"Horse breeding!"

"Yes, because of the matched pair of Thoroughbreds I brought along for you."

Jamil's expression changed to one of boyish delight. "You did?"

Derek chuckled. "Yes. But now that you've mentioned it, why am I here?"

Jamil cringed at the reminder. "It was Omar's idea. I refused at first to even consider it, but he wouldn't give up badgering me about it, and finally I let him convince me to at least ask you. Even so, I would have refused if I weren't certain Selim is behind this plot. He hates me, Kasim, and always has. You know that. You must remember. He was even worse than Mahmud in his spitefulness and cruelty. If he succeeds in eliminating me and comes to power, he would see that my wives, my children, all perish."

Derek did indeed remember Selim. "Yes, I've no doubt of that. So what is Omar's idea?"

"For you to take my place."

Derek was not surprised. He had already surmised this was what he was needed for, the only thing he *could* be needed for. But he wasn't about to become the next Dey of Barikah, even if he was next in line for the position. He simply didn't want that kind of power and the headaches that went along with it. He had lived the simple life of an Englishman too long, even if he had spent a few years embroiled in intrigue and spying for Marshall. It was one thing to have a little adventure, a little risk for the sake of excitement, when you knew you only had to cross the Channel to put it behind you. Here, it would never end.

"I won't succeed you, Jamil. I'll tell you that

right off. As far as anyone here is concerned, I'm dead and forgotten, and I'd like to leave it that way. But temporarily, for the few days it would take to see your family safe if Selim does succeed, of course I'll take your place. You didn't even have to ask. But as long as I'm here, why don't we see that nothing happens to you instead."

Jamil did not show the relief Derek expected. "I think you misunderstood, Kasim. Omar's idea is not for you to impersonate me if I die, but before it comes to that."

For five seconds Derek said nothing, and then he said in a rush, "Jesus Christ! Do you know what you're asking?"

The pain in Jamil's eyes said he did, but he, too, misunderstood, in this case Derek's reaction. "You are right. It is too much to ask, to risk your life—"

"To hell with the—"

"No, no, I should never have brought you here. And I wouldn't have for myself. It is my loved ones . . . but you are right. The danger is still there, whether it is you or me. Omar was a fool to even think of it."

"Jamil—"

"All he is concerned with is Barikah, not the lives he endangers—"

"Jamil, shut up!" Derek finally had to shout to get his attention.

Jamil did. That there wasn't a single person in all of Barikah, not Omar, not their mother, Rahine, not even Jamil's beloved Sheelah, who

112

would have dared speak to him so was irrelevant. Jamil had barely noticed, and Derek wouldn't have cared if he had.

"I'm not concerned about the risk," Derek continued impatiently. "I'm used to risking my life, and for less reason than this. So don't mention it again, Jamil, if you don't want to see me lose my temper. But you're talking about weeks, months maybe, of my pretending to be you! How the hell am I supposed to do that when I haven't seen you for nineteen years?"

Jamil's teeth flashed white in a relieved grin. "But that is the easy part. We would take a week, maybe a little longer, for you to watch me, study my mannerisms, see how I deal with those around me. Omar would instruct you, and he will be on hand to see you make no mistakes."

"And if he isn't always there? If someone should ask me something I haven't the faintest idea of how to answer, then what?"

"Come now, Kasim, you have not forgotten the prerogatives of the Dey. You can dismiss any and all persons from your presence at any time, and no one would dare ask you why. I have done so enough times in these past months that it would seem quite natural for you to order a room vacated of all except my mutes, and even they have suffered from my recent temper."

Derek chuckled. "The confinement getting to you, is it?"

"About three months ago," Jamil replied in disgust.

"All right, so that tells me how I could avoid any ticklish situations that arise, but what about the running of your little empire?"

"Omar is capable of making all decisions. It is his responsibility when I am unavailable."

"Then you don't intend to remain in the palace?"

"No. It is my intention to find Selim, and for this I would enlist the help of his namesake, Sultan Selim. Our half brother was last seen at the Sultan's court. But no one I now have searching for Selim has the rank to get in to see the Sultan, and he does not respond well to letters. So I would go first to Istanbul, and hopefully, from there to wherever Selim is hiding. If the Sultan doesn't know where he has gone, he can find out. My network of spies is nothing compared with his."

"I'm surprised you haven't already done this."

"I wanted to, but Omar wouldn't hear of it, and my councillors all concurred with him. Allah's mercy, they are like a bunch of old women, afraid for me to even step into my outer court, much less outside the palace walls. The trouble is, with more than a thousand slaves in the palace, it is too easy to bribe dozens of my own people to spy on me and report my every move. I cannot leave the palace, even in disguise, without the assassins knowing about it, and that is all they are waiting for."

"Yes, the palace is too easy to watch from without with only one main gate."

Jamil nodded. "Occasionally they grow impatient and send in one or two of their numbers to try and take me. Just last month one got as far as my bedchamber, killed the two guards at the door, and tried crawling across the floor to my bed. Fortunately, my personal guards are more alert than the others, and one spotted the dog before he reached me."

"And all the other guards along the way?"

"Most were drugged somehow, and we have still not discovered how. A few were killed. As far as we could discover, they came over the walls of the third court after poisoning my lions, which are let loose there at night."

Derek shook his head, sighing. "It's a nasty business, Jamil, all of it. I might prefer a little more active part in putting an end to it, but if you think my taking your place for a while will be better, then I suppose I can give it a try."

"You will actually do it?"

"Didn't I just say so?"

"You're sure, Kasim? I really have no right to ask—"

"Christ, don't start that again," Derek said quickly. "And besides, I was asked by my government, unofficially, of course, to do whatever I can to eliminate the threat against you. With the risk of giving you the upper hand in your future dealings with England, I must admit they sort of prefer you to anyone else who might succeed you. And I suppose my taking your place, and thereby taking the threat away from you, will do pretty much what I was requested to do."

"It is annoying that these foreign consuls know so much of what goes on inside these walls and report it to their respective governments."

"They don't know nearly as much as they'd like to, Jamil. But tell me, am I going to have to grow one of those, or are you going to shave yours?" Derek asked, reaching over to tug on Jamil's luxuriant beard.

Jamil sighed. "I suppose it was too much to hope that you would have worn a beard yourself. There will not be time for you to grow one to my length. Allah help me, it is almost too much to sacrifice—"

Derek burst out laughing at Jamil's expression. "Come now, you can see for yourself how you'll look without it," he said, rubbing his own clean-shaven chin. "I get no complaints from the ladies."

"Yes, it does make you appear younger than I," Jamil replied thoughtfully.

"And I almost have to fight the women off."

"Braggart." Jamil chuckled. "You cannot possibly have the same problems that I have with forty-seven concubines,"

"Is that all?" Derek prodded teasingly. "Mustafa must have had at least two hundred before he died."

"Mustafa did not care how many languished in neglect."

A dark brow shot up curiously. "You surprise me, Jamil. That possibly would be a concern of mine after nineteen years among the English—but you?"

"Perhaps we are not so different after all, even with such a long separation."

"Perhaps," Derek agreed, grinning. "Speaking of your women, what will they think when you don't summon them for so long?"

Jamil lowered his eyes before answering, his tone subdued. "But they will be summoned—by you. You must do everything that I would ordinarily do for this to work."

Derek was not so insensitive that he didn't hear the pain in those words. "Don't be absurd!"

Jamil's eyes jerked up in surprise at the vehemence of that response. He had not expected this to be an objection. *He* objected. With every fiber of his being, he objected, for if he was anything, he was a possessive man. He might bemoan the fact that he had more women than he could possibly need or want, but they were *his* women. It was the hardest thing he would ever do, to open his harem to another man, with pride demanding that it be without exception. Were it any other man, he couldn't do it. But this was Kasim, his other self. There was no one he felt closer to, even after nineteen years' separation making them almost strangers to each other.

"It is the only way," Jamil said now with enough force to conceal his own reluctance. "Omar made me see this, and I agree. The eunuchs of the harem cannot be confined. They come and go at will, and you know as well as I that some of them gossip worse than women. And the fact is that I have never ignored my women for more than two

117

or three days at a time. Even when I travel, I take my favorites with me. So if it becomes known that I am suddenly neglecting my harem, it will naturally be wondered why. Consequently, I would be watched more closely. The slightest error on my part, on *your* part, would take on new meaning. Someone might remember that I had a twin who died mysteriously, whose body was never seen by anyone. Do you see now why you must take on my habits as if they were your own, all of them? You must even assume my frustration, and frankly, I have been very difficult lately, which is why anger will be your easiest defense in any situation that arises, for my temper has become the expected, rather than the unusual."

"I suppose I don't have a choice," Derek said, though he was frowning now, "if your freedom of movement is not to be jeopardized."

"Exactly. Neither of us has a choice, if you still agree to do it."

"Is that what you really want, Jamil?"

"I can see no other way."

"*I* could go after Selim."

"Yes, but you do not know him as I do, Kasim. It would take you twice as long to find him, and I could be dead by then. Besides," Jamil added with a wry grin "I will go mad if I cannot get away from here, now that your presence offers me the chance. I don't think I can even bear the time it will take to familiarize you with my habits."

"You'll have to try, brother mine," Derek rejoined. "I'd rather not walk into this thing blind, if it's all the same to you."

Jamil chuckled at that very placid, dry English tone. He would indeed have to try.

Chapter Fourteen

JEANNE MAURIAC glanced curiously around the large room into which she had just been escorted. Pallets lined the floor, most occupied by women with nothing better to do than lie about, counting the passing minutes of each hour even though it was only the middle of the afternoon. Boredom, apathy, fear—she saw it all, but it was nothing new to her. She had gone this route before, three times before, sold and sold again. The only thing surprising to her was the cleanliness of Hamid Sharif's bagnio, the building where slaves were confined together before they were sold. Most bagnios in which slaves already sold were kept as a work force to be hired out, were as filthy as pigsties. But here even a fountain bubbled in the center of the room, and the fretted windows along two walls let in sun and fresh air for what would have made a very nice atmosphere—if it weren't for the boredom, apathy, and fear.

Jeanne found an empty pallet and began to take note of the women. They were her competition, and it was a matter of comparing, at least for her. She knew from experience that the best home to go to was a rich home, and the richer buyers bid only on the prettier women. Happily, she saw there weren't that many women in the room, and none appeared really exceptional except for a black beauty who reeked hostility and was, in fact, chained to the wall. If she was as hostile as she looked, it was doubtful she would be put on the block, but would be sold privately.

Jeanne expected to go on the block. She had done so before, and it was an experience she didn't find quite as humiliating as the other women did; she was proud of her attributes, and having the dark gold hair and blue eyes that were so prized here didn't hurt. She knew that with the right posture and a few sensual looks, she could fire the lust of the bidders and thereby raise her price. She also knew from experience that the more her new owner was forced to pay for her, the more fortunate he would feel in having attained her, and the better she would be treated in his household.

A flash of silver caught her eye and she glanced across the room to a woman she had previously dismissed as being too old, with hair like silver moonbeams. But now that her head was raised, Jeanne gasped, for it was a girl, a very young girl, an incredibly beautiful young girl. Resentment started to rise, then quickly ebbed away as Jeanne realized that this one, like the magnificent black one, wouldn't be put on the block. Beauties such as these were usually always sold by private auction. She wouldn't have to compete against them.

Jeanne stared at this girl, unable to help herself.

120

She was pale, and growing paler by the second. from this distance her large eyes seemed like two black coals against such white skin. They were rounded wide, staring out the window in what was unmistakable horror.

Jeanne followed the direction of the girl's eyes and made a sound of disgust in the back of her throat. In the large, enclosed court outside the room, a public auction was taking place. Jeanne had seen it earlier but had paid it no mind. She had been told she wouldn't be sold until later in the week. Slaves were never sold the first day of their arrival, usually because they arrived in such poor condition they were virtually worthless. That was not the case with Jeanne, but rules were rules.

Jeanne had also been told that twice weekly Hamid Sharif opened his gates to the city for these public auctions, often selling between twenty and thirty souls at a time, more if he happened to be overcrowded with new arrivals. This was undoubtedly why there were so few women left in the women's quarters now. Those to be sold had already been taken out to await their turn on the block.

And it was a block, a tall, square platform in the center of the court that allowed the crowd below to have an excellent view of the merchandise. Slaves came cheap, because there was such an abundance of them. Even a poor man could conceivably save enough to buy a slave or two to make his life easier. A young woman could go for as little as seventy piasters, a strapping man for only slightly more. Eunuchs fetched the most, upward of two hundred piasters, because they were so much in demand and because the Muslims would not castrate a man themselves, castration being forbidden by their religion. The use of eunuchs in a man's harem was not even a Turkish custom, the idea having come from the Byzantines, who had previously ruled Istanbul when the city was still known as Constantinople.

The cheap slaves were those who would be put to manual labor. A woman of fetching beauty was quite a different matter. She would be bought as a concubine and for no other reason, and her price would be determined by how badly a man desired to own her. Jeanne had been sold for five hundred piasters her first time, when she had still been a virgin. But prices had been known to go much higher than that for rare beauties.

She wondered if the silver-haired blonde knew that. Chances were she hadn't been told she wouldn't have to go up on that block, and that was why she was so appalled by what she was witnessing now. A woman and a young child, likely related, were being turned about so the crowd could view them from different angles. Both had been stripped of their clothes; both were crying pitifully. Jeanne wondered if it was better to know exactly what would happen to you by being able to see the auctions firsthand, as these women could, or to be kept away from the slave block and not know in advance what you would have to endure.

She made up her mind and crossed the room, sitting down next to the girl on her pallet. "You won't have to go through that," Jeanne said gently.

"I know," was the anguished reply in Jeanne's own language, though with a slight accent.

"Then why do you look so horrified?"

"It's so degrading, so utterly humiliating. It shouldn't be allowed. It's barbaric and—"

"You're in for a lot of heartache if you go on taking everyone else's misery to yourself, *petite*. You're here. That won't change. And the only way you can get though this is to worry about no one but yourself."

The girl finally looked at her, and Jeanne saw that the eyes weren't black at all, but a dark, glistening violet. "You're not afraid?"

Jeanne almost smiled, but shrugged instead. "I am an old hand at this. It's been nine years since I was first captured and sold in Algiers. I was known as Jeanne Mauriac then, though I've been given other names since. They always change your name, Lord knows why, but to myself, I've kept the name I was born with. And you?"

"Chantelle Burke."

"English or American?" When Chantelle hesitated in answering, Jeanne chuckled. "So you must be English. But don't worry, *petite*. I may be French and our countries may be at war, but we will leave the fighting to the men, yes?"

Chantelle smiled slightly in answer. "How is it you're here if you've already been sold?"

"Ah, a long story that, but then I've time to tell it. My first owner was so infatuated with me that he married me when he didn't have to. Ah, I had it so easy then, my every wish granted, silks and jewels laid at my feet. Unfortunately, he had a first wife who despised me, and when he died, she had me sold into a brothel. Don't look so shocked, *petite*." Jeanne grinned. "I was having none of that. My very first night there, I set fire to the house and escaped. And I almost made it to the French consulate, too, when who should I run straight into but that very son-of-a-dog who first captured me."

"You were taken prisoner again?"

Jeanne nodded with a look of disgust. "And taken right back to the same filthy bagnio that I was first sold from. This time I was bought by a merchant from Istanbul and I spent the next two years in his large harem, completely ignored. Ah, that was nice, too, for a change, to not have to compete with all the other women for the master's notice. He was old, so I didn't particularly want to be noticed. The trouble was, I didn't earn any gifts that way, and so when he died and I was set free, I didn't have the money to buy my passage home."

"You were actually set free at his death?" Chantelle asked in amazement.

"You didn't realize that was possible?"

"No, Hakeem failed to mention that," Chantelle replied with a frown, and at Jeanne's raised brow, added, "He was the one to instruct me on the voyage here, the only one of the corsairs who spoke English. He taught me some of the language, and what to expect."

"Ah, so that is how you knew you wouldn't have to go on the block."

"Yes, but there will still be an auction," Chantelle said miserably. "Hamid Sharif put the word out as soon as I arrived."

"The auction will be private, attended only by those who can afford you, and that will not be so many, *petite*. You will not have to face the hundreds of spectators who just come to watch." At a visible shudder from Chantelle, Jeanne added, "Truly, it will not be so bad, and certainly not like what you see out there in the yard. You will probably not be stripped at all, for these men, serious buyers indeed, will each hope to be the one who will own you, and they will not want you viewed by the others. Do you know when it is to take place?"

"In two more days."

"Then you've been here for some time now? Yes," Jeanne answered her own question. "Sharif would want to allow time for buyers to come from as far away as Algiers and Tunis. And knowing what a prize he has, he has no doubt set a high starting bid. I'm surprised he didn't offer you to the Dey here."

"He did," Chantelle replied. "But Rashid or Reshid, whatever his name is, didn't want me."

"No? Ah, that is too bad." Jeanne sighed. "I've heard he is young."

125

"So much the better, then, that he didn't want me, if I can be set free if the man who buys me dies. I'd prefer an old man, of course."

"No, no, *petite*, never say so. You don't want your first time with a man to be with an old goat who doesn't care if he pleases you. And this will be your first time, yes?" A slow blush creeping up Chantelle's cheeks was answer enough. "Besides, you do not always find yourself free when your master dies. Look what happened with my first husband. And I have not even told you about my second yet."

"You married again?"

"There was not much else I could do when I found myself stranded in Istanbul. But at least I did the picking that time, though without a dowry there was not too much for me to pick from. I became third wife to one of the minor officials at the Sultan's court. He was an older man, too, but handsome at least, and still quite vigorous in . . . anyway, I was competing again to remain in his favor, and so earned myself enough money for a dowry, or passage home, if something should happen to him, and it did. He somehow displeased the Sultan and ended up losing his head."

"You're joking!"

"Not at all. Generally when such happens, the Sultan takes possession of all the condemned man's property, but my husband's oldest son happened to be favored at court, so this didn't happen."

126

"But you weren't property this time."

"That is a moot point here. I was part of the harem, of which all but two wives were slaves."

"Then you were set free again?"

Jeanne made a sound of disgust. "This time I had too much accumulated wealth, and my lord's son was a greedy little bastard. He confiscated everything we women possessed and sold us all, except for his mother. I was bought by a slave trader out of Tripoli. En route, we encountered an American frigate that the *rais* thought he could take. He was wrong."

"You were rescued?" Chantelle gasped.

"Yes, but enjoyed freedom for no more than a week. Late one night we were surprised by one of Hamid Sharif's ships, and so here I am, starting all over again."

"I'm sorry," Chantelle said. "It must have been terrible, to find yourself so close to freedom."

Jeanne shrugged. "It is all the same to me. I have no one in France to return to. If I stay here the rest of my life . . ." She shrugged again. "It is not so bad, *petite*, once you get used to it."

Chantelle found that so unlikely, she refrained from commenting on it. "And the Americans? What happened to them?"

"Ah, they will likely all be ransomed. The Americans, they are very particular about their own countrymen. The American consul was right there to meet the ship, and though Sharif technically owns all prisoners, they were taken to the state bagnio, where they will remain even if they are bought by investors, to be rented out for manual labor. This way, they earn money until their ransoms can be arranged."

"Yes, Hakeem told me something about that."

"It is usually a good investment for a buyer, because negotiations can take years sometimes if the ruling Dey or Bey is one to drag his feet, as most are. I understand things like this move along much more quickly in Barikah—at least this is what the American captain was told. They are fortunate that they have a consulate here. Those who do not are usually bought outright, or they end up spending the rest of their lives in the bagnio."

"The Neapolitans who were captured on our way here must not have a consul," Chantelle said quietly. "I saw them all sold, right out there, and inspected . . ." Her voice died away as another blush climbed her cheeks.

Jeanne smiled to herself, thinking that a girl this young and innocent would have closed her eyes the moment she realized men were going to be stripped down to nothing in front of her. "It is the normal way of things here, *petite*. A slave must be inspected by prospective buyers to see if he is fit and sound, and capable of many years of arduous work. That is all sailors are good for, since they are not eunuchs and so cannot look forward to the lazy life of the harem."

"Yes, I understand all that, no matter how unfair it seems. What I don't understand is why women can't be ransomed, too. I'm an heiress. I can afford to match whatever Sharif may hope to sell me for."

"But women are ransomed, *petite,* and quickly released if they are indeed wealthy or are well connected back home. Does the English consul know you are here?"

Chantelle shook her head. "I was secreted into the city at night."

"Ah, yes, you would be. Women might be ransomed, but rarely ones as lovely as you."

"But if it's a matter of price—"

"It's not. You must realize that Sharif is in the business of selling slaves, not collecting ransoms. To him, you make a rare offering that can only enhance his reputation, which is actually worth more to him than the money. Even if you had been captured by one of the Dey's ships instead of a privately owned vessel, it is likely the *rais* would be smart enough to keep you under wraps until his lord could see you and decide if he wanted you for his own harem or to send as a gift to the Sultan."

"What if I could manage to get word to the English consul?" Chantelle asked hopefully.

Jeanne shook her head regretfully. "Once you enter a harem, your chances of being ransomed are virtually gone, even if your consul should later learn of your presence. Your master need only deny that he has you, and as no man can enter another man's harem, it would be impossible to prove otherwise. The sanctity of the harem is

129

universal here. Not even the Dey would force his way into the harem of his lowest servant."

Chantelle looked down at her lap. "Then I must be freed, or escape."

"*Petite,* it would be better for you if you do not waste your time hoping for such a possibility. True, if a concubine goes to an important house and she has accumulated enough personal wealth, she might be able to purchase her freedom at her master's death. But it is more likely a husband will be found for her, and her wealth used as a dowry, and that is only if she has not made enemies of her master's wives, or his mother, who is the real power in the harem. It is just as likely she will be resold, because she is and will always remain a slave, even if her master takes her to wife should she bear him a son."

"Did you bear your master a son, the one who married you?"

"My case was different. My first master was not an important man, just a rich one, and he already had six sons by his first wife, so he did not care whether I gave him a son or not. But you are likely to go to an important household, perhaps even the royal harem of Algiers or Tunis, and an important man rarely marries a slave unless she first gives him a son." At Chantelle's stricken look, Jeanne quickly added, "You never know, *petite.* The man who buys you may be looking for a wife. Many of the more pretty and intelligent women are actually sought after as wives by local men, either Christian or Muslim." She did not add that that was only if they could afford them, and only a select few would be able to afford Chantelle, but she had mistaken Chantelle's look.

"I don't want a husband here, Jeanne. That would be too—too permanent. I don't think I could bear it if I had to give up hope of ever returning to England."

Those few words had brought tears to Chantelle's eyes, making Jeanne uncomfortable enough to look away. "As I first said, you are more likely to go to an important household."

"And escape? Is that possible?"

Jeanne couldn't bring herself to give Chantelle false hope. "Escape is least likely of all, *petite*. Many harems contain more eunuchs than they do women, and they are there solely to guard the women, to keep outsiders out and the women in."

"Then what is there for me to hope for?"

"You can hope for a handsome master, one you will fall in love with and adore serving."

"And sharing with dozens of other women?" Chantelle bit out caustically.

It was the first bit of spirit Jeanne had noticed in the young girl, and she was surprised enough to say, "But that is the way here. It is the one thing you will quickly get used to."

Chapter Fifteen

CHANTELLE COULDN'T nap that afternoon with the rest of the women. Today marked the fourth auction she had witnessed since her arrival, and she couldn't get it out of her mind.

She had tried to make friends when she had first been brought to this room. She had spoken with many of the women and found they all shared the same fears. It seemed easier for a while, knowing that she was not alone in what she was feeling. But then she had watched those same women she had spoken with be marched out to the yard and sold. She had stopped speaking to new arrivals after that.

The Frenchwoman was the first exception. And Chantelle wouldn't have to watch her being sold. No, Chantelle would be the next to go, in only two more days.

She shuddered at the thought. So often she had tried to look on this as an adventure, but she could never quite manage it. The stumbling block was that she knew she was going to be deflowered by some stranger, and she couldn't get past the horror of that.

At least Jeanne Mauriac had relieved her mind on one count. Ever since she had watched the first sale out in the courtyard, she had been so afraid that she would likewise be stripped down and forced to endure such total humiliation when it was her turn to be sold. One woman had even been drugged, which seemed an even worse crime, for she had lost her last defense in not knowing what was done to her.

As the time drew closer to her auction, her stomach became so tied up in knots with her thinking about it that she became sick whenever she tried to eat.

Jeanne had moved her pallet next to Chantelle's and lay sleeping beside her, and Chantelle envied the woman her blithe acceptance of her fate. But even with one of her worries put to rest, Chantelle still could not relax enough to while away the time in sleep.

Only two more days. God, she would rather stay here, even if this became a prison she could never escape. At least she had been well treated here, and she had come to know what to expect of each day. There had been her initial horror when she had been subjected to yet another personal examination upon her arrival. Hamid Sharif had had to make sure for himself that no one had altered her virginal state on the journey.

But since then, no one had touched her. The eunuchs who had the care of the women were not harsh as long as they were obeyed, and Chantelle didn't have the nerve to argue with such big, frightening-looking men anyway. They even deigned to answer what questions she put to them.

She was able to bathe each morning. The food was good, even if she had lost her appetite these past few days. Yes, she would definitely rather stay here.

She toyed with her dinner that evening while Jeanne kept up a cheerful chatter, exclaiming over the excellent meal. Huge platters were brought in and set on little stools, forming three low tables the women could gather around. The only exception was the black girl who had arrived yesterday and was kept chained to the wall. Not even for eating was she released, one of the eunuchs attempting to feed her by hand. Chantelle had yet to see her eat anything. She either spat it out or refused to open her mouth.

"What's her story?" Jeanne asked no one in particular at their table as she watched the African girl tempt the eunuch's anger.

No one answered, whether the women understood Jeanne's French or not. Chantelle wouldn't have answered either, except Jeanne finally looked pointedly at her.

"She's a princess from some tribe far south of here. She refuses to accept slavery, according to the guards I overheard talking about her."

Jeanne snorted. "She will eventually. We all do." Chantelle had anticipated that attitude from Jeanne, which was why she hadn't wanted to speak of the African girl. She knew exactly how the girl felt. She couldn't accept slavery either. She was just too intimidated at present to say so. And that was Hakeem's doing, by warning her to keep her anger and resentment under wraps. Of course he had been right. She didn't care to be chained up as the black girl was, which would surely have happened if she had reacted as she had wanted to during that second intimate examination of her body.

She changed the subject and managed to get Jeanne to tell some amusing stories of her harem life while they finished eating. It still amazed her, this attitude of the Frenchwoman. She wasn't that much older than Chantelle, perhaps twenty-five or twenty-six, and yet they had such opposite views. Had nine years of living among the Muslims done this to her, or did she truly see nothing wrong with this way of life?

It was only a short while after the remains of the dinner were removed that they had visitors.

"What's this?" Jeanne asked, sitting up straighter as Hamid Sharif himself entered the room.

The slave merchant was followed by a tall, slim man with skin the color of rich coffee. He was as dark as the Sudanese eunuchs who guarded the women, though much older, yet Chantelle couldn't imagine him being a eunuch, thereby a slave, not when he wore a magnificent fur-lined robe of blue silk that glittered with sapphires. Ropes of the same gems hung from his nearly two-foot-high turban.

She sighed, pulling the little gauze veil that was attached to her simple headdress up over the lower half of her face. "This has happened before,"

135

Chantelle said. "Sharif brings in buyers who don't wish to wait for the auction or have missed it. The last time, it was a man whose cook had just died and he was hoping to find an immediate replacement."

She didn't add that these buyers could touch and examine the women at their leisure, open their mouths to check their teeth, or open the little vests that all of them had been given to wear. That little vest was all Chantelle had to wear now, too. She had lost Hakeem's concealing tunic the first time she was led to the baths and her clothes taken to wash. She was given a new set of clean clothes, nearly identical to the others, but Hakeem's tunic was not returned to her then or later.

"But why do you veil yourself?"

"I was told to do so whenever they let buyers in here. Sharif doesn't want anyone seeing me before my sale."

Jeanne sniffed. "I should have been given a veil, too. I don't think I care to have just anyone look me over."

Chantelle almost grinned at such a haughty tone, until she noticed Sharif's client looking directly at her. And then the breath caught in her throat when they both walked toward her.

"Is she the one?" the stranger asked while his chocolate-colored eyes moved dispassionately over Chantelle.

Hamid Sharif, who was a short, squat man of middle years, seemed to shrink even more next to this impressive fellow. For a man who aways

136

seemed to be in complete control of himself—after all, he was master here—Sharif appeared at the height of anxiety tonight.

"But this is so irregular, my lord." Sharif had not bothered to answer the question directly. "I have sent out word of her. I have buyers coming from Algiers and—"

An elegant hand was waved to cut off Hamid Sharif's complaint. "How much?"

"But, Haji Agha, my lord, please, what will I tell the buyers?"

"The truth, or supply them with someone else. Her."

Haji Agha had indicated Jeanne Mauriac, and Sharif's expression relaxed somewhat. The Frenchwoman *was* pretty. He had already been thinking of adding her as a bonus at the private auction, to assuage the bidders who lost out on the Englishwoman. She was older and not a virgin, but at least she was also a blonde.

"How much?" Haji Agha repeated.

"I was anticipating at the very least five thousand piasters."

The black man did not bat an eye. "I will give you three."

"Impossible! I cannot accept less than four thousand five hundred."

"Three thousand five hundred, and my lord's gratitude."

"If you put it that way, of course I cannot refuse," Hamid Sharif said with a bow, and when he raised his head, he was smiling.

"Well! That certainly didn't take long," Jeanne commented as the two men walked across the room to stand over the chained princess.

Chantelle didn't answer immediately. She was slightly in shock. She had just been bought by a man old enough to be her grandfather, by a man with black skin of the like she had never seen until she arrived on the Barbary Coast.

"I—I couldn't understand every word," she said, turning wide violet eyes to Jeanne. "Did that man really just buy me?"

"Yes," Jeanne replied, unable to contain her delight. "And I believe I get to take your place at the auction. Oh, this is much better than I could have expected! And you, *petite*, need no longer worry about the indignities of the sale. It is over. You have a lord and master now."

Over? Yes, there was that. She didn't have to fear being stripped bare before the eyes of a dozen or more men, no matter what Jeanne said to the contrary. Over. Sold. And to an old man. Sold. But he was old. Perhaps he just wanted the privilege of being the one to own her. Would a man that old still call his women to his bed?

"I wonder who he is that Hamid Sharif is willing to risk the wrath of his clients," Jeanne speculated. "He must be very important."

Chantelle was still watching the men, who appeared to have concluded another sale, this time for the African girl. "What does it matter?"

The few Turks and Arabs she had seen since her arrival were swarthy, dark-eyed men, either

138

short and wiry or short and fat, with sharp, aquiline features. There had been only one exception, the Turk looking for a new cook. The friendlier of the two guards who sat outside their door had tried to explain it to her when she had remarked on his very light-colored skin.

The Turks had once been a mixture of strictly Eastern blood—Tatar, Mongol, Circassian, Georgian, Persian, Arabian, and Turkish. But after 1350, when they began stretching their borders into western Europe, the blood of the Greeks, Serbs, and Bulgarians was added, for a civilization as cosmopolitan as those of the Greeks, Romans, and Byzantines. Hakeem had mentioned something about this as well, since it was the same here on the Barbary Coast. In the past centuries, more and more new blood was added, from as far away as England, the Netherlands, and, more recently, even far-off America. But all of it came from the female slaves who ended up in harems and bore their master's children.

Now the more wealthy men, the more important ones, those whose fathers and fathers before them had possessed harems full of fair-skinned concubines, had little Eastern blood left in their veins. It was nothing for the Sultan himself to have red hair or blue eyes. It was nothing for a devout Muslim to pass for a Christian without his turban on. But you were less likely to see this in the teeming streets of the cities in the Barbary States, with the new influx of Arabs and Berbers fresh from the desert, some as dark-skinned as a Nubian eunuch.

Chantelle certainly hadn't seen it in the crowds that filled the courtyard to buy slaves. But she was glad the man who had bought her seemed foreign to her. She would have hated being owned by someone who was so European-looking that she could have passed him on an English road and not remarked on it. She didn't want to relate to this owner of hers in any way.

Jeanne was too interested in the goings-on to have heard Chantelle's question. It was just as well. She didn't want an answer, to be told why it should matter to her when it didn't and wouldn't. Whether she was bought by a sheepherder or the Sultan himself, she was still bought, owned, a slave. No one had asked her if she accepted this role. What she felt about it was not important.

"Ah, you'd better get up, *petite*. I think that's for you."

One of the guards was coming forward with a robe and a yashmak for her to don. She did so docilely. She would save her fight for the important issues, such as if and when they tried to force her into that old man's bed.

Jeanne stood up to embrace her in farewell, even though they had known each other only a few hours. "Good luck, my friend."

"If you wish me luck, Jeanne, then pray I escape."

"Ah, *petite*, you must give up such thoughts."

Chantelle turned away. "When I'm dead and

140

buried," she mumbled to herself as she followed the guard out of the bagnio.

Chapter Sixteen

THE HIDDEN chamber was not unique by any means. One or two could be found in almost any large household in the Near East, many more than that in a royal palace. In the Dey's palace, one could be found overlooking the audience chamber, the throne room, the schoolroom, the council chamber where the Divan met, even Jamil's bedchamber.

As children, Derek and Jamil had often sensed eyes staring down at them from behind the fretted wooden screen high in the wall of the school-room, and had known that one of their parents had come to monitor their studies without disturbing the firm discipline of the class. Mustafa had often punished certain of his wives by forcing them to sit behind the screen in his bedroom while he cavorted with one or two of his other concubines. And attending a meeting of the Divan without the council members being aware of it had been a favorite pastime of many sultans.

Derek stood with one arm braced against the wooden screen that looked out over the large room where Jamil took his leisure. The concealed room was small and dark, without ornament, and extremely hot in the afternoon. Large cushions

141

were piled on the floor to sit on, but Derek rarely used them.

Each morning he was escorted to a similar hidden chamber overlooking the throne room, where he would spend several hours watching Jamil conduct daily business having to do with the palace, disputes among his officials, matters of discipline with the servants, judgments. Even his concubines could seek audience with him there over grievances.

One morning had been spent in another like room above the audience chamber, where Jamil received foreign dignitaries and dealt with matters of the city. Usually this was done four or five days a week, but lately Jamil had cut it down to once a week, attending to only the most important business, and now was not the time to change this recent habit.

In the afternoons, Derek suffered the heat in this tiny room, learning how Jamil dealt with his personal attendants, what amused him, what annoyed him. The early evenings were spent here, too, and Jamil spared himself nothing, concealed nothing; if anything, was extreme in his reactions for Derek's benefit. Omar, who was nearly always at Derek's side explaining things in whispers, insisted more than once that the harshness, the occasional cruelty Derek was seeing, was not the real Jamil.

"His patience is usually unlimited, his kindness renowned. He can be ruthless when the matter is warranted, but also merciful. Even as you

142

see him now, he is still not the tyrant Mahmud was. But what you see is the result of his self-imprisonment. He is a man who worships the outdoors. He would ride for hours each day. When he had to give that up, it was only natural for him to become short-tempered. The situation has simply gone on too long. Since you came, he might have returned to his old self, but he cannot let anyone see it except you and me. Not even his women must suspect that his frustration has nearly gone."

Derek could understand that. He thought that he might react the same way under the same circumstances, and since he was going to be putting himself into those same circumstances, he could only hope it wouldn't be for as long as Jamil had endured it.

To prepare for that time, day and night Derek was witness to his brother's life without anyone being aware of it, even in the bedchamber.

Derek had at first balked at this. As children, he and Jamil might have sneaked into the hidden room to watch their father with his concubines, but that had been as a lark—exciting, dangerous. As a man, he had no desire to play the voyeur. Yet Omar insisted it was necessary for him to know how Jamil behaved toward his women, since they were a very active part of his life.

So far, he had watched Jamil make love to three of his favorites and one of his wives. Each time he was different in his behavior to show Derek the complexities of his nature—tender, forceful, abrupt, even violent. The violence had disgusted Derek, enough for him to get angry, but Omar had explained that this particular woman could not achieve pleasure without it, and so she was called for whenever Jamil needed to work off his frustrations, which had raised her to the status of favorite only recently. She had been whipped, not by Jamil, but by one of his mutes, and then Jamil had taken her brutally. And to Derek's further disgust, she had seemed to enjoy it.

The night Jamil's first wife, Sheelah, came to him was the only time Omar suggested Derek leave before they actually made love. He was almost sorry to go, for she was a rare beauty, with soft sapphire eyes and red hair that reminded him of Caroline. And he noticed the difference in the way Jamil treated his number one *kadine*. He didn't have to be told that this woman was special to his brother.

"He loves her, doesn't he?" Derek had asked Omar as they walked toward the chamber that had been given him for sleeping, and where in total darkness each night he had been sent a slave girl to appease the long abstinence at sea.

"He loves them all, Kasim, but yes, he is *in* love with Lady Sheelah."

"Then it was his idea that I leave?"

"No." Omar chuckled. "Did you not notice his increased testiness today? He knew he would send for her tonight and that you would see her. He would not cut short your instruction for any

144

reason, but he did not like it, that you would see her."

"And I'm supposed to send for her myself later?" Derek asked incredulously. "How can I possibly, knowing how he feels about her?"

"You will have to, Kasim. He sends for her most often. He even goes to her after he has been with one of his other women. Most of them do not sleep with him, but return to the harem for the night. This is normal, because he would rather sleep with Sheelah beside him at night and does. Since you have come he has not, though. What excuse he has given her I do not know, but it would not be the truth. Even she is not to know that you are not him when you take his place."

"So if he has prepared her to expect this change in their routine, I won't have to sleep with her?"

"No, you will not. But you will have to summon her to you, as I said. Of course, what you do with her when you are alone is up to you."

Derek laughed at that. "You sly old fox. Her temporary hurt feelings come second to his peace of mind, correct? Then tell him tomorrow that I won't touch her while he's gone."

"No."

"Then I will."

Omar shook his head. "His pride is at stake here. He hopes that you are a man such as he, that you would not touch another's wife no matter the reason. But for what he asks you to do for him, he cannot deny you anything, even her. Giving you the choice is the risk he takes in leaving you here in his place. He must feel that he risks something, as you do. You cannot take that from him. Besides"—Omar grinned—"this is the incentive he needs to return quickly."

But what agony would he suffer in the meantime? Derek wondered.

Tonight, a half-dozen *ikbals* and all three of Jamil's wives had been invited to take dinner with him. For some, it was the first time they were seeing him with his newly shaved face, which had caused a considerable stir in the palace and did now among his women. Some were surprised, some delighted, which naturally annoyed Jamil, to Derek's amusement. But he could not stay annoyed for long, not surrounded by the crème de la crème of his women.

The atmosphere of competition among the *ikbals* was fierce: who could hold Jamil's attention the longest, find the choicest meat for him, make him laugh. His wives competed just among themselves, it seemed, and only Lady Sheelah had no need to, she who sat next to Jamil and was herself fed by him.

One of the concubines got up and danced to the tune that two blind musicians were playing. It was a sight to delight the senses. These women were the most lovely in the harem, Jamil's favorites. Here, with only his personal attendants on hand, they did not have to veil themselves. All were scantily attired except one, who wore a flowing caftan to conceal her advanced pregnancy. The others were adorned in bright silks, each a

146

different color, and sheer gauzes. Jewels glittered and tinkled about their necks, their wrists, their ankles, some even about their waists, which glistened bare between the short vests and pantaloons.

"Do any take your fancy?" asked Omar, beside him.

"All take my fancy," Derek answered, though with a degree of hesitation.

It was true, however. In beauty of features, in pure sensualty, they were incomparable. If they were each a bit more plump and curvaceous than he was used to, it didn't matter. He had not forgotten the harem he was raised in, where half the women had gone to fat in their lazy existence and the other half would join them eventually. It was a condition prevalent in harems and was no doubt why the Muslim male had acquired a taste for plumpness in his women.

Derek might have been raised to see beauty in the same light, but he had been awakened to manhood by the slim little bodies of overworked English maids, and his taste in women was now decidedly English. Not that each one of Jamil's women couldn't raise his libido, and no doubt many would in the coming weeks. These favorites certainly did. It was just that his preferences were different from his brother's, and he doubted he would find his ideal in Jamil's harem.

Which was just as well. They were, after all, his brother's women. He would not, could not, feel right about taking any of them to his bed, no matter how much Omar, and Jamil himself, insisted it was necessary.

"You will see all of the women tomorrow," Omar told him, wishing he could see Kasim's expression to know exactly what he was feeling, rather than depending on his tone of voice to tell him, difficult to judge when they had to speak in whispers. "They have been invited for an afternoon of games and entertainments in the garden. It will be your opportunity to choose those you favor."

Derek grunted in response. Yes, he would have to learn their names if he was going to summon them to his bed, and it would not be Omar who handled such things later, but the Chief Black Eunuch, the man in control of all those who served the harem.

"What happens to those women I so favor after Jamil returns?" Derek suddenly wanted to know.

Omar did not answer immediately, and then not at all, as a servant entered to whisper a message to Jamil. With a single word from him, his women quickly left. A few moments later, the Chief Black Eunuch came into the room, followed by three of his minions, each dragging forward a woman who was immediately forced to her knees in the traditional prostration of respect before the Dey. One protested this, until her guard jabbed a knee into her back to keep her down.

The Chief Black Eunuch spoke softly to Jamil, bringing forth a chuckle from his master. "So my Grand Vizier was wrong for once."

It was a statement, not a question, and Derek heard Omar stir beside him. "What were you wrong about, Omar, that he finds so amusing?" There was a mumble, and Derek almost laughed aloud, imagining the old man flushing in embarrassment. "Come now, I can't hear you."

"I said," Omar bit out, "Jamil's delighted that I was proved wrong in this instance."

"About what?"

"There was a special slave offered to him before you arrived. He declined as usual. I assumed she would have been quickly sold, so I saw no reason to hurry Haji Agha to the slave markets when Jamil requested some new women, especially since the next slave caravan from the south wasn't due until yesterday."

"He requested new women? I was under the impression he feels he already possesses too many."

"True. These women are for you."

Derek did chuckle now, though softly in understanding. "I suppose the harem is to have some new favorites so that I don't work my way through all of *his*."

"It can safely be assumed that that is his hope, though he will not admit it. And obviously, the special one he previously declined was still available, proving me wrong. Fortunately, these few extra days did not see her sold, or he would not be so amused now."

Which one was supposed to be special was anyone's guess, for all three women were cloaked and heavily veiled, having just come from the city. But Derek was not hopeful and could not dredge up even the slightest interest after having seen Jamil's beauties. The Muslim's idea of "special" was probably "already pleasingly plump," with the fairness of coloring that was so prized here. Anything else would be considered ordinary.

Chapter Seventeen

CHANTELLE HAD made a bad mistake, but she didn't realize it until she was shoved to her knees to pay homage to the Grand Turk, or whatever he was, and she heard Haji Agha address him as "my gracious lord." It was inconceivable that the man she had thought had bought her for himself would show her off to his own master. No, she was very much afraid she had been bought for this other fellow, whom she was at this moment being forced to bow down to.

That went against the grain, and she had very nearly resisted being pushed to the floor until she saw what happened to the black girl beside her, who did resist. It was unfair that brute strength could so easily win the argument. What was the point of going through that when she would only lose in the end and her pride suffer even more? She had put up with enough indignities lately that one more seemed inconsequential.

It would have been nice, though, if she had been told what was going on instead of being left to draw her own wrong conclusions. When she had left Hamid Sharif's, it had been to climb into one of four waiting litters, which had been her first disappointment. She had hoped that she would be walking through the city as she had done before and that there might somehow be an opportunity to slip away. But with all the litter bearers, not to mention a small contingent of mounted guards, that hope had become an impossibility.

She tried peeking out of the curtains that enclosed her in the litter, but was shouted at by one of the guards riding alongside her, so she gave up trying to see where they were going. It was uphill. She could determine that at least. But then the path leveled out, and there was the opening and closing of gate after gate, making her think she was leaving the city, until the litter was set down soon after.

It wasn't until she stepped out of the litter that she saw another girl in one of the other litters, bringing their count to three. And she had only the briefest glance of a courtyard with gardens beyond before she was whisked inside a tall building and down several long corridors, past numerous guards standing at attention before tall doors, and finally brought into this large chamber filled with a half-dozen people. She saw them only in a blur as she was shoved to her knees so fast and forced to lower her head to the floor. She hadn't even noticed the "gracious lord" whom Haji Agha addressed, but she heard him chuckle and mention something about his Grand Vizier being wrong.

Who was he to have a minister with that title? He couldn't be the Dey of Barikah, for that high personage had declined to buy her. Some pasha then? Or some high official in the Dey's could? Would she even be told? That was salt on the wound, that these arrogant Muslims considered women so inferior they didn't have to explain anything to them.

Chantelle gasped when she was suddenly yanked to her feet, and she caught the tail end of the lord's hand gesture that they should rise. What bloody inconsideration! Don't bother with "You may stand, ladies." No, that would be too decent.

Her temper was simmering when her eyes moved from his bejeweled hands to his face, and as instantly as her temper had arisen, it was forgotten. Dear God, one of her worst fears had come to pass. He looked like a European. Worse, with that high brow and sculpted cheekbones, that aggressive chin and aquiline nose, he looked like a bloody English aristocrat! The only thing Turkish about him was his dress—the loose trousers, the long-sleeved tunic of red-and-white printed silk falling just below his hips and sashed tightly to his waist with a large gold clasp. The sash was wide and white, as was his plumed turban, centered with an enormous ruby. His slashing brows indicated black hair, but none was visible, not even a beard. That had been the one thing she had come to expect on all Muslims, a long, flowing beard, or at least a drooping mustache. He had neither, revealing a strong neck, a full, sensual mouth. His eyes were green, dark green, and thickly lashed. He was not short or fat, but just the opposite, as she saw when he rose gracefully to his feet and stepped down from the raised dais on which he had been sitting.

He gave another gesture of his hand and suddenly her double veils and robe were removed, along with those of the other two women. She felt self-conscious now in front of so many people. Besides Haji Agha and the three eunuch guards who stood directly behind each woman, there were three other men and an old woman kneeling near the dais, and two African giants wearing only trousers and short vests, with ugly-looking scimitars hanging from their hips. They stepped forward when the lord did, staying directly behind him on either side.

Chantelle nervously crossed her arms over her midriff. The white cotton of her pantaloons was thick enough and baggy enough to be concealing, but they hung indecently low on her hips, leaving nearly a foot of bare skin between the upper line of the pantaloons and the lower edge of her short fringed vest. She began to relax somewhat when she realized no one was actually looking at her. Everyone's attention was on the tall African girl on her right whom the lord had stopped in front of.

Haji Agha came closer to inform his master: "She claims to be a princess from the jungles to the far south but refuses to name her tribe.

Unlike the other two, she is no virgin, and she still fights her captivity. Hamid Sharif had to keep her chained."

Jamil's eyes moved slowly over the girl, revealing nothing, though he found her magnificent. She was tall, nearly six feet, with large, upthrusting breasts, a thick, hard-muscled waist, and what he imagined would be strong legs, used to running through the bush. Her eyes were a light brown, fired with hate.

"I trust you can tame her?"

"With certainty," Haji Agha assured him.

Jamil nodded, turning his head toward the silver-haired blonde. "I suppose this is the English girl?"

"Yes. She has proved docile, but then she is very intelligent, supposedly of the English nobility. Already she has learned the language well enough to understand most of what we say."

A dark brow shot up. "So soon? From where was she captured?"

"From the English coast, my lord. One of Hamid Sharif's corsairs was hired several months ago to take a passenger there. They had not intended to raid in those waters, but the girl apparently fell into their hands during the short time it took to drop their passenger off on the beach."

Jamil glanced sharply back at his Chief Black Eunuch and suddenly laughed. "By Allah, what irony!"

It was not Haji Agha's place to question his lord's humor or what he found ironic. "Hamid

154

Sharif had sent out word of her far and wide," he continued. "Which is why she was still available. Her private sale was scheduled for two days hence, so naturally he was reluctant to let her go."

"She came expensive, then?"

"Extremely."

Jamil sighed. Next to the African wench, she did not seem tall, though she was taller than most of the women in his harem. And she was skinny, to the point where she looked as if she were starving. Her breasts did not fill out her vest; her stomach was concave, her hips pointy. If that was not bad enough, she was blond, and personally he did not favor blondes because his mother was one, though this girl's hair was so light as to be almost white. But he could see why she would be considered special. Her features were the most exquisite he had ever seen. Not even the dark smudges beneath her eyes could detract from that beauty.

Even so, he was not attracted to her. But then he had not bought her for himself. Whether he kept her or returned her to the slave merchant in time for that special auction was up to Kasim.

"And the last one? Did Hamid Sharif make a fortune off me tonight?"

Haji Agha did not dare to grin, even though he sensed Jamil was not annoyed by the expense, which he could well afford. "No, my lord. One of your own captains brought her in earlier this week, so she cost you nothing. She's Portuguese,

155

of peasant stock, and so quite accepting of her captivity considering her circumstances improved."

Jamil nodded, still revealing nothing of his thoughts. The last girl wasn't exceptionally pretty, but there was a lush sensuality about her that was hard to ignore, which was undoubtedly why Haji had picked her out. And there was the chestnut hair, which the Chief Black Eunuch knew he favored. But then Haji was not aware these women were not for him.

Three to choose from was more than he could have hoped for under such short notice. He was pleased. Whether his brother was pleased had yet to be determined. Jamil was not going to add three more women to his harem if Kasim wouldn't make use of them. With that in mind, he turned his attention back to the African beauty.

Chantelle stole glances at him only when she was sure he was not looking at her. She was too humiliated to meet his eyes directly. To be talked about as if she weren't even there, as if she couldn't understand them, when Haji Agha had explained that she could, just proved further how insensitive were these men. And the lord sounded so indifferent, as if he couldn't care less that he had just bought three new slaves. And he had bought them. His last question to Haji Agha proved that. But why would he buy women sight unseen? Or was the sale upon condition of his approval?

God, let it be so. Let him give her back to Hamid Sharif. She couldn't bear being owned by someone who looked like one of her own coun-

156

trymen. And he was handsome. Lord help her, she wanted to deny it, but couldn't. She found him utterly attractive in both face and form. It was impossible. She could see herself giving in, accepting her enslavement, all because of a unanticipated attraction that she had no business feeling. No! She had to do something to make him send her back before she was enclosed inside his harem and it was too late. But what?

She watched him now, praying an idea would come to her quickly. And then she realized the examination was not over yet. He stood before the African princess, dispassionately studying her face while she stared furiously back, unafraid to let him see her loathing. When he raised a hand and casually flicked open the single clasp on the girl's vest, hot color flooded Chantelle's cheeks, but the princess didn't move, not even to keep the scanty material from falling open.

He stared at the large breasts for a long moment. Chantelle groaned inwardly. She had been proved wrong again. She had actually been relieved at being bought as she was, thinking she wouldn't have to go through a public stripping, yet here it was happening, and in a room filled with people. And the one girl she had thought for certain would resist this debasement didn't. The princess still hadn't moved at all, standing proudly erect, apparently not in the least embarrassed or offended.

It was when the lord finally looked up at her

to judge her reaction that she did react. She spat in his face.

Chantelle gasped in surprise, but it went unheard because of the collective exclamations of shock and outrage in the room. The girl was immediately seized, not by her guard, but by his. The two Nubian giants forced her easily to her knees; then her guard withdrew a short whip from his belt and began to beat her across the back.

Chantelle watched this in utter horror. The lord hadn't ordered the girl whipped, but he didn't stop it from happening either. He stood there totally unmoved, not angry, not anything. One of his servants had rushed to him with a cloth to wipe away the spittle, but he ignored him, choosing to use the back of his sleeve, slowly, while he watched the poor girl writhing on the floor. Not until her pride had finally succumbed and she screamed did he wave a hand to end it.

"A pity," he said, though Chantelle could detect no actual regret in his tone. "Give her to my palace guard. If she survives a night with them, Hamid Sharif can have her back tomorrow." And his attention went to Chantelle.

She turned cold, the blood leaving her face until it was deathly white. Just like that, he had condemned that girl to mass rape, then dismissed her from his mind. And as soon as he had said it, the girl was dragged out of the room. But even with her gone, Chatelle still saw the red welts in her mind, visible even against that dark skin, crisscrossing the area on her back that was bare.

158

Chantelle finally met his eyes, and knew in that instant of total fear that she despised him. The attraction had died for her in witnessing his cruelty. He was a cold, unfeeling man, no doubt capable of unspeakable acts of brutality.

"You're despicable."

The words came out before she could stop them, but he seemed not to hear her, or he didn't understand English or care what she might say to him. She didn't know the word for "despicable" in his language. More's the pity, for there were more appropriate names to call him now that she thought of it.

He was still staring at her eyes, and there was finally some emotion in his expression. It was surprise. Jamil had never before seen this violet color, hadn't known eyes could be this color. He was purely fascinated. They were like glittering amethysts, fringed with long golden lashes that matched her gently sloping eyebrows, of a shade darker than her platinum hair.

What an unusual combination. No wonder she had been so highly prized. With rich food to fill out her curves, she had the potential to rival even Sheelah. And her hair could be dyed . . .

Jamil had to shake himself, remembering her purpose here. She was not for him. But if Kasim didn't want her, he was tempted to break his own rules and keep her for himself after all. It was the thought of Sheelah that decided him against it. This girl might be a rare find, but he loved his first *kadine*. And ever since he had realized that love, he had added no new women to his harem. These two, if Kasim wanted them, Sheelah was not going to understand, at least not until he returned. But that couldn't be helped. No one but Omar was to know about Kasim.

"Shahar," he said suddenly. The moon. It was appropriate, with hair like moonbeams. He turned to his Chief Black Eunuch. "She will be known as Shahar, Haji."

"No," Chantelle said, drawing his attention back to her.

"No?"

"Don't name me. Don't keep me. Send me back to Hamid Sharif."

He was amused. Didn't she realize the decision wasn't up to her? "Why should I do that?"

"Because I don't want to be owned by you."

His eyes narrowed, making her pale. Good God, had she just bought herself a whipping? Couldn't she even state the obvious around here?

But Jamil was annoyed with himself, not with her. He realized it had been a mistake to allow the black girl's whipping, whether it was deserved or not. It was meant as a lesson for the two remaining women, but mostly for Kasim, who had yet to witness such a situation and how quickly those around him would respond to it.

The English girl had been docile and accepting up to that point, and now she was not. He saw now that she was afraid of him, but even in her fear, she couldn't mask the condemnation in her eyes. Kasim was not going to appreciate the fact

160

that he had made her hate him by a simple act of punishment. And Jamil was almost certain that Kasim *was* going to want this girl.

His eyes remained locked on her while he asked the Chief Black Eunuch: "Does she know who I am, Haji?"

Chantelle answered first, insisting, "I don't care if you're the Dey of this whole bloody city."

"You English have a quaint way with words, aways using more than necessary." There was a mocking slant to his mouth as he added, "If you don't care, Shahar, then it will come as no surprise to you that I am in fact Jamil Reshid, Dey of this 'whole bloody city.' "

It was a surprise, but only for one reason. "You declined to buy me when I first arrived, so why am I here?"

He didn't answer for a moment. It was a trial of concentration to decipher her pronunciations and understand exactly what she was saying, though he had to admit her grasp of his language was far superior than could be expected. But even so, he was arrested by the way her eyes and mouth had softened. In her temporary confusion, her fear and revulsion were forgotten.

He surprised her further by replying in perfect French, assuming that if she was of the English nobility as she claimed, then this was a language she would be more familiar with. "It is my prerogative to change my mind."

"Then would you change your mind about that poor girl you had whipped?"

161

"Interesting that you do not ask me to change my mind about you again instead."

"I would have gotten to that."

He almost laughed. It was refreshing to be spoken to with such audacity by a woman. His women did not argue with him, no matter how much they would like to. He might pamper and indulge them outrageously, but their awareness of his power and total control over their lives was never forgotten.

"If I grant you one request, English, which will you ask for?"

Her eyes widened. Was he serious, or was the question only rhetorical? Either way, there was no choice, not one that her conscience would allow. The girl's fate was already sealed; hers was not. And if he was the Dey, then his must be the largest harem in Barikah. He might have bought her, but there was the possibility that he would forget about her once she became lost among so many women. No, her fate was not sealed—yet.

"The girl," she said.

"You want me to keep her instead of sending her back?"

"No, rescind the further punishment you ordered."

He turned and did so, and Chantelle watched in amazement as the order was relayed to a guard outside the door. She glanced back at him, not knowing what to think of this gesture on his part.

"Where is your gratitude, English?"

Now she knew what to think, and it wasn't

162

pleasant. "Thank you," she said, but her tone was clipped.

"What? I have not redeemed myself in your eyes?"

"Her offense was too minor to warrant a beating," she replied in answer.

"In your opinion," he stated. "But she insulted my person, and that is not allowed. You do wish to be aware of what is not allowed, don't you?" It was a warning, and caused her eyes to narrow. "Ah, I see you have remembered that you find me not to your liking. But you will change your mind, Shahar, if I decide to keep you. Shall we determine that now? Will you open your vest, or do I?"

Her whole body stiffened, and there was again that mixture of fear and impotent rage in her expression. But was she cowed enough to heed his warning?

"Will you spit on me, too?" he demanded, his voice brusque now.

She wouldn't. She had wanted to know what she could do to get sent back to Sharif and now she did know, but what came first was unacceptable.

She shook her head, lowering her eyes. And after her earlier resentment, he was surprised to hear her plead, "Please, must you do this in front of so many people?"

"They are only slaves, English, as you are—" he began. Yet what he was doing *was* unusual, and only for Kasim's benefit. "Very well," he

163

amended. "If you will step over here, no one need look at you but me."

He walked over to the side of the room, waving his guard back. She thought it best to follow him, though this was still not what she had in mind. Her back might be to the room now, but others were still present, and she felt outraged that this could happen. He had no right. He believed he had every right. God, she hated this!

She stood with head bowed and fists clenched. He wouldn't allow it, so reached under her chin to force her eyes to meet his.

"Again I do what you ask, English. I am waiting."

"I can't," she said simply, miserably.

"Very well."

It was not a reprieve. Chantelle itched to slap his hand away when it dropped to her vest. But if you could be whipped and condemned to an even worse punishment for spitting on him, what would happen if you slapped him? Would a scimitar be drawn and used instead of a whip?

She groaned as she felt the material drop to each side of her breasts. She looked away, staring at the screened wall in front of her but seeing nothing, feeling only the acute embarrassment that spread color down her chest and made her cheeks burn.

He stepped to her side, saying in a soft voice, "You may cover yourself, Shahar. You will go with Haji Agha. He will have questions about your background for his records."

She turned her head toward him, asked miserably, "Then you won't send me back?"

He didn't answer. He had already lost interest in her, turning his attention to the Portuguese girl.

Chapter Eighteen

"WELL?" OMAR asked when the last girl was led away and Jamil retired to his bedchamber.

"The blonde," Derek replied without hesitation.

"And the other two?"

"I thought the black wench was already dismissed."

"Not if you care to have her."

"And deal with that hostility? No, thank you. Just the blonde will do, and I'll pay for her myself."

"Jamil would not hear of it."

"Then what happens to her when this is over? And the others I summon? You never did answer that."

"They will be given handsome dowries and found good husbands."

"Christ!" Derek swore softly. "Why wasn't I told that before now?"

"Because it can make no difference. Believe me, Jamil will not mind if you use half his harem. He will probably thank you for this excuse to bring his total women down to a number that will not wear him out. You did not really think he would keep those women you favor?"

"I hadn't thought that far ahead. But I'm sure he *wouldn't* thank me if I go through all his favorites."

Omar chuckled. "Why do you think he has provided you with one of your own?"

Derek grunted. "And his wives? Would he get rid of them, too?"

"They are still the mothers of his sons. They would remain in the harem."

"Never to be favored by him again?" Derek guessed.

"That need not concern you—"

"For God's sake, Omar, stop treating me with kid gloves. I'm not going to change my mind about the switch, but I want the truth."

Omar wouldn't look at him. "Then no, he would never again summon them to his bed."

Derek let out his breath slowly. "I had forgotten how bloody possessive a Muslim can be about his women."

"And you are not?" Omar asked with some skepticism.

Derek thought about it for a moment, but he had to admit, "No, I can't say that I am."

"Not even your fiancée?"

Derek chuckled at the reminder that he *had* a fiancée, for in truth he hadn't thought of Caroline for days. "I adore her, Omar, but since I don't intend to be the most faithful of husbands, I can't really complain if she should eventually decide to take a lover or two. It won't change the way I feel about her."

166

"You have become more English than I thought."

"I had ten years here and nineteen there, Omar. Did you really expect me to be exactly like Jamil?"

"No, but you *are* still like him, more than you realize," Omar replied.

Derek wondered, after the whipping he had just witnessed. He had been appalled when Jamil had not stopped it immediately.

Omar hadn't been affected one way or the other. "It is well you had this opportunity to see how quickly his Nubians respond to any threat," he had told him.

"I wouldn't exactly call what she did a threat," Derek had gritted out. "How could he be so severe—?"

"I suppose you refer to her being given to the guards?" Omar inquired, not considering those few strokes of the lash anywhere near severe. "But that is nothing for concern. At most, there will be only a handful not on duty to receive her, and they know better than to abuse such a gift. They will tend her wounds and treat her with care."

He hadn't felt it necessary to add that because she was a nonvirgin slave who was unacceptable to her master, her use was mainly carnal, to be offered to anyone her master chose to give her to. "Besides, it was a lesson for the other two."

A lesson that the blonde was revolted by, if her reaction to Jamil was any indication. She despised him, and not even the concessions he had made for her changed that.

Derek had to force the memory away. "About the whole harem being paraded before me tomorrow," he said now. "It won't be necessary. Just give me the names of the women Jamil won't mind losing."

"Jamil is not going to like it when he comes back and finds he has sacrificed nothing, while you—"

"Don't worry, Omar," Derek interrupted the warning. "I'll be sure to summon at least one of his favorites. That ought to appease him." And he knew exactly whom, for he was certain that one of the women he had seen earlier tonight was the missing Miss Charity Woods.

"Thank you," Omar said, surprising Derek.

"For what?"

"For loving your brother."

Later, after Derek had retired for the night, he found he couldn't sleep for still thinking of the blonde. Who was she? Would he recognize her name if he heard it?

Not that it mattered. Princesses, grand ladies, peasants, they were all the same here if they were unfortunate enough to be captured; slaves, without rights, capable of being used, misused, sold, resold, even killed, all at the whim of their owner. And after hearing Haji Agha's explanation of how this girl had been captured, Derek knew he was indirectly responsible for her being here. How he felt about that he wasn't at all sure. Ironic, as Jamil humorously thought, was putting it mildly, especially now that technically she belonged to him.

What was he going to do with her? He knew what he would like to do. Christ, from the moment her veils had been removed, he had been unable to take his eyes off her. Granted, she was too thin even for his taste. He liked at least a *little* flesh on his women. But that didn't seem to matter when she stood before the screen, so close, and he experienced the most incredible excitement, knowing what Jamil was going to do and waiting for him to step away from her. And when her small, perfect breasts were in his view, his flesh reacted instantly, filling, swelling, aching for her touch.

But would he actually do anything about it? She was a virgin. She was not here willingly. She was English, for God's sake! And more to the point, she held Jamil in abhorrence after what he had done tonight, and he would be taking Jamil's place. How could he in good conscience take advantage of her, knowing all that?

Chapter Nineteen

CHANTELLE SAT with her knees tucked under her, her hands gripped prayerlike in her lap, the whites of her knuckles revealing her inner tension. The dull white of her clothes was stark against the deep blue satin of the plump pillow beneath her. This served as her chair, for there were no ordinary chairs in the room, no chairs in all of Barikah, if what she had seen so far was any indication.

Across a low table, Haji Agha sipped his second cup of the thick, foam-topped brew that was Turkish coffee. Chantelle's first cup was cold by now, untouched. Across the room, a clerk sat on another pillow, his hand poised over his writing tablet, waiting for the interrogation to continue. No one else was in the room. And it *was* an interrogation, a prying into her life from the day she was born until the night she was captured beneath the Dover cliffs.

Her name, family, home, position, even her birthdate were demanded. Her education was picked apart, her accomplished skllls, which included the piano, a fine stitch, excellent horsemanship, sailing, and a passable voice for singing. Only the sailing had drawn a note of interest from the Chief Black Eunuch, who did all the questioning while the clerk diligently recorded the answers.

If she weren't in a state of nervous exhaustion after her ordeal in the Dey's presence, she never would have been so cooperative, answering almost absently anything put to her, her mind still back in that other room, still shuddering in embarrassed memory. When her mind did finally clear enough to wonder about the reason for this interrogation, there wasn't much left to know about her. It was a particular question about her guardian, bringing back an old anger, that snapped her out of her lethargy.

170

"What is the point of all this? I thought it was encouraged to forget the past when you enter this hell!"

The old man smiled at her choice of words. It always amused him, the boldness and defiance these new slaves possessed on arrival, before they learned to fear him. He would give this one a week before her tone became respectful, her manner subservient. She wouldn't dare to question him then.

"You are correct," he deigned to answer her. "But before your past is forgotten, it must be recorded for our information in case inquiries are ever made of you."

"For ransom, you mean, so you know how much to ask for?"

He nodded, but added deliberately, "That is not likely to happen in your case."

"And why not?" she demanded. "I believe I told you I'm an heiress."

"But who, unless Hamid Sharif's ship was seen off your English coast and recognized as belonging to Barbary corsairs, will ever guess you are here?"

She had realized that herself, but to hear him state it so plainly was demoralizing indeed. She almost pointed out defensively that if Barikah's English consul knew about her, then her release would be immediately demanded, but she didn't want anyone knowing that she still harbored hopes of contacting the consul. Those hopes were not very high at the moment. In fact, her only hope

171

at this particular moment was that Jamil Reshid would decide not to keep her.

"Aren't these questions a bit premature?" she pointed out testily. "It hasn't even been determined yet—"

Chantelle broke off when a guard hurried into the room and bent down to whisper a few words to Haji Agha. The old man nodded, not in the least surprised, and stood up.

"Come, Shahar."

He directed her with a wave of his arm toward the door. She didn't move, her limbs feeling suddenly leaden.

"Don't call me that."

"It is all you will be known by henceforth. Chantelle Burke is dead."

"Then—"

She couldn't finish. She didn't have to. The old eunuch nodded again, reading her mind.

"Did you really think it would be otherwise after he was so generous in his dealing with you?"

"Generous!" she burst out, gaining an immediate frown from him.

"Enough," he said softly, but with the stern authority he was known for. "You will follow me or you will be dragged along in my wake. I would think your pride would prefer to walk."

He was correct. She was a Burke, after all, not a sniveling coward, and she was grateful for the reminder. It was bad enough that she had pleaded with his horrid master earlier, and for what? A little modesty? There would be worse things in store for her, she was sure. But, by God, she wouldn't beg again, not for anything.

She followed him out of the room and didn't even blink when his personal bodyguards fell in behind her just beyond the door. She was led back outside the building into the large court where the litters had dropped her off, through an arched gate into yet another garden court, and toward a pair of iron-studded doors at least fifteen feet high.

Her step faltered as she saw the eight heavily armed eunuchs at guard outside these massive doors, intuition warning that this gateway was the last she would pass through. This was the entrance to the palace harem, and once she was beyond these doors, there would be no turning back. Chantelle Burke really would be dead to the rest of the world.

The panic that overwhelmed her had nothing to do with reason and her own wishes. She stopped dead, took a step backward, and would have run like hell if a hard chest hadn't slammed into her back. She was surrounded closely now, two of Haji's bodyguards having moved up on either side of her, and the one behind her shoving gently, but with enough force to get her moving again. Still, the panic was riding her hard and she would have struggled in earnest, screamed and disgraced herself utterly, if Haji hadn't taken that moment to turn and raise a knowing brow at her, as if to remind her how futile were her efforts. There were a half-dozen hulking black men surrounding her, another eight in front of her, two at that moment opening those horrid doors.

Her backbone stiffened, but her knees felt like jelly. The eunuch behind her still had to help her along, and she realized he *was* helping her take those last few steps, his hand beneath her elbow supporting, rather than forcing. And then those heavy doors slammed shut, and there was an echo, an awful, deafening echo, like a death knell. Chantelle closed her eyes, stopping, listening, aching with the knowledge that it was over. She had entered the Babylon of hell, and there was no way out.

"Does it feel easier now, Shahar?"

She opened her eyes and stared at Haji Agha. How did he know? But it was obvious, wasn't it? She was inside. There was nothing left to fight against. She didn't answer him. He represented the authority here. He had picked her out of a roomful of women when he could have picked any one of the others instead. Because of him she was here, owned by a man she found loathsome.

She turned around to look up into the eyes of the man who had helped her not make a complete fool of herself. He was a Nubian like the others, tall and muscular and dark as sin, but unlike the others, he had warm, amiable brown eyes; and when she smiled her thanks to him, he understood without having the words said, and flashed a dazzling white grin at her. It made her feel somehow stronger, more herself, and not quite so lost in this foreign world.

"What was his name?" she asked Haji as they moved away together, his guard dismissed now that they were inside the harem walls.

"He belongs to me, Shahar. His name is of no importance to you."

"Dammit, why can't you just answer my question?" she replied without thinking. "You've got me in here. I'm not going anywhere. Is it too bloody much trouble to just answer a simple question?"

He stopped, making her plow into his back. She jumped back, realizing she might have sounded a bit impertinent. But what the hell. She was the Honorable Chantelle Burke, no matter what they called her. She might as well establish right up front that she wasn't going to be pushed around, ignored, or remain ignorant, as they seemed to prefer their women.

"Well, is it?" she asked in a more reasonable tone when Haji turned to glower at her.

For a long moment he said nothing, and then he resumed walking, expecting her to follow, and she heard a mumbled "Kadar is his name, if you *must* know."

She grinned to herself. "Thank you," she allowed, to which he grunted, picking up his pace.

They moved deeper and deeper into the harem, through countless doors that had to be unlocked and then locked again, through a labyrinth of corridors, alleyways, and richly tiled hallways, down narrow stairways leading to courtyards, along colonnaded torchlit walks, and gardens where small, domed pavilions called kiosks could be seen dimly in the moonlight.

Even at this late hour they passed people along the way, mostly women, and these mostly servants, or rather the harem slaves, recognizable by their white cotton trousers and tunics, which seemed to be the standard dress of the lower menials. But there were eunuchs, too, and young boys in bright-colored outfits who, Chantelle was horrified to later learn, were castrated pageboys.

Those women who were concubines stared at Chantelle in either curiosity, hostility, or plain surprise. The servants, however, fell into an attitude of deep obeisance as Haji Agha plodded by, ignoring one and all.

"Why do they all bow to you?" Chantelle wondered aloud.

"I am the Chief Black Eunuch."

"Really? That would make you the third most powerful man in Barikah, wouldn't it?"

He glanced at her with a degree of surprise. "Who told you that?"

"I had a very persistent teacher on the voyage. I think he hoped I would end up here, and so he drilled me on the hierarchy of the palace. I don't usually forget what I learn, even when it's learned under duress."

"Did he also teach you the hierarchy of the harem?" Haji asked.

"If you mean the caste system, in which certain women stand higher up the ladder than others, yes."

"Tell me."

"I'd rather not," she replied with distaste. "It's degrading, if you ask me, the ways of aspiring to a higher caste—"

"Tell me," he repeated stubbornly.

Chantelle gritted her teeth. "Very well. You have the concubines, or odalisques, on the bottom of the ladder, those women who have not caught their lord's notice. On the next rung you have the *gozde*, a woman who has caught his notice but hasn't been called to—" She blushed here, unable to finish.

"Summoned to his presence yet?" Haji suggested.

"Yes, an admirable way to put it," Chantelle said in relief. "Next up the rung are the *ikbals*, those women who have been 'summoned to his presence,' past and present favorites. And at the top of the ladder are the *kadines*, his official wives."

"And which do you want to be?"

"None of the above," she stated emphatically.

Haji laughed, the first time she'd heard him do so. "You are already *gozde*, but not for long, I think. However, you will find that the caste system in Jamil Reshid's harem is quite different from what you were expecting, inasmuch as the first two lower orders have long since been eliminated."

Chantelle's mouth dropped open, and in her surprise, she didn't quibble words. "Do you mean he beds them all?"

Haji nodded. "Some only a few times a year,

some once or twice a month, but none are neglected indefinitely. He has his favorites, of course, whom he summons more often, but it is his wives he favors most."

Chantelle was frowning when she commented, "Then he can't possess that many women."

Haji smiled at her reasoning. "You bring the total to forty-eight, Shahar. True, it is not very much. His father possessed more than two hundred."

Not very much? Good God! forty-seven women, and he had bedded them all. Talk about a rutting beast. But she was one woman who was not going to aspire to his bed.

"How do I go about getting myself *out* of his notice?" she dared to ask.

Now Haji was frowning again. "You do not. You are here to please him, and when you are finally summoned, you will strive with all you possess to do just that. But it will not be soon. You have much to learn first about the ways of the harem, the ways of a man. It will take many weeks, even though you appear to be a quick learner."

Strive to please that barbarian? Ha! But was that all the reprieve she was to have? No, if many weeks passed, the Dey might forget about her, and it would be up to her to make sure he wasn't reminded of her presence.

Through yet another door they reached a large open court of white marble with a bubbling fountain in its center. Surrounding it were dozens and dozens of tiny apartments, rising three stories high, with wooden balconies running around all sides. Lights glowed from many of the rooms, spilling out into the marbled court. The doorways were hung with material, most open at the moment like curtains, to let in any wandering breeze.

There were dozens of women here, some standing out on the balconies, the sound of many more inside the apartments. One detached herself from a doorway on the ground floor and came forward to meet them, bowing low to Haji Agha. Chantelle's first thought was that she was much too old for Jamil Reshid, though beneath her high turban was a face that still held much beauty. His mother possibly?

Haji introduced her as Lalla Safiye, mistress of this court, where the majority of the women lived. Chantelle later learned that Lady Safiye had been an *ikbal* of Jamil's father and had chosen to remain in the harem upon his death, rather than find a husband at her age or go to the Palace of Tears, a term taken from Istanbul for the house of the widows of a deceased ruler.

Haji left her with Safiye, whose Turkish was much too rapid for Chantelle to understand, but fortunately, she spoke a passable French as well. Chantelle followed her up three flights of wooden stairs to the top floor, where Safiye held open the curtain on the first door they came to.

"You will stay on this floor until you become an *ikbal*," Safiye told her. "Then I will move you down with the others. There would be too much

179

grumbling if I let you join them now, you understand."

The "others" apparently occupied the lower two floors. The top floor was dark and deserted. Across the court and on each of the other two sides, more and more women came out of their cubicles to stare up at the newcomer.

"Here is just fine," Chantelle said quickly, wanting to retreat from so much avid curiosity.

She stepped into the small room, where a single lantern burned next to a tray of food. So she had been expected.

"You knew I was coming?"

"Of course. There is nothing that happens in the palace that we do not learn of very quickly. When Jamil sent word to Haji Agha that you alone of the three had been chosen, another eunuch rushed to tell his mistress, who is Jamil's third favorite, and she told Lalla Rahine, who sent the word on to me so that I could have a room prepared for you."

"How nice."

Safiye seemed not to notice the sarcasm. "In my day," she continued, "this court was used only for *ikbals* no longer in favor. There was a dormitory for the odalisques and another small court for the *gozdes*, but they have been deserted since Jamil came to power."

"Yes, I've already heard how he favors all of his women at one time or another."

Safiye did not let her sarcasm pass this time. Chantelle's upper arm was gripped quite painfully, and the older woman's face pressed close, her expression severely disapproving.

"Do not make the mistake of thinking your impertinence will be allowed here. And do not hold in contempt what you do not understand. Jamil's women are the luckiest women in the empire. They do not know what it is like to live year after endless year without the love of a man, to die a virgin, never knowing a man's gentle touch. But other women do know. It happens often in this country. It happened in his father's harem, where more than a hundred women never even reached the rank of *gozde*."

I should be so lucky, Chantelle thought, but she said instead in a coldly controlled tone, "You can let go of me, Lalla Safiye."

Ordinarily, Safiye would have slapped her to the floor for what amounted to an order, and said so haughtily, too. But this was the first girl Jamil had purchased for himself in several years. That in itself suggested Shahar was going far, and Safiye was wise enough not to make an enemy of a future favorite.

She let go, but compromised by saying, "I hope you understand, Shahar, because your life here will not be pleasant if you do not learn quickly what is tolerated and what is not. We have ways of correcting unacceptable behavior, so you cannot say you weren't warned. Now, tomorrow Lalla Rahine will come to look you over. I suggest you make friends with her, for as the most powerful woman in the harem, she can do much for or against you."

"Is she the Dey's first wife?"

"His mother."

Good Lord, he had a mother after all. Chantelle had somehow thought Jamil Reshid had been spawned by the devil without any help from the gentler sex.

Chapter Twenty

THE GIRL waited patiently, her knees tucked under her, a rich ermine robe lying across her arms. It was never an easy task to dress the Lalla Rahine, for she always had so much on her mind, so many interruptions, forgotten orders to give, supplicants coming and going. But today had been especially trying, as the Dey's mother was anxious about meeting this new slave who had entered the harem last night. Speculation was running rife about the girl, but Lalla Rahine could answer no questions yet. How could she, until she had met the girl for herself?

Two of the Dey's wives had already been here this morning, and three of his favorites. They all wanted to know the same thing: Why had he bought this girl? Had they done something wrong? Was he displeased with them?

Such questions would never have been asked if Jamil Reshid were not their lord and master. But all in the harem knew he was not like other men to crave constant variety in the purchase of new women. They knew his own mother had been forbidden to buy any more women for him either, no matter how beautiful. They had assumed the harem gates were permanently closed.

Lalla Rahine had thought so, too. Jamil might have been pleased with her last purchase, enough to elevate the girl to a favorite, but he had *not* been pleased to begin with.

The servants waiting to finish dressing her might as well not have been in the room for all the awareness Rahine had of them. She knelt on her prayer rug, head bent down, the very picture of a devout Muslim. But she wasn't praying. She had converted to Islam years ago, but there were times when there was another besides God with whom she needed to commune, and she did it so often that it was no longer an unusual occurrence for her to drop whatever she was doing and go to her rug in between calls to prayer.

But peace never came from these impromptu meditations. It never would. She was a woman tormented by past mistakes that couldn't be rectified. And the one person who could forgive her for what she'd done, who could give her peace for the remaining years of her life, she would never see again. It was to him she communed, beseeched, cried, all in her mind, wondering the same thing over and over, time after time, the answer always eluding her.

Oh, God, Kasim, did you forgive me? Your brother did not, and he never fails to let me know it. His love

183

died for me the day I sent you away. I did not even have that to comfort me. And you must hate me, too. Do you? Do you know how sorry I was, how much I missed you, how soon I regretted what I did? It seemed important then to let you go, but I was young and foolish and still clinging to my past, to the father whom Mustafa could not make me forget.

I don't even know if he still lives. Jamil wouldn't tell me if he knew. He's never even told me if you answer his letters. But you are still alive somewhere. I would feel it if you were not. If only I could feel that you have forgiven me. If only Jamil would. But I can't blame either of you, for I cannot forgive myself either.

To look at her was not to know she was suffering, for she had long ago learned how to bury the pain deep inside, to keep it hidden even from Jamil. But for nineteen years she had carried it, for then, as now, her sons were all she had. She had not loved their father. Mustafa had worshipped her. She had merely tolerated him. It was her sons she lived for, and although one was lost to her, she still had Jamil. And she would do anything for him, to assure his happiness, to atone for the pain she had caused him, too.

Which recalled to mind his new slave. She would see her first before she discussed her with Haji. She had already heard that the girl was unique, but that would only explain why Jamil had chosen her, not why he had ordered Haji to search the markets for new women at this time.

And what of Sheelah, whom he had summoned

to his bed last night? Rahine was fond of Sheelah, who was everything she appeared to be—kind, loving, understanding. There was not another woman like her in the whole harem, which was undoubtedly why Jamil had eventually lost his heart to her. And ever since he had admitted to this great love for Sheelah, he had not bought another woman for himself.

So why had he suddenly changed his mind? Was it just the restlessness of his self-confinement in the palace these many months, or something more?

Haji might know, but Rahine doubted it. Jamil was very closemouthed about his feelings. The only one he really confided in was his Grand Vizier, and Omar Hassan never revealed anything Jamil didn't want him to. Rahine was afraid that the only explanation was that Jamil's feelings for his beloved Sheelah might be changing. She hoped not. Perhaps she should talk to Sheelah first, before she met the new slave.

Chantelle wolfed down the meal that had just been brought to her. She had hardly touched the food left for her last night, and the tray had mysteriously disappeared before morning. No locks for the doors. No doors, for that matter. She didn't like that at all, that persons unknown could enter her room while she slept.

Hakeem had warned her that some harem women could be quite dangerous, that jealousy and the fierce competition that existed in all harems were strong motivations, injury and even murder the common results. And she had to allow that although she found Jamil Reshid loathsome, his many women probably did not. Competition here was likely to exist between every single inhabitant, excluding herself.

But would anyone believe her when she insisted she wanted nothing of Jamil, or would they see her as another rival? God, she hoped not. She was going to have enough difficulties in the coming weeks without having to worry about making enemies of her own sex.

"Shahar! How dare you not assume an attitude of obeisance when in Lalla Rahine's presence?"

Chantelle's head snapped up at the first word, that detested name they had given her. She was confronted with two women standing just inside her doorway, one angry, the other wearing an expression very much like her son's, inscrutable.

"I might have if I had known you were even there," Chantelle offered with marked unconcern, ruining the effort by adding, "Don't you people believe in knocking?"

She watched as Safiye's face mottled with red. The woman was so angry she couldn't speak for a moment, and Jamil's mother dismissed her before she could, saving Chantelle what she imagined would have been an earful or worse.

"It isn't wise to antagonize your warden."

Chantelle stood up to put herself on a more even footing with the lady. It didn't work. Lalla Rahine was as tall as, if not taller than, the African princess. She was also an extremely well-preserved woman for her middle years, and she had to be forty-five at the very least to have a son as old as Jamil. She looked a young thirty. It was incredible. And those eyes, just like his, a dark, dark emerald and thickly lashed, but without the kohl that she had seen on every other woman in this harem, even the female servants.

There was a slight resemblance, too, in the high cheekbones, the strong, determined chin, the same arch to the brows, except Rahine's were a dark gold, several shades darker than Chantelle's own. Was she blond? Impossible to tell with her hair tucked up completely under a brilliant blue turban, which happened to have a fortune in diamonds dangling from one side like loose strings. It added even more to her height. She was a sleek woman, tall and narrow, another thing she had in common with her son.

She wore a rich brocaded robe trimmed in fur over a caftan of glimmering blue-and-white silk, with three fantastic diamond necklaces of different lengths about her neck. Belted at the waist, the garb proved not all women in the harem leaned toward the plump side. Still more diamonds glittered from her wrists, her fingers, her ears. Chantelle refused to look down to see if there were any on her toes, too.

All things considered, she should have felt rather intimidated. She might have if Rahine had reacted as Safiye did when they first arrived, but she didn't. Her tone was moderate, with about as much feeling in it as her expression.

"Is that what she is?" Chantelle asked. "My warden?"

"In a manner of speaking."

"And you?"

"I am Jamil Reshid's mother."

Chantelle waved a hand impatiently. "No, I didn't mean that."

"If you want to know what power I have, my dear, it is absolute. I rule the entire harem, in concert with Haji Agha, of course. My son's wives, his favorites, all his women, are ultimately under my care."

Chantelle had already heard from Safiye that Rahine was all-powerful. She supposed what she had wanted clarified was the meaning of "under my care." Safiye might be her warden, but Rahine would have the last word on anything important. No wonder Safiye had suggested she make friends with her.

But Chantelle couldn't quite see herself doing that. There was a coldness about Lalla Rahine much like her son's. They were indeed cut from the same mold, these two. And if he was a cruel, heartless wretch, what was his mother, who had raised him?

While Chantelle was thinking this, Rahine was casually inspecting her from top to bottom, and what she saw confounded her completely. She might not be close to Jamil anymore, but she knew his tastes in women better than anyone, and there was nothing about this girl that would have attracted him. She was nothing but skin and bones. Hollow-cheeked and hollow-bellied. Allah's mercy, was the girl sickly? And she was blond. There was not a single blonde among his many women, and not for lack of availability. Jamil's preference was redheads, but any color would do as long as it wasn't blond. Of the three blondes Rahine had bought for him over the years, each had been promptly gifted to someone else. And she knew why. It hurt, but she couldn't deny it. He disliked blondes because she was a blonde.

She was more confused about this girl now than before she had seen her. Sheelah had been able to supply no clue. Aside from the fact that Jamil had stopped sleeping with her recently, due to a restlessness that was plaguing him at night, his affections for her hadn't changed at all. So why had he chosen this girl? Or was she not for himself?

Rahine would have struck her palm to her forehead if she had been alone. Of course! The girl could be intended as a gift for someone, perhaps even to be included in the yearly tribute to the Sultan. That would explain everything.

As her confusion passed, Rahine began to see some possibilities in the girl. She had exquisite features. That was undeniable. Good bone structure, graceful movements, a certain pride in the way she held herself so erect, but that was not a bad thing. And with a strict diet, her figure could be enhanced, made desirable. Blondes were prized by other men here. Yes, she could be a beauty of both face and body, a gift worthy of the Sultan.

"You're English, aren't you?" Rahine asked suddenly.

"And here I thought my French was superb."

Rahine actually smiled. "Your wit is refreshing, child, but be careful whom you bestow it on. Few Muslims have a sense of humor that would appreciate what is very near impertinence."

Talk about a subtle scolding. "I'll keep that in mind."

"Good. Now Safiye will supply you with a personal servant, and a tutor will be provided to begin your training. I would suggest you apologize to Safiye first, however, or she is likely to find the most lazy slave in the harem to attend you. Give her this." Rahine reached into a pocket and withdrew a small pouch of coins. "A few coins should appease her present annoyance with you. Keep the rest for when they're needed."

"A bribe?"

"Bribery is a way of life here that has gone on so long that the empire cannot operate without it. It is no different in a harem, though we look on it as the 'obligatory gift.' You do not visit someone without bringing a little token. If you want something done, you must pay for it."

"Then how do I see about getting a solid door with a lock on it to replace those curtains?"

Rahine grinned, a remarkable occurrence, though Chantelle didn't know it. She almost wished this English girl would be staying. There was another in the harem, but she didn't possess this lively wit that brought back memories of home.

"You don't, my dear, not in this court any-way. Doors with locks on them are found only in the court of the favorites, where the women have earned the privilege of having a little privacy."

And they still paid for it, with their bodies. Chantelle would have to resign herself to no doors. There was no point in making an enemy of this woman by letting her know of her abhorrence for this place—or her son, at least not until it was absolutely necessary.

Chapter Twenty-one

"I DON'T believe it!" Rahine exploded.

She shot to her feet and began pacing about the Chief Black Eunuch's coffee room, one of numerous rooms in his suite, located near the harem gate. But it was a small room, not really designed for agitated pacing. The marble floor was polished and slippery. And the low divan and round table took up much of the space.

She gave up when her shin bumped the low table and spilled coffee onto the tray of uneaten baklava pastries next to Haji Agha's water pipe. He made no comment when she rejoined him on the divan, even though this display of emotion was quite unlike her.

"Well?" she demanded. "Tell me I misunderstood you."

Haji smiled. This was the fire of the young Rahine whom he had befriended more than thirty

191

years ago, not the calm, unruffled control of the most powerful woman in Barikah.

"I doubt you misunderstood at all, Rahine. Jamil wants her training time cut in half. He wants her ready for him as soon as possible."

"I still don't believe it," she replied, but with less conviction.

"Did you think she wasn't for him?"

Rahine grimaced. "That was exactly what I thought after seeing her for myself. Didn't you at first?"

Haji shrugged and reached for the long stem of his hookah. "Perhaps," he allowed. "But he summoned me early this morning. He did not even trust the order to a messenger."

Rahine leaned back against the silver tasseled cushions. "I don't understand it, Haji. Was I blinded by that bright hair into missing something in the girl?"

"She's undernourished, is all. Plenty of bread soaked in syrup will remedy that quickly enough."

"I did like her," Rahine said reflectively. "She has the sardonic wit of the English aristocracy that brought back so many memories . . . but you know what I meant." She turned her emerald gaze on him. "She's blond, she's skinny—"

"And she doesn't like him."

"*What?*"

"It's true." Haji chuckled. "She might have found him pleasing to the eye at first, but that was before one of the other two girls was unwise enough to spit on him. After witnessing the whipping that

192

followed, Shahar was genuinely revolted by Jamil. She told him to his face that she didn't want to be owned by him. She asked him to send her back to the slave merchant."

"And what was his reaction to that?"

"He was intrigued, I think."

"Then that's it! He's never before met a woman who wasn't instantly enamored of him. She is no more than a challenge."

"I don't know," Haji said thoughtfully. "For some reason he was extremely patient with her. He allowed her to argue with him. He spoke with her at length. He even granted her two requests that she asked of him. But there was nothing in his eyes when he looked at her, not even a little spark of warmth. It was obvious he found the third girl more desirable, yet he picked this blond one instead."

"And now he's impatient to have her?"

"Not so much impatient, Rahine. I didn't sense that. I even had to remind him that he had sent for me. He couldn't recall why for a moment. And when he did, he simply gave the order, as he would any other, then went on to finish the discussion he was having with Omar."

"Very well." Rahine sighed, giving up. "So we are not to know why he wants her or what he sees in her. She will amuse him for a night or two and that will be that."

"She is different from the others," Haji warned.

"I know."

"She is going to prove difficult."

"I know that, too!" she snapped. "Why do you think this has upset me? All the trouble that is going to be caused, and just for a passing fancy."

"Maybe he has finally decided it is ridiculous to put a limit on the number of women he owns," Haji suggested.

"Do you think so?" Rahine asked hopefully, but in the next instant threw up her hands. "Ah, Haji, what is the difference? Our duty is to his pleasure. Whatever he wants, whatever the reason, he shall have it."

Even while Rahine bemoaned it, trouble had already begun, for Safiye was feeling magnanimous after the generous gift Chantelle had bestowed on her and decided to take the new slave to the baths that morning, before they became crowded. She thought Chantelle would appreciate the privacy while she became accustomed to the ritual of the baths, rather than having to endure dozens of curious eyes watching her every move.

And Chantelle was grateful when told that today was a exception, that tomorrow and thereafter she would have to go to the baths in the afternoon with the other women. "But you will come to enjoy it once you lose your modesty. Many of the women spend the entire afternoon in the baths, even eating their dinner there."

Chantelle could understand why one might not want to leave. The *hammam* of the harem was nothing like the single large room used for bathing at the bagnio. It was peaceful here, and immense, with countless chambers, one leading into the next. There were steam rooms, and rooms with hot and cold showers, rooms with sunken pools of cool water, and massage rooms.

The first chamber after the vestibule, where she had to leave her clothes, was the largest room. Its surprising beauty almost made her forget her nudity. It was octagonal, with a high vaulted cupola from which hundreds of tiny openings let in long bars of steamy sunlight, shooting in every direction, illuminating the green tiled walls with an illusion of being underwater. Here the concubines would gather to gossip while their slaves labored to beautify them, sitting on Turkish rugs they had carried with them or on cool marble benches, or lying on the large round slab of marble in the center of the room that was heated from below.

She was not to stay in this room, however. The four bath attendants whom Safiye had handed her over to led her into one of the smaller rooms, where she was washed thoroughly this first time with an abrasive soap until her skin felt raw all over. She stood there and let them, mostly because she was mortified when they insisted that *they* do the washing. She didn't even object too strenuously when the down was removed from her body with a depilatory substance. Every woman here went through the same procedure, they told her. Did she expect to be any different?

No, of course not. She wanted to be the same, to blend in, to be unnoticeable and so forgotten. And if they had stopped there everything would have gone all right, and she would have finished the purification process. But they didn't stop with just the pale blond down covering her body, and Chantelle raised holy hell when they went after her pubic hair, intending to pluck out every curly strand.

When Safiye arrived after being hastily summoned, it was to find Chantelle backed into a corner with a pot of hot melted wax in one hand and the brazier of coals that had heated it in the other.

"And just what do you think this will accomplish?" Safiye demanded. "I have only to summon a eunuch or two, and you will be subdued."

"They wouldn't leave me alone," Chantelle replied angrily, glaring at the now nervous slaves who had refused to listen to her objections.

"So you intend to burn them?"

"Whatever it takes, madame."

Safiye sputtered furiously at this calm retort. "You're mad! Mad! What do you think you protect, you stupid girl? Your hair is to be removed, not your hymen!"

Chantelle blushed but did not back down. "I let them remove enough of my hair already. No more."

"It is not up to you. Your body is no longer your own, and pubic hair is sinful! It must—"

"Who says so?" Chantelle demanded. "My body is as God meant it to be, so how can anything that grows on it be sinful?"

"A very good point," Lalla Rahine said quietly from the doorway, having come in unnoticed. "And when you learn our ways, Shahar, you may see our point, too. But for now, all this fuss is unnecessary." Then she frowned, adding reproachfully, "You have burned your hands, haven't you?" She snapped her fingers, and a slave immediately ran for salve. "Come, Shahar, put those down and let us attend your burns before they blister."

Chantelle had barely felt the stinging on her fingers. "They're not plucking any more of my hair," she insisted stubbornly.

"No, they will not. You will finish your bath and return to your room, where your training will begin."

"But—" Safiye began, to be silenced by a sharp glance of those emerald eyes.

Only now that the controversy was over did Chantelle realize she had been standing there stark naked with her two meager weapons. "Could I have a robe or something—"

"Of course, my dear." Rahine flicked a wrist and another slave ran off. "But you really must work toward abandoning this modesty of yours, especially here in the *hammam*, where many of the odalisques lie about unclothed for the better part of each day. Go now with the attendants and let them finish their duties."

As soon as Chantelle was led off to the next room, Rahine's tone changed to frigid displeasure as it lashed into Safiye. "You fool! There is ample time to take care of such things before she is summoned by my son, and ample time for her to adjust to the changes expected of her. There was no point in letting her become so upset that she feels she must fight us. In future if she balks over something, bring the matter to me." And she swept out of the room without allowing Safiye any defense at all.

Chapter Twenty-two

"WELL, WHAT do you think?" Adamma asked.

Chantelle picked up the hand mirror to study her face thoughtfully. She was not surprised that she could hardly recognize herself under so much cosmetics. It was the kohl lining her eyes, giving her an exotic appearance, that would take time getting used to.

"It looks like someone punched me in both eyes."

Adamma giggled. "It does, doesn't it. You are just too fair. I think all you need is a very thin line, yes, just enough for emphasis."

Chantelle would prefer nothing at all. "What's the point of all this?"

"You want to be beautiful, don't you?"

"No, I don't."

"But every woman does."

"I'm not every woman, Adamma," Chantelle replied patiently.

"Ah, I see. You want to look different, to stand out—"

"No," Chantelle interrupted hastily, for that was the last thing she wanted. "Go ahead and do your worst."

Adamma smiled with satisfaction, thinking she had made her point. Chantelle let her think what she would. She had already discovered it was not easy arguing with Adamma. The girl was just too cheerful and easygoing. Nothing fazed her.

Adamma had been brought to her that morning, before the unfortunate incident in the baths. She was skilled in the art of applying cosmetics, or so she claimed. Her mother was a Nigerian slave who worked in the kitchens. Her father was one of the palace guards, though neither she nor her mother knew exactly which one he was. That this didn't seem to bother the girl was not surprising. It was just another of the many differences in outlook here that would take getting used to.

She was pretty, with her exotic coloring and delicate features. She might not know who her father was, but he had to have been fairly light-skinned to bequeath the African girl her golden coloring and light amber eyes. And she was sweet, eager to please, and ecstatic about her new position. Chantelle had liked her immediately.

Adamma had previously worked in the *hammam* more or less as a maid, running back and forth from the kitchens with refreshments for the concubines who lazed the day away in the baths. It perhaps explained why her young body was still so coltishly thin at her age of sixteen, giving her a certain clumsiness. Chantelle certainly wouldn't

199

run her so ragged, but that wasn't the only reason Adamma was delighted to belong to her now. Being the personal slave of one of the Dey's concubines was a position to strive for among the slaves not so lucky to be bought to share the master's bed.

This Adamma had happily explained to Chantelle while she was applying her makeup. Chantelle felt the girl was more lucky not to have to share the Dey's bed, but she didn't say so. That she would rather be a simple servant like Adamma was not going to be understood, so there was no point in trying to explain it.

Adamma had just finished removing most of the black kohl from Chantelle's eyes when another young girl entered the room. This one was no servant, however, or so her clothes and jewels indicated. Chantelle was instantly annoyed that she had just walked in, without asking for permission to enter.

"I am here to explain sex to you."

"You must be joking," Chantelle said dryly, for the girl looked several years younger than she.

"This is normal, *lalla*," Adamma piped up. "She will explain all things sexual to you."

Chantelle frowned to see her sitting there avidly waiting for the instruction to begin. *She* might have to listen to this scandalous information, but sixteen-year-old virgins did not.

"You may go, Adamma."

"But—"

"Go!"

Chantelle regretted her tone instantly, for Adamma scurried out of the room so quickly she didn't have a chance to tell her that she wasn't displeased with her, but with this lesson she must endure. She would apologize later. She wasn't going to have a servant of hers living in fear of displeasing her mistress, which every other slave in the palace did. When death could be the result of such displeasure, this fear was understandable, but Adamma would learn that was one fear she need no longer have, at least while she remained Chantelle's servant.

She returned her attention to the girl, who had plopped down on a pillow across the low table from her. Bangles clinked loudly on her wrist as she reached for a sweetmeat that Adamma had provided earlier. There was about her an air of superiority and condescension, a petulancy around the soft mouth. She was voluptuous, for all that she looked so young. She had a round, full-bodied figure that was truly on the plump side, with heavy breasts, thighs, and hips, and a thick waist. That this was supposed to be a desirable figure Chantelle found amusing. Safiye had already told her that she would have no hope of being summoned by the Dey until she gained some weight.

Understandably, Chantelle had not touched a single one of the rich sweetmeats Adamma had tried to tempt her with. She knew she had lost a considerable amount of weight since her ordeal began, and she fully intended to gain it back, but

201

not an ounce more. Exercise was the key, and she would throw herself into it each night after she was finally alone. Let them wonder why the rich diet they had planned for her wasn't working. She would keep her exercising a secret.

"You were expecting me, were you not?"

"I suppose," Chantelle replied with a sigh. The sooner this was over, the better.

"I am called Vashti," the girl supplied, adding haughtily, "It means 'the beautiful.' "

She was that, Chantelle had to allow, but the girl's attitude was rubbing her on the raw. "How nice."

Vashti shrugged, mistaking sarcasm for a compliment, but no amount of flattery was going to endear the Englishwoman to her. She despised her already, for *she* had been bought by Jamil himself, while Vashti had been purchased by his mother and had enjoyed his bed only once in the eight months since she had entered the palace harem. She was jealous of his wives, jealous of his favorites because she had not become one of them, and jealous of this newcomer who was causing such a stir of speculation.

She thoroughly resented being given the chore of instructing a virgin on what to expect in her master's bed. She needed instruction herself, for she had obviously not pleased Jamil enough to be summoned back, but had Safiye taken that into consideration? No. She had simply snapped at Vashti to tell the English bitch what it was all about. Very well, she would tell her, and she hoped she would worry herself sick in anticipation of it as Vashti had done after that spiteful Yasmeen, her own tutor, had made sex sound so horrible. Vashti smiled smugly, thinking about it. She didn't know that her very lack of experience was what had prompted Safiye to choose her for this instruction; the older woman was furious with Shahar after what had happened in the *hammam* and the setdown she had received from Rahine because of it. If she hadn't already given her Adamma, she would have supplied the most lazy, good-for-nothing slave she could find. Vashti was the next best thing, for the girl's spitefulness and jealousy were well known.

Chapter Twenty-three

THE MOMENT Derek entered his new bedchamber, he tossed off his turban and heavily jeweled caftan. Omar, following him, smiled to see him shed the unaccustomed raiments of the role he had finally assumed.

"It was a successful diversion, will you not agree?" Omar remarked.

"Oh, ho," Derek snorted. "For someone who argued as loud and long against it as you did, you're sounding mightily pleased now."

The diversion had been Derek's idea, and Jamil had gone along with it, though Omar had not. But it had worked splendidly, with Derek appearing in the outer court as Jamil, ostensibly to examine his new matched pair of Thoroughbreds, long enough to gain the notice of everyone present so that Jamil, dressed in the same burnoose that Derek had worn when he'd entered the palace, could slip out the main gate unnoticed.

Just showing himself was all that was necessary to be the immediate center of attention, for it had been months since Jamil had appeared in public. But Derek had gone one better, mounting the white stallion and spending nearly an hour putting him through his paces, to the delight of the surprised crowd, and thereby allowing Jamil ample time to reach the harbor and the ship that would take him to Istanbul. But this also gave any would-be assassin the opportunity to kill him, if any were fanatic enough to try it with so many guards about. None were, and Omar had nothing left to complain about.

But he did redden slightly at the reminder that his dire predictions had been proved wrong, and he defended himself. "It *was* dangerous, and I still say another diversion could have been staged without your involvement."

"Yes, but this one served more than one purpose. Jamil made it safely out of the palace, the public got a good look at the Dey's beardless appearance, and the assassins have valid proof now that their target is still in residence. Besides, it assured that no one would follow Jamil if they decided he looked worth following, which was a distinct possibility if I hadn't been on display as a distraction."

"True, true, all true," said the Grand Vizier with a sigh.

"And, Omar?"

"Yes?"

"I enjoyed it."

This time Omar snorted. "Let us hope you find less dangerous ways of enjoying yourself in the days to come."

"Oh, I intend to." Derek grinned. "Beginning immediately. You did say there's nothing for me to attend to today?"

"Nothing that will require your presence."

"Good. Then do I send for Haji Agha, or will a messenger serve to bring Shahar to me now?"

Omar's brows shot up. "Now?"

"Is there anything wrong with the time of day?" Derek wanted to know.

"No, of course not, but . . . she won't be ready for you this soon, Kasim. You know how lengthy the training period is."

"I don't care," Derek insisted. "Unlike Jamil, I'm used to untrained women."

"But she's only been here four days—"

"Was she bought for me or not, Omar?"

Omar cringed at the brusque tone, so like Jamil's of late. "You know she was."

"And if I want her today, right now, why should I wait?"

There were a number of reasons that would make it unadvisable, but Omar sensed Kasim didn't want to hear them. Omar couldn't remember the last time he had been this impatient for a woman. He couldn't remember ever being this impatient. But then he wasn't young and lusty anymore, and he hadn't deliberately deprived himself of a willing bedmate these past four nights, as he knew Kasim had foolishly done.

Still, he felt it expedient to point out, "There are dozens of other women to choose—"

"Omar."

The old man threw up his hands. "Then you had best summon Haji Agha. This particular summons coming from anyone else will not be believed."

Haji Agha had not moved so quickly in twenty years. Immediately, Jamil had said. How to interpret "immediately"? Was there time to dress the girl properly? Pray Allah she was already bathed. But it was late in the afternoon, so a bath was hopefully the least of his worries.

He burst into Rahine's apartment, so out of breath it took him several seconds before he could get out, "He wants her now."

"Who?"

"Shahar."

"*What?*"

"There is no time to wonder about it, Rahine. He said immediately."

Rahine opened her mouth to argue, but the word "immediately" changed her mind. Jamil had never demanded one of his concubines immediately before.

She took a deep breath to calm herself, then

206

turned to the women gathered around her. "You heard Haji Agha. There is no time to dawdle. Kalila, go to the wardrobe mistress. Tell her something in lavender, to match Shahar's eyes. Saril, fetch one of my jewel boxes, the one with the pearls, I think. Oma, my scented oils, quickly. Come along, Haji."

The old man smiled as he hurried after her. "You're taking this very well, Rahine."

She ignored the comment. "Did you at least *try* to tell him she wasn't ready?"

"Of course."

And he had still said immediately, she realized. "But why the rush? She's going to be denied the preparation ritual that is so important for her self-esteem. To be the chosen one is an honor—"

"Do you really think *she* will consider it such?"

Rahine stopped cold, paling. "Allah help us, what if she resists him?"

"That is a distinct possibility."

"I should have spoken to her myself, should have warned her what could happen if she displeases him."

Omar continued walking, saying over his shoulder, "He has called for her before she is ready, Rahine. He will have to take that into consideration and have patience with her."

She hurried to catch up with him. "But *will* he? You know how short-tempered he has been—"

"Which is why there is no time for this speculation. We only have time to see her properly dressed."

On inquiry of Shahar's whereabouts, they were directed to the *hammam*. Thank Allah for small favors. But Rahine had recalled by now that Shahar had not been denuded of all her body hair. She decided not to mention this appalling fact to Haji, since there was nothing they could do about it now. There was no telling what Jamil's reaction would be, but again, he had to accept what he got when he allowed no time for preparation.

Rahine sighed to herself. She couldn't even be annoyed with Jamil for breaking tradition because of this unprecedented impatience on his part. He was under a strain. He was not himself, and hadn't been for months. If Shahar could take his mind off his troubles for a while, Rahine would be thankful for it. She was just afraid that this particular girl was going to add to his frustration, rather than appease it.

They found her stretched out on a bench in the main chamber of the *hammam*, her head resting on her crossed arms, her eyes closed. The girl who had been given to her knelt beside her, gently running a brush through that wealth of platinum hair, spread down her back and over her hips. If Jamil could see her like this he would find no fault with her no matter her attitude, for her skinniness was hidden beneath a caftan that covered her completely, falling to the floor on each side of the bench. She presented a sensual picture, with a dreamy smile on her lips in her relaxation.

A light coating of cosmetics had already been applied to her face, a very light coat, Rahine noted, and realized it suited her fairness. She made a mental note to reward Shahar's servant for having her in a state of readiness even though she was still in training. *That* circumstance had abruptly changed. Now for the battle that Rahine fully anticipated.

Chantelle's eyes popped open as she heard the surprised gasps all around her and the quickly uttered greetings to the Dey's mother and his Chief Black Eunuch. But then she groaned, seeing that the pair were moving directly toward her. What now? she wondered with a distinct flare of irritation. Had Vashti complained of her surliness? But that wasn't her fault, for that haughty little twit gave her a very real headache each time she showed up for Chantelle's "lessons in the arts of love."

As she sat up, she glanced briefly at the culprit in question and saw Vashti preening in what was supposedly a provocative pose, naked from the waist up, her large melonlike breasts looking grotesque with the nipples hennaed, as many of the women's were; they used henna not only on nipples but on hands and feet, too. One lady had even put the red dye around her hairless pubic region, a sight which Chantelle had had to pinch herself to keep from laughing at, it had looked so ridiculous.

The nakedness in the baths was not unusual, for half the women in the room were partially clothed as well, and there were about twenty concubines present at the moment. Chantelle had even managed not to feel quite so disturbed by it today, so she supposed this was one thing she was quickly getting used to, though she refused to lie about in such a state of indecency.

"Lalla Rahine, Haji Agha." Chantelle gave them the barest semblance of a nod to allow them their due respect. "Is there something you require of me?"

"What is that scent you are wearing?" Rahine asked abruptly.

"Attar of roses."

"I would have preferred something more sensual, but it will do, I suppose." Rahine waved the girl Oma away when she rushed up behind her with her own box of scents, and directed her next question to Adamma. "Was she thoroughly bathed today?"

Adamma was in a frozen state of shock, as well as rendered speechless, at being spoken to by Lalla Rahine for the first time ever. Chantelle's eyes narrowed at these pointless questions. As far as she was concerned, her cleanliness was no one's business but her own. Did they have to pry into *everything* here?

Irritation prodding her, and after having listened to nothing but allusions to sex for the past three days, she drawled, "Why, *lalla*, you could eat off me, I'm so clean. Is that what you wanted to know?"

Rahine's lips twitched despite herself. "You must inform Jamil that he has that option, Haji."

"He might find it a unique experience," the old eunuch agreed, his grin more obvious.

"Now just a minute—" Chantelle began, but was distracted by another servant running toward her, arms laden with the sheerest silk she had ever seen, in the most exquisite shade of lavender.

The material was laid out carefully on the bench beside her, and now Chantelle saw that it wasn't just material, but a finished product, an outfit in the same design as what she was already used to wearing. The silk pantaloons were shot through with silver thread, making them glitter at the slightest movement. And she gasped to find that the little vest was trimmed with silver-mounted amethysts. There were also transparent veils in the same color, but of gauze; a stunning head circlet of silver, pearls, and much larger amethysts to attach the veils to; and satin slippers studded with still more purple gems.

It was an outfit unlike any she had seen in common wear around the harem, an outfit worthy of . . . the Dey's pleasure. Her eyes flew to Rahine with that horrid thought, but she could sense nothing in the older woman's expression to panic her. Besides, she had been assured that she wouldn't be summoned until her training was completed, and it had only just begun. She had also been assured she wouldn't be summoned until she put on some weight, and at the most she had gained back only a pound or two, enough to take the gauntness from her face.

"Is this costume for me?" Chantelle asked Rahine.

Rahine had not missed the brief moment of fear that was revealed in Shahar's expression. But then she had been anticipating a battle royal, only it was a battle the girl couldn't win.

For a long moment, she actually debated lying to Shahar about where she was going. That would get her dressed quickly, get her all the way to Jamil's apartment without incident, and also keep the girl from hating her, and she realized with a degree of surprise that she didn't want Shahar to hate her.

Rahine sighed, for she knew she was only fooling herself. In no way could they leave the battle to come on Jamil's doorstep. The results of that would affect the whole palace, and that was something she couldn't risk, even if she was willing to cause Jamil's displeasure, which she wasn't. Besides, lying to the girl would undoubtedly gain her hate anyway.

But they could at least get her dressed first. "Do you like it?" Rahine asked with a smile. "I knew the color would suit you the moment I saw it. And I thought you deserved something nice, now that you've settled in without any more disturbances."

Chantelle glanced at Haji, distrustful of that unlikely statement, but when he didn't dispute it, she smiled, too. "Then I thank you. It *is* lovely."

"Well, then, what are you waiting for? Go and

212

try it on so that I may see how you look. My women will help you."

"No," Chantelle declined, politely but firmly. "I have Adamma now to help me."

Rahine looked at the girl in question, still on her knees behind the bench. "Very well, but, Adamma, be quick about it," Rahine warned, adding for Shahar's benefit, "I'm pressed for time."

If Chantelle didn't understand, Adamma certainly did, and she was too frightened of the Dey's mother to warn her mistress, though she wanted to. From certain comments that Shahar had made in the past days, Adamma realized why Lalla Rahine was avoiding the truth until the last moment. Even when they removed themselves to one of the small chambers off the main room for privacy, she said nothing, praying silently instead, for she too realized that her mistress was going to balk at what had come about much sooner than anyone had expected.

With Rahine's warning uppermost in mind, she had Shahar changed in record time, then just stood there in amazement at how such fine raiments could enhance her mistress's pale beauty.

"Is it that bad?" Chantelle asked with a grin.

Adamma started. "Oh, no, *lalla!* His highness will find you more beautiful than the hummingbird's song, more beautiful than—"

"Oh, don't start with all that silliness, Adamma. And his highness's opinion doesn't count anyway, since he's not going to see me. But I would like to see for myself. Didn't you say there was a mirror in Safiye's apartment? How much do you think it will take to bribe her to let me have a peek in it?"

"I—I—"

"Oh, never mind. Perhaps Lalla Rahine can arrange it."

And with the intention of asking that favor, Chantelle returned to the main chamber. Only she was brought up short upon finding the room deserted of the other concubines, leaving only Rahine, Haji, and two other eunuchs who had entered while she was gone. One was Kadar, but Chantelle didn't spare him even a fleeting smile. Her eyes locked with the emerald gaze of the Dey's mother.

"The color does indeed suit you, Shahar."

Chantelle continued forward. "Thank you, but would you mind telling me why you have sent everyone away? It is your doing, isn't it?"

Rahine took the last step that brought her close enough to kiss Chantelle's cheek. "I'm sorry, child, but Haji will take you to Jamil now."

"Is that normal? I thought I wasn't supposed to see him until . . ." The words trailed off as the color left Chantelle's face. "No." It was barely a whisper.

Matter-of-factly, Rahine stated, "Jamil owns you. This is a fact even you can't dispute. And he has decided not to wait until your training is completed. It is his wish that you come to him now."

"I won't." Still in a whisper.

"Yes, you will," Rahine insisted. "You have no choice in the matter."

214

It was the words "no choice" that broke through Chantelle's horror to ignite her temper. "Like bloody hell!" she shouted, forgetting herself enough to speak in English. "I won't go anywhere near that—that—that *man!* You'll have to drag me there and hold me down for his depravity—"

"That can be arranged," Rahine replied coldly.

"You wouldn't," Chantelle faltered.

"On the contrary."

Chantelle's eyes widened accusingly as she exclaimed, "You're speaking English!"

"I am English."

"Then he's half English? Oh, God, that just makes it worse."

"I don't see why—"

"You don't see anything! You've been here too long. You think like them now, you act like them. You're no longer English, or you couldn't force me into this!"

"It is not I who am forcing you, Shahar, but the circumstances that brought you here. You lost your freedom of choice when you were made a slave. Now you do as your master wishes, or you suffer the consequences."

"Rahine," Haji interrupted finally. "There is no time for this."

"I know." Rahine sighed, turning away. "Take her. If she angers Jamil by resisting him . . . other women have died for less."

Chapter Twenty-four

Magic words, "do or die." Until Chantelle could determine if it was true, she had to give in. She might be furious and terrified in turn that it had come to this, but she wasn't stupid. There were a lot of things she would do to preserve her maidenhead. Dying wasn't one of them.

She barely heard Haji Agha as he hurried her down the long corridor toward the Dey's private apartments. The last-minute instructions and warnings fell on deaf ears. She was too aware of what was going to happen. Vashti had taken her through it step by step, and those were the words she kept hearing.

"It is over with very quickly. He will stick his thing in you and you will feel the terrible pain as it rips through your hymen. If his mood is good, he might allow you time for the pain to subside —most likely not, since what you feel does not concern him. Then he will thrust and thrust and finally cry out his pleasure. He will take a few moments to recover; then he will move away, and that is the end of it. Simple. All over quickly, and he sends you back to the harem. Rarely does he keep a concubine with him all night, since he prefers to sleep with his wives."

Those words had haunted Chantelle ever since, intruding on her other lessons, in which her instruction had begun in the arts of enticement and seduction, but mostly pleasure. How to please a man. Not just any man, but one man in particular.

Chantelle had had to see a little humor in it or she would be fast on her way to going crazy. For so many people to be concerned with one man's sexual delights was the height of ludicrousness, yet that was exactly the case here. Every single woman in the harem, every single eunuch, every slave, was concerned with only one thing, the Dey's pleasure. If it weren't so ridiculous, Chantelle would cry about it. But it wasn't so ridiculous now, not when she was about to become the main course on tonight's menu.

It had come about. It was actually happening. *No, it's not. It's just a dream.*

"You do not rise until he bids you to."

"Rise?"

She was facing a door. Slowly she turned to see Haji Agha's eyes narrowed at her.

"Shahar, have you heard nothing I've said?"

"I—I'm sorry, but I don't think so. If you'd like to repeat it—"

"There is not another moment to spare," he said in annoyance, fully aware she was playing for time. "Just remember to prostrate yourself before him and stay down until he bids you to rise. Do exactly as he says and all should go well.

We can only pray he has not become annoyed with the delay."

"What delay?"

"He wanted you here immediately."

"Why?"

Haji sighed. "Allah only knows."

Abruptly, he yanked away the short veil that had covered her lower face, then opened the door and escorted her to the center of the large room. Not trusting her to do as he said, Haji tugged on her arm until she sank to her knees. Satisfied to see her lower her head to the floor as well, he backed out of the room.

It was not out of respect that Chantelle prostrated herself. She had kept her head bowed and her eyes on the floor upon entering the room and would continue to do so for as long as she could, for the simple reason that she didn't want to look at the Dey. In this position she couldn't, and that suited her fine for the moment.

Where he was she didn't know. He might not even be in the room—she didn't hear him, couldn't sense him. Or could she? Yes, she did feel as if she were being watched, and it wasn't a pleasant feeling.

Derek remained quiet, not trusting his voice just yet. It seemed as if he had waited forever for this moment, though it had only been four days. Four days of misery and hoping he could later laugh at himself for building something up out of nothing. But it was later now, and there was nothing to laugh at. She was more lovely than he remembered: ethereal, willowy—and his.

But a virgin. He had to keep that uppermost in his mind, or he would carry her straightaway to his bed.

"Sit up and look at me."

Not "Let me look at you"; he was already doing that, damn his eyes.

Chantelle had tensed at the sound of his voice but didn't move otherwise. Not that she didn't want to. She was just afraid that once she did, her defloration was going to proceed at an alarming pace.

"You know that you must obey me in all things, Shahar, though all I ask is that you look at me. Is that so unreasonable a request?"

His voice was calm, gentle even, and yet it was the same voice she remembered from before, slightly husky, with a deep timbre, a voice that could condemn a girl to brutal rape one moment and then rescind the order and ask without really caring if he hadn't redeemed himself in her eyes. This man could never redeem himself in her eyes, no matter what he did.

But now that she was reminded of what a cold-hearted bastard he was, she felt she could meet his eyes without showing her fear. It was her loathing she wasn't so sure she could hide.

When she sat back on her heels, she saw not only Jamil but also his two bodyguards, standing with their backs to the wall on each side of a large four-poster bed. Jamil was at the foot of the high bed, resting his hips against it, his arms crossed over his chest, his legs stretched out before him and crossed at the ankles, the pose so bloody English in its casual nonchalance that Chantelle nearly gasped in surprise. Thank God for the Eastern dress that made the effect incongruous, reminding her that there was nothing English about Jamil. Since he'd been raised a barbaric infidel, blood didn't count.

"You are allowed to speak, you know."

Her gaze dropped back to the floor. Her fingers worried at one of the four ropes of pearls Rahine had draped over her head just before she'd been led out of the baths.

"I have nothing to say."

"Do not retreat, Shahar. Return your eyes to me, or better yet, come closer."

"May I walk?"

"Don't be impertinent. If I wanted you to crawl, I would say so."

Color singed her cheeks. He would, too, the swine. But she was warned by the abruptness of his tone that she had better keep her flippancy to herself for now.

With acute dread which was accelerating her pulse, she rose slowly to her feet and closed the distance between them. Still, her eyes wouldn't meet his again, and whether he was getting annoyed with this continued defiance on her part she couldn't tell.

She watched him push away from the bed so that he was standing when she stopped an arm's distance away. Legs straight and spread, an arrogant stance if she'd ever seen one, his arms unfolded, and then she felt fingers gliding across her cheek.

Fire was her impression, his fingertips were so hot. Amazingly, she kept from flinching, but her gaze remained locked on the deep V of his white tunic and the large tiger's eye medallion that rested against his skin there. It was bronzed skin and sparingly dotted with crisp black hair near the point of the V, which made her realize with a flare of irritation that he didn't have to suffer his hair being plucked and scraped away. On top of that thought was the further realization that she wasn't completely denuded of hair either, though she was supposed to be. What would his reaction be to that? she wondered, and in the wondering knew that she had already accepted the fact that he would soon be in a position to discover her apparently sinful state.

"Will you take dinner with me?"

The incongruity of that question, when she had expected at any moment to be tossed onto his bed, brought Chantelle's eyes flying up to his face. "Dinner?"

"If you like," he said softly.

He was staring at her mouth. His thumb moved to trace the line of her lower lip. And then his eyes locked with hers. Emerald fire. There was nothing indifferent about *his* gaze.

"Dinner would be nice . . . I mean wonderful

. . . I'm famished, actually," she ended on what she hoped was a note of sincerity.

He laughed, amazing her. The sound was deep and pleasant, and she imagined that she could feel its reverberation inside her own chest.

"You are so transparent, Shahar. Did you think I would ravish you the moment you walked through the door?"

Exactly, but she didn't say so. She didn't have to. The blush soared clear to her hairline this time, visible even with her head bowed.

"This shyness is allowed, but your eyes are exquisite, little moon. I want to see them."

And everything you want you get? She thought with annoyance, then tossed caution to the wind and said it in English.

His emerald gaze narrowed the tiniest bit. "English is unacceptable here, Shahar. Your French is superb, but it is not a language everyone is familiar with. You may use it while you are with me, but otherwise you will practice the mixture of Turkish and Arabic that is the common language of the palace. Eventually, that will be the only language you will speak."

She said nothing. What could she say? That was tantamount to an order. And she learned one thing. His mother might be English, but she obviously hadn't taught him to speak it. He proved it by his next words.

"Now, what was it that you said to me?"

For a split second she considered lying. But his hand had come beneath her chin, forcing her head back up, *Forcing* her to meet his gaze. She decided on the truth, hoping it would annoy him enough to take his hand off her.

"I asked if you get everything you want."

He didn't take his hand away. The other hand came up, and he cupped her face in his palms. He obviously wasn't offended, but then the instinct for self-preservation had kept the derision out of her words this time.

"Of course," was his husky reply. "Everything, Shahar. Why should it be otherwise, when everything you see belongs to me, including yourself?"

She tried to pull away. He countered by holding her firmly and stepping closer until his hips just touched her. Her nostrils flared with the scent of him, musk and sandalwood, nice, so nice.

She blinked. Good God, he was hypnotic, with those dark green eyes so close, his breath warm against her lips. She groaned, and instantly she was released.

"We will eat here," he said, walking away from her, as if he hadn't been on the verge of kissing her, as if she hadn't been on the verge of wanting him to.

"Here," she saw as she followed him, was an enclosed garden just outside the room. The sun had already sunk below the high walls surrounding the little area, but it still shone brilliantly against the palace above their heads, leaving the grounds shaded and cool. Tulips, roses, and carnations abounded in quaint little groupings. A single tree offered an even cooler shaded area, with a bench beneath it. A fountain in one corner bubbled like a waterfall into what she saw was a fish pond made entirely of small blue tiles, large orange fish a striking contrast.

Large square pillows had already been laid out around an engraved brass table, set up right on the grass. It was peaceful here, romantic even, and the effect of what was nearly an English picnic was relaxing in its familiarity.

She let him lead her to one of the pillows, but she didn't sink down on it until she knew how close he would be sitting, for with so many pillows there for the taking, she could lean either way to allow more distance between them. She needn't have worried. He moved around the low table until he was directly across from her.

"What do you think?" he asked when the trays of food began arriving.

"I think it wouldn't have mattered if I wanted to eat with you or not."

She shouldn't have said that. Did she *want* him angry? But he wasn't. He waved the servants back and filled her plate himself.

"True," he said after a thoughtful moment. "The asking was a mere courtesy for your benefit."

"And if I had declined?"

"I would have insisted."

"I see."

He glanced up at her and smiled at the stiffness in her expression. "No, I don't think you do. I can insist as the Dey, and no one dares to defy me. Or I can insist as the man, Jamil, and see how persuasive I can be."

Her brow rose skeptically. "Am I to believe, then, that I have some choices? I was told that I did not."

"On some things—perhaps."

She couldn't quite bring herself to ask if one of those things was sharing his bed. Somehow she doubted it, and to introduce that topic now would give her indigestion.

It was a quiet meal, once they began eating. If she didn't know better, she would think Jamil was as nervous as she. On her part, she tried to ignore him, concentrating on the food he had piled on her plate. For the main course there was roast kid and guinea fowl, as well as *pideli kebab*, which was lamb enclosed in flat, oval bread. And if none of those were tempting enough, there was also a turkey stuffed with rice, liver, currants, and pine kernels. The side dishes were just as numerous—sweet peppers stuffed with flavored rice and meat, artichoke hearts, sheep's brain, white beans, asparagus, and two different salads.

Several drinks were also offered for her to choose from: *kanyak*, a Muslim's sole vice, which was a combination of brandy and wine; almond milk, made from crushed almonds, sweetened water, and orange blossom extract; a sweet Cyprus wine; and tart cherry juice. She noted that Jamil chose the almond milk, her first indication that he adhered to the Islam strictures that forbade the drinking of intoxicating beverages. She took the *kanyak* herself, anything to help her get through the rest of this ordeal, and would have drunk the whole bottle, but Jamil allowed her only a glass and a half.

When the desserts were brought in, Jamil again served her, putting one of each offering on her plate. There was a pastry rolled in sugar syrup, baklava, the one layered with walnuts and syrup; *helva,* a ground-up compression of sesame, butter, honey, and nuts; and lastly, the jellied sweets called *rahat lokum,* meaning, "giving rest to the throat," and oh, God, it did. The Turkish coffee was served now, too, brewed by the coffeemaker right there at the table; sweet, hot, with thick foam on top. She was actually beginning to acquire a taste for it.

Looking around her, Chantelle realized that she had eaten more at this sitting than she had in weeks, but she wasn't thinking of keeping her weight down any more. It was too late for that. She would have eaten another full course or two, anything to keep the meal from ending. But it was ended. The servants who had streamed in with their heavily laden trays now took everything away.

Jamil's hookah was brought, but he made no move to partake of it. He was reclining on several pillows, propped on one elbow facing her. His black hair was in disarray from the slight breeze that worked its way over the walls, several locks falling over his forehead. She hadn't thought he would have such thick, luxuriant hair, what with having to wear a turban constantly. She wished he were wearing the turban now. He looked too English by half.

As if his own thoughts were running along the same vein, he said, "I want to see if your hair is as silky as it looks. Will you come nearer, Shahar, and let me feel it?"

It would have been churlish to say no. But it was such a simple request, how could she refuse? She came around the table on the pillows, stopping on the one next to the one he leaned on. His right hand reached toward her immediately, first removing the jeweled circlet that had rested on her forehead and still supported the longer veil that only half covered her unbound hair. He tossed this aside, and then she felt his fingers sliding along her scalp, but only for a moment. He raised his hand, letting her hair glide slowly through his fingers for at least a foot's length; then he twisted his wrist, catching a handful, but he didn't tug on it.

Chantelle turned her head to see him rubbing her hair between his fingers, and she was mesmerized for a moment. It seemed such an intimate thing, those dark fingers caressing her hair, and that was what he was doing, caressing, memorizing the feel and texture of a single lock. She was leaning toward him to give him an easy reach. She had the option to move back at any time—or so she thought.

"I was wrong," he said, drawing her attention back to those dark green eyes. "It's even softer than silk. Is your skin the same?"

227

Oh, God, did he want to touch her now? She tried to sit up straight, but he was still holding her hair and wasn't letting go.

"Come, Shahar, slide onto my pillow," he coaxed her. "You may rest your head on my knee." When she didn't budge, he added, "You must get used to lying next to me, but it is only your skin that interests me at the moment. And you have enough exposed that I will not ask you to remove any clothing."

That should have relieved her, but it didn't. She knew she couldn't really deny him these little requests, because her body belonged to him. He didn't have to ask for anything. He could just take. Whether she could let him plunge his "thing," as Vashti had called it, into her when the time came, without any resistance on her part, she didn't know, but she had no need to panic yet, not until he suggested they go inside.

For a man who had wanted her here immediately, he was certainly taking his time with her now. She was grateful for that, and that today, he seemed nothing like the man she had first met.

"Shahar . . ." he prompted, not impatiently, but to let her know she was not reprieved by her hesitation. He was waiting.

She moved, twisting to slide over his pillow in front of him. But she couldn't lay her head on his bent knee as he had suggested. That was too intimate by far. She rested back on her elbows instead, aware that this position thrust her breasts forward, but unable to help it. She didn't have

228

large breasts, though she didn't think they were that small either. But in comparison to those of his other women, they were small, and so she hoped he would not even notice them.

He didn't. He was staring at her midriff, and Chantelle groaned inwardly. She supposed it had been too much to hope that when he had mentioned her exposed skin, he was thinking of her bare arms. He wasn't. His hand dropped slowly toward her belly, and when it finally rested there, she sucked in her breath, for it felt so hot she imagined herself branded.

"What?" he asked, and her eyes flew to his face, finding his eyes had been drawn to hers with the sound she had made.

"Nothing," she squeaked and, hearing the sound, groaned in embarrassment.

"You will come to no harm under my hand, Shahar, but you must relax."

"I—I can't."

"Why?"

His fingers had spread wide over her belly, covering nearly the entire area. And his hand moved now, in a slow, soothing circle. But it wasn't soothing. Her muscles were contracting, as if they could jump away from the contact of his flesh on hers. Even her insides seemed to be leaping in an attempt to escape . . . .

"Why?" he repeated with more insistence. "Have I given you reason to fear me?" Then he added with a touch of annoyance, "Today?"

229

She thought about it for a moment, but there was only one answer that was truthful. "No."

"Then what is wrong?"

Everything, she thought, but said only, "No man has ever put his hands on me like this before."

"I know," he said, surprising her. "Your innocence is why we are here instead of in there." He nodded toward his bedchamber.

Chantelle immediately took hope that the day of reckoning had not actually arrived, that this meeting was for her to become used to him and no more. He was quick to disabuse her of that notion.

"Do not mistake me, Shahar. We *will* go inside—when you are ready."

She would never be ready. She almost told him so but thought better of it. What would he consider readiness on her part, anyway? She wasn't going to appear so, whatever it was.

He sighed then and caught the hand that rested next to his side, pulling it out from under her. "You cannot relax unless you lie back."

"I don't want—"

"Lie back, Shahar."

It was an order, given in such a tone that she obeyed it instantly, afraid to do otherwise. And what else could she do, anyway, with him so close that he could easily *make* her obey him? But if he thought she could relax, he was crazy.

She laid her head on the very edge of his knee, keeping as much distance between them as possible. She was acutely aware of his hips so near her shoulder, and one of the things Vashti had taken particular delight in telling her about pleasuring him came to mind, and with it a scalding blush. But his position didn't change. His hips were nearly flat against the pillow. Only the upper portion of his body was twisted to face her.

"I am going to taste you now, Shahar."

That softly murmured warning caused her to bolt straight up, only to have him push her right back down. Visions of him biting her flashed through her mind, and she tried frantically to remember if she had seen the scars of his teeth on any of his other women. But before the thought was even finished, his hand moved to grip her side and his mouth opened on her navel. She jerked, a scream welling in her throat, only to feel his tongue, not his teeth.

She relaxed so completely then that he chuckled. "Did you think I meant to devour you, little moon? I must confess I do have the urge to, though I promise you it would not hurt. Another time, perhaps."

His mouth returned to her navel, making her desperate to leap up and away from him. But she couldn't, not with his right arm lying across her rib cage with enough pressure to keep her from rising off the pillow. She tried closing her eyes and concentrating on something else. Her eyes popped open immediately, for with them closed she felt his tongue too intensely. But even so, there was a wealth of agitation just beneath his mouth, as if she were trembling deep inside.

She didn't recognize the sensations he was causing her to experience. She wanted to push his head away. She wanted to hold it to her. Irrational —God, what was wrong with her?

She heard his sigh, deep and fanning over her wet skin, making her shiver. "You still won't relax, will you?"

"I'm sorry, but I can't," she nearly wailed, afraid of his displeasure after being warned never to cause it.

"If I stop tasting you here"—and his tongue delved once more into her navel—"will you accept my lips in a more conventional place?"

"Yes." Anything to get his mouth away from her belly.

Too late did she wonder where that more conventional place was, and there was no time to ask. Before she could even draw another breath, he had scooped her up and placed her in his lap, covering her lips with a scorching kiss that was painful in its intensity. She couldn't lessen the pressure, for his hand had slipped up beneath her hair to hold her head still for this ravishment.

And then, seemingly from far off, she heard him groan and was terrified again that she had displeased him, or hurt him somehow, when she was the one hurting, his kiss was so passionate. But he didn't stop what he was doing. On the contrary, his other arm tightened around her back, smashing her upper torso against his chest until she became light-headed from lack of breath.

And then, abruptly, all pressure ended. "I'm sorry, Shahar, but you cannot know—"

Derek stopped when he realized what he was saying. Christ, what was wrong with him? Jamil would never have apologized, for any reason, and he was supposed to be Jamil in every way. She was not to know otherwise, yet he hadn't truly played his role since she'd walked into the room.

Jamil would never have waited this long to carry her to his bed. He would have done so the moment he felt the urge, and Derek had felt it even before she had arrived. But he hadn't acted on it, not completely. He couldn't bring himself to rush her through this experience, her first experience with a man. Her innocence demanded more consideration from him than that. And yet he didn't consider waiting until another day. He couldn't deviate from Jamil's character that much —or so he told himself.

He had also told himself that he was doing this for the girl. True, *he* was the one benefiting by her dilemma, but he wasn't going to lose too much sleep over that, for she would benefit, too, in the long run. He had thought long and hard about it the first night he'd seen her, and had finally concluded that if he didn't take her for himself, Jamil would when he returned. She would then be just one of so many, a circumstance that he knew any Englishwoman with a lick of pride would find utterly abhorrent. Then, too, Jamil's heart was already taken. Derek just couldn't see such an exquisite beauty taking second place to anyone. She deserved to be loved and cherished, and this way she would be found a husband for herself. Derek could insist it be a man with no other wives. He could do that much for her.

But that was for the future. Right now he had probably just frightened the daylights out of her, and he wanted nothing more than to explain that it wasn't intentional, that he had simply lost control of his passion. Only, Jamil wouldn't explain his actions, especially not to a woman. But Derek could make amends in other ways.

He sighed and bent his forehead to hers. Her breathing had quieted, but she was stiff in his arms.

"Shall we try this again?"

She immediately strained against him. "No, please—"

"Shh, little moon. I can be gentle, too. Put your arms around my neck and I will show you."

"I don't want—"

"Do it, Shahar."

He regretted the tone that made her leap to obey him, but Christ, this was pure torture, denying himself for so long. Much longer, and he was going to forget his good intentions. He had to reach her. He had to make her want him, now, before his natural inclinations took over.

Chantelle braced herself for the onslaught of his mouth again as it lowered toward hers. She felt his breath instead, and then his tongue, whisper-soft, smoothing over her upper lip, then the lower, soothing the soreness from his previous kiss. One hand was holding her head again, but the other had come up to warm her cheek.

He leaned back and she caught the full potency of his emerald gaze. For some reason, it made her feel strange this time, almost as if his mouth were still pressed to her belly, causing that trembling inside.

And then his forefinger was tracing the same path his tongue had. "Open, Shahar. I want you to feel what it is like when a part of me is inside you."

"But—"

His finger slipped inside her mouth the moment she opened it to protest. Her natural reaction was to close her lips against it and try to push it out with her tongue.

"Be still." His lips rested on the corner of her mouth. His finger was moving against her tongue, acquainting her with the salty taste of it. "I want you to suck on it . . . no, Shahar, don't question my motives. Forget what you have been told in training. It is my tongue I want you to accept in your mouth, no more than that. But you must know what to do with it when it is there." At her groan, he smiled. "No one has instructed you about kissing yet, have they? I imagine they were only concerned with one thing. But kissing comes first, Shahar . . . or would you rather we move on to the lessons you *have* learned?"

She immediately began sucking on his finger. She heard his deep chuckle but didn't care. And then, before she knew it, his mouth had covered her lips and she was sucking on his tongue instead.

"Gently," he said after a moment. "Yes, now try to catch it." He began plunging his tongue in and out and around, so she couldn't get a grip on it. "Now give me yours."

The sounds she was making deep in her throat only he heard. She was obeying him mindlessly, caught up in something she had no control over. How long it lasted she didn't know, but finally she was aware of something other than the rushing, rolling maelstrom inside her. She was aware of his hand where it shouldn't be.

"How is it you were able to keep this soft bush, little moon?"

She moaned in embarrassment, trying to hide her heated face in his shoulder. And she felt the fingers delving into the curls, touching that most intimate part of her body. It was too much. She went cold, suddenly remembering everything about him that she despised. How *could* she have let him do these things to her? She should have resisted from the very beginning, and the devil take the consequences.

"Don't!" she gasped, reaching for his forearm to yank it away from her.

He let her, but when she tried to rise from his lap, his arms locked around her. "What is it, Shahar?"

"I can't do this!" she cried, squirming desperately now to break his hold. "I hoped I could, but I just can't, not with you. Please, let me go!"

236

If she hadn't said "not with you," Derek might have tried to calm her. But he was remembering the same thing she was, her meeting with his brother, and how Jamil's actions had appalled and disgusted her. It was going to take more than one meeting with her to make her forget her first impression. Only that meant letting her walk out of here now, when he was aching so badly to have her that he could barely think straight.

Understandably, his voice was rather harsh, as were his hands on her arms as he pushed her away from him. "Go, and do it quickly, before I change my mind."

Chapter Twenty-five

Across the corridor from Jamil's rooms, a eunuch was waiting for Chantelle, sitting there Turkish fashion on the floor. He scrambled to his feet when she burst through the door, putting out an arm to detain her. It was Kadar.

He made no comment on her haste. "I will take you to my master."

She nodded. At least he didn't ask what had happened. Haji probably would, though, and so she was dragging her feet before she reached the harem.

Kadar led her to Safiye's apartment, where Haji was having a good gossip while he waited for her. But he wasn't expecting to see Chantelle this soon.

"So he truly was impatient, was he?"

Chantelle stood in the doorway, cringing to hear Safiye laugh at this observation. Her fingers worried at the pearls around her throat, and she seized on them as an excuse to avoid giving a reply.

"Will you return these to Lalla Rahine with my thanks for the use of them?"

Haji Agha took the pearls from her, but his expression turned thoughtful at such an obvious evasion. "Did all go well, Shahar?"

She bowed her head to avoid those searching eyes of his. "I would rather not talk about it."

He accepted that, thinking she was merely upset over the loss of her virginity. "Very well, you may go to your room and rest. Perhaps we will talk later."

God, she hoped not, but she hurried away before he changed his mind and decided to interrogate her now. Before she reached her room, she was trembling. She dismissed Adamma with a sharp word and curled onto her narrow pallet. The trembling increased.

Oh, God, what had she done? Would the next person to appear at her door be the executioner? Was her stupid virginity worth her life? God, no! She had already discovered that she could survive its loss. She had thought herself raped on board ship. She had felt miserable and shamed, but it hadn't been the end of the world.

But this just might be. He had been so angry! *If she angers Jamil by resisting him . . . other women have died for less.* Other of Jamil's women, or had Rahine been speaking in generalities? As if it mattered now. She had done the one thing she had been told she could not do. She had refused the lord and master the use of her body. *If she angers Jamil by resisting him* . . . She had done both.

Stupid, so stupid! If only she could go back and do it over. So she despised him. So he was a ruthless, coldhearted barbarian. What did that count next to her life? But she couldn't go back. She could only leave the harem by his summons, and that was unlikely to ever come again. After all, what use did he have for women who found him detestable, when so many adored him.

At this very moment another woman was probably in his bed; Chantelle hadn't mistaken that rigid bulge she had been sitting on for what it was. Jamil wouldn't wait long to relieve it, for his rampant desire had been the very reason he had been furious with her resistance.

Even if he didn't order her death, even if she were only punished for today's defiance, it was doubtful she would ever see him again after she had told him plainly that it was he she objected to. She was going to perish in this horrid place, forgotten, forsaken, wretched.

The self-pitying tears had dried a half hour later when Rahine stormed into her room. In fact, Chantelle had cried herself to sleep, so she was understandably disoriented on being awakened so abruptly, and so loudly.

"You foolish child! In all my years here I've never seen anyone with such a total lack of self-preservation!" When Chantelle paled at those words, Rahine added tightly, "No, you are not to die yet, though I wonder if that isn't the answer. Jamil could be told you had succumbed to sickness, and then he would no longer be infuriated by you, as if he doesn't have enough to inflame his temper already."

"I—I couldn't help it."

"Don't give me nonsense, Shahar. You may be stupid, but I am not. You were warned, yet still you refused my son what is rightfully his. And he is in such a temper now that he has ignored his councillors and left the palace to go riding. Riding! Putting his very life in danger! And all because you think you are too good for the Dey of Barikah."

"That isn't why," Chantelle insisted.

"Isn't it? Or is it that you think you are better than every other woman here? They all came to my son as virgins. Is your virginity more prized than theirs?"

"No, of course not."

"Then what did you think you were saving it for?" Rahine demanded, her fury rising again, mixed with the anxiety she was feeling for Jamil's safety. "Did you forget so soon that you are here to stay? The only man who *can* take it is Jamil, and if you think he will still want it after today, you are mistaken."

"I realize that," Chantelle said in a whisper.

"Do you? Then you will agree that you are no longer fit to grace this court, let alone the court of the favorites, which you could so easily have aspired to. Let us see if you find the kitchens more to your liking."

"Is that to be my punishment?"

"It will be your life's sentence, if Jamil is wise enough to forget about you. But that is assuming he returns to the palace unharmed tonight. If not, then you may be sure your life *will* be forfeit for causing his recklessness."

Derek rode hell-bent over the plain, at last able to give the Thoroughbred his head to gallop full speed. He hadn't bothered to dress for the excursion other than to strap on his own boots for riding. He had been too impatient to get out of the palace, away, anywhere. He didn't care about the panic he left behind. His impersonation of his brother was on temporary hold. It was Derek who needed space, who needed the wind in his hair, the surge of a powerful animal beneath him— the distance to keep him from doing something he would regret, for he had been that close to having Shahar brought back to him and forcing her to his will.

Damn her own strength of will for enabling her to deny the potent sensuality he had aroused in her. And damn Jamil for the impression he had made on her that made her deny it. She *had* enjoyed his kisses. She had melted in his arms, mindlessly giving of herself and taking what he offered. He wasn't mistaken about the complete, unrestrained response that had revealed her true nature, and he was convinced it was an extremely passionate nature, if it could overcome her abhorrence and distrust of him.

But only temporarily. The slightest distraction had sparked her resistance and her determination to reject any pleasure he might give her. Stubborn English perversity in all its annoying glory. If she were of any other nationality, would she persevere with such tenacity? No. Only the English dug in their heels even on lost causes.

Derek slowed the stallion when the desert finally stretched before them and brought him to a halt. He barely noticed the beauty of such barren emptiness lit in blue shades of moonlight. He sat there for a moment, letting his thoughts fan his hot temper, rather than cool it.

If he was honest with himself, he wasn't so much angry at Shahar's obstinacy as he was with himself. This lustful impatience on his part was a new experience, one he didn't like at all. Shahar couldn't be blamed for her reaction to him, or for her reluctance to part with her innocence. If he could tell her it was in her own best interests to consummate their relationship, and what the future would hold for her if she did, she might give in gracefully, even with gratitude.

But he couldn't tell Shahar that. And when he thought of how long it was going to take to break through her resistance on his own, without the truth to make it easier, he groaned in frustration. How was he ever going to last? Certainly there were any number of women he could summon to his bed, but his ache was for Shahar, and until she relieved it, he doubted anyone else could, not completely. To hell with half measures. He would wait.

In the meantime, he would put his impersonation to the test and meet his sisters-in-law, all three of them, and his many nieces and nephews. These summonses were expected and might as well be gotten out of the way now as opposed to later. Shahar would need a few days alone anyway, to contemplate his displeasure. If fear could make her more agreeable, he wouldn't prevent its manifestation, though he wouldn't add to it either. He would prove to her afterward that there had never been any reason for her to be afraid of him.

With that resolved in his mind, he turned about and headed back to the city. He had ridden only a few yards when he noticed the vague outline of two of his guards finally catching up with him. He chuckled, his mood improved. Their desert mounts had never had a chance of keeping up with an English Thoroughbred sired by a champion racer. It was in his blood for the stallion to leave all comers in the dust.

Derek should feel contrite about his thoughtless actions, but he didn't. He had needed this time alone, with nothing but the stars and the wind and the quiet to keep his temper company. The danger of going off alone had been the least of his concerns. In fact, he would have welcomed a would-be assassin—he had been in the mood to hurt. But that mood was over now that his loins had cooled off. Imagine being ruled by his sex.

That, too, was a new experience he found disconcerting.

Derek pulled up on the reins when the approaching riders got closer and he made out the
flowing gray robes, not exactly the uniform of
the palace guards he had assumed them to be. He
frowned, wondering if he was going to get his
wish after all, to meet a few of Jamil's enemies.
Not that he minded. It just would have been
convenient if he had thought to carry a weapon
or two on him for this mad dash out into the
countryside. But he hadn't exactly been thinking
when he'd left the palace. He had been propelled
along by hot, frustrated emotion and nothing else.
A rather stupid thing to do after his many so-
journs across the Channel as one of Marshall's
spies. Old Marsh would be appalled by such care-
lessness.

The riders didn't slow down until the very last
moment, giving Derek fair warning that he did
indeed have a fight on his hands. The thing to
do would be to take off and outrun them. There
was no chance in hell they could keep up with the
white stallion. But he didn't do that.

The decision was made in the split second before a scimitar cut the air in front of him, slicing
toward his head. He ducked, noting that the assassins weren't smart enough to come at him from
each side. As the first man passed him after an un-
successful swipe, the second came up on the same
side, only this one tried to leap onto Derek and
knock him off his horse. He met Derek's foot

squarely in his chest, kicking him back into his saddle and nearly over it. He dropped his weapon in the fight to regain his balance and breathe at the same time.

Derek immediately dismissed him as incapacitated for the moment and swung about to face the other man, who had had time to turn around for his next assault. Several yards away, Derek was able to rear the stallion up on his hind legs and bring the front legs down at the crucial moment. The scream told him the stallion's hoofs had hit something vital on their descent. The man's horse had suffered, too, the front legs buckling, which sent the assassin tumbling over the animal's head. He didn't try to rise, squirming on the ground with one hand pressed to his right shoulder, yelling loudly now in his pain.

Derek whipped about again to see what the other one was up to, only to grin as he caught the man's shadow in flight, already far away. He dismounted then and picked up the dropped scimitar before he moved to stand over the fallen man. The fellow immediately started blubbering for mercy, but Derek had no intention of killing him. He did intend to take him back to the palace, however, and turn him over to Omar. There was a slim chance that this one might know something more than the other would-be assassins who had been caught.

Swiftly, he brought the hilt of the scimitar down on the man's turbaned head. Silence was immediate. Derek moved to check the fellow's horse,

which had since risen and was standing by docilely. Bruised, undoubtedly, but the animal seemed
capable of carrying a prone burden back to the
city. If not, Derek would just as soon drag the
luckless fellow behind his own mount. For someone who had just tried to kill him, he couldn't
dredge up much sympathy.

Chapter Twenty-six

THE OTHER slaves didn't know what to make of
Chantelle's presence among them. Some were
spiteful, some sympathetic, some fearful of speaking to her at all. Apparently, a concubine from
the royal harem had never before been sentenced
to kitchen labor. And from the few derogatory
remarks she overheard, she knew she was singu-
larly unique in not wanting to win the Dey's favor. With every other woman going out of her
way to please him in any way possible, it was no
wonder punishment such as she had incurred was
rare.

She was considered a freak, her crime heinous.
God, what absurdity. She hadn't done anything
wrong as far as she was concerned. Of course she
hadn't thought so two days ago, when she'd been
brought to the cavernous kitchen area and turned
over to the Chief Cook, who was now in charge
of her. At that time she had been so terrified, the
large, overbearing woman had taken one look at
her and turned away in disgust, ranting that she

would never get any work out of such a pale, skinny wraith.

But Chantelle's fear had been very real after Rahine's parting shot. She didn't know why the Dey's life should be in danger if he left the palace, but that he had, and that it was, horrified her, for she did think she was responsible, and she believed absolutely that if he didn't come back, her life would be forfeit.

She hadn't slept that night, for no one had bothered to let her know that Jamil *had* returned safely to the palace. She'd learned of it the next day, when one of Noura's servants, Noura being his second wife, came through the kitchens bragging to anyone who would listen that her mistress had been summoned for that night. Chantelle had then felt such keen resentment that it surprised her. She'd told herself it was because of her sleepless night, all for nothing, that Rahine could at least have had the decency to send word that her life was no longer in danger, even if her punishment wasn't to be rescinded. Her umbrage certainly wasn't because Jamil was going to spend the night with one of his wives. He could have a bloody orgy for all she cared, as long as she wasn't included. And it didn't look like she would be, ever. He sent her to labor as a kitchen slave and blithely went on with his customary lechery, the swine. Rahine was probably right—she would be forgotten in this dreary, unfriendly place.

Well and good. It was what she had originally hoped for, wasn't it, to end up anything but a concubine? But it would have been nice if she hadn't spent those first few days as a concubine, which accounted for the outright resentment of some of the other women who shared her new existence. Not all, though. She had met Adamma's mother yesterday and found her as likable as her daughter.

Fayolo was a beautiful Nigerian who seemed much too young to have a daughter Adamma's age, but she had informed Chantelle unabashedly that she had been a ripe thirteen when she began catching the eye of the palace guards. That the kitchen slaves had access to other parts of the palace was news that Chantelle pounced on, until the Chief Cook snapped that *she* wasn't to have such freedom, by Rahine's orders, which just added another dose of resentment to that which was already brewing.

The large chamber was to be her prison and, with a pallet on the cold floor, her bedchamber as well. Jamil had sent her here—she didn't doubt that. He had obviously left the order before he'd stormed out of the palace. If it had been left to Rahine to punish her, she would more likely have been severely beaten instead, the lady had been that angry with her. No, Jamil had put her here, probably thinking that this would shame her more than anything else, that she would regret losing her pampered existence in the harem and wish she had been more agreeable to him. Hah! He had done for her what she hadn't been able to figure out how to do for herself. He had put her out of his reach. Well, not exactly, but if enough time passed, he *would* forget about her. And as she had already concluded, why would he bother with her again when he had so many women who prayed to have his notice?

She had to count her blessings. It might not be a pleasant place to work, but thanks to her stay with Aunt Ellen, a kitchen was at least familiar ground. And they had made their own meals. The blustering cook, who was so quick with the slaps and the shouts, might not be an easy taskmaster, but Chantelle would eventually get along with the woman if it killed her. The main thing was, here she didn't have to worry about being summoned to share her lord's bed. For that relief she could put up with anything, the hostility, the ridicule, the constant work, even a slap from the Chief Cook when she did something wrong. Also, she would have a much better chance of escaping from the kitchens than the harem, whose every door was guarded. But that was for later, when she was acclimated and no longer under curious observation from nearly everyone.

Yesterday had been a normal workday, yet even with so many slaves on hand, Chantelle had still been kept busy, for this kitchen fed all the concubines and favorites of the Dey. Fayolo informed her that only the eunuchs' kitchen, one building over, was as busy, since there were three times as many eunuchs, but that the ideal kitchen to work in was Lalla Rahine's, which served only her.

"But what of the place guards and the slaves?"

Chantelle had wondered aloud. "Isn't their number even greater?"

"Much greater," Fayolo told her. "But their food is simple fare, requiring much less actual preparation."

Today Chantelle found out just how much preparation could go into one meal, and this for only ten people. She was awakened before dawn to help Fayolo get a young sheep ready for roasting. *Mechoui*, the dish was called, and Chantelle, so used to bringing home already butchered meat from the market, lost the leftover pastry she had quickly downed as her breakfast when she watched Fayolo plunge a knife into the carotid and blood spurt out. She had time to recover, however, since they had to wait until all the blood was drained, but then a hole was made with the knife point above the knee joint on one back leg and the skin loosened there. With nausea fast returning, she had to take turns with Fayolo blowing through this hole until the air reached the forelegs so the sheep could swell and stiffen.

Fayolo took pity on her and did the skinning, but the Chief Cook insisted Chantelle participate in scraping and rinsing the tripe, as well as singeing and cleaning the head and trotters. She was twice sick again before they finished, over which the cook and half the women there laughed heartily, but finally the sheep was impaled from tail to throat for slow roasting and basted in olive oil.

It would take five hours for the skin to become crackly and the flesh juicy, but Chantelle was not

250

given a respite. She also had to help cut up camel meat for the *tajin*, a stew that was so thick it was eaten with the fingers, while Fayolo made the couscous, a delicious-smelling dish of semolina with chicken and two sauces, one to moisten the semolina and one to spice the dish, with vegetables cooked down to a paste.

But the most arduous time was spent helping the Chief Cook with the *bstila* to round out this feast for ten. Never had Chantelle seen such a complicated dish for so few in number. Three actual pounds of butter were needed, thirty eggs, four pounds of flour, six pigeons, twelve ounces of sugar, a pound of almonds, and then the exact measurement of cinnamon, ginger, pimentos, onions, saffron, and coriander. What it turned into in the end was an enormous stuffed flaky pastry with one hundred and four thin individual layers of crust.

The *bstila* took all day to make, but Chantelle only had to help with the crusts in the afternoon, after the previous helper had fainted from the heat. During the few hours that she was under the cook's watchful eye, she received two separate slaps when she broke two of the thin crusts when setting them aside. Fayolo tried to change places with her, for she was the one basting the sheep, a much easier job, but she got a slap for the offer. Chantelle thought the cook was just being spiteful, until she heard one of the other women giggle that Noura had specifically requested that she have a hand in each preparation. And then she learned that this feast was Noura's idea, a surprise for the Dey, to be attended only by his wives and favorites.

For a split second, she wished she could get her hands on some poison. But by the time this magnificent feast was carried out, she wished only for her pallet. She was wilted, her hair and clothes damp with the sweat that had run off her all day, and so tired she could barely keep her eyes open. She was certainly too tired to eat her own dinner, which wouldn't be served for several hours yet, since the kitchen slaves didn't rest until the last concubine had been fed.

Fortunately, the cook must have found an ounce of pity in her large frame, because she sent Chantelle to bed, rather than ordering her to another table where food was still being prepared for the other ladies of the harem. Or maybe she just realized that Chantelle simply couldn't do any more today without dropping. The reason didn't matter. Chantelle was asleep the moment her head touched the pillow, her last thought of Jamil's second wife and how she would have liked to see her roasted instead of that poor young sheep, which she hoped they all choked on, especially Jamil.

Chapter Twenty-seven

"I'M NOT sure I want to invite you in with that long face, Haji," Rahine remarked when her old friend appeared at her door. "Didn't Jamil like Noura's surprise feast?"

"He seemed pleased."

"But not enough to mend his temper?"

"On the contrary, he seemed in very good spirits," Haji replied as he curled his old frame onto the pillow next to Rahine.

She sighed in exasperation when he said no more than that. "Spit it out, then. What did not happen as expected?"

"He wondered why Shahar was not among his favorites to enjoy the feast with him."

"What?" Rahine gasped. "But he must have been joking! A concubine cannot reach the status of favorite until she has found favor in his bed."

"He knows that, Rahine. But this situation is rather unique, you must agree. Never before has a new slave been summoned by him and then returned to the harem a virgin. As far as he is concerned, that first summons changed Shahar's status, regardless of how their evening ended."

"More deviations from custom?"

"So it seems."

"But doesn't he realize the confusion and resentment this will cause among the other women? You did point that out, didn't you?"

"Certainly."

"And?"

"He said he would rectify the situation tonight."

Rahine groaned. "No! How can he do this to me? Did he think I would do nothing when the girl defied him and made him so furious that he recklessly risked his life? Only by the grace of Allah and Jamil's own skill did he return that night unscathed. Does he think Shahar has been languishing in comfort just waiting for him to summon her again? He knows me better than that!"

"Perhaps with everything else that is on his mind right now, he simply didn't consider the possibility that you would punish her," Haji offered.

"Possibility!" Rahine shrieked the word. "There was no uncertainty involved. The girl deserved to be punished. I am only surprised that Jamil didn't attend to it himself."

"Perhaps that alone should have given us pause, Rahine. The fact that Jamil didn't punish her himself, especially when he has been so quick to deal with the slightest offense lately, should have made us at least hesitate—"

"You agreed with my decision at the time!" Rahine pointed out scathingly.

"I know, I know, and what is done cannot be changed. At least she has been in the kitchens only two days. How much damage could have been done in so little time?"

"But he doesn't know, does he? Or did you have the courage to tell him where I put her?"

Haji shook his head. "Maybe she won't mention it," he said hopefully.

"Don't count on it, Haji. I will have to tell him myself."

"Don't be a fool, Rahine. Why stir the pot to boiling when it is only simmering? If she mentions it, that will be soon enough to bear the brunt of his anger. And you only acted in his best interest. Perhaps these few days have changed the girl's dispostion. If so, he will have reason to be grateful, not furious."

"Perhaps." Rahine sighed. "But Allah's mercy, Jamil hasn't been the same since he first laid eyes on this girl. He has become completely unpredictable."

"Which is not a bad thing at this time," Haji remarked. "If we cannot predict what he will do next, neither can his enemies. He certainly surprised them the other night."

"But Omar was unable to learn anything from that cutthroat Jamil brought back with him. I still shudder to think how close they came to succeeding in killing him. He had no weapon on him, Haji! When has Jamil ever left the palace without a weapon before?"

"Which only proves the power this girl has over him, if she could upset him that much. I think it would be wise to be extremely careful in our dealings with her henceforth."

"I will see she has anything she wants if she is deserving of it," Rahine said with glowering irritation. "I won't change my policies in dealing with his women just because he has."

Haji shook his head at such stubbornness, but Rahine wouldn't be Rahine without it. "Will you at least strive for your renowned control where she is concerned? She seems to have the power to make you lose it, as well as your son."

Rahine made a very unladylike sound that caused

the eunuch to grin before she demanded, "I assume that you have already set things in motion and sent someone to fetch her to the baths?"

"Of course. The feast won't last but a few hours."

"Again we are expected to work miracles. So be it. What color did you select for her?"

"Blue, to soothe her nerves and his temper, should it arise again, Allah forbid."

Rahine's lips quirked finally. "Very appropriate, but then you can aways be depended upon to think of such things. I will bring along my sapphires to complement your choice. Hopefully the next time he summons her, she will have her own jewels."

"Your attitude is already improving, Rahine."

"Let us pray hers has as well."

Their prayers were not to be answered. One of the bath attendants met them before they reached the *hammam.*

Breathless from running, the girl cried fearfully, "You must hurry, *lalla!* Kadar is having difficulty restraining the English girl without hurting her!"

"Restraining? Why?"

"She is fighting him, *lalla.*"

Rahine scowled darkly. "Was someone stupid enough to tell her she had been summoned by the Dey?"

The girl's horrified expression was answer enough. "You can't blame them, Rahine," Haji said reasonably, though he was frowning now, too.

"It's an honor, after all, that anyone would assume—"

"The whole harem knows why she was banished to the kitchens! You can't keep secrets here." But then Rahine groaned. "Oh, never mind. What's done is done. So much for hoping she might be more agreeable this time." And then, determinedly: "Haji, you had better fetch something to calm her, and quickly. With all that we have to do to prepare her, there is no time for this silliness. I'll meet you there."

Rahine ran the rest of the way to the *hammam,* which was fortunately empty at this time of the evening except for a few attendants. The sight that met her eyes at first glance seemed an embrace, for Haji's slave, Kadar, had his arms wrapped around Shahar, her back to his chest, his head bent to her ear. It was only when Rahine saw Kadar's hands gripping the girl's wrists, which were crossed in front of her body, and the two bleeding stripes on Kadar's cheek, as well as the many smaller scratches on his arms, that the illusion ended. Shahar's face was also beet red from her straining with all her might to get free of Kadar's hold. She appeared not to hear at all the calming, beseeching words he was whispering in her ear.

"So we resort to violence again, do we?"

Chantelle glanced up to see Rahine's disapproving countenance and snapped, "Go to hell, madame!"

Rahine clucked her tongue. "I hope we aren't

257

going to rehash the same arguments, because the consequences of resisting your master still apply, you know."

"My so-called *master* isn't here, but if he was, you can bloody well believe I'd—"

The rest of that tempestuous statement was squeezed off as Kadar tightened his arms around her midsection. Rahine stepped closer and lifted Chantelle's chin to meet pure fury in the narrowed violet gaze. If eyes could snarl . . .

"So you obviously are incapable of learning from your mistakes. You are not ready to be returned to more comfortable quarters?"

"Never!" Then Chantelle accused, "You said he would forget me!"

"Wishful thinking on my part, I'm afraid," Rahine returned dryly.

"What happens this time when I resist him?"

"I honestly don't know, my dear. You've sorely tested his patience already. He isn't used to waiting for what he wants."

"Too bad," Chantelle sneered with such derision that Rahine actually chuckled. That only increased Chantelle's outrage. "I'm not going this time! Tell him I fell into a vat of stew and drowned!"

"Don't be ridiculous, child, You know very well that you have—"

"No choice?" Chantelle spat out. "Hah! You'll have to carry me there this time, and I swear I'll blacken Jamil's eye, too, if he lays one hand on me!"

"Too?" Rahine said in bemusement, glancing up at the eunuch, who met her look with a grimace. "Why, Kadar, is that actually swelling around your eye?"

He stoically refused to answer, but there was indeed a slight puffiness, though with his dark skin, no bruise was visible yet. Rahine shook her head in amazement.

"You're just full of surprises, aren't you, Shahar? But this really can't continue, you know."

"No, indeed," Haji said from behind her, having heard enough to realize that Rahine was wise in deciding to drug the girl. Rahine had never approved of resorting to drugs, not that it had ever been necessary since Jamil had come to power. But for her sake, he tried one other tack first, hoping to terrify the girl into compliance. "As long as we must carry her to Jamil, it won't matter too much if she has a taste of the bastinado first."

It didn't work, for Chantelle turned her lethal stare on him, screaming, "Go ahead! I don't give a bloody damn anymore what you do to me! It can't be any worse than submitting to that monster you all worship, that two-faced whoremaster, that bloody tyr—"

The word was choked off as Haji took advantage of her open mouth to shove a vial halfway down her throat. Fortunately, it wasn't made of glass, for Chantelle bit down so hard in reaction, she would have broken it with her teeth, cutting her mouth horribly. But Haji was the one to get hurt as she bucked and strained violently to shake the thing from her mouth. One foot caught him brutally on the shin, making him leap back. Chantelle immediately spat out the vial.

"You bas—tard." Her eyes closed slowly, then popped back open. "Damn you—" The eyes closed again.

Rahine gripped Haji's arm in alarm, watching Chantelle fight to keep her eyes open. "By the Prophet's beard, how much did you give her? It has never taken effect this quickly!"

Haji was himself alarmed. "No more than necessary."

"Did you take into account her frailty?"

"Frailty?" he snorted, rubbing his shin before he frowned. "No, actually, I was in too much of a hurry to recall her skinniness in comparison—"

"Forgive me for interrupting, master," Kadar cut in as Chantelle sagged in his arms, "but I was told by one of the kitchen women that the girl was worked from dawn until dusk preparing the Dey's feast. She was sleeping in a corner when I arrived to fetch her, so exhausted that the noise of two dozen chattering women could not keep her awake."

"By Allah, and still she fought like a demon," Haji said with a degree of admiration. "How does she do it?"

"She's English, Haji," Rahine said in answer, as if that were answer in itself.

Haji gave a snort of disgust for the pride he detected in Rahine's tone. "English or not, she can't be trusted to remain unconscious for long, no matter how tired she is. The girl's will is much too strong to succumb to mere exhaustion, even with the help of the relaxant I gave her. We had better take advantage of her incapacity and get her bathed and ready while we can." He nodded for Kadar to carry Shahar into the nearest bathing cubicle, motioning the cowering attendants as well as the terrified Adamma, who had arrived behind him with her cosmetic tray, to follow.

"We might have an easy time preparing her now," Rahine said, "but you realize Jamil is going to be furious if she arrives in this condition."

"We will have to get some coffee into her to counteract the drug," was all Haji could suggest.

"Will that work?"

"It should," he replied, hoping against hope that it actually would.

His assurance relieved Rahine, enough to send her thoughts onto a different path. "At least I can take this opportunity to get rid of the rest of her body hair. Thank Allah, Jamil didn't proceed far enough last time to discover her sinful state—"

"Rahine," Haji interrupted, "he did proceed that far. He even mentioned it to me, wanting to know how it was possible that she retained the curls between her legs."

"Did you tell him?"

He nodded, though his expression now held a touch of bemusement. "He actually laughed."

Rahine's brows shot up. "Laughed, as in amusement?"

He frowned at her own levity. "Yes, as in amusement," he retorted. "And he specifically ordered me to see to it that those silver curls are left alone."

Rahine found no humor in that. "But it's forbidden."

"Nothing is forbidden the Dey," he reminded her unnecessarily.

"The other women will see it when they bathe with her."

"Yes, and will want to grow their own hair back to emulate the current favorite."

Rahine sighed. "Do you really think Shahar will reach that status, to become his first *ikbal?*"

Hiji pursed his lips before replying, "If Jamil doesn't kill her in a fit of fury before he beds her."

Chapter Twenty-eight

CHANTELLE HAD to be guided down the entire length of the wide corridor, a hand firmly supporting each elbow. Her feet were moving of their own accord, but she was barely aware of it, and she couldn't seem to recall where she was being taken. Not that it mattered; her mind flitted from one undisturbing subject to another, between lapses of total blankness during which she actually slept on her feet.

The coffee that had been forced down her throat had revived her enough to leave a pleasant lassitude. Even when she was shaken to awareness and told that they had arrived at Jamil's door, she couldn't dredge up much interest, let alone fear. Jamil who? she wondered briefly before she was pushed to her knees; then her head dropped down and she promptly fell asleep.

Derek waited for Shahar to stir after Haji and Kadar bowed out of the room, but when several minutes had passed without even a little fidgeting on her part, he sighed. So he was going to have to start over again, to force each and every concession out of her. But had he really thought they could begin tonight where they had left off before? His body had certainly hoped so.

"Shahar, you may rise—and henceforth, I don't want to see you on your knees again. I will so inform Haji." If Derek thought this would please her, a privilege afforded only to Sheelah by Jamil, he got no immediate reaction. " Shahar?" he repeated, and when she still didn't respond: "Shahar!"

"What?" she replied in an irritated tone as she rose to her knees. Unfortunately, she came up so quickly she toppled right over. Derek stared at her in bemusement as he heard her giggle and ask, "Now, how did that happen?"

Derek didn't answer. He closed the distance between them and offered her a hand to help her rise. She took it immediately, surprising him further, and once again giggled.

"Thank you kindly, sir."

"You're welcome," he replied hesitantly, peering down into her face. "Are you all right?"

"Couldn't be better." She gave him a smile that took his breath away.

His fingers were instantly drawn to trace the line of those curving lips. But the moment he touched her, she pulled back.

"What do you think you're doing?" she demanded indignantly, shaking loose the hand that still held hers.

She took another step back, only to get tangled up in her own feet and sway dangerously before she righted herself. Her indignation was gone and she was once again giggling.

"My, that was clumsy of me, wasn't it? I really think I ought to sit down." She swept the room with a glance, swaying dangerously again and making him start to reach out to steady her, but he stopped when her eyes lit on him and she said in what amounted to a confiding whisper, "I hate to say so, sir, but you need a decorator. Not a single chair? Where's a body to sit itself, I ask you?"

Derek's brows were already narrowing as he suggested, "You might try the bed."

"Absolutely not!" The indignation had returned. "Whatever would Aunt Ellen say?"

It was the last straw. He grabbed her hand and yanked her to the bed, which she fell back on with a small shriek. He stood there glowering down at her, only to watch her eyes slowly close and to hear a contented sigh as she settled more comfortably into the soft mattress.

"Oh, no, you don't!" he growled, leaning over to shake her shoulders. "Look at me!" he commanded harshly, and when she did, he asked, "Do you know who I am?"

She stared at him with keen concentration for nearly a half minute, her eyes moving over every inch of his face, before she finally said, "Yes."

That wasn't good enough. "Who am I?"

"You're that bloody cold fish who condemns innocent women to fates worse than—."

She said it without rancor, but still he put a hand over her mouth to silence her. Christ, Jamil probably would have slapped her unconscious before she got past the "bloody," not that it would take much to render her unconscious at the moment. Her eyes were already closing again.

He let go of her, swearing under his breath, then grabbed her and shook her furiously again. "What the hell did you take to make this easier? Answer me, dammit!"

She blinked at him. "Take?"

"Don't play games with me, woman! I want to know what you drank and who gave it to you!"

She discovered her indignation again. "Are you accusing me of being drunk, sir? I'll have you know—"

"Arghhhh!" The scream exploded from his lungs.

He came off the bed in a towering rage, barely able to recall the silent language of the mutes, which he had learned as a child, in order to send one of them after the Chief Black Eunuch. A stream of epithets followed as he waited for Haji's return, pacing in front of the bed. Every few moments he cast Shahar a fulminating glare, which she was blissfully unaware of since she was now soundly asleep.

He felt like wringing her neck. How dared she attempt to escape him in this way? My God, Jamil would have the skin off her back for such audacity, and off her accomplice's, too, for she couldn't have obtained whatever she took on her own. And knowing what could have happened to her if his brother were here instead only made him more furious with her. The stupid little half-wit!

Haji burst into the room out of breath, took one look at Shahar sprawled half on the bed and then at Derek's murderous expression, and dropped to his knees. "It was necessary, my lord, I swear! She was so out of control that we feared she would harm herself. I gave her only enough relaxant to calm her. I just didn't know she was already so tired—"

"Then she didn't do this deliberately?"

"No, Jamil, no. I take full responsi—"

"*Why* was she out of control?"

Even though the question was snapped out, Haji was able to breathe again. The murderous look was gone, replaced by one of only extreme aggravation though that was nothing to relax over. Jamil aggravated was as quick to issue punishment as Jamil in a towering rage these days. And Haji was afraid that the "why" he wanted answered was going to tip the scale again.

"You will not like the reason," Haji warned, to ease the suspected reaction.

"I don't suppose I will, but tell me anyway. . . . No, don't. I can well guess." He gave the girl another baleful stare before shouting for a servant, who fortunately appeared immediately. "I want some *kanyak* and plenty of it." To Haji, when he noticed the old man's surprised look, he said, "I need it." And he bloody well did.

Christ, so much for hoping fear might bring Shahar around. Or did she no longer fear him? Perhaps he should have punished her in some small way instead of simply sending her back to the harem, which obviously made her think there were no consequences to suffer by defying him. But, dammit, he couldn't bring himself to punish her in any way. She couldn't be blamed for her reaction to him. It was perfectly natural after what Jamil had forced her to witness. That he wasn't Jamil made no difference. She thought he was.

"Son of a bitch!"

"My lord?"

"Oh, get up, Haji," Derek snapped. "You're too old to be wearing out your knees on the floor."

Haji got hesitantly to his feet, not understanding Jamil's present mood at all. Jamil never touched spirits, never. His brother Mahmud had, and had been known to order the execution of luckless innocents while under the influence. Mustafa had occasionally drunk, too, in his later years, on a moderate scale. But Jamil? That he intended to drink himself into a stupor with so

267

much ordered *kanyak* was not only alarming in its unusualness but unnerving given his unpredictable temper. And that he should think he needed it . . .

"Let me summon Sheelah, my lord. She will ease—"

"No," Derek cut in bitterly. "My desire is for this one." He flung a hand in Shahar's direction, following it with another look at her relaxed body, which only served to increase his frustration. "So she didn't even wait this time until she was here to let loose her stubborn defiance? Did you know the English were so stubborn, Haji?" He glanced back at the old eunuch and gave a harsh laugh at his bemusement. "Of course you know. You've lived all these years with the most stubborn Englishwoman of them all, haven't you?"

Haji knew better than to defend Rahine to Jamil. "Shahar's presence annoys you, my lord. Let me remove her."

"She stays."

Haji didn't dare argue with that tone. "Of course, my lord."

"But you may go—as soon as you tell me exactly what my little *ikbal* did that you feared would cause her harm."

Haji was incredulous to hear Shahar called his lord's favorite still, but he wished the question hadn't been worded exactly that way. He had a reprieve, however, when several bottles of the very potent *kanyak* arrived on a tray with a single glass, which the servant quickly filled before scurrying

268

out of the room. Then Haji's eyes bulged to see the glass drained and Jamil refill it himself this time.

"Well?"

Haji cleared his throat. There was no help for it. "She fought most violently the moment she learned you had summoned her."

"Who did she fight?"

"My slave, Kadar, and he bears the marks of her resistance. But I swear he was as gentle as it was possible to be in restraining her, my lord. She simply refused to give up the fight."

"Didn't you think to inform me instead of drugging her? If she's going to fight anyone, I prefer it to be me."

"But, my lord!" Haji was appalled by the suggestion. "You would then have been forced to punish her—"

"Like hell I would!" Derek snapped, forgetting himself. And then he sighed. "Never mind. You may go, Haji. And compensate your Kadar for his trouble."

"He would never accept, my lord," Haji protested, explaining, "He likes the girl."

Derek had to remind himself that it was a eunuch and not a whole man who liked his Shahar, though why he should even think of this annoyed him. "Does he?" he grunted, but after a moment added, "Send him here, Haji."

"Now, my lord?" Haji questioned, afraid his slave would receive the brunt of Jamil's displea-

269

sure tonight, since he was obviously determined to direct it away from the girl.

"Yes, now."

"As you wish."

Derek had finished yet another glass of the brandy-wine combination before the younger eunuch knocked for admittance. The door opened hesitantly to his growled command to enter, but the giant black man who stepped inside displayed no fear, though his eyes refused to focus on Derek. He bowed with a measure of dignity, rather than prostrating himself. Derek couldn't have cared less, for he was too fascinated with Kadar's battered face.

"By Allah, she's a regular little wildcat, isn't she?"

And he burst out laughing, surprising Kadar enough that their eyes met now.

"The little English, my lord?"

"Yes, the little English," Derek replied, a smile settling on his lips even as he shook his head incredulously. "Did she really give you that black eye?"

"She did not mean to," Kadar protested quickly.

"Oh, I'm sure, just as she didn't mean to leave those gouges on your cheek."

"Truly—"

Derek stopped him immediately. "You don't have to protect her with excuses, Kadar, not to me, but I'm glad to see you try. In fact, I'm going to make it your sole responsibility, protecting her."

"I don't understand, my lord."

"I believe I can persuade Haji Agha to give you to Shahar. Would you like that?"

"To serve the little English?" Kadar beamed. "It will be my greatest pleasure, lord. Thank you!"

"I wouldn't thank me. I doubt it will be an easy job, serving such a contrary female, but that wasn't what I had in mind. She'll have others to serve her. Your job will be to see that she comes to no harm when she's not with me."

And when she is with you? Kadar wanted to ask but didn't dare. "I will protect her with my life," he said instead.

"That's all I can ask. But see that you protect her from herself as well."

"My lord?"

"She panicked tonight. I don't want that to happen again. The sooner she accepts me, the sooner she will accept life here and find a degree of happiness. Do we understand each other?"

Kadar was afraid they did, though he didn't know how *he* could persuade the little English to accept her lord when no one else had been able to, including Jamil Reshid.

Chapter Twenty-nine

DEREK CAME awake slowly to a tickling on his chest and an unfamiliar weight resting against him. He reacted badly for a moment, with no memory coming forth for an explanation until he raised his head and saw the platinum locks spilling across his chest. He relaxed back into his pillow, a strange contentment settling over him.

At least in sleep Shahar didn't hate him. She wasn't exactly curled up next to him, but she was using his chest as a pillow, her knees bent and braced against his hips, one hand pressed flat against his side, the other somehow tucked under his back. His hand had been resting on her side, too, just beneath her breast. He didn't move it, didn't move at all, afraid she would wake up and pull away.

He hadn't meant to sleep with her. At some time during the evening he had placed her under the covers, removing only the jewels she wore. Removing anything else had been out of the question with how he had been feeling. She hadn't wakened then, and he had sat on the bed a long time just gazing at her, until he'd remembered that he wasn't alone with her.

The ever-present Nubians had been in their customary positions on each side of the bed, so silent it was no wonder he had forgotten their presence in the room. They might not hear his conversations with Shahar, but they had eyes, and they were able to communicate with anyone who knew their silent language of hand signals and body movements, which meant just about anyone raised in the palace. Which was also why he had concluded he would sleep with Shahar. It was either that or send her back to the harem, for Jamil would never give up his bed, even if it was occupied with a passed-out concubine. And Derek had been loath to have her carried away, regardless of how disturbing her presence was to him.

But it had been a long time before he'd been able to bring his body sufficiently under control, enough to trust himself to lie next to her. The *kanyak* certainly hadn't helped, and he had given up on it when he was still cold sober, after the first bottle had been emptied. Which was fortunate now, for he felt no aftereffects, but hadn't been fortunate last night, for it had taken a hell of a long time for him to finally fall asleep, as well as to will away the tumescence that had sprung to life again with his proximity to the sleeping beauty.

He could feel it happening again, more strongly than ever. Derek groaned, unaware that he squeezed Chantelle's side, enough to waken her.

Her reaction was much worse than his had been upon waking. She was frankly horrified at the sight of bare skin beneath her cheek, and she didn't have to wonder whose it was. She knew instantly. She just couldn't account for how it had gotten there.

"So you are awake?"

Had she moved? She thought she was too paralyzed to move a muscle. Or had the fact that she had stopped breathing given her away?

His hand left her side to glide into her hair. "I know you are awake, Shahar. It is no use pretending otherwise."

She raised her head just enough to turn it toward him. She found no answers in his expression. "Did we—did you—"

"When I do," he interrupted, lips twitching, "you won't have to ask."

"I don't believe you," she said daringly, chagrined that she couldn't remember.

"You are still wearing your clothes, if you care to notice. Do you really think I would bother to redress you after I had made love to you? I assure you I wouldn't."

She glanced down at her chest. Every button was still closed on the little blue vest, and now she could feel the material against her legs under the cover. She looked back at him, her eyes still narrowed accusingly.

"Then what am I doing here?"

He smiled at her. "In my room, or in my bed?"

"Oh, God!"

His laughter caused her chin to bounce against his chest. She sat up immediately, glaring back at him.

"I don't see—"

In a second, Chantelle was flat on her back with him leaning over her, though not so close that she panicked—yet. "You don't see anything, Shahar, because you don't remember anything, do you? What the devil were you doing yesterday that so exhausted you?"

As if he didn't know. No, she had to be fair. He might have sent her to the kitchens, but it was his second wife who had seen to it that she'd had no rest yesterday. The day before, she had been able to take several short naps to make up for her sleepless night. But yesterday . . . She wondered if Noura had known that Jamil would send for her last night, or if Noura had just been spiteful. What did it matter, however, in light of what had happened in the baths?

It was slowly coming back to her, and with the memories, a bone-chilling fear. If she hadn't been so tired, she never would have reacted the way she had when she reached the *hammam* and was told why she was there, but that was no excuse. She had actually balked and fought against being brought to Jamil again. Good God, she could have been really hurt for such behavior, beaten or worse. Gone completely had been the logical conclusion she had reached before, that her virginity wasn't worth her life.

What had been his reaction? He must have been furious. He had to have demanded an explanation for her condition. So why hadn't she awakened chained to a whipping post instead of lying comfortably in his bed, using him for a pillow?

She had been staring at him with wide eyes, trying to glean something of his thoughts, anything, but there was nothing, just those dark green eyes watching her. Such a look brought to mind the way he had been when she had first met him, and when he was like that, he was capable of anything. But she reminded herself that he had smiled earlier, and laughed, too. His mood couldn't be that dangerous, although his last question had been rather harsh. And she wasn't going to answer

him. Even if he wasn't aware of why yesterday had been particularly grueling for her, he did
know she had been working these past two days,
so he had no business questioning her fatigue. She
wasn't about to bring up the subject of her last
punishment when she didn't know yet what her
new punishment would be.

"Were you angry?"

It was as if he had only been waiting for her to
speak for his expression to relax and his eyes to
warm. "Extremely."

"I don't feel as if I've been beaten."

Derek chuckled. "Perhaps because you haven't
been."

"Yet?"

"No, little moon." He was smiling, his voice
low-pitched, a soothing timbre. "It would be a
crime to mar this tender skin."

As he said it, his hand smoothed a path down
her arm. On reaching her wrist, he picked it up
and brought her fingers to his lips. He kissed one
and gently bit the next one. Gooseflesh shot up
her arm and spread down her back.

"Do you remember what I taught you about
kissing? Put your finger in my mouth, Shahar."

He didn't wait for her to do it but caught
the third finger with his lips and sucked it inside
his mouth. The strangely pleasant sensation was
immediate and alarming, making her snatch her
hand away.

"I agree," he said, leaning toward her. "Tongues
are much better."

Her hands came up to stop him, lodging against his shoulders, but she needn't have bothered, for his mouth reached hers anyway. His tongue pressed against her lips. which she refused to open. He leaned back, his expression half chagrined, half amused.

"I see you have forgotten after all," he allowed, instead of mentioning her resistance. "But remember where you are, sweetheart, and that I can just as soon amuse myself with other things quite easily."

One hand slipped behind his neck to draw his lips back to her now-open mouth, but he could barely oblige her for chuckling at this swift reaction to his not-so-subtle threat. "I am . . . delighted by . . . your . . . enthusiasm, but . . ."

The thought was lost when her other hand tentatively touched his cheek. Derek groaned, claiming her mouth completely for a long dueling of tongues that left him burning with need. Her innocence was the farthest thing from his mind. This flame had consumed him once too often. It took control now, throbbing in his groin until he thought he would die if he couldn't have more of her.

Chantelle was melting under his gentle attack. Her limbs seemed to have liquefied, her strength flowing away, leaving a fire behind that frightened her, and yet she had no desire to halt its course. Far from it. What she was feeling was so delicious, so intoxicating, she couldn't question it. She just wanted it to go on forever.

Senses reeling in discovery, she was barely aware of the hand that had slipped beneath her vest to squeeze the flesh there. It was warm, but so was the belly pressed to hers, so was the leg that covered her own, so was the mouth that had taken control of her will. Then that mouth left hers and exploded in white-hot heat against her breast.

It was too much, one new sensation too many, especially when this one was the most powerful. His mouth enclosing over her nipple, his tongue softly stabbing at it, was a violent shock that brought her hands flying to his head to jerk him away.

"Don't."

The low growl stopped her in an instant. It also stiffened her body. Fear was all she felt now, but still she would stop him again if his mouth returned to her breast.

It didn't. He was aware that the desire he had ignited in her had disappeared. He had gone too far too fast again for such an innocent. But realizing that didn't ease his pain.

Derek dropped his forehead to her chest, desperately fighting the urge to ignore the fact that she had become cold and unyielding, to simply take her and end his torture. It was going to happen eventually. Why the bloody hell should he wait and suffer like this?

Because he didn't want her to hate him any more than she already did. Because he wanted her soft and willing and wanting him with equal fervor. Anything less and he would feel cheated. But knowing that didn't cool off his body any quicker either.

He felt her hands at his shoulders, pushing very gently but insistently. She wanted a distance between them. He only wanted to get closer. He considered for a moment that in the role he was assuming, his wishes were the only ones that mattered. The trouble was, he couldn't play that role without alienating her further. With anyone else it didn't matter. With her, and only her, because she didn't really know the true Jamil, he could be different, more himself. But not too different. Women gossiped and compared notes, after all, and every other woman in the harem knew Jamil intimately. He couldn't have Shahar wondering about her deferential treatment or mentioning it to anyone.

"I am trying very hard to ignore the fact that I have you exactly where I want you, Shahar. But if you can't find some patience and be as still as possible to make it easier for me, I am going to give up the effort."

Her hands fell away from his shoulders, but for some reason, he resented her quick compliance this time. That she would do anything to keep him from making love to her was blatantly apparent and shattering to his ego. He wondered just how far she would go to delay the inevitable. He wondered if he could withstand putting her to the test.

He leaned back to pierce her with his emerald

gaze. "I will assume that you object to being made love to in the bright light of day, rather than that you find my touch offensive. Am I correct?"

His displeasure was so obvious to her that she was afraid to accept the excuse he offered, let alone deny it with the truth, which wasn't that his touch was offensive, just that its effect on her was frightfully disturbing. She simply didn't understand what happened to her when he touched her, why it felt so good when he kissed her, why her skin became so sensitive it felt as if she burned, why he should affect her at all.

"You don't answer."

She groaned inwardly, hating this new mood of his that could attack with such calm deliberation. "Please, can't I just leave now?"

"No, we are going to talk, you and I, to discuss things that interest me, such as how you can be so warm and wet for me one moment, then turn cold and unyielding the next."

"I wasn't—I didn't."

"Oh, but you did, and I want your secret, Shahar. Perhaps then I can control my passion as easily. I can't, you see, at least not where you are concerned. So tell me. I truly want to know."

Just from the way he said it, she knew instinctively that nothing would satisfy him except the truth. And it wasn't secrets he wanted. She knew that. He wanted to know why she had stopped his lovemaking when she had.

"I was frightened."

"Of what?" His tone softened a degree. "Haven't you realized yet that I won't hurt you?"

"But it did hurt."

"What did?"

"The heat."

He stared at her for a long, curious moment. "Is your skin really that sensitive, Shahar? Does this burn you?"

She sucked in her breath and began to squirm as his hand closed over her breast. She had been completely unaware that it had been bared to him all this time, ever since he had lifted the vest to taste of it.

"Please—"

"Did it burn?" he repeated, though he took his hand away and even tugged the little strip of thin cloth back down to cover her.

"No," she admitted, closing her eyes against the acute embarrassment she felt about this subject. "It—it was your mouth."

He smiled at her, though she didn't see it. "The mouth is known to be a rather warm part of the body, little moon. Perhaps you were only startled by its heat, since you are not yet accustomed to it. But I do assure you that you are not burned, and what you felt was natural, if a little extreme. It will not be such a shock to you next time."

Her eyes flew open at that. "Next time?"

He thought better of smiling at her consternation. "Your taste is sweetness itself, Shahar. Do you really think I will deny myself your nectar now that I've discovered it?"

"I—"

"Shh. Tell me what you felt before I shocked you. You liked it when I was kissing you, didn't you?" She started to shake her head, but he stopped her again. "Don't lie to me, Shahar."

That he already knew the answer rubbed her on the raw. "Then don't ask me what I felt!"

He was surprised by her vehemence, but he shouldn't have been. It wasn't going to be easy to make her admit to any pleasure she experienced at his hands, not as long as she was so set against him.

"Then I will tell you," he said softly, placing his hand on her belly. "You felt warm and weak and trembling. Your pulses raced, your senses throbbed, and heat unfurled in your vitals."

"How did you—" She caught herself on that revealing question, but too late.

"Because I felt it, too," he replied, his hand circling her belly in a warm caress. "It's called desire, and it has a will of its own that cannot be denied. Do you feel it now?"

He looked down at his hand on her skin and she did, too, and panicked, because she *did* feel that heat unfurling inside her again. "No!"

She reached out to pull his hand away, only to have her fingers locked in his. She tried to pull her own hand away and ended up having it pinned to the bed. She began to struggle in earnest then, until she heard his deep chuckle and realized she was accomplishing nothing.

"If you think you can fight me as you did

Kadar, you are welcome to try it. But I warn you, he was very limited in what he could do to restrain you. I am not." And then his brows narrowed, seeing her fear. "Don't look at me like that, woman. Have I hurt you even once? Did I punish you when you refused me before? No, and I will not this time either. Doesn't that prove anything to you?"

Chantelle caught her breath. Had she heard him right? Of course she had. So he was not the one responsible for her kitchen duty. His mother was, and he obviously didn't know anything about it. And if he did know? She had a feeling he wouldn't like it, because for some reason he was trying to impress her with his benevolence, and petty punishments would ruin that impression. But someone else could tell him if he or she dared. Chantelle wasn't about to risk his anger, even if it wasn't directed at her, especially in her present precarious position of lying half beneath him in his bed.

"You seem surprised, Shahar." He was watching her thoughtfully. "Don't you believe me?"

Believe him? What had he said? Oh, that he hadn't hurt her. Yes, she supposed that was true —so far. But there was more than one face to this man, and she had seen the face that could terrify her.

"No, I—I'm not surprised—just confused—yes, confused. The one thing that has been repeatedly told to me is that I can't refuse you the use of my—well, I can't refuse you. Now you're telling me that it's all right. Who do I believe?"

"Me, of course," he said with an engaging grin that had her staring at his mouth for in inordinate amount of time. When her eyes returned to his, they seemed to be smiling at her, too. "Ah, sweet girl, what am I going to do with you? I can't have you thinking that it is all right to refuse me. It will upset the whole balance of my harem. I did not say it was all right, only that you wouldn't he punished."

"Then—"

"Let me finish. You will not always refuse me. You will accept me of your own accord when the time is right." He put his hand to her cheek to stop her from shaking her head to deny it. "You will, Shahar, I promise you. You felt desire for me this morning. You felt it the other evening. It is not something that you can ignore for long." His fingers moved to her throat to caress the pulse there. "Even now my touch excites you."

"That's fear," she murmured breathlessly.

He chuckled. "What a little liar you are. Of course, I will allow it is easy to mistake the one emotion for the other when they are so similar. But I believe you know the difference by now. Just don't deceive yourself for too long, Shahar. What we will have together will be beautiful, if you will just let it happen."

He was telling her, without saying the words, that he had only so much patience. She supposed she should be grateful he had any at all. She certainly hadn't expected it of him. But then she hadn't expected him to be so considerate of her feelings either. How was she to deal with such unpredictability?

She didn't know how to answer him, so she didn't. But he was waiting for her to make some comment after those last disturbing statements. Perhaps she could put him on the defensive for a change.

"Won't it seem strange, your keeping me here so long? I was told you spend the night only with your wives."

He turned away from her to sit on the side of the bed, giving her his back. She was relieved to see that although he had removed his tunic to sleep, he had worn his trousers to bed. For her sake?

She was almost sorry now that she had annoyed him with her question, and she certainly had. The muscles along his back were taut, and she could see one hand where it gripped the edge of the bed, the knuckles white. Why should that particular question bother him?

"No one questions what I do, Shahar." He said this without glancing at her. "They would not dare. You will not question me either."

Her eyes flared, as did her temper. What bloody, autocratic nerve! "In other words, you can ask me anything you like, no matter how improper, but I can't ask you anything?"

"Exactly."

Her mouth started to drop open, but she

285

snapped it shut, grinding her teeth for a moment. She had the powerful urge to hit him square in that hard back he was still presenting to her, but her anger hadn't quite overridden good sense yet.

Tightly, she asked, "May I go now—your highness?"

She was not going to call him "my lord," as most everyone else did, for that would only reinforce their positions. And she knew "highness" was just one of many names that were acceptable to call him, though she could think of numerous others she would have preferred to use.

She watched his shoulders droop almost tiredly, though his tone was still curt. "Yes, go."

Thank God she was dressed. It would have been mortifying to have to wait to put her clothes on, but then it would have been mortifying to wake up naked in bed beside him, too. And that could have been a distinct possibility, considering that she had passed out in his bed.

Realizing that he could have done anything he liked to her unconscious body, but hadn't, took a little steam out of her indignation. Finally standing up and seeing the two Nubian guards for the first time knocked the remaining wind out of her.

Good Lord, they had been there all along, even when Jamil was—when he . . .

Hot color flooded her cheeks. How could she not have known, or sensed their presence so close? But, of course, her attention had been captured by Jamil from the moment she had awakened, to the exclusion of all else. And they might not be look-

286

ing at her now, their focus straight ahead, might not have glanced at her as she lay next to Jamil, under him, letting him . . .

With a small sound of dismay, Chantelle made straight for the door. But to reach it, she had to come around the bed and pass in front of Jamil, who still faced in that direction.

"Shahar?"

She stopped, groaning inwardly. She might have dismissed him temporarily from her mind, but he apparently had not dismissed her, even though he had seemed to.

"You are forgetting something."

His voice didn't sound quite so brusque now, but she still turned around hesitantly, to be met with the powerful image of him sitting there nearly naked on the bed. Wariness receded, replaced by pure fascination. She hadn't really looked at his bare chest before, but now she couldn't help it. Sleek muscles were visible, as well as a faint scattering of black curls across his breastbone. Even though he wasn't sitting perfectly straight, there was no rippling of skin across the hard stomach. And the shoulders seemed so wide in that position, with his arms still braced on each side of the bed. They were powerful arms, deceiving when adorned in his rich tunics, but so obvious now as to be disconcerting. When she had thought of his power, it had been in relation to his authority, not to his physique. His height might have been daunting, but he had seemed so lean, his movements so graceful, she had not imagined there might be hard strength beneath the surface.

She saw him now as a man, not as the Dey, and a very impressive man. She once again felt the overwhelming attraction she had experienced when she'd first laid eyes on him. Fortunately, it was that self-same body that both aroused this new attraction and helped to tamp it down, for it was blatantly clear now that there was enough strength there to force her to his will if his authority could not.

Annoyed with herself for allowing him to see her fascination with his body, Chantelle dragged her eyes up to his, treating him to the contradiction of her emotions, blazing eyes and a trembling lower lip, which she stilled by sucking a portion beneath her teeth a moment before asking. "What did I forget—your highness?"

That slight pause was enough to bring his brows together. Her refusal to call him anything less impersonal was deliberate, and now he knew it. She didn't care. The only thing she could have forgotten was to bow herself out of the room, and if he was going to be so arrogant as to insist on it, she felt she would scream.

He said simply, "Come here."

"Must I?"

"Come here," he repeated without raising his voice.

That he completely ignored her flippancy was the only reason she didn't consider refusing. She moved toward him, albeit very slowly, but stopped several feet away.

"There," he said.

Chantelle looked down where his hand indicated, to see a bundle of material on the floor by his feet, clothes, she assumed, that he had discarded before getting into bed. But resting on top, as if on a bed of white silk, was a small pile of sapphires. She'd never seen them before to her recollection, and could only think that he meant to pay her for sleeping in his bed, even if nothing had come of it.

Indignation stiffened her spine, and her eyes flashed back to his. "I don't want them."

A single brow rose at this response. "Interesting," he said, and after a long pause, "but irrelevant." He bent down to retrieve the jewels, and once dangling from his fingers, they were revealed to be mounted in silver, three tiers of different sizes and cuts, forming a magnificent necklace that had to be worth a fortune.

Cheeks reddened with the assumption that he meant to buy her affection, she repeated stiffly, "I don't want them."

He surprised her by smiling at her, as if he found her show of indignation amusing. He did, she realized, when he said, "A necklace such as this might be presented to a woman on the birth of a child, not for what you are thinking. As it happens, you arrived wearing it, and so you will leave wearing it, to return it to its rightful owner."

"Your mother," Chantelle said, flushing even

more as she realized her mistake. "She lent me the pearls, so she must have . . . You can return them to her as easily as I," she finished, not wanting to take even a single step closer to retrieve the necklace from him.

He had other ideas, leaning forward enough to catch her arm and bring her right between his knees. When she tried pulling back, his hold tightened.

"Are you that afraid of me?"

She heard the anger in the question but didn't care. Pride made her snap back, "No," even if it wasn't true.

"Then be still," he ordered. "I only mean to put the necklace on you, since it was I who took it off. You will leave here as you came, Shahar."

He released her, daring her to step back. She didn't. An image had come to her from his words, of him removing the necklace, touching her skin, while she slept blissfully unaware. The unfurling of warmth in her belly surprised her so, she gasped. How could that happen from an image?

"I'm waiting."

Recalled to herself, she didn't understand for a moment what he was waiting for, and when she did, she balked. Since he hadn't stood up to put the necklace on her, he obviously wanted her to kneel down before him. It was too much, too subservient, too demeaning.

"I don't have to wear the necklace to return it." She held out her hand for him to simply give it to her.

"I insist."

"Well, you can just go—"

In whatever direction she had meant to send him was lost in a small gasp as one of his feet came around to press against the back of her knees, buckling them, and his hands on her sides forced her down and kept her down. She had to look up to see him, and she did, murderously.

"Are you happy now?" she demanded shrilly.

"I will be happy when you stop fighting me," he replied with a tinge of regret, then added softly, "This was not meant to humble you, little moon. I will grasp any excuse to wrap my body around you, to feel—"

"You said I could go!" she cried, eyes flaring.

"And so you can. I still mean only to put the necklace on you. Lift your hair for me and it will be done."

She did not know what to make of him. Wrap his body around her? God, how weak that image made her feel . . . .

Quickly, to get it over with, she lifted the weight of her hair off her neck. He picked up the necklace from where he had dropped it on the bed. And then he stared at her for a long moment before he slowly, very slowly, slipped the cold metal around her neck.

Chantelle shivered, not so much from the coldness, but from the warmth of his fingers that were there, too. Then he leaned closer to fasten the clasp, and she did find his body wrapped around her, his arms, his chest, his knees pressed to each side of her hips.

The cold, the heat, the contact of her cheek against his chest, all combined to make her forget her anger. It was like being enclosed in a warm, safe cocoon. Safe? Yes, somehow she did feel safe for the moment. He had said she could go, so she had nothing to fear from this embrace except perhaps her own reaction to it. God, it did feel good to have him surround her like this.

The regret she felt when he removed his hands from her neck was real. She looked up at him in bemusement, to find him smiling at her.

"Was that so hard?"

She refused to answer, pride pushing away what he had made her feel. "Can I go *now?*"

"Yes." But his hand on her shoulder stayed her when she started to rise. "As soon as I have your word that you will come to me tonight when you are summoned."

"But—"

"Your word, Shahar, or you don't leave me now."

"Nothing has changed," she told him plainly.

"I did not think it had, but you will come here anyway, and we will see what happens. Your word?"

She bit her lip in indecision, then finally nodded. This brought his hand to her cheek for a soft caress and an even softer warning. "Save your fighting for me, little moon. If you have not noticed, I have accepted the challenge."

When she rushed from the room, it was with a certain degree of dread, but something else as well. She wasn't ready to admit it might be anticipation.

Chapter Thirty

CHANTELLE COULDN'T work up much interest in her new "prison cell." She now had two rooms instead of one, and both were three times larger than her previous cubicle. Very nice, she supposed, with Rhodian tiled walls and marble floor in the anteroom, where large pillows surrounded a low table. There was even a little fountain in the center of the room, and latticed windows facing a large court of pink marble.

In her bedchamber, she had a rose canopied bed instead of a pallet, and a large chest already filled with a dozen of the skimpy outfits she thought of as underwear. There were shelves behind a lacquered screen for her cosmetics, oils, and perfumes, and a magnificent Turkish carpet of crimson and gold covering most of the floor. Here there was another window, this one overlooking the walled-in garden of the favorites, where a larger fountain gurgled among beds of carnations, tulips, and dark purple lilies. A jasmine shrub just below the window allowed the sweet scent to drift in with the breeze.

She had been brought here directly from Jamil's apartment, where Kadar had again been waiting for her out in the hall. She had been too ashamed to look at the giant eunuch with his battered face that she was responsible for, and so hadn't really noticed where he was taking her until she stood in the doorway of her new abode. Adamma was there beaming at her, but so was Haji Agha, so Chantelle didn't see anything out of the ordinary in being brought here.

It was Kadar who enlightened her. "This is yours now, *lalla*, as am I."

Chantelle whirled around to see him grinning from ear to ear. A gambit of emotions crossed her own features, guilt on seeing the evidence on his face and arms of the violence she was capable of, anger that Kadar could be given away so easily, suspicion as to the reason, and finally amusement, for his grin was so infectious, she couldn't help but return it. But only for a moment, and only Kadar was treated to her brief smile.

Haji Agha got the brunt of her suspicion. "Is this true? Does he belong to me now?"

The older eunuch nodded hesitantly, taken aback by her feral tone. He was unused to such directness in a society that insisted on the exchange of pleasantries before any discussion, no matter how serious. And he certainly had never before been attacked when a concubine was informed of her improved status in the harem.

"You are not pleased?" Haji stated the obvious.

Chantelle waved her arm impatiently. "What has that to do with anything, when it's never before mattered if I was pleased or not? I want to know why you're giving Kadar to me."

"It was Jamil's wish," he replied simply.

"His wish? Oh, of course," Chantelle sneered. "How foolish of me to forget that your great master can do anything, even force you to give away your own slaves."

"I was well compensated," Haji tried to tell her.

She was quick to snap, "Good for you."

Haji shook his head at this attitude. "If you don't want Kadar—"

She cut him off. "You still haven't told me why he's been given to me."

"Every favorite has her own personal eunuch. You must know that by now." He said this with surprise.

Chantelle surprised him further. "I'm not a favorite, Haji." She was too angry to address him with the respect he was due. "I know how things are done around here, and I know that no concubine can aspire to be a favorite until she has first—" Embarrassment nearly choked her. "Suffice it to say I don't meet the criterion yet."

"Then you haven't—"

"No, I haven't."

"I thought surely this morning—" He stopped at the emphatic shake of her head. "This is amazing," he added incredulously.

"Hardly," Chantelle snorted. "You've been presumptuous, is all."

"Not quite, Shahar."

She didn't like the obvious pleasure he found in contradicting her. "I've told you—"

"It doesn't matter. You are here because Jamil ordered me to move you here. You are now his first *ikbal*, regardless that you have yet to share his bed. It is unusual, certainly, but we do not question the Dey's wishes."

"And if I don't want to stay here? No, forget I asked. I'm sick of being told I don't have a choice." In the midst of her rancor, another thought occurred to her. "If Kadar belongs to me, then I can set him free, can't I?" That Haji *and* Kadar both shouted, "No!" simultaneously made her cringe. "Oh, for God's sake, all right. Where did I get the ridiculous idea that I could do something *I* wanted to do?"

"*Lalla*, if you don't want me, Haji Agha will find you another."

She turned to Kadar and felt ashamed that her mood, which had nothing to do with him, had wounded him. "No, Kadar. If I must have my own eunuch, I'm glad it's you, honestly I am, though I don't see how you could be pleased about it."

But he was. His renewed grin told her that. And Haji seemed pleased now, too, as he took his leave of them, no doubt thinking he had weathered this storm without too much damage.

Chantelle tried to hide her dissatisfaction when Adamma insisted on showing her everything, bubbling over with her own enthusiasm. But Chantelle simply wasn't interested in her new apartment.

She couldn't help concluding that Jamil was too confident, that he had put her here because it was just a matter of time before she did in fact give in to him. Hadn't he told her he had accepted the challenge? But the wretch fought dirty. He was letting the whole harem think her defloration was a fait accompli, for who would believe that he would elevate her status before he had actually bedded her?

"The only things you do not have that the wives have are an extra room or two and your own private garden," Adamma was telling her happily. *"This* is the best apartment in the pink court. Mara herself had it."

"And what happened to her?"

"She was moved back to the court of the *gozdes*. And what a fuss she made!" Adamma giggled. "But there is room here for only six favorites."

"So she was the least favorite but had the best room," Chantelle commented skeptically.

"Mara had enjoyed her position just recently, but because she served a purpose, she was given special treatment and got whatever she demanded."

"What purpose?" Chantelle asked, only to have Adamma turn away and try to change the subject. She was having none of that. "What purpose, Adamma?" The young girl was still reluctant to answer. "Must I ask Jamil's mother?"

"No! You mustn't do that. Lalla Rahine never approved of Mara."

"Well, then?"

Adamma bent her head. "Her—Mara, that is— her nickname is 'the whipping post.' "

Adamma expected that to explain it. It did. "The . . . you mean Jamil beats her?" Chantelle gasped.

"Not him," Adamma said quickly, and then was now to add, "But his mutes do."

"Why, for heaven's sake?" Chantelle exploded. "Does the girl cause trouble?"

"Not at all," Adamma assured her. "She is just peculiar in that she gets no pleasure out of sex without some form of violence done to her first."

"That is preposterous!"

"It's true, *lalla*. She goes to the Dey smiling and comes back smiling. The bruises mean nothing to her. My mother says it is because Mara's first experience with a man was violent, but she still found pleasure in it."

"You mean with Jamil?"

"No. Mara was raped by the slave master who brought her to Barikah."

"But I thought all of Jamil's women were virgins when they came here."

"Mara was still a virgin," Adamma replied. "She was raped in a different way."

The image that arose didn't bear thinking of. "But Jamil still has her beaten before he— before—"

Adamma nodded, saving Chantelle from finishing. "She cannot experience pleasure otherwise. And the Dey only summons her when his mood is terrible. She is happy and his anger is relieved.

298

So you see the purpose she serves? His bad moods are not taken out on his other women, and Mara gets what she wants, too."

"It's despicable," Chantelle said, but quietly.

"But who is hurt by it, *lalla?*"

No one, apparently, though Chantelle couldn't help being appalled. Yet she had no business being surprised. She had seen with her own eyes that having a woman beaten was nothing to Jamil. She was almost grateful for the reminder of how cruel he could be. Forgetting that had made her dangerously enjoy his embrace this morning. But no more.

"Lalla?"

"Yes?"

"You will now be able to select three more slaves for yourself. If I may suggest—"

"Wait a minute," Chantelle interrupted in surprise. "Who said I am to have more servants?"

"It is customary."

Chantelle frowned at the girl. "You heard me tell Haji Agha that my being here defies custom, Adamma. I have not *earned*, shall we say, any special privileges, nor do I intend to."

"You mustn't say that, *lalla*. If the Dey stops summoning you, then we will be moved back with the unimportant concubines."

From the look on Adamma's face, that move was to be avoided at all cost. Chantelle understood the girl's desire to remain here. When a concubine moved up, her servants also advanced in the hierarchy of the slaves. But the servants didn't have to deal with the Dey. She wished Adamma could understand her desire *not* to remain here.

"Lalla Shahar?"

Would she get no peace today to sort out this new situation. Chantelle turned, glowering at the newcomer who stood framed in her doorway. She had not seen him before, but he was undoubtedly a eunuch, for no other type of men were allowed in the harem, servants or not. Only this man was fair-skinned, and looked very important in his flowing fur-trimmed clothes and high turban.

Through the windows she could see several *ikbals* standing out in the court watching him. They were unable to hide their curiosity. Neither could Adamma. Kadar had also reappeared and stood directly behind the fellow, but Chantelle detected no curiosity in him, merely a watchfulness that disturbed her for some unknown reason.

"What is it?"

The man bowed formally. "I come from Jamil Reshid." He extended his hands, on which rested a thin rosewood box at least a foot square in size and rimmed in mother-of-pearl. "With the Dey's compliments, *lalla*."

Chantelle was still frowning as she took the box, but that was nothing compared with her scowl when she opened it. Inside, and spread out on white velvet to show off every single gem, was a two-tiered necklace of amethysts, with a single jewel the size of an an acorn right in the center. It was a necklace every bit as magnificent as the

sapphire one she was still wearing, and undoubtedly just as valuable, what with the enormous size
of that purple-hued stone in the middle.

What had Jamil told her? That such a necklace was for a woman who gave birth. So what
was he doing honoring her with such a gift? The
first assumption she had made this morning was
obviously correct. The Dey was going to try to
buy her affections now.

She started to hand the box back when the
servant said, "There is also a message, *lalla*, if
you will allow me. The Dey said to tell you, 'With
your own jewels, you are less likely to forget them,
but . . .'" The man's brow knitted, his eyes
closed, his teeth clamped down on his lip, and
then his eyes popped open as he finally remembered. "Oh, yes! 'But I hope you will continue to
forget them.'"

Why should that message bring color rushing
to her cheeks? No one understood it except her,
but she was afraid she understood it too well. Was
this Jamil's way of telling her he knew she hadn't
really objected to their last intimate embrace? How
could he know?

Chantelle did thrust the box back now, only to
find the messenger gone.

Chapter Thirty-one

IT WASN'T long before word ran through the
harem that Chantelle had been chosen for tonight.

It came as little surprise to anyone, since it was customary for a new favorite to be summoned several days in a row, sometimes longer. What was speculated about was why she hadn't become a favorite the first time she had visited the Dey, for only a select few knew that she hadn't lost her virginity then. Only those same few knew she still hadn't lost it, but this was not information they wanted bandied about.

If Chantelle thought no big to-do would be made over her this time, she was mistaken. She was still escorted to the *hammam*, this time under the supervision of Lalla Savetti, a Serbian of middle years who was Mistress of the Pink Court. Haji Agha was there waiting with several of his eunuchs, obviously taking no chances. Kadar also accompanied Chantelle, though she had to wonder whose side he would be on if she happened to panic again. But she wasn't panicked, at least not where it showed. And she had given her word to Jamil. She had to go through the extensive preparations and be presented at his door. After that was another matter.

Unfortunately, the baths were not empty this time. It was early yet, and from what Chantelle could see when she first entered, it appeared the entire harem was present in the main chamber, or very nearly so. And unlike Safiye, who was reserved in her manner, Lalla Savetti was the exact opposite, and nothing would do but that she introduce Chantelle to the other favorites, as well as to Jamil's three wives.

Chantelle was utterly unprepared for this meeting. She had seen a few of the favorites before in the baths, but to see them all together, for Savetti called them over to her, was enlightening and disconcerting. They were every bit as beautiful as could be expected of the elite of the harem. One had black hair, one had dark brown, but the other six had red hair in a multiple of different shades. It wasn't difficult for her to conclude that this color was Jamil's preference. Glancing about the rest of the room revealed more than half the women present were also redheads.

These eight women were extraordinary, making Chantelle feel inferior, washed out, and plain dowdy by comparison, not to mention sickly. Her body seemed like a stick next to theirs. Not one of them was the least bit fat, just depressingly curvaceous. And she had never seen so many jewels in all her life as sparkled on these eight women, even in the baths, for God's sake.

It was fortunate that there was no time to chit-chat, for Chantelle felt completely tongue-tied in their presence. It wasn't that she detected any animosity, not even a little jealousy, which might be expected. They were in fact all friendly toward her, including Noura, the black-haired one with the sultry dark eyes to match her glorious mane. Noura's attitude might be suspect, but the others seemed to genuinely want to welcome Chantelle into their little group.

She didn't know how to relate to that. They obviously loved Jamil and were selflessly willing to share him with one another. What could you say to women like that? *I think you're crazy. How can you love such a beast?* Not one of them could empathize with her.

But she was rescued by Haji's remarking on the lateness of the hour and then whisked off for the full treatment. She didn't know if she had gone through this last night unaware, but this time she wasn't only bathed, shaved, and shampooed, but massaged, oiled, and perfumed, too, as well as having her teeth polished, her gums inspected, her nails dyed, and her breath sweetened. They would have attacked her hair and face if she hadn't called a halt, insisting Adamma would attend to the hairdressing and cosmetics.

Haji had to give in to her wishes, since she was being so cooperative. Chantelle knew he was expecting trouble from her, perhaps had planned for it, but he didn't know she had given her word, and she didn't feel like relieving his mind by telling him so.

When she returned to her room, the Mistress of the Wardrobe was there waiting with a new creation of rose- and shiny silver-striped "underwear." Chantelle did protest this time, for she had already chosen a much less revealing outfit from her own new clothes, but she was informed quite haughtily that what she possessed was too ordinary for a visit to the Dey, that her clothes were to be worn only in the harem. It wasn't worth arguing over, especially after she requested a caftan to complete the costume and was reluctantly granted it. She could merely sigh when it was fetched, and it turned out to be so transparent it was barely noticeable.

The color of this outfit, Adamma pointed out, matched her amethysts perfectly, and Chantelle had to wonder if her morning gift wasn't known to everyone by now. She had intended not to wear Jamil's jewels. She wished now that the thief she had heard about who had been stealing items of value in the harem had paid her a visit today, because when Adamma brought the necklace and everyone stood there waiting to see how Chantelle looked in it, what could she do? It would be breaking her word to make a scene, but she'd be damned if she would give her word again.

She was almost ready to go when Rahine showed up. She was surprised that the older woman dared to face her, or did Rahine not know that she was aware she had overstepped her authority by having her punished?

"If nothing else pleases you, Shahar, are you at least happy to have a door now that is quite solid and lockable?"

"You are correct, madame," Chantelle allowed. "The door is the only thing here that pleases me." Adamma was still fussing with her hair, but Chantelle waved her away and waited until she was alone with Rahine before asking, "Did you know that Jamil didn't want me punished?"

Not a muscle moved on Rahine's porcelain features. "I didn't know then, but I do now. Why didn't you tell him?"

305

Chantelle used the excuse of her hand mirror to avoid those green eyes. "What makes you think I didn't?" she asked offhandedly.

"We would all have heard the results of his temper if you had. You aren't going to tell him, are you?"

The question was asked with such confidence that there was no point in denying the truth. "No."

"Why?"

"I would just as soon have stayed in the kitchen, if you must know. No harm was done."

"Stayed in the—? Do you hate him that much?"

The incredulous tone snapped Chantelle's temper.

"I don't want to be his next whore!"

"My dear, you could never be that," Rahine said gently. "No concubine could when she is restricted to only one man's attentions. But you must know that Jamil already prizes you. He breaks customs for you. He appears obsessed with you in every way. Can you truly find no tender feeling for him?"

"Why do you do this?" Chantelle cried.

"Because I live for his happiness. What else do I have to live for?"

Oh, God, how pathetic. Chantelle couldn't stay angry with the woman after hearing that. "Can't you go home? Why do you lock yourself away in here when you don't have to? You're his mother. He wouldn't keep you here if you wanted to go, would he?"

"No, but I have nowhere to go. This *is* my home now, Shahar. Jamil, his children, his women, they are my family. This is my life. There is nothing for me anywhere else."

"You're not an old woman. You could still find another husband."

Rahine smiled at that. "I can do that here, Shahar, if that is what I want."

Chantelle gave up. "Very well, so you like it here. Kindly accept the fact that I don't and never will."

"I wonder if you will still feel that way, say, a week from now."

Rahine didn't wait for a reply but left Chantelle alone to wonder what could happen in a week that might change her mind. It didn't take much intelligence on her part to guess. Rahine was warning her that Jamil's patience wouldn't last any longer than that. So be it. She had known, deep inside, that he would get his way eventually, one way or another. She knew her days were numbered. But she would still hold out to the bitter end, and her feelings weren't going to change when that end came.

Chapter Thirty-two

IF CHANTELLE didn't know better, she would swear she was being courted. During the past five days she was summoned to Jamil every evening, and each time was the same. He was charming, witty even. He told stories about his childhood in the harem, some that even made her laugh. They would walk in the garden or play games, and once they read to each other.

It was all very proper by her standards, which was why she was learning to relax in his company, at least for most of each visit. But before the evening was over he would inevitably make his move, and she would inevitably resist it, though God knew it was getting harder each time to do so. When Jamil turned amorous, he was plainspoken, telling her exactly what he wanted to do to her. She would have not only his hands to contend with but his words, too, and what they could make her feel. But she prevailed, despite her traitorous body's reaction to him.

Amazingly, she was not treated to another display of anger, even when she rejected his advances. She almost wished it were otherwise, for her image of the cruel tyrant was receding more and more, especially when little gifts would arrive during the day, or notes to remind her that he was thinking of her.

Last evening had been the same as the others, except he had been drinking when she arrived. That had made her extremely nervous, until she realized he wasn't drunk, just different, more relaxed, more—well, truth to tell, he seemed more English than ever. This "courtship" seemed more English than ever, too. If she didn't have to return to the harem, filled with women who belonged to him, she could almost forget who he was and where she was.

But the women, his many women, could never be forgotten. He might spend his evenings with her, but she didn't know with whom he spent his nights. No one else was summoned to him; any enemies she had in the harem would have made sure she knew about that. But he was known to spend his nights with one of his wives, to go to her apartment rather than have her brought to his. This could be done in secrecy, so Chantelle couldn't know what he did after she left him.

That she should wonder about it at all disturbed her. She shouldn't care about whom he slept with, as long as it wasn't with her. But if she was going to be honest, at least with herself, she had to admit she didn't like the notion that his patience with her could very likely be the direct result of his getting his pleasure elsewhere.

This made her less agreeable toward his wives, who had since paid her several visits. Noura she hadn't liked before they'd even met, and that opinion was reinforced at their second meeting, when the black-haired beauty showed her true colors. She had an attitude of superiority that was only more pronounced by her conceit and imperious manner. She might have reason to be so condescending, since, according to Adamma, Noura was the only woman in the harem who was not a slave, having been given in marriage to Jamil to seal a treaty with some desert pasha. But that was no excuse for such overweening arrogance, or for her cutting remarks. Noura could turn her spite on anyone who gained her attention.

The other two wives were totally different. Sheelah, especially, was hard not to like. The hummingbird that the first *kadine* had given her was indicative of her generous and friendly nature. In fact, Chantelle couldn't find a single reason to dislike her—except that she was Jamil's beloved first wife, and that reasoning was so illogical that it didn't bear close examination.

There was a certain anticipation today as Chantelle prepared herself for her sixth consecutive evening with Jamil Reshid. She accredited it to nerves, because she knew her time was running out. That she might be looking forward to his company was not considered.

For tonight she was dressed in a delicate pink muslin that softened the color of her eyes and went well with her platinum tresses. Those Adamma still arranged loose, pinning only the front locks away from her face. She now had earrings, two bracelets, hairpins, and a large amethyst ring to go with her necklace, gifts that Jamil still sent her even though she hadn't earned them in the traditional way.

"You will take his breath away, *lalla*," Adamma assured her happily.

"Do you think he will expire from suffocation, then?" was the hopeful reply.

Adamma giggled. She didn't take Chantelle's disparaging remarks about Jamil seriously anymore, perhaps because Chantelle only said such things from habit now. A week ago she might have looked upon his demise as her salvation and felt not a moment's sorrow. Now she might still pray for escape, but not through his death.

It was Kadar who took her to the Dey each evening and waited for her return. He had become like her shadow, escorting her everywhere she went, guarding her door when she was in the apartment, sleeping in the front room with Adamma at night. She had wondered whose side he would take if she were to refuse Jamil's summons again. He seemed completely loyal to her, but she wasn't quite ready to put it to the test. After she had figured out a way to escape, she was going to need help, and she was hoping Kadar would supply it. But it was too soon yet to trust him completely.

Tonight she found Jamil standing by the garden doors. He never received her in any room but this one, with the ever-threatening bed close by. But he had had large pillows brought in to form a cozy couch by the windows, through which moonlight would filter in. Not that the room wasn't always well lit to begin with. Yet somehow the lighting seemed to dim before the evening ended, as if invisible servants came to extinguish each lamp. She wouldn't know if they did. Jamil always claimed her attention so completely, an army could march through and she probably wouldn't notice.

He was wearing a dark gold tunic in a rich Venetian brocade that molded across his chest and shoulders. The typical loose trousers were white Persian silk and tucked into high boots of a European design. The wide sash about his waist was gold tissue and held a dagger that was lethal in its unadorned simplicity. The only jewels tonight were his rings, a large amber stone and the emerald that he always wore. And as usual, he was without his turban. She hadn't seen him turbaned since they had first met.

She wished it were otherwise, for with that smoothly shaved face and the thick black hair that parted in the middle and fell in waves to his shoulders, there was nothing Eastern about him from the waist up. How often had she gazed at him and thought how normal he would look in an English drawing room. She had pictured him in a well-cut coat, tight knee-high breeches, with a silk cravat at his throat, and knew he would cut a dashing figure. He cut a dashing figure anyway, damn him.

At Jamil's insistence, she no longer prostrated herself when entering the room. But she never approached him either, remaining by the door until he called her forward. Tonight he didn't say anything at first, though he stared at her with those penetrating green eyes of his. Perhaps he was merely waiting for the recital to finish. A Reader of the Koran sat in a corner, reading aloud from the book on his lap.

When the little Muslim's voice rose suddenly, Chantelle turned toward him, unable to ignore him any longer.

312

Those you fear may be rebellious,
admonish; banish them to their couches
and beat them. If they then obey you,
look not for any way against them; Allah is
All-high, All-great.

Your women are a tillage for you;
so come unto your tillage as you wish,
and forward for your souls; Allah is
All-mighty, All-wise.

Chantelle caught her breath and glanced back to see Jamil still watching her. He dismissed the Reader of the Koran with an abrupt motion, never taking his eyes from her.

Chantelle waited until the little man had bowed himself out; then one silver brow rose sharply. "For my benefit?"

"But of course."

His sudden grin was so mischievous, she couldn't help laughing. "You forget I'm a Christian infidel who doesn't follow your prophet's teaching."

"I never forget for a moment what you are, Shahar." He walked toward her while he said this, and brought her fingers up to his lips before he finished with, "What you are is mine."

Her mind might shy away from her attraction to him, but her body did not. It responded immediately to his touch and possessive tone. But before she could even think of a reply, he was leading her to the couch of pillows. He dropped down there, pulling her next to him.

They had never sat this close so early in the evening before, not that they were actually sitting. The pillows were so large they were like a bed when formed together. Jamil reclined back on one elbow, with one knee bent so that he leaned partially toward her. She rested on both elbows for the moment. He had always managed to work his way closer to her gradually, in effect forewarning her when he was about to make an advance. That the rules were suddenly changing was unnerving.

Slowly, so as not to be obvious about it, Chantelle scooted back until her spine rested on the pillows that were set up against the wall. At least their thighs weren't touching this way, and she had the advantage of being able to look down on him, which settled her nerves a little, until she saw him smile. She hadn't been subtle at all.

He chose not to comment on her discomfort, saying instead, "What shall we do tonight?"

"A walk in the garden?"

Chantelle immediately started to get up. An arm across her thighs prevented her.

"What would you like to do—here?" he clarified, and to her relief removed his arm.

"I—I don't know. What would you—" He cocked his head to look up at her, and his grin was so blatantly wicked, she didn't have to finish the question. "Besides that," she added a bit sharply.

He gave the barest of shrugs, his gaze traveling slowly down her body to end at eye level on her lap. "Have you learned to dance yet?"

She knew what kind of dancing he meant. She had watched one of the *ikbals* practicing in the courtyard, and it was like nothing she had ever seen or could even imagine. It was a dance designed solely to arouse male passions, with sinuous belly and pelvic movements that were not just seductive; as far as she was concerned, they were obscene.

"Your Eastern dances are too . . . foreign for my tastes," Chantelle said.

"But I would very much like to see you dance, Shahar," he replied, and ran a finger down the top of her thigh to her knee, where his hand then rested. "Will you learn for me?"

He looked up for her answer. The heat in his emerald gaze caused her throat to tighten. Her belly was already turning flip-flops from his touch.

"I—I couldn't."

"You could," he murmured thickly, and his finger started a trail back up her thigh. "You choose not to. But it is not something that can be forced. You have to want to inflame my passions—

"Jamil!"

She grabbed his finger before it could go any farther. He startled her by yanking it away and sitting up. When he glanced back at her, she knew she had displeased him from the tight set of his features. She assumed it was because she

315

had stopped him. It was a surprise to find out differently.

"You may call me anything but Jamil."

"I beg your pardon?"

"Call me Derek."

"What?" she said incredulously.

"It means 'beloved.'"

She blinked. What the devil had come over him?

"In what language?" she asked skeptically.

"Never mind what language!" His voice rose in his irritation. "Will you call me Derek?"

"No," she replied simply, and saw his jaw stiffen.

"In another language, it also means 'bastard.' *Now* will you call me Derek?"

It was too much. She grinned and the laughter followed, until she was bent over with it, clasping her sides. When she finally leaned back, she saw him watching her with his own lips curled.

"Oh, God." She sighed, wiping tears from her eyes. "If I'm not permitted to call you Jamil, you only had to say so. Derek indeed. The name's as English as I am."

"So is my mother, Shahar," he pointed out. "Perhaps she gave me the name."

"Did she?"

"No," he said truthfully, for it was his grandfather who had named him Derek.

He reclined again, bemused by his irrational reaction to hearing her call him by his brother's name. What was a name, after all? Just because it belonged to someone else . . .

316

Chantelle was watching him curiously. "What was that all about, then, if you don't mind my asking?"

He glanced up at her, suddenly aware that her humor had relaxed her guard. That would change, however, if he claimed his prerogative not to answer.

He shrugged offhandedly. "My frustration, rising to surprise us both."

She could believe it, but was loath to pursue *that* subject. "Oh, well . . ."

He chuckled. "Where's your courage, English? Aren't you curious why I'm frustrated?"

"No!"

"It's not what you think."

"Isn't it?"

"I want you in my bed, yes, but I want other things as well."

Before she realized what he meant to do, he had hooked his fingers in the top of her pantaloons and tugged, gently enough so that the buttons on each hip didn't snap off, but enough to bring her sliding down the silken pillow until she lay flat on her back next to him. She brought up her hands immediately to ward him off, but he didn't lean over her as she had expected.

"That's better," he said. "I was getting a stiff neck looking up at you."

If that was meant to reassure her about this new position, it didn't. "I don't think—"

"Shh, don't you want to know what I want to

do to you?" She shook her head emphatically and he gave her back her own words. "Besides that."

"No matter," she insisted. "It can't help to talk about it."

"How do you know? And how do you know you won't like what I want to do to you?"

She closed her eyes with a little groan, only to snap them open as she felt him lean closer. His face was now above hers, a mere breath away. His hand, still holding the band of her pants, turned so that she felt his palm against her skin. It wasn't as warm as the smoldering heat of his gaze.

"I want to put my fingers inside you, Shahar."

"Oh, God!" she got out before his mouth slanted across hers to add to the whirling of her senses that his words had caused.

Still, she reached for his arm, wrapping her fingers about his wrist. That there was no strength to her tug was not surprising.

"If you don't give me something, woman, I am going to go mad," he said against her lips.

His kiss turned fierce, possessive, as if he meant to devour her. She became even weaker under this onslaught, until her hand fell away. His hand immediately slid into her pants, the fingers parting her curls, moving down, finally doing what he said he had wanted to do.

Her reaction was to soar up against him, which allowed his fingers to press even deeper inside her. She clung to him, reeling in the most delicious sensation, mindless of anything except that pleasure.

"Oh, love, you're so hot, so wet."

Chantelle melted to his words, wrapping her arms around him, kissing him back with a frantic need. That he had spoken in English didn't penetrate, she was so inflamed. And he continued to work his magic, not letting the fever abate for even a moment.

And then suddenly he was lying between her legs and there were no clothes between them. How he had managed it, she didn't know, couldn't recall at all. What had brought her to an awareness of it, she wasn't sure. Perhaps the overall heat of his skin pressed to hers, belly to belly, chest to breast. Perhaps the vulnerability of having her legs parted to accommodate him. Perhaps because he had stopped kissing her for a breathless moment.

But there was no time for panic or fear to take hold. He had only waited for her awareness to crystallize, to see it in her violet eyes, and then he was kissing her again, his tongue plunging deeply. At the same time she felt the exquisite pleasure of his fingers inside her once more . . . no, not his fingers this time, but him, that part of him she had feared but feared no more.

Slowly, so slowly he entered her, and with such ease, for she was hot with waiting, moist with needing. There was a fullness unlike his fingers, a tightness that was much more delicious for her knowledge of what it was, and then a strange sensation as if something had popped inside her, not actually hurtful, but startling, then an even greater fullness so deep inside her.

His groan mingled with her own as he continued to kiss her, gently now, but no less passionately. He moved in no other way for a moment, and she didn't mind, savoring this new feeling, knowing instinctively that there would be more. And there was. When his hips began a slow thrusting against her, her heartbeat seemed to pick up the same tempo, accelerating as he did, faster and faster, until she was jolted with a thunderbolt of liquid sensation so extreme she cried out, her arms tightening around him as he gathered her even closer, his own pulsating climax joining hers.

Chapter Thirty-three

CHANTELLE HAD drifted into a wondrous limbo where no thoughts could intrude, just a surfeit of feelings, all of them nice. Skin to skin tingling, a pleasant weight, a moist heat at her breasts, a slow heartbeat in her loins, so nice. She could have stayed like that indefinitely, if Jamil hadn't started to tease, drawing circles around a nipple with his tongue, then blowing cool air on it until it puckered into a hard little nub.

This surge of feeling, though still pleasant, wasn't quite so relaxing. It seemed to force Chantelle's hands to that head above her breasts to bring the warm mouth back to her nipple.

"So you are awake?"

She smiled dreamily as he now began to suckle very gently. "I wasn't sleeping."

Her fingers delved into his hair, marveling at the baby-fine feel of it. He was lying on her, with his belly pressed into her groin. Finally realizing that sent a sweet sensation curling through her.

Suddenly a hand cupped each breast, and his chin rested between them. "Are you angry with me, little moon?"

She raised an arm to support her head so she could look at him. Angry? Was he serious?

"Do I look angry?"

"I took advantage of you."

Her lips twitched upward a tad. "Did you?"

"I believe you were sure this would not happen unless we were in my bed."

"Aren't we in your bed?"

He grinned at her. "You see my point."

"Very well, so you took advantage of me."

"And you liked it?"

"Will you have me drawn and quartered if I don't give the right answer?" A squeeze to each breast made her forget about teasing him. "Yes, you conceited man. Is that what you want to hear?"

His smile nearly melted her heart. "Do you know how much pleasure it gives me, to know you belong solely to me?"

"I might, if you belonged solely to me as well." After a moment, the blush spread up her

321

cheeks. God, where had that come from? "What I mean—"

"No, I won't let you take it back," he interrupted with a chuckle. "I was right. You English cannot share, can you?"

Whether she could share or not, she didn't share his humor now. "If you mean we believe in one man for one woman, yes, indeed, we do," she snapped. "But a man who possesses nearly fifty women wouldn't understand that!"

"Are you jealous, little moon?"

"Certainly not!"

"Then why should it bother you, how many women I own?"

"It's indecent!"

"By your standards. By mine, the number is actually quite small."

She couldn't argue about that, not when his very religion sanctioned bigamy for the men of this country. He would never understand her views, and would ignore them anyway, so why waste her breath? But it infuriated her, honest to God it did, that his faithlessness was a matter of course here, but Allah forbid if one of his women should even be looked at by another man.

"I think," she said with stiff hauteur, "that I should return to the harem."

"Now you are angry with me."

"Not at all," she insisted, though the tight set of her lips put the lie to her words. "I was only anticipating your wishes, since I was told that

322

when you've finished with one of your women, you send her away immediately."

How she had dared to say that, when everything else Vashti had told her about this first time had proved untrue, Chantelle didn't know. And Jamil apparently didn't like what he was hearing either. His hands tightened on her unconsciously as he leaned backward, and his expression turned dark and ominous.

"Who told you such a thing?"

Chantelle's irritation withered under that tone. She might not like Vashti, and had even more reason not to like her now that she knew the girl had deliberately lied to her, but she wouldn't wish Jamil's anger and retribution on anyone, knowing full well what forms of punishment he could so casually have administered.

"What does it matter?" she evaded.

"Who?"

"I don't recall."

His eyes narrowed even more at her stubbornness. "And what else were you told?"

"Nothing," and then more firmly, "Really." But she might as well have saved her breath.

"Things to make you fear me?" he guessed correctly. "Who do I have to thank for prolonging my frustration? Who was assigned to instruct you?"

She knew he could find out easily without her telling him. If he was going to be furious with anyone, it might as well be with her. Vashti's lies had not accounted for all her fears, after all.

"You're wrong, your highness." She reverted

to formality, their intimate position forgotten for the moment. "Nothing that was told to me could have made me fear you more than your own actions had done."

"You still think I would hurt you?" he demanded, more in amazement than in anger.

"You're hurting me now," she replied quietly.

He finally became aware of the flesh he was squeezing in his agitation and released her breasts, instantly contrite. But she didn't give him a chance to apologize.

"However," she continued, "that was still not the cause of my reluctance to share your bed. I was raised to believe that no virtuous woman would give her virginity to any man other than her lawful husband. To do otherwise would cause shame and ruin."

"I am your lawful master."

"That doesn't matter."

"The only man available to you, Shahar, the same as a husband to you."

"No, not the same. You bought me. You didn't marry me."

"You want me to marry you?"

She was appalled by the very idea. "And be your fourth wife? No!"

She was further appalled to realize too late that she had just insulted him in the worst way. But thankfully, he chose not to take offense, saying only, "So there is yet another reason for this reluctance of yours to make love with me?"

She glanced away before replying in a tiny voice, "It made it—final, my enslavement."

His own voice softened in understanding. "It became inevitable the day you were captured, Shahar. Surely you did not delude yourself otherwise."

"Until it actually happened, there was still hope. You have a large harem filled with beautiful women. And since you rarely enter it, you could easily have forgotten about me."

He smiled, turning her face back to him with a hand on her cheek. "You are not the type of woman who can ever hope for obscurity, little moon. A man has only to gaze on you once to never forget you. Don't you know that?"

She shook her head. "By your standards, my body is much too thin to be found attractive."

A teasing light entered his eyes. "You might be lacking in padding, but what you have is everything that I could want."

"You don't want me to put on weight?"

"I want you to remain just as you are."

"Then if I do put on weight, you won't want me anymore."

He chuckled, following the direction of her thoughts. "I could have sworn I heard you say you liked what we just did. Or have you perhaps forgotten so quickly that you no longer have your virginity to protect?"

She blushed, for she had indeed forgotten for the moment that that monumental transformation had occurred to change everything, especially her outlook. How she felt about it she wasn't quite sure yet. But one thing was disconcerting. She hadn't expected to enjoy it so completely. But it was foolish of her to admit liking it, especially to him. The man had her at enough disadvantage as it was without giving him that, too.

Having gone from satisfied languor to anger to dejection to confusion was also disconcerting. She wanted nothing more than to leave so she could be alone to think more clearly about her loss. She certainly couldn't think clearly with Jamil still settled comfortably between her legs. Why *was* she still here? That he slept with only his wives was not one of Vashti's lies, but fact that she had heard from numerous sources. Of course, he didn't appear to be ready to sleep.

"You have become pensive, little moon." His voice drew her gaze back to those probing emerald eyes. "I will not allow you to regret your surrender."

His arrogance was almost amusing. "You might own my body, your highness, but my feelings are still at my own command."

"Are they? And your senses, are they at your command, too?"

He dipped his head to suck a nipple into the warm recesses of his mouth. Chantelle closed her eyes as the delicious thrill traveled from her breast to her belly, and from there to her loins. The other breast was given the same thorough attention, until her fingers moved into his hair, answering his question more plainly than words.

Abruptly he left her, only to scoop her up into his arms and carry her to his bed. The momentary respite to her senses brought her out of her daze long enough so that the bed beneath her triggered a memory, and she immediately glanced behind her. How could she have forgotten about his guards? But the hot flush didn't have time to spread. The wall behind his bed was empty.

"Where are your mutes?" she asked as she looked back at Jamil and then gasped, finding him staring down at her, his eyes slowly traveling the length of her body.

"Banished to the garden in deference to your modesty."

He himself was playing havoc with her modesty, since he spoke without ending his slow perusal of her body. That same modesty forbade her a like examination of him. Though he stood beside the bed in full view of her, her eyes wouldn't move below his chin.

"Am—am I to understand you aren't finished with me yet?"

Even that question didn't bring his eyes back to hers. "Oh, no, little moon," he said with feeling. "How could you think that? Such frustration as you have caused me will take a long time appeasing."

"I find this frustration you keep expounding on hard to believe when you have so many women available to you."

It was her terse tone that finally got his attention. He smiled and joined her on the bed, stretching out next to her so that she felt the heat of his body along her entire side. One hand cupped her cheek and slid up into her hair to bring her mouth to his for a disturbingly gentle kiss.

"You think another could put out the fire you ignited?" His lips moved on to the side of her neck, ending by her ear, causing an explosion of hot, liquid pleasure that shot clear to her toes. "I have been able to think of no one but you since my eyes first beheld you. How then could I invite another to my bed, Shahar? Only you would do."

She chose to believe him, because those words were as inflaming as the tongue delving into her ear. Once more all thoughts deserted her as she gave herself up to the pleasure of his touch.

Chapter Thirty-four

"Do you mind if I join you?"

Chantelle shrugged without raising her cheek from the heated marble slab. "Not at—" Her head snapped up, for that was her own language she had heard, clear and precise. "Are you from England, too?"

It was Jamila, one of the other five *ikbals*, who unself-consciously opened her robe and lay down next to Chantelle on the warm marble shelf in the center of the communal chamber. She was naked beneath the robe, and her full, young breasts jutted out as she anchored herself on both elbows. That Chantelle was just as naked beneath her robe to enjoy the heat was precisely why she wouldn't assume that position.

"I thought someone would have told you," Jamila said with a smile. "My family is from Gloucester, though I was pretty much raised in London."

"No, no one mentioned it. I thought Rahine was the only other Englishwoman here. Why didn't you say something when you came to visit me the other day with Lady Sheelah?"

"It was Sheelah who taught me to speak Turkish, but it's taken me so long to learn that she still insists I speak nothing else until I get it right. She's so patient with me, but I was never very good at languages. My French teacher almost despaired of me."

"But this is wonderful, to hear the mother tongue again. I'm so glad—" Chantelle flinched. "I don't mean that I'm glad you're here. I wouldn't wish this enslavement on anyone."

"No, I understand. I was sorry to see you arrive, and for the same reason."

"How long have you been here?"

"Not long, really. Just over six months. I was the last woman to enter the harem until you arrived. And there was such a row over that, I thought surely there wouldn't be any others. Everyone thought so, too, which was why you were such a surprise."

"A row?"

"Oh, yes." Jamila grinned, remembering. "I can laugh about it now, but I was terrified at the

329

time. The Dey was so furious with his mother, he didn't even wait until they were alone to chastise her, but came right into the harem to do it. I was sure I would be sold again or worse."

"But why should you be sold again if he bought you? What was he angry about?"

"*He* didn't buy me. Lalla Rahine did." And then Jamila frowned. "I thought you knew. The Dey hasn't bought a woman for himself in five years, not since he came to realize how much Sheelah meant to him. More than half the women here have been given to him or purchased by his mother. It was when she bought me that he finally laid down the law and told her absolutely no more." She giggled. "He's not like those other Turks and Arabs who think the more the merrier. He actually exhausts himself to assure that none of his women are neglected for any great length of time. So you can see why he might be upset to find his harem growing any larger."

Chantelle refrained from snorting at that observation. What was she doing here, then, if he didn't want any more women to wear him out? She recalled their first encounter and how he had seemed so indifferent to her. If he had stayed like that, she could understand what Jamila had told her. But there was last week. There was last night. There were his words that she had believed and still did, that he hadn't made love to any of his other women since he'd first seen her.

Yes, last night. He hadn't let her go until the dawn, and neither of them had slept at all during the long hours of the night. She had lost count of how many times they had made love, how many times his voice and touch had stirred the embers that he never quite let die out. She had returned to her rooms to sleep the morning away, exhausted, but with a contentment she hadn't tried to analyze yet. She still hadn't really thought about it, preferring to savor a while what she was feeling before she picked it apart to understand why she wasn't upset or even a little disappointed at her own easy surrender.

"You can understand why there's so much speculation since he's bought you," Jamila continued, playing with a lock of her dark brown hair, flicking it against her cheek and lips. "Everyone's wondering if he simply couldn't resist you or if your coming signifies a change, that there'll be more after you to fill the ranks."

Chantelle was not about to consider that when there were so many other, more important questions she was avoiding. A change of subject was in order.

"Do you miss home, Jamila?"

"Oh, yes. I can't seem to get used to the inactivity here. I was always so busy at home, making the rounds, you know. There never was enough time in a day to fulfill all of my commitments. Here there's too much time with nothing to do. I was convinced the boredom would have me fit for Bedlam, but of course, that was because it took so long for the Dey to get over his anger and finally notice me." She leaned closer and lowered her voice to confide, "I've only been an *ikbal* this past month, but it's made all the difference. Now there's the anticipation of never knowing when I might be summoned, but knowing I will be because the Dey never ignores his favorites for more than a week. The wait is exciting, the day I'm actually summoned so thrilling, with everyone so envious. But you know that now. He's such a wonderful lover, isn't he?"

Yes, wonderful. There was no denying it to herself, and certainly not to any of his women who knew firsthand that it was so. Chantelle shied away from that thought, remembering again Jamil's words that had assured her he had been with no other woman.

Jamila hadn't waited for confirmation of her last statement. She was still rambling on. "Poor Sheelah doesn't know what to think, as you might imagine. She loves him so."

"Do you?" Chantelle couldn't resist asking.

The brunette shrugged. "I don't know, really. Each time I'm with him, I think surely I must love him. I was so relieved when I first saw him, that he wasn't old, or fat, or ugly. And having seen him, I thought I would die, waiting for him to notice me. Actually, I can't think of a single man of my acquaintance in England who can compare with him, he's so handsome. But—" She paused for a moment and glanced around to make sure no one was within hearing of them before she whispered, "If I could be ransomed tomorrow, I wouldn't be disappointed to leave

332

here. The Dey is wonderful and kind and so sexy, and I've been so lucky that I was bought for him rather than someone else, but I'd rather have a man I could call my own, who would be available to me anytime I wanted him. I guess I'm a little selfish."

"Not at all," Chantelle assured her. "It's the way we were raised."

"Then you don't like it either, having to share him?"

Chantelle didn't care to answer that. She said instead, "All our lives we've taken it for granted that we would marry, and naturally we expected to be our husband's one and only love."

"Exactly." Jamila beamed. "No one else will admit that. But then they've all been here so much longer and are accustomed to this arrangement. I suppose we will be, too, when the years start rolling by. But it's a shame." She giggled and rolled her eyes. "With what I've learned here, I don't think any husband of mine would be bored and out looking for a mistress too soon."

Chantelle grinned despite herself. "No, I don't think he would."

"But I'm not likely to ever find out." Jamila finally laid her head down on her crossed arms with a sigh. "Sheelah was the lucky one. I thought surely the Dey really loved her. Oh, he gives to the rest of us of his body, but to her he gave from the heart. It was so romantic watching them together," Another sigh. "You could see the difference last week, though, when he joined us all for Noura's little party. It was the first time I'd ever seen him divide his attention so equally between us when Sheelah was present. She was crushed."

Chantelle frowned. She had spoken with the first *kadine* several times since that infamous feast that she had helped to prepare, but not once had she sensed any great unhappiness in her.

Jamila's eyes were closed now, so she didn't see how this bit of gossip had affected Chantelle. She blithely continued. "I wouldn't be surprised if Noura had hoped something like that would happen. She's always hated Sheelah for being the Dey's first wife and would do or say anything if she thought it would hurt her. I ought to warn you if no one else has, to watch out for Noura. Everyone swears she tried to kill Sheelah's son after her own was born, but it could never be proved."

"Are you serious, Jamila?"

"Mmm." Her eyes popped open. "Oh! I didn't mean to frighten you. You surely don't have anything to worry about, at least for a while. Noura's worst spite is reserved for those who have born the Dey's children. I just wanted to warn you so you wouldn't take anything she says to heart."

"I appreciate it, but I've already taken her measure. A more vindictive woman I've never met."

"That's Noura." Jamila grinned. "You just have to learn to ignore her, as everyone else does."

"I will," Chantelle replied. "But what about

Sheelah? Why was she so nice to me when she must hate me—"

"Oh, no! You mustn't think that. She isn't capable of hating anyone, not even Noura. Sheelah just isn't that way."

Why did that make Chantelle feel terrible instead of relieved? "If you say so."

"Oh, dear, I've upset you, haven't I? I didn't mean to, really I didn't."

"It's all right, Jamila."

"Are you sure? You're not just saying that?"

"Not at all."

"Good, because I was so hoping we could be friends. But you mustn't feel guilty about Sheelah. She wouldn't want that. And it's not exactly as if you were the 'other woman.' " Jamila chuckled here. "How could you be when there are so *many* other women?"

"But she's his wife."

"One of three wives, and we're his favorites, and he doesn't neglect the other concubines for long either. That's life here. Whoever he favors for the moment is the lucky one. You must enjoy it while it lasts."

Meaning it wouldn't last? Chantelle didn't voice that question. "I don't like being the cause of someone else's hurt."

"Oh, but you're not," the girl assured her. "Why, Jamil summoned Sheelah the day before he first summoned you to him. And she'll likely be the first one he wants as soon as he gives you a rest, so don't worry about her. Even if he does

335

come to favor you above her, she'll still be next after you. After all, she bore him his first son and he absolutely adores the boy. She's only been upset by the difference in the way he has behaved toward her since you've been visiting him. She just wasn't expecting it."

Chantelle hadn't heard much after that second sentence. "Do you mean that he made love to Sheelah after he bought me?"

"Well, of course he did," Jamila said in surprise. "You were in training, if you remember, so he couldn't very well summon you, though that was certainly cut short, wasn't it? But as I recall, he still called Sheelah to him the night he bought you. And actually, I had the next night, which was a relief to me, because I thought I'd be the first to go when you became a favorite. As it turned out, Mara was sent back instead. It was only after he first summoned you that he called no one else to him. You don't know how lucky you are, Shahar, to have him to yourself for a whole week. I managed only two days in a row my first time before Sheelah was back in his bed."

Chantelle closed her eyes and counted silently to ten. She mustn't let this news disturb her. Just because it appeared Jamil had lied to her didn't mean he actually had, or that it had been deliberate. He hadn't precisely said that he hadn't made love to anyone else. He had asked her how he could invite another to his bed. Well, he could, obviously. He had only implied that it wasn't likely.

No, no, she mustn't think he deliberately meant

336

to deceive her. Perhaps he had meant to say that he hadn't been able to think of anyone but her since he first summoned her, rather than when he first saw her, and Jamila had just confirmed that that at least was true. And besides, hadn't she assumed he was still sleeping with his wives even while he was seeing her? She hadn't let that stop her from surrendering to him. Oh, but it had been so romantic to hear him say that only she would do from the moment his eyes had first beheld her.

Those words were more than a little responsible for her contentment this morning and had gone a long way toward making her ignore the fact that she wasn't Jamil's only concubine. Everyone here was sharing him with her, but that she hadn't as yet shared him with anyone made a great deal of difference. It made all the difference, actually.

She would just have to ask him about it when she joined him tonight. If he could assure her that there wouldn't be anyone else . . .

"Oh!" Jamila squealed suddenly, only to end on a less ecstatic note. "Oh, dear. Are you sure?"

Chantelle glanced at her to find a servant squatted next to her and whispering in her ear. "What is it?"

"I've been summoned for tonight," the brunette said in amazement. "I wasn't expecting . . . well, no one would have expected . . . he must be angry with Sheelah for some reason to ignore her like this. Yes, that must be it." She sat up, grinning delightedly. "Oh, but I certainly can't complain. I thought I would have to wait weeks and weeks to have my turn again, what with you here now." She placed a hand excitedly on Chantelle's arm. "Be happy for me, Shahar. I do so like this business of making love." And then she was off, pulling her servant along toward the bath cubicles.

Chantelle didn't move or even breathe for a moment, until she realized her stupid eyes were starting to water. *Oh, God, don't you dare!*

She put her head down and managed to inconspicuously wipe each eye against her forearms before she jumped up. She had to get out of this crowded room immediately, and she didn't dare risk the long walk back to her rooms along paths just as crowded. No one, not anyone at all, was going to be able to say she had seen Chantelle the least bit disturbed by how quickly the Dey had lost interest in her. Quickly? No, most everyone thought she had been sharing his bed all week, which would make it even worse if the women believed she was upset to lose that privilege now. *Privilege, ha!* God, what an utter fool she had been!

She stood there for a moment, agonizing that she couldn't think of a single place where she could be alone long enough to get herself under control. And then it came to her, where the steam was so thick that even if she wasn't alone, no one could see her clearly enough to discern her emotions.

Quickly, Chantelle made her way toward the steam rooms, swallowing against the knot that had formed in her throat, praying that no one noticed her departure or at least couldn't see her eyes, which were already filling with moisture again. One of the steam rooms was empty, thank God. She stretched out on a bench in the corner and buried her head in her arms. The tears were impossible to hold back.

That rotten, perfidious, lecherous sod. She hated him, despised him. Oh, God, it hurt, and it was her own fault. She was so stupid! To think for one moment that he might have had feelings for her other than simple lust. How naive could she be? And how quickly he showed his true colors the moment he got what he wanted. But never again. If the Burkes did anything, they learned from their mistakes. So she had been seduced. So she was silly enough to have formed some romantic notions about the man. Thank God those would be nipped in the bud before the relationship got serious and she imagined herself in love with him. She couldn't begin to think how she would feel now if that were the case. This was bad enough.

What was so appalling was that she had truly deluded herself. She should have expected this. Hadn't she had enough warnings? Just about everyone had told her how much Jamil loved Sheelah, but was he faithful to his first wife? Not even a little bit. So what in hell had made her think it would be any different in her case? He didn't love her. Even if he did, he wouldn't give up his other women for her, the mothers of his children, his Sheelah. She had been harboring

339

impossible dreams, so she had no one to blame for what she was feeling now but herself.

A moment later, Chantelle heard voices outside the room, getting louder. *Let them pass, please.* But if they didn't . . .

She sat up and quickly dried her face with the sleeve of her robe. She had to be grateful for small things inasmuch as Adamma hadn't applied her cosmetics yet, so there was no telltale kohl smeared by her tears. Stupid tears. How dared she cry over that son-of-a-camel's-turd? A giggle almost escaped. She would have to stick to English curses. She didn't have the flair Adamma had for Turkish ones.

The steam in the room wasn't quite as thick now, so it was probably one of the attendants coming . . . no, that tone was too imperious for an attendant. ". . . want no more excuses! It should never have taken this long!" There was a man's soothing voice in reply, but he was speaking too low for Chantelle to hear what he said. The woman's angry voice was quite clear, however, as she continued. "Take this and sell it. If that doesn't buy some courage, I'll have to—" There was an interruption by the man. "What about the boy?" Another mumbled reply, and then the woman said. "Yes, go ahead and arrange it. Nothing else has been able to draw him out of the palace, so maybe that will. But if it does, there had better be results. No more bungles or I will take it out of your hide. And don't you dare shush me, Ali! No one is—"

Chantelle barely heard the last, for they did indeed pass on down the hall. Too bad, for whatever they were arguing about was just getting interesting. Not that she had made head or tail out of it, but it had served to get her mind off herself for a moment, and now she felt she could safely make it back to her rooms.

She didn't notice the two people standing at the end of the hall when she left the steam room, but they noticed her.

"Do you think she could have overheard?" the eunuch asked.

"No, but just in case . . ."

"I'll see to it personally, *lalla.*"

Chapter Thirty-five

CHANTELLE WAS blurry-eyed when she entered the baths the next afternoon, but nothing could have kept her away, not her queasy stomach, not Adamma's warnings that everyone would be talking about her today, and certainly not her own desire to hide herself away. She had too much pride for that, and besides, she had herself in hand now. As far as anyone could tell by looking at her, she wasn't the least bit upset over what had happened yesterday.

But Adamma hadn't exaggerated. She was the center of attention. If she had been favored by Jamil for only a day or two, that would have been normal and not worth more than a passing comment. But she had been summoned not only before her training was even near completion, but also for six nights in a row, which was apparently a new record for Jamil. Because of that, a definite reaction was expected.

Well, she had reacted all right, and exactly how it was hoped she would by those who were envious of her. But she'd be damned if anyone here would know it. So she endured the sneers and gloating looks, the whispers and outright laughter when she came near, though to be fair, she realized not all the women were so petty in their jealousy. She even managed to smile through a run-in with Noura, who couldn't wait to tell her that Jamila was so exhausted that she was still sleeping at this late hour.

That had hurt, because she had felt the same way yesterday morning. She was exhausted today as well, but for a different reason. She had found no pleasure in last night's sleeplessness. The whole evening had been a miserable experience. She had refused all visitors and so suffered only Adamma's company. And the girl had behaved as if she were the one out of favor, moping around with a long face.

Misery loves company, but Chantelle would rather have done without last night. She hadn't been able to eat more than a few bites of her dinner, thanks to her emotionally distraught state, and even that much she had lost later in the night. Her stomach still didn't feel up to nourishment, which was another mark against Jamil. The bloody sod had given her indigestion.

Chantelle had just left the baths to enter the communal chamber when Adamma rushed in, wreathed in smiles, to tell her she had been summoned for tonight. And the girl couldn't have said this quietly. No, she had to practically shout it, deliberately, Chantelle suspected. But Aunt Ellen would have been proud. Chantelle didn't even bat an eye. She did no more than nod and calmly leave the *hammam* to return to her rooms, giving the impression that she accepted the summons as a matter of course. But she didn't. No, not in the least.

Once in her quarters, she went straight into her bedchamber and did not come out. She could hear Adamma pacing on the other side of the curtain that separated the two rooms. She hadn't said a word to the girl, so she was no doubt anxious to begin the preparations. But Chantelle had nothing to prepare for.

Adamma waited no more than twenty minutes before she finally poked her head through the curtain. She found her mistress in front of the window, staring out at the garden.

"*Lalla?*"

"Yes?"

"Shouldn't we begin—"

"No."

"But—"

"I'm not going, Adamma."

Shahar hadn't turned from the garden. Her

voice hadn't been raised in the least. Adamma chewed on her lower lip. She should have expected this, but hadn't.

"Are you ill, *lalla?*" she asked hesitantly.

Chantelle glanced over her shoulder. "Ill?" She smiled tightly. "No, but that excuse will do as well as any to avoid a battle royal. Have Kadar inform Haji Agha so the Dey can make other arrangements for tonight."

Adamma groaned and rushed to the front door to find the black eunuch in his customary post outside it. "She's not going!" the girl blurted out.

Kadar came instantly to his feet. "Is she ill?" He asked the same question.

"No, but you must tell Haji Agha that she is."

"It won't work, girl."

"You better hope it does, because she means it. She's not going."

Kadar grunted and hurried away. He should have known the little English wouldn't remain docile for very long. She was too proud, that one, and too willful for her own good. Perhaps Haji Agha would believe that she was ill.

"I don't believe it," the Chief Black Eunuch said after Kadar had delivered his message. "What is wrong with the girl now?"

"I should think that is obvious, my lord."

Haji frowned. Yes, it was obvious. Shahar was no doubt upset that she had been ignored yesterday. The Europeans aways took longer to acclimate themselves to the way of things here. She would be angry and jealous, and her jealousy would probably be worse than her previous defiance had been.

"The Dey will never believe she's ill," Haji said more to himself, for he had already concluded that he had to at least try this way. Without the use of drugs, that left only force, and Jamil would not like having her "delivered" to him.

"Perhaps he will accept it even if he doesn't believe it," Kadar suggested. "He knows her temperament by now."

"We can only hope," Haji grunted. "By the Prophet's beard, the girl is more trouble than she's worth," he added as he departed for the Dey's apartments.

He should have known it wouldn't work.

"Is she ill?" Derek asked suspiciously.

Haji could only stammer, "I—I haven't seen her myself, but—but her attendants assure me—"

"Ill or not, have her here at the appointed hour, Haji."

And that was that.

Chapter Thirty-six

CHANTELLE WAS the one pacing now. She was still in her bedchamber, but she was no longer calm. Kadar and Adamma both had been browbeating her for the past thirty minutes. Jamil had been told that she was ill, but he didn't care. He insisted she make an appearance. She refused.

"If you do not go, the Dey will come here," Adamma told her.

"No, he won't. You said he rarely bestirs himself to enter the harem because of the commotion it causes."

"But if he does? And if he does, he will be furious."

"Good," Chantelle snorted. "Anger loves company just as much as misery."

Both servants grimaced simultaneously at such a sentiment. They had been warned to get results or else. It was the "or else" that kept them trying, but they were getting nowhere.

Haji Agha waited in the outer room, too old and set in his ways to resort to mere cajolery with a concubine when so many other options were usually available to him. But all they could do was argue in this case, after the Dey had ordered no punishments for the girl.

"Soon the Keeper of the Jewels will be here," Kadar said now. "The Mistress of the Wardrobe, too. Do you want them to think you are pouting because you weren't summoned yesterday?"

That infuriated Chantelle. Pouting? The very idea!

"I'll have you know—"

"It will make no difference what you say, *lalla*. The harem will draw its own conclusions."

"I don't care."

"Don't you?" they both asked together.

Chantelle glared at them. How the hell had they

346

gotten to know her so well so quickly? Damn, but pride could be bloody awkward.

"All right," she said testily. "But if I get my head chopped off tonight, you'll be as much to blame for forcing me to see him."

"That won't happen, *lalla*."

"Won't it?" she snapped. "If he so much as touches me, I'll scratch his eyes out. We'll see how long my head holds up after that."

Adamma paled, taking her seriously. Kadar repressed a grin. The little English was angry, not stupid. And besides, the Dey was not an insensitive man. He knew she did not want to see him, and so he would be expecting the worst.

Derek was indeed expecting the worst, and had been even before Shahar had tried tendering an excuse of illness. The wise thing to do would be to give the girl a few days to get over her pique, which was what he had originally intended to do. But that was yesterday, when he had decided to send for Charity Woods, when he had thought he had gotten enough of Shahar to last him for a while. He realized differently last night. He had had the lovely Charity at hand, could have easily availed himself of her charms, and they were nice charms indeed, but instead he had spent the evening playing chess with her, and losing, because all he could think about was Shahar and her reaction to his supposed perfidy.

But there had been no help for it. He had had the option of putting off summoning Charity

Woods until later or getting it out of the way now. Later might have been too late, since there was no telling when Jamil would return. And unless it was recorded in the harem records that the favorite known as Jamila had been summoned to his bed, she wouldn't be released when this was over.

If she wasn't one of Jamil's favorites, Derek could have simply asked for her release. As it was, with Omar's insisting he had to make love to at least one of Jamil's women, it had worked out ideally. But getting it out of the way now had put him back to the starting point with Shahar.

He'd bungled the whole thing, really. Shahar wouldn't be upset now if he had seen to Miss Woods earlier. But no, he had let his body rule him then, and he was doing it again today, and why? What was it about Shahar that put him into a fervor of impatience? She muddled his thinking. She controlled his body more than he did. Why her, especially when there were dozens of other beauties available to him who would be more than willing to appease this hunger that one silver-haired blonde had created?

He couldn't figure it out, but one thing was blazingly apparent. He had become obsessed, and he had to get over her before Jamil returned. His future was mapped out. It did not include a beautiful concubine who technically didn't even belong to him. He had the use of her temporarily, but that was all. So there was nothing for it but to wallow in her charms while he could and hope that an overindulgence would soon have him bored and free of this obsession.

Derek dismissed the Nubian guards ahead of time, as well as his other attendants. Dinner for two was prepared and already served. Roses graced the low table set before the garden doors, an English touch for Shahar's benefit. Muted music drifted over the garden walls.

They would be alone once she arrived. Derek wanted no witnesses to the argument he anticipated, not when he was supposed to be Jamil, and Jamil wouldn't tolerate any argument at all. Derek was going to be more than tolerant. He would do anything short of groveling to appease the lady he wanted in his bed.

Her entrance was subdued, after he had almost expected her to be carried in kicking and screaming. But he should have known she'd have more control than that. She was in fact stiffly regal in her posture, as if she were cloaked in dignity rather than the silver tissue in which she had been dressed. From her hair to her silver sandals, she was all aglitter, with sequins banding her skimpy costume and diamonds circling her neck, wrists, and ankles. She had worn not a single jewel that he had given her, which was a telling statement. She nonetheless took his breath away with her beauty.

She stood in the center of the room, her head held erect, her hands at her sides forming little fists. She stared straight ahead, not even bothering to locate him in the room. She looked like she would break if he spoke too loud.

He came up behind her. "I trust you have recovered from your illness?"

She didn't reply at once. "Actually . . . I'm feeling rather nauseated."

Derek grinned at the bold-faced lie. "Too ill to share a meal with me?"

It was on the tip of her tongue to refuse to dine with him, but the fact was, she was famished now that her stomach had settled itself. "A meal would be nice," Chantelle allowed.

He moved in front of her and, with an arm, motioned her to proceed to the low table behind them. She wouldn't look at him other than to follow his direction. And once seated on a plump pillow, she stared only at the many platters of food spread out before her.

It was disheartening that she didn't even comment on the roast beef and Yorkshire pudding that had been obtained from the English consulate especially for her, as well as the cook to prepare them. Sir John Blake was undoubtedly wondering what Jamil Reshid was up to, but then the Dey didn't have to explain himself to the English consul, who wouldn't dream of refusing such a minor request as a raid on his larder. But Derek would have liked at least some acknowledgment, when he had gone to the trouble just to please her.

It was not to be, however. Her manner was stiff, cold, uncommunicative, so he wisely decided to forgo conversation while they ate. Humors were generally improved on a full stomach, and by her attitude, he needed all the help he could get.

But when he poured her tea, also acquired from Sir John's household, he finally ventured to ask, "Was the meal to your liking?"

"The meat was a bit tough."

Derek gritted his teeth. So it was. Mr. Walmsley, the Marquis's butler, would have been appalled. But what did she expect here in Barikah, where the main staple was sheep?

"It was the best I could arrange under such short notice."

She didn't reply. She sipped her tea, keeping her eyes lowered.

Derek was becoming distinctly uncomfortable under this treatment, not to mention annoyed. He would have preferred she just lay into him and get it over with, though he still wasn't sure what he could say to her when he couldn't tell her the truth. And that, too, was annoying.

He stood up abruptly. "Come."

Chantelle ignored the hand he offered and stood up by herself, moving over to the couch of pillows. But she didn't sit down there. She couldn't. She stared at the setting of her seduction and experienced again the full fury of her stupidity.

Derek came up behind her and took matters into his own hands, pulling her down onto the cushions with him and then straight into his arms. Her reaction was to immediately push away from him and scoot back several feet. He allowed this after a brief connection with her eyes. They

351

were glittering as brightly as the diamonds she wore, but with hostility.

"This won't do, Shahar," Derek said after a moment's indecision. "It is my right to touch you."

"And my God-given right to fight you, and I warn you I will."

He had her full attention now. She had come up on her knees to face him, her fists clenched on her thighs, tensely ready for any move he might make.

Derek sighed and gave her a smile that was vaguely apologetic. "But you cannot win, so there is no point in even trying. You will only expend your energy, when we can put it to a much better use."

She caught her breath. "No! Never again!"

"Never?" He shook his head, as if the word were alien to him. "You are angry, but at least be realistic, Shahar. You know full well that when I want you, I will have you."

"And I will fight you!"

"So you have said. Shall I show you how little good it will do you?"

There was a brief flash of fear before she exploded. "Damn you, have you so little pride that you would force yourself on a woman who despises you?"

"Do you really think force will be necessary?"

She bristled at the confidence in his tone. "Just try anything, and you will—"

"Oh, I intend to, English, and soon. I will

352

make you purr for me again. You do remember—"

"Stop it!"

"I see you do," he said with a devilish grin. "I do as well. So why are we wasting time—"

"Oh!"

Chantelle shot to her feet, only to have his arm snake around her legs and pull them out from under her. She landed half on him, half on the pillows, but in only a moment she was flat on her back, his body covering her, his hands capturing hers and stretching them far above her head. She was trapped, and no matter how hard she exerted herself to dislodge him, it did no good.

"Don't stop," he murmured thickly by her ear. "I can feel your body's movements with every part of my own." She went still and he chuckled. "You are so predictable, English. I believe we have played this game before."

"Let me up," she gritted out between her teeth.

"I prefer you like this," he said, grinding his hips into her. "It brings back such wonderful memories."

"I hate you."

He shook his head slowly in answer. "You are angry with me. You don't hate me."

He was amused. She saw it in his eyes, in the slight twisting of his lips. He wasn't taking her seriously. Or if he was, he felt confident he could charm her around. But he couldn't, and she was afraid when he realized that, he would finally get angry, too.

"Don't presume to tell me what I feel, your highness," she said tightly. "You can't command feelings the way you do everything else."

"I thought I was fairly good at it the other night."

She gasped at this pointed reminder of how easily he had made her want him. "That was before you lied to me!"

At last he frowned, demanding, "What are you talking about, woman?"

"You led me to believe that you had not been with another woman since you first saw me. I know now that the very night you bought me you spent with Sheelah, and the next night you summoned—"

"Enough!" Derek cut in sharply.

Christ! And he thought he only had to explain away Jamila. What could he say? Certainly not that while he had lain in his empty bed thinking of her, his brother's bed had not remained so empty. He couldn't defend himself without giving up the game. He couldn't tell her the truth about Jamila either. For Miss Woods to be released, everyone had to think he had taken her to bed, including Omar—including Shahar. Bloody hell. He hadn't lied to her before, but now he would have to lie through his teeth.

"You accuse me of lying, Shahar, when I spoke from the heart. I wanted only you. From the first moment, you excited me as no woman ever has before."

"That didn't stop you from—"

"You were untried, woman! You were innocent in mind as well as in body. I couldn't summon you immediately, as was my desire. You needed at least a little instruction so that you would know what to expect and not be afraid of our coming together. Or did you want to share my bed that first night?"

"No," she replied stiffly. "And I don't care who did. Nor do I care why someone did. The point is that you told me no one did, and I believed you. It made a difference in the way I— well, it made a difference." And then, bitterly: "But that's what you intended, isn't it? That's why you lied to me."

"Did I lie? Or did I tell you the truth, that you were all I wanted, all I could think about?" He didn't wait for an answer, taking advantage of the momentary doubt he detected in her eyes. "Did I allow you months of training? Did I listen when I was told you were not ready? Who knows better than you that I did not, that I could not wait to see you again? And then you rejected me. Do you know how that made me feel?"

"I—"

Chantelle fell silent, at a loss for words. She hadn't expected to find herself on the defensive. She hadn't expected to experience this feeling of guilt, either, that was tightening in her chest. But he was right, damn him. He hadn't actually lied to her, hadn't actually said specifically that no other woman had shared his bed. And she had thought

355

of that, that she had simply misinterpreted his words, or that he had just phrased them wrong.

I spoke from the heart. You were all I wanted. There was no misinterpreting those words, and damn it to hell, she believed him again. Then why didn't it give her joy?

Derek relaxed somewhat, sensing that he had won this round. He didn't give Shahar a chance to throw up the next hurdle, hoping he might bypass it entirely with a little luck and a lot of skill, which he immediately brought into play with a kiss meant to shatter the last of her defenses. And it worked. She didn't turn her head away to avoid his lips. He could feel her arms going slack, her body fitting more snugly to his. As she yielded, he let go of her hands and felt her fingers drift into his hair. And then suddenly she yanked.

"Ouch! By Allah—"

"I warned you," Chantelle cut in furiously. "If you wanted a willing bedmate, you should have summoned Jamila again. She would—"

Derek clamped a hand over her mouth. He didn't take into account that he had convinced her he wouldn't hurt her physically, or that he had told her he'd accepted the challenge of subduing her. It simply turned his blood cold that this anger of hers could make her so heedless of its consequences.

Jamil would have been flattered by it, and amused, but not for long, and certainly not enough to allow her to actually fight him. Derek wasn't amused. He knew that she had come to trust him, which was why she had finally surrendered, and now she was feeling betrayed.

But thank God Jamil's tastes were different from his own and his brother hadn't decided to keep Shahar for himself. She wouldn't have passed a week without some serious punishments which would have eventually broken her spirit. She didn't realize how lucky she was, nor could he tell her. But what was the point, when she only had him to deal with?

That he had been concerned for her welfare was a natural reaction, but it gave a hard edge to his voice now. "If I had wanted Jamila, I *would* have sent for her. I wanted you, Shahar. I wanted you yesterday as well, but foolishly thought you might be grateful for a day of respite after I was so relentless in giving you none the night before."

She pried his fingers away from her mouth to snap, "Don't you dare claim it was for my benefit!"

"I also thought you had too much pride to succumb to jealousy."

Her eyes flared at this new attack. "Jealousy? Not on your life! It was just brought home to me that this is no more than a whorehouse, and you are the—"

"Don't say it!"

"Why not? If I made love to a different man every night, that is what you would call me. And don't tell me it is different for a man, that you are allowed, that *you* in particular are allowed. Your world might think so, but mine does not."

"Does it not?"

It enraged her further that he smiled when he asked that. "Then let me put it this way. *I* do not. Now will you . . . let . . . me . . . up!" She shoved at him again, but he couldn't be budged.

"I will let you go, Shahar, when you forgive me for hurting you."

She made the mistake of meeting the warm glow in his eyes. That and his husky timbre sent a shiver along her nerve endings.

"You didn't hurt me," she insisted, turning her head to the side. "I just ignored a few basic truths for a while, but I am back on the right track now."

"Don't do this, Shahar." He took advantage of the throat she exposed to him, nuzzling his lips there. "It meant nothing to me." His lips moved toward her ear, and he took a moment to draw her earlobe between his teeth. "I cannot even recall what I did or said last night, it was so insignificant." He was murmuring right into her ear now, so that each breath affected her. "But I can remember every single moment I spent with you."

Chantelle's thoughts had scattered, and she couldn't seem to get them back. "You—you can't be faithful. You don't know how."

"If that is what it will take to have you willing again," he promised recklessly.

She shrugged him away from her ear, doubting her hearing. "You don't mean that," she scoffed. "My God, I have even been told you exhaust yourself in order to satisfy everyone. You should be glad that at least one of the women you own won't feel neglected if you ignore her."

"It would devastate me if that were so, but you know it is not. Now that you have tasted the pleasures of the body, you would miss this." He slid a hand between their bodies to capture a breast. "Even now I can feel your nipple hardening, begging for my kiss."

"Sto—" The word turned abruptly to a scream, for suddenly behind him there loomed a dark shape, but all Chantelle actually saw was the flash of a dagger raised above the Dey's head.

Chapter Thirty-seven

IF DEREK had stopped to think, that would have been the end of it. The knife would have found its target, plunging through his back straight to his heart. And the blade was long enough to have passed through him, going on to impale Shahar as well.

But he didn't stop to think. Shahar's scream was laced with fear, not outrage at his seduction, and his instincts demanded immediate response, not questions.

He rolled, taking Shahar with him, right into the legs of the assailant. The man lost his balance, falling over them, his knife sinking so sharply into the pillows it pierced right through, the tip breaking off on the marble floor beneath. But the weapon was not made any less dangerous by losing its point. It was still deadly enough to slash through flesh and bone, and was swiftly brought into play to do just that.

Derek only had time to shove Shahar away from him, the man was on him so quickly. He couldn't even spare a glance to see if he had abandoned her to other assailants, though professionals weren't likely to bother with a woman until their objective had been met, and he was that objective. But the man didn't get immediate help. He was strong enough not to need any, as Derek painfully found out. And if the blunted, jagged edge of the dagger didn't have difficulty breaking through his skin, it would have sunk deeper than a mere half inch before his own strength forced it out, his hands nearly breaking the man's wrist before it was jerked away.

The second stab was deflected with his forearm, and that gave him a chance to land a fist on the assassin's jaw. But in his position on the floor, there wasn't much power behind it. Mere seconds passed before the knife was back, slashing at his throat this time. But the longer reach of his arms saved him, and a palm to the chin of the assassin so he couldn't see his target.

The blade fell short of its mark, and Derek was able to latch onto the wrist again, determined not to lose it this time. Now it was simply a matter of strength, and an awareness that there could only be one survivor in this contest.

Chantelle crouched on the floor, both fists

pressed to her mouth, her eyes riveted to the deadly scene before her. She didn't think to run for help, nor did she wonder why there wasn't any help forthcoming after her piercing scream. Her instinct was to do something herself, but she was terrified to take her eyes off the grappling pair even for a moment, afraid that it would be over if she did. And the assailant was so huge, now that she could see him clearly. There was solid bulk filling his robes, a broad back, thick shoulders, and arms that were probably just as thick. How could Jamil, who might be strong but was so much slimmer, hold him off for very long?

She had to do something and quickly, before the fear she was experiencing paralyzed her even more. She stumbled to her feet, glancing frantically about for a weapon that would make a likely club or . . . . Her eyes flew to the table as she suddenly remembered the long knife Jamil had used to carve the roast. No servants had come in to clear the table. The knife was still there, but could she use it? Could she actually kill a man? What would happen if she didn't?

Jamil could die, of course, and that gave her the incentive to run to the table and snatch up the knife. But she was more terrified than ever with the lethal thing in her fist. How could she do it? How could she not? She didn't want Jamil to die, did she? *Did she?*

She acknowledged the answer only on a deeper level, for she was already moving toward the deadly struggle on the floor, and before she could question the right or wrong of it any further, she raised the knife to plunge it into the assailant's back, just as he had meant to do to Jamil. But she had gotten too close to them. A leg jarred her, ruining her aim, and somehow that broad back wasn't there to receive the blade, but Jamil's head was.

Chantelle blanched even as the momentum prevented her from drawing back, it all happened so quickly. She saw the knife nick Jamil's ear as she fell against the assassin. And then she went crashing into the wall, unaware that she had knocked the large man so off balance that Derek was able to change their positions, and she got thrown over in the process.

The pillows set up against the wall cushioned the impact, so that Chantelle wasn't even stunned. But she had lost her knife in the fall. And when she looked back, the two combatants were still. No, oh, God, no!

"Jamil?"

He raised his head, and Chantelle crumpled with relief, sinking back into the pillows. *Now* she felt bruised and battered. But what must he be feeling?

"Are you all right, Shahar?"

"Me?" she choked, and then sucked in a gasp as he stood up. "You're bleeding!"

It came out as an accusation. Derek glanced down at his chest but knew the cut was too minor to be concerned about.

"It is nothing."

"But why did he . . . how could this . . . where the devil are your guards?" she finally got out, anger replacing her fear.

"I believe I told them I would skin them alive if they interrupted me tonight for anything. They obviously took me at my word. But they are mutes, after all, and would not have heard anything."

"I screamed loud enough to alert the guards at the end of the hall."

"So you did." Derek grinned. "But even if they would have responded to a woman's scream, which is doubtful in your case, since the entire palace knows what trouble I have with you, the guards at the door would not have let them in."

She ignored the insinuation that her screams could only mean he had lost patience with her. "Then how *did* he get in?" She looked at the man lying motionless on the floor and shuddered, seeing the dagger protruding from his chest and the wide pool of blood around it.

"A good question."

Chantelle watched him march to the door, only now realizing that the guards outside must be dead. But they weren't. They came in the room, followed soon by many others. And the Dey's personal guards weren't dead either. They were still in the garden where he had banished them, which left both entrances guarded, but obviously not very well. It was no wonder the mutes were so upset on finding the dead man in the room. They were guilty of either inattention or collusion.

But then the rope was found, dangling next to the garden doors, explaining at least how the assassin had gotten this far into the palace, but not how the two Nubians could have missed seeing him shimmying down from the high roof.

"It is my own fault." The Dey exonerated them to an older man who had come in after the guards and seemed more upset by the incident than anyone else. "I warned them to stay away from the doors and simply patrol the garden walls."

"You deliberately left yourself vulnerable?" the old man asked incredulously.

Jamil said something that Chantelle didn't hear, but she blushed furiously when the old man looked at her with disgust afterward. Whoever he was, he blamed her, and no doubt everyone else would, too.

Some physicians came to fuss over the Dey's wound. The dead man was also examined. A heavy bag of coins was found in a pocket, but nothing else.

Chantelle stopped watching the proceedings. Her anger had turned to guilt, and the full realization of what had happened hit her hard. Jamil could have died. My God, *she* had nearly killed him.

She glanced up to see one of the doctors dabbing something on the Dey's ear and she paled, her stomach turning over. What if he thought she had done it intentionally, that she had taken advantage of the moment to free herself of him? Hadn't she just told him tonight that she hated him? She had no reason to help him, none that she could think of, none that he would think of, certainly nothing that made sense.

The body was carted from the room, the blood wiped up from the floor, and those pillows that had been stained by it exchanged for new ones. Chantelle moved over when the pillow she was sitting on was taken away, but she didn't get up, even when the room began to empty. She was recalling her angry remark to Kadar that she was going to get her head chopped off tonight, and experiencing the full dread of its being a distinct possibility now.

Finally only Jamil and the two Nubians remained in the room. The Dey drained a glass of *kanyak*, which he had requested, then abruptly dismissed the two black men back to the garden. They nearly balked at this; in fact, they did seem to argue with him. Chantelle couldn't understand one bit of the sign language they used, but she did understand that they didn't want to leave Jamil alone again. But of course the Dey was finally obeyed and left alone—with her.

"Why did you send them away?" she asked as he approached her. "Or do you mean to kill me yourself?"

He dropped to his knees in front of her, his eyes narrowing. "What silliness is—"

Chantelle didn't give him a chance to finish. In a panic, she threw herself at his chest, nearly knocking him over, and clinging tightly when he righted himself.

"I'm sorry!" she wailed against his throat. "I didn't mean to hurt you, I swear I didn't. I was aiming for his back, but I tripped and—"

"I know."

"His back wasn't there any—" She pulled away to look up at him. "What do you mean, you know?"

He laughed at the umbrage that had slipped into her tone. "What happened to 'I'm sorry'?"

"Then you don't think I was trying to kill you?"

"Were you?"

"Of course not!"

"Then give me credit for knowing the difference between help and hindrance, and timely help at that."

"Timely?"

"My arms were nearly ready to give out from trying to hold him back when your fall unbalanced him enough so that I could get him off me. You probably saved my life."

"I did?" she said in awe, but after a long moment of thought, she added, "Then you owe me a great boon, don't you?"

"If you are thinking of asking for your freedom, little moon, do not. I want you too much to let you go, even in gratitude for my life."

If he had said anything else, his earlier declarations would have rung false. As it was, that answer didn't disappoint her as it should have.

"Could I ask for something else?"

"What?"

"Constancy?"

"You wouldn't rather be showered in riches?" At the shy but negative shake of her head, he gathered her close. "You will wish you had chosen the riches when you beg for mercy and find none."

Chapter Thirty-eight

"DID YOU have him hung from the palace gate?" Derek asked Omar.

They were on the way back to Jamil's apartments after a morning spent in the audience chamber, a long morning, since it was only Derek's second attempt at dealing with the foreign dignitaries in his brother's stead. The first time he'd been nervous about meeting men of importance who had dealt with Jamil before and could so easily detect any difference in his behavior. But he'd handled it rather well this time, being more comfortable with the role he was playing. He'd even seen more petitioners than he'd planned on, though he had refrained from making any concessions without Omar's advice to guide him.

The older man frowned at the question, his expression indicating he was still touchy over the subject of last night's assassination attempt. "Yes, he is hung out to rot where all can see as they come and go from the palace. But no one has come forward to collect the reward for identifying him."

"Did you really think they would? At this point in the game, it would take a fool to admit to knowing anyone even remotely involved, let alone one of the actual assassins. And the story has probably spread far and wide already that another one has failed in the attempt. That's two since I have been here, and how many more before that?"

"Five attempts, eleven dead," Omar grunted.

"There you are. They are bound to get discouraged eventually, just from sheer loss of numbers."

"Or more desperate and suicidal."

"Come, now, the money behind this plot has to run out sometime. You will have to agree that the risk is too great to come cheap."

"Selim left Barikah bitter, not poor. But you are right about the risk being great, though it is no greater than the unnecessary one you have been taking. You prefer the danger, don't you?"

"Do I look crazy?"

"You look like a man thoroughly enjoying himself," Omar replied disgustedly.

Derek chuckled. "So you have found me out. But it's no more than a little excitement to break the monotony."

"I thought the woman was all the excitement you needed. Or did you use her only as an excuse to leave yourself vulnerable to attack?"

Derek grinned despite Omar's very real displeasure. "It was exactly as I said. Shahar could never have relaxed in my company with those Nubians looking over my shoulder. But no harm was done last night." At Omar's fierce glower, Derek laughed again. "Let it go, old friend.

I promise to be alive and kicking when Jamil returns."

"*Inshallah,*" Omar retorted before leaving him.

There was that, but Derek no longer believed wholeheartedly in the concept that every man's fate was predestined. Muslims did, however. It was what led them fearless into battle, the belief that if it was their time to die they would, and if not, nothing could harm them. He liked to think his own destiny was a little more controllable, that his own skill and decisions could alter its course.

But Omar was right insomuch as Derek had welcomed that little skirmish in the desert last week, just as he had thrived on the challenge last night. It wasn't that he needed life-threatening danger. He really wasn't suicidal. He just needed excitement of any kind to keep him from falling into the same rut Jamil had experienced.

Jamil at least had had normal business to attend to. But it had occurred to Derek just this morning that with no real responsibilities, no actual decisions to make or worry over, he had nothing of importance to occupy his time. It was no wonder, then, that his concentration had focused on a woman. Could that be the sole reason for his obsession, why he had made *her* so important? It was likely, and it went a long way toward relieving his mind. When it was time to leave, it wouldn't be that difficult for him to put this episode of his life behind him. He would remember Shahar fondly, but that was all.

In his rooms, Derek motioned his dresser forward to shed him of the raiments of office. The rest of the day was free now, and he had every intention of sleeping through part of it. But that was not to be. He was informed a servant from the harem was waiting to see him, and he finally noticed the girl cowering in a corner, fearful of actually being in the Dey's presence.

Derek sighed in genuine irritation. "I had very little sleep last night. I haven't even eaten yet today. Can this not wait?"

Hearing that, his own attendant dismissed the girl immediately, and she was more than happy to have the matter taken out of her hands, running in her haste to vacate the room. Derek frowned at that.

"What was she afraid of?"

His dresser shrugged. "She was probably the bearer of bad news. Your brother Mahmud was famous for imprisoning, and sometimes executing, anyone who brought him news he did not care to hear."

Derek's frown darkened. "Go find out what that was about, then."

The man returned in a moment, hesitant himself now to deliver the message. "She was sent by the eunuch Kadar, my lord. Your slave Shahar has been . . . poisoned."

"God, no!" The color drained from Derek's face. "She can't be dead!"

"She is not . . . yet, but—"

He didn't wait to hear the rest, calling over his

shoulder as he rushed out of the room, "Send my own physicians to the harem immediately!"

"But, my lord, they cannot enter—"

Derek ran the length of the corridor that the women used to reach the Dey's apartments. He stopped when he caught up with Kadar's messenger, and then only because he didn't want to waste time asking directions. He knew how to reach the Pink Court from childhood, but not where Shahar's rooms would be.

The girl was terrified to be stopped by him, thinking the worst, and fell to her knees at his feet, crying loudly for mercy. Derek had to bend down and shake her just to get her attention.

"I mean you no harm, dammit!" His tone was not reassuring. "Just take me to Shahar."

"You mean to enter the—"

He cut through her amazement with a sharp "Now!"

She flinched and ran ahead of him. She was not as quick as he would have liked. And once they entered the harem there were the crowded pathways to be contended with, the shrieks of surprise, the crashes as trays of food slipped out of nervous hands, and every single soul dropping to the floor so quickly that a sprained wrist, two cracked ribs, and a dislocated jaw would later be reported.

Shahar's apartment was easy to find after all. It was where all the favorites and wives were gathered outside, along with their servants and eunuchs, waiting to hear more news, good or bad.

Again his sudden appearance caused a commotion, and he actually had to step over several prone bodies to reach the door. Then he stopped dead for a moment, hearing an anguished cry coming from inside.

Oh, God, don't let her die. Please, not her.

He stopped at the door to the bedchamber, where the curtains were tied back to allow for all the comings and goings. The room was filled with women, most of them the old ones who tended to the minor illnesses in the harem. Kadar was there, too, kneeling by the bed, his hands fisted in his hair as if he meant to pull it out in his despair. A young girl was on the other side of the bed, tears running down her cheeks as she applied cooling compresses to Shahar's forehead.

Dread slowed his steps now as Derek approached the bed, seeing nothing but the pitiful form lying there. She lay on her side, curled in a tight ball, arms locked over her stomach. Blood beaded on her lower lip where she had bit it, scarlet against the ashen hue of her face. Her eyes were squeezed shut, the lashes wet with tears. She was whimpering . . . .

"How long has she been in pain like this?"

Kadar's head snapped up as he recognized the quiet voice. There were tears in his eyes, too, but they weren't so blurry that he could mistake the stricken expression the Dey unknowingly revealed.

"I thought you were not coming, my lord," Kadar said, a note of accusation in his voice that he didn't care if the Dey detected or not. "I sent word hours ago."

"That idiot girl did not bother to find me. She waited for me to return to my apartments, which I only just . . . How the hell could this happen?"

It was a stupid question, he knew, and so he didn't expect an answer. Poison was one of the commonest methods of doing away with rivals, and had been used for hundreds of years in hundreds of harems all across the Turkish empire. What he really wanted to know was why it had to happen to his Shahar.

"We are not certain of the poison used, but it would have been an easy matter for someone to tamper with her food in the kitchen, and all servants have access there."

"Where is Haji Agha? He should have informed me of this himself."

"In the city, my lord. This is the day he customarily visits the bazaars. He has not returned yet."

"And what has been done for her?"

"She was given a purge, but because we do not know which poison was used, or how much, it is impossible to tell—"

"Has she gotten worse? Better?"

Kadar hesitated a long moment before he was forced to admit, "Worse."

Derek closed his eyes. For all the power at his disposal, he felt completely helpless.

"My lord?" someone said behind him. "The

physicians are at the gate, but the guards are refusing them entrance."

"Dammit to hell! I summoned them. Were the guards not told that?"

"No men have ever entered the harem before, my lord," was the tremulous reply. "The guards will not accept their word that they come by your order."

Derek turned back to the eunuch. "Kadar, I give you leave to act in Haji Agha's stead. Blindfold them if necessary, but get them in here fast. And I want this room vacated, and those women outside gone, too," he added angrily. "This is not a deathbed to be hovering over."

Derek shook his head when Adamma started to leave, too. She moved out of the way, however, when he sat on the edge of the bed, amazed to see the hand he stretched toward Shahar's cheek tremble.

"Can you hear me, Shahar?"

"Jamil?" She didn't open her eyes. Her voice was hoarse, her throat raw from repeated vomiting. She moaned, then tried to stifle the sound by clamping her lips together. When the cramps lessened, she asked, "Am I going to die?"

"No, love, I won't allow it."

She meant to smile, but it came out as a grimace. "Arrogant . . . as always."

He smoothed the silver locks back from her temple. Her hair was damp, her face covered by a fine sheen of cold sweat. With a finger he wiped the blood from her lip.

"Look at me, Shahar."

"Chantelle," she whispered. "Call me Chantelle at least once before I—"

"Dammit, woman, you are not going to die!"

Her eyes slitted open to glower at him. "Don't shout at me!"

"Then fight back. Resist it. Put your infernal stubbornness to good use."

"What the bloody hell do you think I'm doing, damn you!"

Adamma was appalled, listening to them, that the Dey would torment a dying woman like this. And yet color had returned to Shahar's cheeks, and her voice was strong again. His provoking her had done what all their tender care had not.

Rahine, who had been in the back of the room when the Dey entered and hadn't left with the others, was disturbed as well, but for a different reason. She had never seen Jamil behave like this. She knew he fancied this girl, but to show his feelings for anyone and everyone to see was not his way. Even when Sheelah had had difficulty with her second labor, he had kept his concern hidden.

He was different. Was it Shahar's doing, or simply the strain from all these months of danger? Whatever it was, she shouldn't have gone out of her way to avoid him since his displeasure with her over Jamila's purchase. It seemed she didn't know her own son anymore.

Chapter Thirty-nine

DEREK FINALLY noticed her when he turned at the physicians', arrival, but he didn't recognize her. It was because she was still there after he had ordered everyone out that made him wonder who she was to defy him. And then he met her eyes, as emerald green as his own, and he knew. And the knowledge nearly undid him.

Christ, he had been racking his brain for a way to see her without her being aware of it, but it was easy to spy on him, not so easy on the women in the harem. He had wanted to just summon her to his presence, but Omar had talked him out of it, because if anyone could see through his impersonation, it would be his mother, and they had agreed, Jamil included, that no one, not even Rahine, was to know about the switch. And that meant Derek couldn't talk to Rahine, at least not until it was over and Jamil was safe.

But here she was, only a few feet away, changed surely, older, reserved now, not the impetuous young woman he remembered, but, God, still beautiful, still regal in her bearing, still able to see into the soul with those eyes. They were probing his now, wondering no doubt why he was staring at her like this. What had Jamil said about her?

Not much, because Derek wasn't supposed to run into her.

He should have turned away and just ignored her. He couldn't do it. He walked up to her, aching to embrace her, yet knowing full well it wasn't something Jamil would do. But, dear Lord, she was just what he needed at the moment, the one person from whom he could accept comfort. If she told him Shahar would be all right, he would believe her. She was his mother. He felt like crying . . . .

"Are you certain you want these men to see Shahar?"

Derek pulled himself together to see that the two doctors were just standing there, their blindfolds still intact. The traditions of the harem suddenly disgusted him, that no man, not even a desperately needed physician, could look on another man's women.

"I don't give a damn who sees her, as long as they cure her."

"They understand, Jamil," Rahine said gently. "But it would be wise if you came into the other room. They are too nervous to do anything with you glowering at them."

He nodded and followed her only because he knew she was right. And then, too, he wanted some answers, and not where Shahar could hear them.

"You know these women better even than I. Who would want to kill her?"

Rahine hesitantly joined him by the window

that faced the marble court. The area was empty now, the sun turning the spray in the fountain to diamond drops. He hadn't asked anything of her in so long. She was gladdened that he did now, but at the same time wretched because she couldn't help him. And he was obviously upset by this incident, enough to make him behave out of character.

"Your women are not as vicious in their jealousy as they could be, Jamil. I honestly don't know. Noura is the most spiteful, but then you know that. If she were going to have anyone poisoned, it would be Sheelah. It is the position of first *kadine* that she covets, not your bed."

"Who else?"

"Mara lost her position when Shahar moved to the Pink Court, but I don't think she would kill to get it back. She knows she serves a special purpose that no one else can fill."

"Who else?" he repeated.

"Have you considered your own enemies?"

He glanced sideways at her, but only for a moment. "I presume you mean my *main* enemy?"

"Yes. It is no secret outside the palace that you are very well pleased with your new concubine. It is said you are content to remain inside the palace walls now that you have this new slave to entertain you. So it is not unreasonable to suppose that you might be distressed should anything happen to her, even careless enough to attend the funeral."

"All right," he said curtly. "You have made your point."

"Haji Agha will, of course, have the harem searched. If we can find the poison—" She paused, ending with the obvious. "It is doubtful anyone would be so stupid as to not get rid of it."

After a short silence, he said, "I want her moved to my apartments as soon as she is able."

Rahine was so surprised by this, she thoughtlessly touched his arm to draw his eyes to her. "If it is a matter of protection, we can do that better here, now that we know it is needed. What can you be thinking of, Jamil? There are so many other variables to be considered outside the harem; in particular, the number of times the assassins have managed to get as far as your apartments. Was Shahar not in danger just last night?"

He conceded, placing his hand over hers. "I know. I just cannot seem to think clearly where she is concerned. Can you promise me this will not happen again?"

Rahine felt an unexpected moisture gathering in her eyes. Twice now he was asking for her help, and this time trusting her to protect his most prized possession. She couldn't remember the last time he had wanted anything of her. And he hadn't touched her, actually touched her, since she had sent Kasim away.

"Jamil . . ." No, she couldn't bring herself to mention his brother. It had always thrown him into a rage whenever she tried to broach the subject. He was already too distraught over Shahar.

"Yes, I can promise you there will be no more poisoned food. I will make my own cook and food tasters available for her henceforth. My people have been with me more than twenty years. There are none more loyal."

He nodded, relieved on that score at least. It had been irrational for him to think of moving her out of the harem anyway. He had already made too many unusual precedents for her. Jamil wouldn't return for weeks yet. He had to stop doing things that Jamil wouldn't do, or risk giving himself away. But damn, he wanted to protect her himself, not leave it in the hands of others.

He glanced back out of the window. There was nothing more to say to Rahine. He had a thousand questions, but none could be asked now. Yet he was loath to end this rare moment with her.

"Tell me she isn't going to die, Mother."

"Oh, God!"

He caught her arm when she swayed back. "What is it?"

"Nothing, nothing," she assured him. But she turned aside. She wouldn't look at him again. "You must not fear for her, Jamil. You said yourself she is stubborn. And she brought up everything she had eaten, so whatever poison remains is minimal."

"But she is in pain."

"As likely from the purge as from the poison. Your physicians will give her something to ease

380

it. She is probably better already. Go and see for yourself."

He didn't have much choice, since she quickly left him then. But he knew he had upset her. He just didn't know it was because he had called her Mother, something Jamil hadn't done for nineteen years.

Chapter Forty

"ARE YOU feeling better now?"

Chantelle stopped Adamma from fussing with her pillows and motioned her to leave. Rahine sat on the other side of the bed. It was she who had made the inquiry.

"I'd hate to tell you what I really feel like, madame."

Rahine smiled at the surly tone. "Much better, I'd say."

Chantelle started to glower but didn't want to waste the effort. She felt like her insides had been wrung out to dry. There was a horrible taste in her mouth, every bone seemed to ache, and she was as weak as a kitten. But this was nothing compared with how she had felt earlier. At least Rahine was speaking English for a change, so she didn't have to tax herself by translating.

"Did you come here to pay your last respects?"

Rahine laughed outright. "Don't be absurd, child. You'll be as good as new in a few days."

Chantelle closed her eyes against such good

humor. No one should be cheerful while she felt so miserable, at least not in her presence.

"Am I to take it you're glad I'm still among the living?"

"Very glad, Shahar. I don't know what it is about you, but you have completely changed Jamil, and for that I thank you. It's almost as if I have my son back."

"I wasn't aware you had lost him."

"That's a . . . long story, and nothing for you to be concerned with."

That evasion should have aroused Chantelle's curiosity, but she had other things on her mind. "Did I dream it, or was Jamil here?"

"He was here most of the afternoon."

"But I thought he never enters the harem."

"You will allow the circumstances are unusual, my dear. It's the first time one of his women has ever been poisoned."

So much for thinking he might care for her more than he did for any of his other women. "How did I get to be so lucky?"

"It's doubtful we will ever know who wished you harm, but you needn't fear it will happen again. Your food will come from my own kitchen from now on, and Haji Agha has assigned you two of his own bodyguards. You will never be left entirely alone."

"Wonderful," Chantelle said bitterly. "More the prisoner than ever."

"You mustn't look at it that way."

"No? I should be grateful, I suppose, that someone wants me dead?"

She would never be able to escape now, but worse, she wasn't sure she wanted to, not after last night. She didn't want Rahine to know that, however, not after she had predicted just that happening. Chantelle didn't have the temperament to hear a smug "I told you so."

How had Jamil done it? How had he gotten around her anger and hurt and made her want him again? And so much! Dear Lord, they had made love all night long. After how close he had come to death, it was as if *she* couldn't get enough of him. If anyone had been ready to beg for mercy, it was Jamil.

She should be utterly ashamed, but she wasn't. At some point during the night, she had forgiven him for Jamila, and he had assured her it wouldn't happen again. She would believe him because she wanted to, because she wanted him. It couldn't be any simpler than that. Like a silly twit in love, she had gone and become contented with her enslavement. Was she in love? Good Lord, that would be a ridiculous thing to do. Love a man who owned forty-eight women? Best not to delve too deeply into that.

Then Chantelle was reminded that during all those pleasant hours she had spent with him last night, she had never gotten around to asking him about the attempt on his life. Was it related to her own near brush with death?

"—don't you think?"

"I'm sorry, what?"

"I said you should be grateful you're still alive. It was very close for a while today."

Chantelle made a face. "I was there, remember?"

"Has anyone ever told you that you don't make a very good patient?"

Chantelle finally smiled grudgingly. "Am I being especially trying, Rahine?"

"And impertinent."

"No one else is around, *madame*."

Rahine had to suppress her laughter this time. "You are incorrigible. Very well, you may call me Rahine—when no one else is around."

"Then will you call me Chantelle—when no one else is around?"

"You are supposed to forget your previous life," Rahine began but was quickly interrupted.

"Did you?"

"I—think you need your rest."

"Not yet." Chantelle sat up more against her pillows. "First tell me who that man was last night who tried to kill Jamil."

"We'll never know that."

"Then you don't know why he attacked him?"

Rahine stared at her for a moment in amazement. "Do you mean to say . . . but you must have heard something about Jamil's troubles since you have been here."

"I don't know what you're talking about."

"But I mentioned it to you myself, didn't I, the

night you drove him to recklessly leave the palace? I told you he had put his life in danger."

"That's all you told me. But I beg to differ that I *drove* him to leave the palace that night," Chantelle added tightly. "I'm not responsible for his hot temper."

"Whether you were or not is a moot point now. But he *was* set upon that night. It was inevitable, since they watch the palace constantly. By Allah's grace, however, Jamil wasn't harmed that time. Even without a weapon, he disarmed one assassin, and the other was too cowardly to face him alone."

"Assassins? This sounds like a conspiracy," Chantelle said in alarm.

"So it is, and it began nearly a half year ago with the first attempt on Jamil's life. There have been numerous attacks since then. Twice now they have even gotten as far into the palace as his private apartment. Whoever wants him dead seems to have an endless supply of fanatics willing to brave impossible odds to collect the promised reward."

"Then you don't know who it is?"

Rahine shrugged. "Everything points to Selim, Jamil's younger half brother, because he went into hiding about the time of the first attack and he still hasn't been found."

"Fratricide?" Chantelle frowned in distaste. "That's—"

"Fairly common in the Turkish empire, my dear, where children are exposed early to the rivalries and petty jealousies of the harem. But as I said, everything points to Selim. That doesn't mean that it couldn't be someone else, although Selim is next in line to succeed Jamil."

"But Jamil has sons," Chantelle pointed out, though that subject wasn't one of her favorites.

"True, but they are all much too young. This is not England, child. A brother who has reached manhood will nearly always be chosen over a son too young to rule. Of course, there have been extreme cases in which a mother has bought the support of the army to elevate her son, but that has never happened in Barikah."

"Then Sheelah—"

"Never Sheelah!"

Chantelle frowned at the interruption and obvious support for Jamil's first wife by his mother. But then her eyes widened.

"Noura has the second oldest son, doesn't she?"

"Yes, but . . . that is ridiculous, Shahar—"

"Chantelle."

Rahine pursed her lips. "Very well—Chantelle. Speculation of this sort is pointless. And besides, Jamil has yet another half brother under Selim. Do you realize how many would have to die before Noura could come to power through her son? It would be much too obvious, even if the other deaths could be made to appear accidental, especially if Jamil should die first."

A chill passed over Chantelle, hearing it said so plainly. If Jamil should die. . . . She hadn't known he was in such danger.

"I wish you hadn't told me about this."

Rahine shrugged. "You asked, child. But I really thought you knew about it already. Why do you think we were so intent on keeping you from angering Jamil? His temper has been abominable these past months due to the restrictions imposed on him by this threat." Rahine leaned over to squeeze Chantelle's hand. "We have you to thank for taking his mind off it, even if you have done so in an unacceptable manner."

Chantelle knew very well she was referring to her defiance, even up to last night. Did Rahine also know it had ended last night? Of course she did. She knew everything.

Cheeks heating with color, Chantelle was ready to change the subject. Rahine did it for her. "I really shouldn't have stayed this long. You are to have complete bed rest for a week—"

"A week!"

Rahine couldn't help smiling. "At the very least, several days without exception."

"Jamil isn't going to like that."

"How so?"

Chantelle looked away in embarrassment before answering. "He promised me he wouldn't summon anyone else."

Rahine's brow shot up because she knew Jamil was dining with Sheelah at this precise moment. How could he possibly have made such a promise? But to be fair, he hadn't exactly broken it. He hadn't summoned Sheelah but had gone to her instead. Had he thought no one would know of it just because he could reach his wives' apartments without entering the main harem?

When Rahine said nothing, Chantelle glanced back at her. "Does he keep his promises, Rahine?"

"When at all possible, yes, of course he does." What else could she say?

Chapter Forty-one

DEREK GENTLY cradled the infant in his arm. It was getting easier. He could even smile now about how nervous and out of his element he had felt the first time he had held one of the babies, and there were three still in swaddling.

Rather than disrupt the harem as he had done today, over the past weeks he had had Jamil's children brought to his apartment in groups of two and three at a time. Getting to know his nieces and nephews had relieved the tedium of the long afternoons when his lack of activity was most acutely felt, but he surprised even himself by how much he enjoyed the time spent with them.

The little girl in his arms had flaming red hair like her mother's, and bright emerald eyes. She was adorable, but then all of Jamil's children were. And what was so fascinating about them was that Derek could see himself in each one. His own children would look like this, especially like those who most resembled Jamil. And if he had been born first, instead of a few minutes after Jamil, he would likely have just as many children by now, instead of none.

It was ironic and lamentable that he was being coerced into marriage to get just one great-grandson for Robert Sinclair when Jamil had given him sixteen great-grandchildren, four of them sons, but none of which the Marquis could officially acknowledge without bringing the scandal of Melanie Sinclair's enslavement down on his name. England thought that Lady Melanie was dead. Rahine had long since given up that name.

But that was beside the point, and he was experiencing a moment of bachelor's indecision, was all. It was time he married. "Lamentable" was much too harsh a word for it, and only his long years of delightful lechery making a last protest. And he hadn't truly been coerced. He hadn't even protested overmuch, not with Caroline as the obvious, compatible choice.

With his copper-haired Caro as the mother, his own daughters could look exactly like the infant he was holding. In a complete reversal of mood, he decided he couldn't wait. And then he wondered what his and Shahar's children would look like, and he frowned. Jamil possessed no blond concubines, so he could make no comparisons for likeness. And he shouldn't have had the thought in the first place.

"Are you still worried about her? "

Derek glanced up to find Sheelah staring at him, and he quickly smoothed out his features. "Not at all." He handed the baby back to her nurse. "I have been assured Shahar will make a complete recovery."

"I'm glad."

She was sincere, he realized. What an amazing difference between her and his little English, who stubbornly denied her jealousy even as she seethed with it. Sheelah truly accepted Jamil's other women. She would accept anything if it made him happy.

Bloody hell. He should never have let Omar convince him that he couldn't continue to ignore Sheelah without arousing suspicion. She would expect him to stay and make love to her tonight. He wasn't about to get anywhere near her. Nor could he allow the two of them to be left alone together, even for a moment. That was why her three children were present, as well as their nurses. He refused to let them leave. He wanted witnesses so that Jamil could have no doubts that Derek had stayed here only for dinner.

But Sheelah wasn't going to understand. She knew Shahar was unavailable tonight. He was here. To her way of thinking, he had no reason to leave. So when he did leave, she was going to be hurt.

Damn Omar for putting him in this situation. "Sheelah, I thank you for the superb dinner, but I—I must go now."

"No, wait!" She came around the table so quickly, she was practically in his lap before he could stop her. "Let me help you, Jamil. Your distress is my own."

"I know that," he replied, gently taking her

hand from his cheek and returning it to her lap. "But I cannot—"

She pressed her lips to his. He drew back instantly, panicking in the worst way. The nurses giggled across the room. Sheelah misunderstood.

"I'll send them away—"

"No! What I mean is—" He collected himself with an effort. "I don't want this, Sheelah, not tonight."

"Not to—"

She didn't finish, her large sapphire eyes widening, her mouth dropping open. What the devil had he said, Derek wondered, to get this reaction? And it was worse than he thought.

"You are not Jamil," she said in an incredulous whisper. "Who are you?"

Bloody hell. "Are you mad, woman?"

Sheelah bowed her head, contrite. "I'm sorry, my beloved. Forgive—" Her head snapped up, her eyes narrowing. "No, you are *not* Jamil. I know the man I love with all my heart too well. He comes to me for comfort. You refuse—"

"Be quiet," he hissed. "Do you know what kind of rumors you could start with such nonsense? Look at me and tell me who else I could be."

"I don't know." Tears were gathering in her eyes. "Just tell me—tell me he is not—"

Derek put a finger to her lips. He glanced at the others in the room, but they were still far enough away not to have overheard. He looked back at Sheelah, his expression softening. Damn women's intuition. He couldn't leave it like this.

"You have nothing to be distressed about. Nothing. Will you believe that, Sheelah?"

She nodded and rose with him to walk him to the door. "I do not understand."

"You will. Just be patient and all of your questions will have answers." And then he gathered her close for a moment. She was his sister-in-law after all. "You know you are loved, Sheelah. Have faith in that."

She gave him a hesitant smile in parting, enough to convince him he had relieved her mind, if not her suspicions.

Chapter Forty-two

A CHAIR arrived along with today's summons. Chantelle found that amusing, but also a little embarrassing. She wasn't an invalid. She felt fine now. But Jamil obviously didn't want her overtaxing herself on the long walk to his apartment, and she knew why. So would everyone else who saw her carried through the harem. But of course, every woman summoned was expected to share Jamil's bed. She would have to get over these feelings of discomfiture each time it was her turn, especially if Jamil kept his promise and she was the only one.

When she arrived just after evening prayer, it was to find Jamil not alone. The old man she had seen the other night was there, arguing with Jamil about something. When she had described him to Adamma, the girl had thought he sounded like the Dey's Grand Vizier, the second most important man in Barikah. She hoped not, remembering the way he had glowered at her that night. He did it again now, plainly annoyed that Jamil had motioned her to stay when their business wasn't finished.

"I don't see that it makes any difference, Omar." Jamil was saying. "He was my brother. I have to go."

"No one will expect it, not after this most recent attempt on your life. And you, you didn't even know—"

Jamil made a sudden slashing motion with his arm and Omar glared once again at Chantelle. "Send her away until we are finished."

"No. We are finished now. It is my duty to attend the funeral, the *Dey's* duty," Jamil emphasized.

"Duty be damned. The Divan has voted unanimously against it. You must heed the advice of your councillors!"

"Must?"

Omar threw up his hands. "Allah save us from a man who loves danger. Do you think these fanatic assassins will respect the sanctity of the funeral procession? No, they will be in the crowds, just waiting for you to appear. They cannot afford to let such an opportunity pass. Nothing else has been able to draw you out of the palace."

Chantelle frowned. She had heard that before, those exact words, or almost those exact words.

"Jamil?"

He didn't even glance at her. "Be patient, Shahar. This will only take a moment more."

"But, Jamil, I've heard that before."

Now he turned around. "What?"

"What he just said to you, that nothing else has been able to draw you out of the palace. Only she said 'him,' instead of 'you.' "

"You are not making much sense, Shahar. Come here and tell us what you are talking about."

She approached, but reluctantly. Omar wasn't frowning at her now. Jamil was. She should never have interrupted them. From what she had just overheard, apparently one of Jamil's brothers had died. He had to be upset already. But there was nothing for it now.

"Well?" he demanded.

"I am sorry about your brother," she began, but he waved that aside, so she told him what she remembered. "It was a few days ago in the baths. I was alone in the steam room when I heard someone outside. It was a woman and a man, I think. I never heard his voice clearly, but she called him Ali. I assumed he was a eunuch. I could hear the woman plainly, though, because her voice was raised in anger. She told him she didn't want any more excuses, that it should never have taken this long. And then she gave the man something and told him to sell it. She said, 'If that doesn't buy some courage, I'll have to—' But the

394

man interrupted her then, and . . . oh, my God!" Her eyes flared in sudden understanding.

"What?"

"None of it made sense to me, so I forgot about it, but I didn't know someone was trying to kill you then."

"So? What you have said does not signify, Shahar. The woman could have been talking about anything."

"I know that, but . . . was your brother young? Was he just a boy?"

"Yes, but what has that to—"

"How did he die?"

Chantelle could see he was fast losing patience with her by the tightening of his mouth, but he answered her just the same. "He appears to have suffocated. But whether he choked on a piece of food—he was apparently eating at the time—or whether someone smothered him to make it appear so has not been determined."

"Do *you* think it was murder?"

"He was not a strong boy. It would not have been at all difficult for a man to hold something over his face until he expired. There was an emergency that drew his servants away. When they returned, they found the table in a shambles and Murad lying beside it, dead."

"And if it was murder," Omar told Jamil at this point, "it was arranged specifically to lure you outside the palace. There is no other reason to kill the boy."

"Omar—"

"But, Jamil, he's right," Chantelle insisted.

"No one can know that for certain—"

"Will you just listen?" she said in exasperation. "After the woman was interrupted, she asked Ali, 'What about the boy?' and when he answered her, she said, 'Go ahead and arrange it. Nothing else has been able to draw him out of the palace, so maybe that will. But if it does, there had better be results. No more bungles or I will take it out of your hide.' Ali must have told her to lower her voice then, for she got even angrier at him, but they moved on and I couldn't hear any more."

Jamil exchanged a long glance with Omar. The old man was smiling now. Jamil wore a half-amused, half-chagrined expression that bemused Chantelle.

"It seems 'our friend' has made a useless trip to Istanbul," Omar remarked.

"It does look that way, does it not?" Jamil agreed, before his emerald eyes fell on Chantelle again. "Who was the woman, Shahar?"

She grimaced, having to admit, "I don't know."

"But you saw her?"

"No, the door was closed."

"Damn—"

"But I think I would recognize her voice if I heard it again."

"That is something anyway, and how many eunuchs can bear the name Ali?"

"Dozens, unfortunately," Omar supplied.

"Then I leave it in your capable hands to narrow the number down to our culprit. And I think that is enough on the subject for now."

Omar nodded in agreement but had to add, "You will not go to the funeral?"

"No. Arrange it so I can pay my respects here."

That this was Omar's original suggestion made his expression quite smug as he left. Jamil wasted no time in drawing Chantelle into his arms.

"Thank you," he said sincerely. "Without your help, we would have continued to flounder, suspecting the wrong man. Will you help again and listen for the voice?"

"Of course, but, Jamil, why would one of your women wish you harm?"

"Who can guess what is in a woman's mind?" he said with a shrug.

Chantelle snorted. "I could say the same thing of a man's mind."

"But women are so much more contrary and unpredictable. And speaking of women . . ." He pulled her closer, meshing their hips together. "I have missed you."

She gave in gracefully to the change of subject. "It was only one night—"

"And two days. We will have to make up for it."

"Is that so?"

"Unless you are too weak."

"Do I look weak?"

He grinned at her. "Just to be sure, I should get you off your feet."

And he did, carrying her straight to his bed.

Chapter Forty-three

WEEKS PASSED, but Chantelle had no luck in hearing that angry voice again. Jamil kept her informed of the progress he made, but he had reached a dead end, too. The number of men called Ali who were still suspect had been reduced to five, and these five were watched constantly, but nothing came of it. Short of having them all tortured, which Jamil forbade Omar to do, it became a waiting game, for one of them to make a mistake.

The women these men belonged to were also watched. The money to finance the assassination was taken into account, and which woman was favored enough to have accumulated a sizable fortune. But that wasn't a deciding factor, not with the recent rash of thefts in the harem, the amount of jewelry stolen also amounting to a fortune.

It was really up to Chantelle, and she became anxious, realizing that. Jamil questioned her each night she saw him, and that only made her frustrated for having nothing to tell him.

Of the five women under suspicion, Chantelle knew only two of them. One was a current favorite named Sadira, a woman due to give birth in less than a month. Chantelle couldn't picture her plotting anything other than the happy future of her child. How could a woman order death while her body nurtured life? Sadira couldn't. She was not in the best of moods as her time approached, and her voice was often raised angrily against her servants. It wasn't the right voice.

But the other woman Chantelle knew out of the five was a different story. Noura was that other woman. Chantelle was not surprised. She had already thought of Noura before that overheard conversation had meaning for her. But Noura's voice, that was the undeciding factor. Chantelle had heard Noura speak in many tones, from peevish to gloating smugness, though not once in actual heated anger. And unless she could say positively that Noura's voice was the one she had heard, she wasn't going to say anything.

She became Noura's shadow, watching, always listening. She even tried to prick Noura's temper, but the desert beauty wouldn't take the bait. Once or twice it was close, yet Noura was quick to collect herself, almost as if she knew what Chantelle was doing and was determined to show herself as being above falling for the same snare she was renowned for setting herself.

Chantelle was almost at her wit's end. She was afraid Noura knew she was under suspicion and so would be careful to make no mistakes. She finally asked Rahine's advice on how to get the second *kadine* to lose her temper. Rahine, who was, of course, aware of the latest turn of events, was no help at all.

"It would only be a waste of time, Shahar."

"You don't know that."

"I know Noura," Rahine said with quiet conviction. "It isn't her."

"I disagree. One of Jamil's brothers is dead now. What if the other one is, too, and that's why he hasn't been seen since the attacks started? That would leave only Jamil and his oldest son to stand in the way of Noura's boy, wouldn't it?"

Rahine frowned. "We don't know that Selim is dead. True, it no longer appears that he is behind this plot, but—"

"Rahine, don't argue with me," Chantelle cut in impatiently. "Just tell me how I can get Noura to lose her temper. If she isn't the one, I'll know it when I hear her voice raised in anger. What can it hurt to try?"

"Very well." Rahine sighed. "The last time she threw a temper tantrum was when she had prepared for weeks to give a recital for Jamil's pleasure, she and a half-dozen others. She had memorized an exceedingly long but beautiful poem, and she insisted on her turn being last, so as to make the best impression. But after an hour's time, when the other women had all recited their pieces, Jamil was called away. Noura plain and simply had a fit, I think mainly because it was due to her own instigation that she was last on the program."

"Did she ever recite that poem?"

"Yes, a few nights later, and Jamil was naturally pleased, so she was completely pacified."

"Then that won't do. Think of something else, Rahine."

"She loves Chinese shadow plays. Come to think of it, I have the sketches for a new play in my apartment."

"But will she agree to perform it?"

"She would be delighted."

"Then that's it. And when it's time for the play to begin, Jamil can walk out, or fall asleep, or something equally annoying."

"Yes, I suppose it wouldn't be too difficult for Jamil to be annoying." Rahine grinned.

Chantelle grinned, too. "Will you suggest she do it, then?"

"Me? It was your idea."

"I've thrown so many barbs her way lately that she's liable to bleed if I get near her. She certainly wouldn't be open to any suggestions coming from me."

"Yes, I've heard the complaints of your recent bitchiness." Rahine chuckled. "Noura recommended I send you back to the kitchens."

"Oh, she'd love that, so she can order another feast and make sure I have to prepare it again."

"I'm sorry," Rahine said soberly. "I didn't know about that."

Chantelle shrugged. "My aunt always said a little hard work never hurt anyone. And it was no punishment, Rahine. At the time, I was delighted to be in the kitchens."

"But you wouldn't be now."

Chantelle gave a very unladylike snort. She had

known that "I told you so" would come around eventually.

Chapter Forty-four

THE DAY of the shadow play rolled around only three days later. Due to Jamil's letting it be known that he needed a distraction, Noura spent day and night learning the required moves and put on a preview performance for the ladies that morning, which was a success. Even Chantelle had enjoyed it. Now if everything went according to plan tonight, Noura would be exposed before the day was out.

But that was many hours away. Chantelle took advantage of finding the pool empty to while away one of those hours. She enjoyed the pool. Actually, she had come to enjoy the entire *hammam*. It was a lazy place, where soothing hands were aways ready to massage tired muscles back to life or rub sweet-smelling oils into already soft skin. But Chantelle didn't laze about in this room, where the sunken body of water was so reminiscent of the ocean to her. She used it for exercise, swimming laps back and forth and beneath the water, pushing her muscles to the limit just for her own satisfaction. The water wasn't deep. Few of the harem ladies knew how to swim, so the water at the deepest point only reached her breasts. But it was cool and invigorating, and Chantelle could almost imagine that when she surfaced from the water, the Dover cliffs would be there to greet her.

Today when she came up for air, her imagination took second place to water-clogged ears. She left the pool to dry off, shaking her head to clear it, but still there was only a loud droning in her ears.

Oh, this is just wonderful. Noura has her one and only angry fit tonight, and my ears are too clogged up to hear any of it.

Impatiently, Chantelle quickly donned her robe and bundled her hair up in a towel, then bent forward and turned her head to the side, wiggling her earlobe. There was a pop, and then the amplification of the water lapping at the sides of the pool.

And then the voice, clear and irate. "I should have known the pool wouldn't be empty. It never is. But shouldn't you be primping before a mirror by now? Or did Jamil finally summon someone else?"

Chantelle didn't answer. She was too dumbfounded. She sat there on a bench staring at the woman in the doorway, not knowing what to think. How could it be her? Her eunuch's name was Orji, not Ali. And she would have nothing to gain by killing Jamil. It made no sense.

Yet the voice was the same, even more recognizable when she snapped, "What are you staring at, Englishwoman?"

"A murderess," Chantelle replied boldly as she came to her feet. "I was so certain it was Noura, but it was you, wasn't it?"

"You're crazy! I haven't killed anyone."

"Perhaps not with your own hands, but there isn't much difference when your coin paid to have it done."

"I don't know what you are talking about," was the haughty reply.

"Yes, you do. I heard you and Ali outside the steam room the day you ordered poor Murad's death. Did you see me leave? Is that why you had me poisoned, Mara?"

That was a guess, but it paid off. The woman gave up all pretense of innocence, sneering, "Too bad it didn't work. I could have used the few extra gems the Dey's rage and grief would have brought me."

"Yes, it must be getting harder and harder for you to steal them now that everyone knows what a clever thief we have among us."

"I was up to the challenge. I found it quite thrilling, actually."

Chantelle shook her head in amazement. The woman was bragging now. She didn't seem at all fearful of having been found out.

"All to kill Jamil? Why, Mara? It can't be the whippings, because I was told you enjoy them."

Mara became enraged suddenly. "What do you know about it, you stupid bitch? I hate him! I hate all men, but especially Jamil, for discovering my shame and using it against me. Do you think I am proud that I can receive pleasure only through pain? If I could find the man who made me like this, I would chop him into little pieces, slowly, so

404

that he would survive to the end. But first I would roast his balls and his—"

"I'm sorry for that first experience that affected you so . . . bizarrely, but Jamil hasn't done anything to you that you haven't let him do. You could have put an end to it at any time by simply making your feelings known."

"No one refuses the Dey what he wants."

"I did."

"For how long?" Mara sneered.

Even though Chantelle's cheeks tinged with pink, she still insisted, "That was different. I was seduced, not threatened. And it could never have happened if I were not attracted to the man."

"How splendid for you, but he sickens me," Mara bit out. "And Orji told me I had no choice."

There were those two words again that Chantelle despised. *No choice.* She had been told the same thing. She could understand Mara's dilemma. And yet—when it came right down to it, Chantelle had not been forced. They were only hollow threats used to make women give in gracefully. Why should it be any different in Mara's case? Jamil was not the cruel tyrant she had first thought him to be.

"You should have tried stopping it instead of letting your resentment build to this level. Jamil is basically a very gentle man. How often did he make use of you before you plotted to kill him?"

"One time was too many!"

"But you only increased your own suffering by

sending assassins after him. Or didn't you consider that that would happen?"

"It was worth it to have him dead."

"That is so stupid!" Chantelle said angrily. "If Jamil dies, we will all of us become the property of the new Dey, to be disposed of or not. That will be Selim, and from what I have heard, they don't come more brutal or merciless than he. You think he won't learn of your weakness and take pleasure in using you the same way? Some men enjoy inflicting pain, and he appears to be one of them."

Mara laughed. "I am not *that* stupid, English-woman. Selim can no longer practice his vicious-ness on anyone. He has been dead all these months, murdered and disposed of by one of his own slaves while he was in Istanbul."

Chantelle gasped at this startling disclosure. "How do you know that?"

"The guilty slave was foolish enough to return here, and stupid enough to get drunk and brag about what he had done to an old friend. The old friend happened to be Ali, who had sense enough to get rid of the man so the information would not go any further."

"Yet he told you, didn't he?"

"Of course. He knew how much I hated Jamil. He saw this as the perfect opportunity to get rid of him, knowing that Selim would be the natural one to suspect. And dead men cannot defend themselves."

"But why would this Ali involve himself in your

problems? He's a eunuch, isn't he, and not even yours to command?"

"So? Just because he was given to Noura does not mean he has to love her. He loves me," Mara said smugly. "He would do anything I asked of him."

"Love? He cannot—"

"Cannot?" Mara cut in. "That shows how naive you are. Castration does not cut out the heart, nor does impotence always put an end to longing. Ali can love just as fiercely as a whole man. He just can't do anything about it."

"You say that as if you don't care."

"I don't. I might not feel threatened by his love, but he is still a man, worthy only of my contempt. My loathing for all men allows no exceptions."

"Too bad he didn't realize that before he let you embroil him in treason," Chantelle replied. "But his being duped by you won't save him."

"He isn't in danger of discovery any more than I am. You don't really think I will let you leave here after telling you all this, do you?"

That Mara was blocking the doorway wasn't too alarming. That she made the threat so confidently was.

"You cannot stop me, Mara. I have bodyguards just outside."

Mara smiled as she pulled a short dagger out of her caftan. "There was no one outside this room, or I would have been alerted to your presence here. Your guards must not be very diligent today."

"You're lying!" Chantelle cried as Mara kicked the door shut behind her.

There was an unconcerned shrug. "Go ahead and scream if you doubt me. Your guards won't come, nor will anyone else." Mara gave a short, ironic laugh. "I could not have picked a better place for this little discussion if I had planned it. Did you never wonder why this room is so far away from all the others? It's because the women make so much noise when they gather to play in the water. A scream or two coming from here is not a matter for concern—it is normal."

"And I suppose you think I am just going to stand here and let you stab me with that thing?"

Chantelle said this as Mara started to approach her. She backed away. There was a good fifteen feet between them, and if she could just get around to the other side of the pool, she could use it as a barrier. If Mara tried following her around it, then Chantelle would have a clear path to the door. But she couldn't take her eyes off that dagger long enough to turn around and run.

She had never been in a situation like this before. It wasn't quite like the night she had looked over Jamil's shoulder to see a dagger about to descend on them both. She hadn't been alone then. She was completely alone now and had no skills to draw on to use against this threat. That the threat came from another woman wasn't exactly reassuring. Mara might not be as tall as she was, but the woman was much heftier, stronger, and her life was in the balance. If she couldn't kill Chantelle, she knew she would have to face Jamil's justice, so Mara had to be extremely desperate, which would give her added strength. That she was so calm about it was what was so frightening.

Chantelle wiped her sweaty palms on her hips. Mara had already closed the distance to only ten feet. "You—" She paused to clear the squeakiness from her throat and swallow. "You don't have to do this, you know. You could escape. Ali could help you, couldn't he?"

"After you give the alarm? Hah!"

"I am only looking at all the options you have!" Chantelle snapped.

She couldn't believe she had actually said that. Mara couldn't either, for she shook her head, snorting, "You talk too much, Englishwoman."

Chantelle tried a different tack. "Have you ever done this before, killed someone with your own hands? It's not like having someone else do it—"

"Shut up!" Mara shouted, making Chantelle's heart slam even harder against her chest.

Why hadn't she screamed already? She was a coward after all, wasn't she? But she was afraid if she did, it would bring Mara leaping at her all the sooner. She would be dead before anyone came, if anyone heard her. If she could just talk Mara out of it instead. . . .

The distance was down to eight feet. "I've never done anything to hurt you, Mara. You know that. Can you live with my death on your—"

Chantelle finally shrieked as she backed into a bench and lost her balance. She had forgotten about the damn thing, which was set so near the edge of the pool. She fell back on it, and before she could rise, Mara was standing over her and it was too late to scream or do anything else. She was paralyzed with heart-stopping terror, unable to move or breathe as she watched the dagger rise up for its descent. It was a repeat of that other night, only without Jamil's body lying between her and death. Jamil would have known what to do. He would have . . .

At the last instant, Chantelle remembered what Jamil had done and rolled to the side, right into Mara's knees. And just as it happened before, knife and attacker went tumbling forward. As Chantelle hit the hard floor, she heard a thud and then a splash on the other side of the bench. But she didn't bother to see how quickly Mara could climb out of the pool. She leaped to her feet and ran out of the room.

"Kadar!" she shouted as she ran down the hall, only to have him appear right in her path, so that she crashed into him. She pushed away the hands that came up to steady her, demanding shrilly, "Where the devil were you?"

"Here, *lalla*," he replied in an offended tone. "Where else would I be?"

"Then she lied? God, I should have—no, it doesn't matter now." Chantelle gripped his arm tightly, her fear not quite diminished yet. "It was Mara all along, not Noura, and she just tried to kill me, too, or again. She admitted she had me poisoned because of what I had heard." When he just stood there staring at her, she snapped, "Do something! She's still in the pool room, and she has a knife!"

He set her aside then and moved toward the door she had left wide open. When he slipped inside, she should have taken off in the opposite direction, the only wise and safe thing to do. She followed Kadar instead, the silence drawing her partly, but also a need to see Mara apprehended so the last of her fear would go away.

But she went no farther than the doorway. Kadar was bent over Mara, who lay by the side of the pool. She wasn't moving, and pink-tinged water ran down her forehead onto her face and the tile beneath her head.

Kadar glanced up and said in a quiet voice. "She is dead, *lalla*."

Chantelle looked back at the pink water and finally saw it for what it was. Bile rose in her throat and she bent over, unable to stop its exit. After a moment, hands lifted her and she turned her head against Kadar's shoulder.

"Oh, God," she cried. "If I hadn't been so cowardly, I would have looked to see that she didn't surface from the water. I could have pulled her out before—"

"It would not have made any difference, *lalla*. She cracked her head on the side of the pool. She was already dead when she slipped into the water."

"But that doesn't matter. I made her fall."

"Why?"

"Why?" She looked up, startled. "It was either that or let her stab me."

"Then why are you searching to place blame on yourself when there is none?"

"It's just not fair. She was a victim, Kadar, from the very start. She was abused, defiled, and then abused again by . . . She should have had help, care, understanding. Instead—" Chantelle fell silent a long moment before she said in a tiny voice, "I tried to justify to her the way Jamil treated her, but it can't be justified, can it? He is sensitive, perceptive—at least I thought he was. Why couldn't he see that she hated her weakness, and hated him for exploiting it?"

"Is that why she tried to kill him?"

Chantelle could only nod at this point. She was crying in earnest now, and barely aware when Kadar led her away.

Chapter Forty-five

"NOW THAT the money source is gone, the informants are lining up at the gates," Jamil told Derek. "It will not be long before we have every last man who has been involved."

He had returned to the palace late last night, but learned in the harbor that his trip had been for nothing. It was his longing for Sheelah that had brought him back. He had intended staying just the one night, then going on to Tripoli, where an informant had suggested Selim might have gone after leaving Istanbul. He knew now how false that idea was.

But Jamil had put off everything until he had straightened things out with his beloved Sheelah, and that had taken all night. Not telling her his plans in the first place had been a mistake. He understood that now, and his only excuse was that he hadn't been himself when he left.

He had had a long conference with Omar this morning, and then he had joined Derek in the secret room, which he had returned to last night.

"Then it really is over?" Derek said.

"Did you think it was not? Ali gave his cutthroats a paltry sum to risk their necks, with the big prize promised only for the men who succeeded. Of course, there never was a fortune waiting for the culprits to collect. I paid Mara extremely well for her services, but the whole thing went on too long, draining everything she had. There were men to be paid for their constant vigil outside the palace. There were all the men to be paid who intercepted my couriers, and that was just to throw us off the scent. It was why Mara had to resort to stealing jewels from the other women. If someone *had* actually succeeded in getting to me, Ali planned to kill him when he showed up for the prize."

"And now that it has been made known that the instigators are dead and the money gone . . ."

"No one is going to risk his life without reward.

I am as safe outside the palace as I am within," Jamil finished.

"And I can go home."

Jamil laughed at Derek's sigh. "And here Omar assured me you had been having a wonderful time."

"Only at certain times of the day," Derek grunted. "I have learned firsthand how quickly boredom can set in for the balance."

"And how is the skinny little blonde who relieved that boredom?"

"Not talking to me, actually, ever since she had that confrontation with Mara. She seems to think the whole thing was my—your—fault, for not sensing that Mara was seriously troubled by her abnormality."

Jamil frowned. "I suppose I might have sensed it under normal circumstances, but the fact remains that the woman did everything possible to ensure that she *was* punished, by deliberately insulting me or disobeying me, and when that didn't work, by attacking me. However, she was never whipped for long, nor even very hard, but when it was over, she was savage in her lovemaking. You saw this for yourself. And I suppose I came to expect it, and so summoned her whenever I had need for such violence, which was more and more often after the weeks of self-imposed confinement turned to months."

"Your own frustration was abetting your assassination. A vicious little circle—ironic, to say the least."

414

"It was ingenious. Suspicion would never have fallen on Mara. We had overlooked the harem entirely until Shahar overheard that conversation. Even then Mara didn't come under suspicion."

"I'm glad you're putting credit where it's due," Derek replied. "You owe her a lot."

"I am not denying that, Kasim. But I thought you would want to name the reward, considering she has been 'our' exclusive favorite all these weeks." At Derek's grimace, Jamil chuckled. "All the time I was gone, I thought you would be giving me the excuse I needed to weed out my harem."

"Don't give me that, brother. You were worried sick about it."

"A little, perhaps. But I did hear that you found one of my favorites to your liking. Strange that it was only the Englishwoman who should attract you, and Jamila being the source of so much inquiry from the English consul."

Derek grinned. Jamil had seen right through that one, so there was no point in delaying his request.

"You won't mind letting her return to England with me, then, since you will be wanting to get rid of her anyway?"

"Your people would be pleased, I suppose?"

"They wouldn't take it amiss."

"Very well," Jamil replied. "And your Shahar? Will you make the same request for her?"

"Actually, I don't know what the hell I want for her." At Jamil's raised brow, he admitted, "I thought taking her to my bed would assure her a husband of her own when you returned. English-women are particular about that, you know, having a man all to themselves."

Jamil was surprised. "You mean you never intended asking for her freedom?"

"I think I deliberately didn't consider it because I needed an excuse—"

Derek didn't finish and Jamil smiled knowingly. "That she was a virgin was a problem, was it?"

Derek sighed. "A bloody big problem."

"I was afraid her first meeting with me would have made things more difficult for you."

"Oh, it did, but nothing I couldn't get around. It just took longer. And . . . oh, who the hell am I kidding? Of course I want to take her out of here with me. It's what she would want, and she deserves that for solving your little problem." He didn't add that the more he thought of it, the more he didn't want to see her married to some other man.

"Then should I tell her, or do you want that privilege? Perhaps she will talk to you again after you give her the good news."

Derek scowled, watching Jamil trying to hold back his amusement. "Actually, the longer I can get away without telling her the truth, the better. She can think she is sailing with you. She doesn't have to know where."

"But why?"

"For a few extra weeks of peace. The lady is

going to raise holy hell when she learns I'm as English as she is, believe me. And it's not going to be pleasant being confined with her on a ship once she realizes that I could have obtained her freedom without taking her to bed."

"You are much too indulgent where women are concerned. You should be—"

"More like you?"

They both laughed, and Jamil admitted, "I do have quite a few women to placate after your single-minded pursuit of the new favorite left them all neglected. It will take me at least a month to bring contentment back to my harem."

"I hear you started last night."

"Sheelah is and always will be my main concern. And, Allah be thanked, she understood. She also begs your forgiveness if she made things more difficult for you. She said she sensed your guilt in not being able to tell her the truth."

Derek shrugged that off. "It's over and everything can get back to normal, including my own life."

"Yes, you have that fiancée waiting for you, do you not? And Shahar? Will you keep her, too?"

Derek's lips turned up at the corners. "Now that you mention it, that's not a bad idea."

Jamil snorted. "As if you had not already thought of it. But will she agree?"

"I got around her aversion to you. I can get around her aversion to being my mistress. After all, she will see herself as ruined and unsuitable for a decent marriage now."

"Is she?"

"As beautiful as she is? Are you kidding?"

Jamil grunted. They might be twins, but their tastes in women just weren't the same. "I wish you luck, then. But as you say, you will have to get around her anger first."

Derek made a face. "Yes, there is that."

Chapter Forty-six

"SHAHAR, YOU are to pack your things. You are sailing on the evening tide with Jamil—you and Jamila." Chantelle stared at Rahine as if she had lost her mind. "Did you hear me, child? You are going on a trip."

"Where?"

"Where?" Rahine repeated. "What does that matter? This is an honor—"

"Where, Rahine?"

"Actually, I don't know. Not even Haji could find out. But it really doesn't make any difference. Jamil wants you to accompany him, and so you will."

"And so will Jamila. If he's taking her, he doesn't need me along."

"Are you jealous?"

"Certainly not!"

"Then you must be pouting because Jamil visited Sheelah last night."

"Rahine—" Chantelle began warningly, only to have the older woman chide her.

"Then don't sound like it. It's you he's taking with him, not Sheelah."

"And Jamila."

"You *are* jealous!"

"No . . . I'm . . . not! She can have him. They can *all* have him. He's everything I first thought he was and more. I hate him!"

Rahine pursed her lips. "So you're still upset about Mara? I tried to tell you there was more to it than just what she had told you."

"You deny what he did to her every single time he summoned her?"

"No."

"Then what more can you tell me? So he needed an outlet for his temper. Other men punch walls." Rahine nearly choked trying to hold back a chuckle. Chantelle saw this and scowled. "Go ahead and laugh. It's very funny that that woman was victimized to the bitter end."

Rahine sobered. "No, it's not funny. It's tragic. But Jamil isn't to blame."

"He—"

"Shahar!" Rahine cut in sharply. "You're going to listen to me this time whether you want to or not. Jamil was provoked. Mara deliberately forced him to punish her each time she was summoned. Did she tell you that?"

"No, but I don't see how that leaves him blameless. He should have realized something was wrong with her and left her alone. Instead he called for her more often, using her as his whipping post. Do you know how disgusting that is?"

"I can see there is no getting through to you." Rahine sighed. "It makes no difference that she gave every impression of wanting to be abused? There are women who enjoy that sort of thing, you know."

"She hated it afterward."

"Then she should have said something."

Chantelle couldn't disagree with that. She had told Mara the same thing. But she didn't want to see Jamil's side of it, especially now. For five days after Mara's death he had summoned her, and she had turned away from him. *He* could have told her what Rahine just did, but he hadn't bothered. He'd simply got angry when she wouldn't talk to him. And then he had gone to Sheelah. Well, fine. Wonderful. He could continue going to Sheelah. Chantelle wanted nothing more to do with him.

She turned away, mumbling, "Why doesn't he take Sheelah with him on this trip instead?"

"He usually does take her whenever he leaves Barikah, but this time he wants you. It is your chance to make up with him, Shahar," Rahine pointed out hesitantly.

"And if I don't want to?"

"I imagine that's why Jamila is going along, too," Rahine said deliberately.

Chantelle swung back around, eyes narrowed and glittering violet. "He can just—"

"Enough, Shahar! I really don't have time to argue with you anymore. Jamil has sent for me, and I'm late now. Pack your things. Be ready to

420

leave by this evening. And if I don't see you again before you leave . . ." Rahine stepped forward to embrace her. "Allah go with you, and hopefully, he will help you come to your senses."

Rahine had to rush now to Jamil's apartment, but she had wanted to tell Shahar of the trip herself. She had hoped it would cheer the girl up, the honor of being chosen to accompany the Dey, but apparently it hadn't. At least Shahar had listened this time about Mara. She was intelligent. She wouldn't continue to blame Jamil for Mara's sickness. But she was stubborn, too. For too long she had been the one and only favorite. The jealousy she had tried to deny was going to fester for a while. And if Jamil grows impatient with her and makes use of Jamila on the ship, that jealousy will magnify, she thought.

She should mention it to Jamil. She was still thinking about it when she arrived and found him alone in the room. That was unusual. He usually had a half-dozen attendants at hand. But her being here was unusual as well. He hadn't summoned her to his rooms in years. She couldn't even begin to think of a reason for it now, and so hadn't tried to, afraid whatever it was wasn't going to be good.

To put it off, she went right to the subject that might distract him. "I just came from seeing Shahar to tell her of the trip."

"How did she take the news?"

"She knows Jamila is going, too."

Derek laughed. "So she didn't take it well. No

matter, Mother, she will have other things to get in a snit over once we sail."

There was that heart-stopping "Mother" again. Rahine was so unnerved at hearing it that she almost missed the fact that Jamil was speaking in English. For her benefit? Not likely. He rarely used English except with foreign diplomats who spoke nothing else, the reason being he didn't speak it very well—or at least he didn't used to speak it well. He had obviously mastered the language since the last time she had heard him speak it, when he was a child.

"Where . . . is your destination?" she asked hesitantly. "I haven't been told."

"To England, and I want you to come with me."

"I want you to stay, Mother," Jamil said from the garden doorway.

Rahine looked between the two and said only, "Oh, God," before she started to collapse.

Derek leaped forward to catch her. "Dammit, Jamil, I thought you were going to give me a few minutes to break it to her gently!"

"And let you steal her right out from under my nose?" Jamil accused him.

Derek asked incredulously, "Are we going to fight about this, of all things?"

"Perhaps," Jamil replied, moving to help Derek get Rahine to the bed. "You don't need her. I do. She keeps peace in my life."

"Does she know that? Have you ever told her?"

Jamil answered with anger. "You should have

warned me you were going to ask her to return with you. I would never have allowed this meeting."

"You couldn't have prevented it, Jamil. I never would have left here without seeing her again. The first time didn't count. She thought I was you."

They got her to the bed, but when Derek tried to stand back, he winced at how tightly Rahine gripped his arm. He glanced down at her to find her emerald eyes fixed on him, wide and shimmering with tears.

"Kasim—oh, God, Kasim? Is it really—" She looked to Jamil on her other side, then back to Derek. "It is," she said with a catch in her voice. "Oh, God, it really is.'

Derek sat down beside her, putting his arm around her. "You're not supposed to cry about it, Mother."

In response her crying became quite noisy. She hid her face in her hands, ashamed to have lost control like this, only to cry even louder when Derek wrapped his arms around her.

"Mother, please don't do this. I thought you would be happy to see me."

"I am!" she wailed.

The two brothers exchanged a look of mutual helplessness. Typical of their gender, they could deal with almost any situation—except this one.

"Can we get you something?" Derek asked gently. "Brandy? *Kanyak?*"

"She doesn't drink spirits," Jamil answered for her.

"How would you know?" Derek snapped back with impatience. "Just because you don't—"

"You mustn't fight," Rahine interrupted, pushing herself away from Derek's chest. "Brothers must never fight."

"Were we fighting, Jamil?" Derek grinned.

"Not at all," Jamil replied with the same grin.

Rahine tried for an expression of disapproval but couldn't quite manage it. She still doubted her faculties, her sight, her hearing. Kasim here? Jamil showing concern and saying he needed her? Again she looked from one to the other. So identical. So beloved. Her heart felt as if it would burst, it was so full of emotion.

She swiped impatiently at her tears, then wet Derek's cheek with her fingertips the next moment. "Why? When?"

"For some time now," he replied, "so Jamil could safely search for Selim without an assassin turning up at every corner. Of course we didn't know it was a pointless endeavor."

"No, you couldn't know he was already . . . Then it was you—ever since—" She tried to think back, but so many things were whirling through her mind, it wasn't easy. "Ever since Shahar was bought . . . no, since you first summoned her. That was when you began acting differently. And I never guessed."

"You were not supposed to," Jamil said, bending down in front of her to take her other hand in his. "No one knew except Omar, since it was his idea to bring Kasim here to take my place."

424

"You didn't even tell Sheelah?"

"No, not until I returned last night. I thought of telling you—"

"We both did," Derek interjected.

"But in order for the deception to work, it was better if no one's behavior deviated in any way."

"Except your own." She smiled, squeezing his hand in understanding.

"Yes, well, my behavior was already unpredictable, and had been for months. Any mistakes Kasim made could be attributed to that unpredictability. But even now no one else is to know that he was here. He doesn't want to be resurrected or called on to succeed me should something happen before my sons reach their manhood."

There was the potent reminder that tore at Rahine's heart. She turned to Kasim, her eyes brimming with tears again.

"Your life is . . . tolerable, then?"

"More than tolerable, Mother." He smiled at her. "It suits me admirably."

Her throat constricted; she did not know whether to believe him or not. "I—I'm so sorry, Kasim," she whispered brokenly. "I regretted sending you away almost as soon as you were gone. I prayed and prayed that you knew it— somehow sensed it. I never thought I would see you again to tell you."

"I did know it, always," he assured her. "And I understood once I met your father. I came to love

425

him as much as you did. Of course, he's grown rather dictatorial in his old age."

She smiled at the humor in her son's eyes. "Has he?"

"I'm to get married or else, don't you know. He's even sent a ship here to fetch me home. Didn't trust me to find my own way." She laughed as he had intended; then he said tenderly, "I have no regrets, Mother, so you mustn't either."

"I don't deserve your forgiveness. Jamil never—"

Derek cut in curtly. "Jamil is a pigheaded fool."

"No, you mustn't say that—"

Jamil interrupted this time. "He's right, Mother." Rahine's chest swelled with pain as he suddenly buried his head in her lap and she heard his anguished plea: "Can you forgive me?"

"Please—Jamil—please don't." She was unable to stop the tears spilling down her cheeks again. She lifted his head to her breast. "I understood your hurt and anger. You two were as one, and yet I severed the cord. I had no right, and I certainly never blamed you for hating me."

"But I did not—I could not. And when I finally understood that, I resented you for the barrier between us that I had created. I was wrong—"

"But it's all right now, Jamil, truly."

Derek broke in at this point, saying crossly, "I suppose this means you won't be returning home with me."

Rahine had to laugh at his tone. "Come now, Kasim, you didn't really think I would. I don't exist there, any more than you do here. Surely I am assumed dead after all these years."

"There was mention of it to account for your long absence," he was forced to admit.

"There, you see. We have both made different lives for ourselves that are all we want now."

"You could make a new life, assume a new identity—see your father again."

"That's unfair," she scolded gently. "He has you now. He doesn't need me. But Jamil does."

"Stop arguing with her, Kasim," Jamil snapped irritably. "She's staying."

Derek gave in gracefully, knowing when he was outnumbered. "Just see that she knows she's appreciated from now on, brother, or I'll take a leaf from the Marquis's book and send a ship back here for her."

Jamil snorted in response, but later was to assure Derek that Rahine would never want for anything again, emotionally or otherwise.

Chapter Forty-seven

CHANTELLE LASTED several weeks before the boredom got to her. She had thought this voyage would be different from her sea journey into captivity, but it wasn't, not by much. She was still locked in her cabin, denied the sights and sounds of shipboard activity that could have made the slow passage of time more bearable. The little man who brought her meals was English, probably a slave, and disgustingly cheerful about it. The only other person she saw was Jamil, and it was getting more and more difficult for her to put him off when she was starved for company.

At least on her first voyage she had had Hakeem drilling her with information nearly every waking hour. That and her anxiety for the future hadn't allowed her time to be bored. Now she would even welcome Jamila's company. But they had been parted as soon as they had reached the ship, given separate cabins no doubt so Jamil wouldn't disturb one by visiting the other. And she wasn't about to ask him if she could visit Jamila when she was still barely speaking to him.

But he was undoubtedly visiting Jamila. Oh, he came by to see Chantelle each evening, but that was no more than courtesy now, for he had stopped trying to talk her out of her pique. What he did after the visit, she had no way of knowing.

He had changed since they'd set sail. Not only his appearance but his very temperament seemed different. Gone were the robes and tunics she had become used to, even the Turkish pants. He wore lawn shirts an Englishman would envy, and tight buff pants with knee-high boots. All that was missing was a cutaway jacket, but the warm weather could account for its absence.

She couldn't imagine why he was dressing as a European now, and was too stubborn to ask. His mood change was even more curious, but that, too, she didn't comment on. There were no bursts of anger or frustration over her continued rebuffs. It was as if he were walking on eggshells around her, glad that she had so little to say to him.

Her dinner arrived right on time as usual, and the little sailor who answered to the name of Peaches was all smiles this evening. "We make port tomorrow for fresh provisions, miss. No sea biscuits and Gundy's 'put anything into it' stew tomorrow night."

He said this as he set her tray down. Chantelle came forward to note there was a bottle of wine tonight to make the bland fare more palatable. Gundy had stopped providing any variety in the meals a week ago.

"What's the name of this port we're stopping at, Peaches?"

"I couldn't pronounce it right even if I tried, miss. It's one of those foreign names. But it's just a little harbor halfway along the coast of Portugal. No place of any importance."

Chantelle stared at him incredulously. "Do you mean to say we've actually left the Mediterranean?"

"Why, that's right, you would've missed the Straits, being as we came through in the dead of night. Surprised Sinclair didn't tell you, though."

"Sinclair?"

"Why, the gent you're—"

"If you don't have enough tasks to keep you busy, Peaches," Derek said from the doorway, "perhaps I should have a talk with the captain to rectify that."

429

"No need for that, milord. I was just having a little friendly chitchat with the lady."

"So I heard."

"Right you are."

Derek closed the door as soon as Peaches hurried out, then leaned back against it, arms crossed over his chest. Chantelle narrowed her eyes at him.

"Did my ears just deceive me, or did you speak to him in perfect English, Jamil?"

"I doubt he would have understood a word of my French."

"Then you lied to me. You *do* know English!"

"Of course," he replied with a careless shrug. "It's Jamil who doesn't speak it, at least not very well."

"Jamil who doesn't . . . oh, I see. I suppose you've changed identities along with your clothes."

"Something like that."

"You could have said something sooner," she replied peevishly. "If you're traveling in secrecy—"

"Whatever gave you that idea?"

Her brows drew together suspiciously. "Have you been drinking?"

"Not at all." He grinned at her.

"Well, you're not making any sense. If you don't want anyone to know who you are, then this trip must be secret."

"But it's not, Shahar, and everyone aboard knows who I am. Derek Sinclair, present Earl of Mulbury, at your service."

"Derek?" The name struck a chord of memory. "Didn't you ask me once to call you . . . wait a minute. I know the name Sinclair. It's the family name of the Marquis of Huntstable, who lives not four miles from my home."

"My grandfather."

"Like bloody hell," she snapped. "I'm not a fool, Jamil."

"Of course you're not. I think your difficulty lies in getting past one simple fact. I'm not Jamil Reshid. I took his place for a while because he needed my help."

"You're lying again. How could you impersonate someone everyone knows? You would have to be his twin."

"That did make it easier."

She could have spit at that point, she was so exasperated. "If you can't be serious, get out! I don't like being toyed with!"

Derek came away from the door and pulled out a chair at the little table the cabin was equipped with. "Sit down and I'll explain, Shahar. It's time we got this out of the way."

She did, and when he had finished, she could only stare at him. "Then you really aren't the Dey of Barikah? You were raised in . . . you're a bloody Englishman?"

"Yes, if you must put it that way." He was so relieved that she was only surprised, he didn't care what she called him. "You don't mind?"

"I don't know," she replied truthfully. "I

431

haven't really . . . if you aren't Jamil, then you don't own me, do you? In fact, you never did."

"You were bought for me, Shahar. When I took Jamil's place, his harem was also at my disposal. And since any woman I favored would be married off at his return, you could say he hoped that with a concubine of my own, I wouldn't be tempted by too many of his women, at least those he didn't care to part with. And so I wasn't."

"Jamila?"

"I already knew about her before I arrived. I was asked to get her out of Barikah if I could. But because she was one of Jamil's favorite's, there was the chance he wouldn't let her go even if I asked him."

"So you summoned her to your bed."

"Actually, I didn't touch her, but I couldn't tell you that at the time. For her to be released, everyone, especially Jamil, had to think she shared my bed."

"Then you told her who you were?"

"No. She was rather piqued that she couldn't tempt me. She's a precocious young woman. But I counted on her vanity to keep her from telling anyone that all I wanted was to play chess with her. And she didn't."

Chantelle frowned as another thought occurred to her. "Just when did you change places with your brother?"

Derek grinned, reading her mind. "The very day I first summoned you."

"Then . . . that was Jamil who bought me, not you?"

He nodded. "That was the only time you saw him."

"Then you didn't . . . it was he who . . . and Mara! It wasn't you!" She shot out of the chair to throw her arms around his neck. "I'm so glad! I could never reconcile myself to the cruelty you—he displayed. I couldn't understand how I could—"

When she lowered her eyes without finishing, he prompted, "Don't stop there. Could what?"

"Never mind," she evaded. "What about Shee-lah? I haven't forgotten that you—"

"Not me, Shahar. That was the day Jamil returned, and he went straight to his wife. He does love her, you know."

"Then you kept your promise?"

"Actually, I told you the truth when I said I hadn't been able to think of anyone but you since my eyes first beheld you. There still hasn't been anyone else, Shahar—only you."

She looked up, eyes sparkling, and then she kissed him. He didn't let her stop there. It had been weeks since she had let him get this close, weeks of his worrying about her reaction to the truth. He certainly hadn't expected it to be like this.

He scooped her up and carried her to her small bunk. She helped him to remove her clothes and his as well, and then he was lying beside her and doing all the things to her that he had only been able to dream about recently.

Chantelle reveled in the sweet promise of his touch. He knew her body so well, every sensitive place that made her burn for him. How she had missed this, and how blissful to know that she need never deny herself again. He had been true to her. He must love her. Deciding that gave her more joy than she had ever imagined possible.

"I should have told you sooner," Derek said, between nibbles at her throat and breasts.

"Why—didn't—you?" she asked breathlessly.

"I was afraid you would be angry."

She caught at his face and showered it with kisses. "That you're not Jamil? That you kept your promise to me? That you're taking me home? You *are* taking me home, aren't you?"

"Yes." He grinned. "Home with me. You don't think I'd bring you all this way just to let you go, do you?"

As he said this, he pinned her to the bed, coming home now to the warmth he craved. She was ready for him, welcoming him inside with a passion made more powerful by her love for him. God, it was so nice to finally accept it, to have no doubts about his worthiness, to give her heart into his keeping. It made all the difference in the world, which she discovered when their bodies joined in climax to achieve a pinnacle of pulsating ecstasy never reached before.

Chapter forty-eight

DAWN WAS slowly creeping through the port-hole when Derek finally rose from the bunk. He had spent the night, but not to sleep. Chantelle stretched luxuriously as she watched him dress and splash cold water on his face. He was tired, while she felt smug that she wasn't. Not yet anyway.

"Are you certain you wouldn't like to stay just a little longer?"

Derek glanced over his shoulder to find her leaning back on both elbows, her uncovered breasts thrust provocatively forward. He groaned and looked away.

"A man has his limits, Shahar," he said in an aggrieved tone.

"Are you begging for mercy, my lord?"

"Yes," but he quickly amended, "Until to-night." He came back to sit on the edge of the bunk. Those sweetly thrusting breasts were almost his undoing. "Then you can be as merciless as you like. I will insist upon it."

She laughed throatily. "It's your own fault for ignoring me for so long."

"Me?" He mustered up some indignation in his tone. "You had me practically on my knees."

She turned on her side so her pelvis pressed against his hip. She trailed one finger slowly up his arm.

"You would never grovel, my lord. You're too used to getting your way and relying on your seductive powers."

"None of which did me much good recently."

"Oh, I don't know. It wasn't easy trying to ignore you, especially when I adore this fine strapping body of yours."

"Minx," he said as her hands slipped inside his open shirt.

"Give me a kiss and I'll let you go without further protest."

He did, but when her tongue thrust inside his mouth and one hand started a slow descent down his chest, Derek turned the aggressor. "I wouldn't have believed it was possible, but I'm not going anywhere."

"What a shame. You kept me up all night, you know, and I'm suddenly feeling quite—" At his growl, she giggled. "Well, when you put it that way, I suppose I can stay awake for another hour or so."

It was nearly an hour later when Chantelle again watched Derek dress, but this time she yawned, sleepily content to make no protest. Tenderly, he bent over to give her a last kiss.

"I'll see you this evening, little moon."

"You'll see me sooner than that," she replied dreamily. "Or don't you think it's time I had a little fresh air and exercise up on the deck?" When he didn't answer, she opened her eyes to find him frowning. "Well, don't you?"

"Actually," he replied hesitantly, "I would rather you continue as you have."

She was fully awake now. "Locked in? You must be joking." But at his deeper frown, she exclaimed, "You're not joking! Why?"

"It would be better all around—"

"For who? Not for me, so it must be for you." And now she was frowning. "Is there something you haven't told me?"

"Why do you say that?" he hedged.

"Because you obviously don't want me talking to anyone else on the ship. And as I recall, you mentioned something last night about thinking I would be angry. What exactly was I supposed to get angry about?"

"Very well," he said tightly. "The captain and half the crew know that I have a fiancée awaiting my return to England. She was with my grandfather when he made the arrangements for this ship to pick me up in Barikah."

"I see," she replied with admirable calm. "A fiancée. Now tell me you intend to break the engagement."

"Break it? You just don't break an engagement to the daughter of a duke."

"You could," she said angrily.

"No, I couldn't," he snapped back.

"Why? No, don't answer that. You love her, don't you?"

"Of course I love her! I've known her most of my life!"

"What has that to do with it?"

"What has—" he started to shout, but thought better of it, lowering his tone to a persuasive level. "The point is, this has nothing to do with us, Shahar."

"Don't call me that! Your brother gave me that name and I always hated it. And there is no 'us,' my lord, nor will there be if you marry your Duke's daughter."

"You expected me to marry you?"

"After you said you were taking me home with you, yes, I suppose the thought did cross my mind!"

He stared at her for a long moment. "Then I'm sorry, but that wasn't the arrangement I had in mind." Chantelle's eyes flared wide as it dawned on her what he *did* have in mind. "You wanted me to be your *mistress?*"

"You needn't say it like that. A mistress is perfectly respectable these days."

"That's the best I can hope for, is that it? You ruin me for a decent marriage, then hope to benefit—" It hit her suddenly what she was saying, and her eyes flared even wider. "My God, you were in a position to . . . you could have obtained my freedom without . . . you bloody bastard! You didn't have to make love to me. You could have left me untouched as you did Jamila."

"That wouldn't have gotten you your freedom, Shahar."

"Don't—call—me—that! And don't lie to me."

"I'm not lying. Jamil owned you. You got your freedom as a reward for helping him. Otherwise, he was within his rights to keep you."

"He never wanted me. He bought me for you. He would have let me go if you had asked him. All you had to do was ask him. He was your brother, for God's sake. Don't you dare tell me he would have denied you anything after you had traveled all that way and risked your life for his sake!"

"Perhaps not, but I couldn't take the chance. I couldn't see you buried in that harem forever, just one of so many women, especially when his love was already taken. I thought at first to insist you be married to a man with no other wives. I felt you deserved to at least be a first *kadine*. But that couldn't be arranged unless I bedded you first."

"If you're trying to tell me you did it for my sake, I'll—I'll—"

"All right!" he angrily interrupted her sputtering. "That was just an excuse to salve my conscience. The plain truth is I couldn't leave you alone. I wanted you too much and I still do. And, by God, you *are* going home with me, woman. I'm keeping you, one way or another. If I have to turn this ship around and live out the rest of my days in Barikah so I can keep you locked in a harem, I'll do it."

"I won't be your mistress!" she screamed at him as he stalked out the door. She got no reply

439

other than the key turning in the lock. "I won't," she added softly for her own benefit. And then she started to cry.

Chapter Forty-nine

IN THE end, Chantelle did let Derek take her to the Huntstable estate with him, but only because she had finally recalled the dilemma she had left behind in England. It was *not* that she had agreed to be his mistress, though he steadily worked on changing her mind. It was simply that he could help her locate Aunt Ellen and assess the current situation much easier than she could, and he owed her that much.

He wasn't too happy about learning who her father had been, especially when he learned his grandfather had been acquainted with him. Nor did he listen to the rest of her story calmly. That he was angry for her sake surprised her. That he agreed to help her without having to be coerced into it surprised her even more.

She met Caroline the first day of their arrival. It was an uncomfortable ordeal in every way. Even the new clothes that Derek had purchased for her in Dover didn't give Chantelle the confidence to face up to this beautiful, and splendidly attired, woman. She was wearing plain blue linen. Caroline was adorned in Chinese red silk.

The seamstress who had relinquished the two already finished outfits that needed only a few minor adjustments to fit Chantelle was upstairs waiting to fit her for the complete wardrobe she had agreed to let Derek order for her, but that didn't help her now. Seeing Caroline and Derek together was like watching long-lost friends re-united. They didn't seem at all like lovers, yet Chantelle still hurt to see that Derek really did have true feelings for this woman.

What he told Caroline about her after their brief introduction, she didn't know. She didn't care to stay and watch this reunion any longer than she had to, and quietly slipped away unnoticed—or thought she did.

Derek watched her leave but didn't try to stop her. Seeing her with Caroline, he was more confused than ever, and he had been in a state of continuous confusion where his feelings were concerned ever since he had had the expected row with Chantelle on the ship.

He was glad to see Caro, delighted in fact, having missed their special closeness. He very nearly blurted out his dilemma with Chantelle, as he would have done before their engagement, to ask her advice. It was then that it hit him, the differences in his feelings for the two women. He loved Caroline. He adored her. She would make an ideal wife in every way but one, and it was that one factor that he had never considered before. He had no real desire to bed her. He could do it if he had to, but the simple truth was he would rather not.

Christ, how had he missed it before? They

were *too* close, more like siblings. In fact, what he felt for her, he now realized, was distinctly brotherly.

What he felt for Chantelle, on the other hand, was the exact opposite. He couldn't keep his hands off her. She exasperated him, frustrated him, made him crazy. She also fired his desire with just a look or a touch. He not only wanted her in his bed, he would be perfectly happy if she never left it.

Bloody hell. What did that tell him? Just that he had deluded himself too long. He was marrying the wrong woman, and there wasn't a thing he could do about it except hope that Caroline would call it off herself. He couldn't. He had tied her up for nearly a year with this engagement. And at twenty-five, she was considered quite on the shelf. He couldn't hurt her like that, even for the sake of his own future happiness.

Four days later Aunt Ellen arrived, thanks to the efforts of a dozen servants sent out to locate her. Chantelle was so happy to see her she cried for twenty minutes without getting a single word out. Ellen was only half as emotional. She managed to tell her news first, that their cousin Charles was dead, challenged to a duel after having been discovered cheating at cards. The bad news was that his son, Aaron, now had guardianship of Chantelle.

"And if you felt the need to hide from Charles, you can be sure it is much more imperative that you stay out of Aaron's hands. He wouldn't marry you off, my dear. He would keep you an old maid and permanently under his protection, if you know what I mean."

Chantelle did, and that left her in the same predicament, exchanging one rotten apple for another. But she wouldn't think of that now. Derek had promised to help her, and she would wait and see what he had to say after he finished his investigation into the American Burke's affairs.

Right now Chantelle had her own story to relate, and she did so with a lot of missing pieces that she couldn't bring herself to confess to her aunt. Unfortunately, her abridged story left Derek smelling like a rose. Ellen saw him as nothing less than a glowing hero, and after she met him, she couldn't sing his praises loud enough. It made Chantelle positively sick.

She met Derek's good friend Marshall Fielding that evening, but when Caroline showed up for dinner, too, Chantelle managed to drag Ellen away shortly afterward with the excuse that they hadn't caught up yet on everything that had happened over the summer. Ellen knew Chantelle well enough to discern immediately what was wrong, and when they got upstairs and Chantelle pleaded tiredness suddenly, that confirmed it. But she also knew Chantelle wouldn't talk about it until she was ready. She wouldn't press her.

Downstairs, Marshall rudely requested a private word with Derek, leaving Caroline abandoned to the Marquis's company in the drawing room. That he and Marshall hadn't had a chance to talk since his return wasn't the only reason Derek agreed. He was uncomfortable in Caroline's presence now. It was absurd, but nonetheless true.

Derek filled two snifters with brandy before taking the chair opposite Marshall in the small library. "Did Miss Woods get back to her people all right?"

"Yes, and is giving out some ridiculous story about having escaped from the corsairs and finding succor from some Christians until you rescued her."

Derek chuckled. "If that's what she says . . ."

Marshall made a face. "She's not a very pleasant young woman, is she? Too prim and starched for my tastes."

"You should have met her before she found out she was going home. A more charming and agreeable girl you couldn't ask for."

"And your guest? What's her background?"

"The same as Miss Woods'." Derek grinned. "After all, I found them together."

"Beautiful girl," Marshal remarked. "Stunning, really."

"Yes," Derek agreed tightly. He thought so, but damned if he liked Marshall's noticing.

"And you traveled all that way with her?"

"You could say she was as unpleasant as Miss Woods once she realized she was free."

"Really? Strange reaction, that. But you've done your part, more than was asked of you. I'll take her off your hands, if you like."

Derek sat forward, his humor gone. "Chantelle

Burke is not your concern, Marshall, so stay out of it."

"Touchy, aren't you?"

"It's none of your business."

"I beg to differ. Caroline can't be too happy that you've brought another woman home with you."

"Caroline understands perfectly, and what the hell has this got to do with you?"

Marshall backed down. He hadn't expected to get into an argument with Derek over it. He thought he would be relieving a ticklish situation by offering to help. What the devil *was* Derek so touchy about?

And then it occurred to him. "Is there something going on between you and this girl?" But at the storm gathering in Derek's expression, he again backed down. "Forget it. I just don't want to see Caroline hurt, is all."

"She won't be," Derek replied curtly.

"Good, good, delighted to hear it." A change of subject was definitely in order. "Now, about your activities in Barikah—"

"Didn't you read my report?"

"Come on, Derek, you call those two sketchy pages you sent round to me a report?"

"I summed it up rather nicely, I thought. The problem was internal and has been taken care of. England can enjoy Jamil Reshid's reign without further worry."

"That's putting it mildly. According to a report that arrived from Sir John just this morning, in the first few days of Reshid's return to normal business, he granted us six concessions, two of which the French previously had exclusive rights to."

"So he was a little grateful—"

"Don't be so bloody modest. A little grateful? You must not have heard yet about the Barikahian ship that arrived a full week before you did. It was filled to the brim with exotic gifts for His Majesty, gems to put the crown jewels to shame, silks, brocades, parrots, ostriches, two *live* panthers—"

"A drop in the bucket, Marsh. He's not exactly an impoverished ruler, you know."

"That's not even the half of it, Derek. There were also twenty female slaves—" At Derek's burst of laughter, Marshall frowned. "Would you mind telling me what you find so amusing? It was a bloody embarrassment."

"I don't doubt it. So he found an excuse to weed out his harem after all."

"His harem? They claimed to be from his household—but his harem? No wonder each of them possessed a personal fortune even a duke would envy. But doesn't he realize—"

"Of course he does. He knew full well they would be set free."

"Then why didn't he just free them himself?"

"Come on, Marsh, you know that isn't the way things are done over there. Slaves are given away quite frequently and for any number of reasons, but rarely are they granted freedom without

446

recompense. They're just too valuable a commodity."

"But in effect he freed them."

"Yes, but in the guise of gratitude. There is a difference." And then Derek grinned. "Besides, he probably thought I would appreciate the gesture." *Since I failed to do the weeding for him.*

"Which brings us back to your modesty. You must have done something more than simply point him in the right direction."

"Not at all. They were getting nowhere by suspecting Selim. I might have turned suspicion elsewhere, but it was one of the Dey's own concubines who discovered the true instigator of the plot."

"So you claim. Chantelle Burke, by any chance?"

"I don't recall giving any names in my report."

"As uncooperative as ever." Marshall sighed. "You're just not going to tell me the whole of it, are you?"

"There's nothing else to tell. England is happy. Barikah is happy. What more could you want?"

"A little honesty between friends," Marshall grumbled.

Derek stared at him for a long, thoughtful moment; then he finally said, "He's my brother."

"Good God! That explains . . . no wonder . . ." Marshall cleared his throat, his expression almost comical in his embarrassment. "Sorry, old man, for being so bloody persistent. As you say, there's nothing else to tell, is there? Shall we rejoin Caroline and your grandfather?"

Derek suppressed a grin. "By all means."

But his own discomfort returned on finding Caroline alone in the drawing room, the Marquis obviously having deserted her, too. She was finishing a piece on the piano, a melancholy tune that didn't suit her at all. It suited him, however, when he thought of how disturbed Chantelle had been during dinner and how stubbornly she had tried to hide it.

Of course he knew why, but there was very little he could do about it. He had her tucked in under his roof where he wanted her, and would do everything possible to keep her there. But Caroline thought of this as her second home, and she would be popping around more and more often as the wedding day approached. Meetings between the two would be unavoidable.

The music had ended and Marshall's voice broke into his thoughts with a surprising "Rather off key, weren't you, Lady Caroline?"

She stood up, smiling tightly. "I didn't realize you were tone-deaf, Lord Fielding."

"And I didn't realize you were so unaccomplished at the piano."

Caroline's gasp was heard clear across the room. "How dare you!"

Marshall shrugged carelessly. "Just pointing out what everyone else is too polite to mention. You would have saved your music teacher a good deal of frustration, I imagine, if you had just told your father that you had no interest in learning the piano. But that wouldn't do, would it? You've never made a decision on your own in your whole life."

Derek couldn't believe what he was hearing, and it didn't stop there. Caroline got angrier, and Marshall became even more insulting, and they both seemed oblivious that he was in the room, the sparks flying between them hot enough to singe the carpet. It occurred to him that he and Chantelle behaved in much the same way when they couldn't come to terms with their feelings, and suddenly he burst out laughing.

He received two furious scowls that choked off his humor, and he managed a very conversational response. "Would this antagonism end if I left you two alone?"

Caroline was the one to answer, her voice still sharp. "I don't know what you mean."

"Actually, I believe you do. Perhaps I should have asked instead if a broken engagement might improve the situation."

She blushed, but it was Marshall who replied. "You can't expect her to answer that. The woman doesn't know her own mind."

"I do so!" Caroline snapped.

Derek crossed the room to put an arm around her shoulders. It was all he could do to keep from grinning.

"Perhaps you were a bit hasty in accepting my proposal, Caro."

In a ridiculous emotional about-face, she glanced up at him meekly. "Do you think so, Derek?"

He nodded. "I'm a cad and a scoundrel, but I'm going to ask you to beg off."

"Are you sure that's what you want?"

"Don't argue with him, Caroline!" Marshall said impatiently.

She threw him another scowl before she smiled at Derek. "Very well."

He finally let the grin loose and leaned down to whisper, "Don't let him get away, love. I think this is the one you've been waiting for."

"But how did you know?" she whispered back.

"Intuition—and the same problem."

"Chantelle?"

"You guessed it."

"I like her, but I don't think she likes me."

"She will, love, once she hears you're going to marry someone else and not me. And if you don't mind, I'd like to tell her now."

"Of course. And, Derek, thank you."

"Not at all." Then he turned to Marshall. "You should have said something, old man."

"I—ah—I thought I did," Marshall replied in embarrassment now.

"Not seriously enough. And don't just stand there like a clod, or you're liable to lose her again. Talk about indecision."

"I couldn't have said it better myself," Caroline agreed with a grin.

Chapter Fifty

CHANTELLE WAS just about to extinguish the last lamp in her room when the door burst open. "She's in love with Marshall!"

Chantelle jumped, startled, even though she recognized that voice before she saw him. The very reason she was going to bed so early, just so she wouldn't have to think of *him* anymore. And more annoying, he was all smiles as he stood there waiting for her to say something.

Despite herself, she asked, "Who is?"

"Caroline."

She stiffened. "Well, good for her."

He ignored her peevish tone and closed the space between them to draw her into his arms. "You don't understand, love. We can get married now."

"That's what you think."

"Chantelle, I'm serious."

"So am I," she retorted and pushed away from him, furious that he should ask her *now*. "I've heard the story, Derek. Your grandfather wants you married and you don't care who as long as you please him. Well, no, thank you. I don't care to be second choice now that your first one has deserted you."

451

He had expected her to be as delighted as he was. It infuriated him that she wasn't. "Dammit, you have never been second and you know it! Is it my fault that I was already committed when I met you? Caro is one of my best friends and always has been. How could I break off with her if I thought she would be hurt by it?"

"It was all right to hurt me, though, wasn't it? It was all right to rip out my heart and trample all over it with your miserable suggestion that I be your mistress!"

"Do you think I would have loved you any less in that position?" he shouted back.

"What?" she asked, stunned.

"You heard me! How else was I to keep from losing you?"

Her eyes blazed when she realized she had obviously misunderstood him. That was all he was worried about, that he wouldn't have the use of her body anymore. How could she have thought otherwise, even for a moment?

"Why am I even arguing with you? I've given you my answer. Now will you kindly get out of my room?"

He started to do just that, he was so angry with her. He got as far as the door and stopped. He had left the damn thing open. He closed it now and turned back toward her. If feelings counted for nothing, maybe logic would succeed.

"You need a husband, Chantelle."

"The devil I do."

"Have you forgotten your guardian?"

Her eyes narrowed. "What about him?"

"The only way you can get out from under his rule is to marry." That wasn't exactly true. He had already talked to his solicitor about the options she had available to her, but he wasn't about to tell her that now. "Or did you intend to hide from him until you came of age?"

"Why not? It was what I had planned to do before I got influenced by a vacation in Barikah."

He hated it when she got sarcastic. "Don't you want the pleasure of kicking him out of your house?"

"Not enough to put up with you for the rest of my life."

Derek gritted his teeth. "Why the bloody hell are you being so stubborn about this? You love me. I love you. There is nothing to prevent our getting married now. That *is* what people usually do when they—"

"All right."

"What?"

"All right, you have convinced me."

It took him a moment to realize she was smiling at him. He approached her again, slowly this time.

"Was it that bit about having to stay out of circulation?"

"No."

"Was it the part about kicking your cousins out?"

"That was a nice thought, but no."

She was grinning now. When he made no move to embrace her, she took matters into her own hands, slipping her arms around his neck. He was the one to resist now.

"Wait a minute—"

"Shh." She began nibbling at his chin. "Have you forgotten so soon how easily passion can flare between us?"

"So that's it? All you want is my—"

"Silly man. All I wanted was your love. All you had to do was tell me."

He turned the tables on her, grabbing her hips to press them into his own. "I thought I was always quite demonstrative in that area."

"I didn't mean that!"

"Didn't you?" he teased. "What about this?" And he captured her lips until her legs gave out from under her.

"That was always nice," she said breathlessly, "but I wanted the words."

"Silly woman." He gave her back her own words. "I knew you loved me. Why weren't you as intuitive? If I didn't love you, would I have put up with your willfulness, your temper, your jealousy?"

"I was never jealous!" she retorted.

"Of course not." His chuckle was warm and caressing. "Are you sure you want the words, love? You're going to hear them so often you'll be begging for mercy."

"That's what you think. We know who always ends up begging for mercy, don't we?" But then she sighed, holding him close, so happy she could barely stand it. "Oh, Derek, I love you so much. How soon can we be married?"

He grinned at her impatience. "Not until morning, at least. I have other plans for tonight. "

"Do you, my lord? So do I, now that you mention it." And she brought his lips back to hers.

A note on the text
Large print edition designed by
Kipling West.
Composed in 16 pt Plantin
on a Xyvision 300/Linotron 202N
by Marilyn Ann Richards
of G.K. Hall & Co.